LUCCA

JENS CHRISTIAN GRØNDAHL is one of the most celebrated and widely read writers in Denmark today. Born in 1959, his literary work includes thirteen novels, essays and several plays. *Silence in October*, published recently by Canongate, is being translated into sixteen languages.

ANNE BORN has translated many works of Danish, Norwegian and Swedish literature, including *Letters from Africa* by Karen Blixen, *The Snake in Sydney* by Michael Larsen, *Vita Brevis* by Jostein Gaarder, and *To Siberia* by Per Petterson. She has published twelve collections of her own poetry, and many Scandinavian poets in translation.

LUCCA

Jens Christian Grøndahl

Translated from Danish by Anne Born

CANONGATE

First published in English in Great Britain in 2002
by Canongate Books Ltd,
14 High Street, Edinburgh EH1 1TE

This new edition published in 2003

First published in Danish in 1998 by
Rosinante, Copenhagen

2

The publisher gratefully acknowledges general
subsidy from the Scottish Arts Council towards
the Canongate International series

The English translation was supported
by The Danish Literature Centre, Copenhagen

British Library Cataloguing-in-Publication Data
A catalogue record for this book is available on
request from the British Library

ISBN 978 1 84195 397 7

Typeset by Palimpsest Book Production Limited,
Polmont, Stirlingshire

Printed and bound in Great Britain by
CPI Group (UK) Ltd, Croydon, CR0 4YY

www.canongate.tv

Part One

One evening in April a thirty-two-year-old woman, unconscious and severely injured, was admitted to hospital in a provincial town south of Copenhagen. She had concussion and internal bleeding, her legs and arms were broken in several places, and she had deep lesions in her face. A petrol station attendant in a neighbouring village, beside the bridge over the motorway to Copenhagen, had seen her car take the wrong slip-road onto the carriageway and drive at high speed against the oncoming traffic. The first three approaching cars managed to manoeuvre around her, but about 200 metres after the junction she collided head-on with a truck.

The Dutch driver was admitted for observation but released the next day. According to his statement he started to brake a good 100 metres before the crash, while the car approaching him actually increased speed for the last stretch. The front of the vehicle was totally crushed, part of the radiator was stuck fast between the carriageway and the lorry's cow-catcher, and the woman had to be cut free. The spokesman for the emergency services said it was a miracle she had survived.

On arrival at hospital the woman was pronounced close to death, and it was 24 hours before she was out of danger although still critically ill. Her eyes were so badly damaged that she had lost her sight. Her name was Lucca. Lucca Montale.

Despite the name there was nothing particularly Italian about her appearance, from the photograph on her driving licence. She had auburn hair and green eyes in a narrow face with high cheek-bones. In build she was slim and fairly tall. It turned out she was Danish, born in Copenhagen.

Her husband, Andreas Bark, arrived with their small son while she was still on the operating table. The couple's home was an old farmhouse in an isolated woodland setting seven kilometres from the site of the accident. Andreas Bark told the police he had tried to stop his wife from driving. He thought she had just gone out for a breath of air when he heard the car start. When he got outside he saw it disappearing along the road. She had been drinking quite a lot, he could not remember how much. They had had a marital disagreement. Those were the words he used, and he was not questioned further on that point.

Early in the morning, when Lucca Montale was moved from the operating theatre into intensive care, her husband still sat in the foyer with the sleeping boy's head on his lap. He was looking out at the sky and the dark trees when Robert sat down beside him. Andreas Bark merely went on staring into the grey morning light with an exhausted, absent gaze. He seemed to be slightly younger than Robert, in his late thirties. He had dark, wavy hair and a prominent chin, his eyes were narrow and deep-set, and he wore a shabby leather jacket.

Robert rested his hands on his knees in the green cotton trousers and looked down at the small perforations in the leather uppers of his white clogs. He realised he had forgotten to take off his plastic cap after the operation. The thin plastic crackled between his hands. The other man looked at him and Robert straightened up to meet his gaze. The boy woke up and asked where he was, bewildered. His father stroked his hair slowly, mechanically, as the doctor spoke.

When he got home Robert had a shower, poured himself a whisky and walked about the house for a while. Apart from a faint twittering, the only sounds were those he made himself, the parquet blocks creaking under his bare feet and the ice cubes clinking in his glass. He never went straight to bed when he came home after a night shift. He sat on the sofa as it grew light outside, listening to the new recording of Brahms's third symphony bought last time he was in Copenhagen. He gave in to fatigue and imagined he was floating on the peaceful, swelling waves of the strings, studied the palings of the fence at the end of the garden, the birch leaves fluttering in the breeze, and the hesitant little hops on both legs of the sparrows on the cement paving stones, between the plastic garden furniture on the terrace outside the wide panorama window.

The house was actually too large. It was intended for a family with two or three children, but it had been going at a favourable price. Moreover, Lea came home every other weekend. He had furnished a room for her with everything she might need. She had gone to buy the furniture with him and chosen the colours herself. He had given her a bicycle too, which awaited her in the car port, and a ping pong table he had set up in what was intended as the dining room. He preferred to eat in the kitchen. Lea was becoming a dab hand at table tennis, she could beat him now every other time. She was just twelve.

He had become used to living alone. It wasn't as hard as he had feared, he worked long hours. He had moved out of Copenhagen two years ago, when he was divorced. At that time he and Lea's mother had worked at the same hospital. Six months after the divorce Monica moved in with the mutual colleague she had begun a relationship with while still married to Robert. He didn't like constantly coming across them in the corridors.

He had moved to this particular town by chance, never having envisaged taking a job at a provincial hospital, but he liked his work, and although the town depressed him with its red-brick suburban houses and provincial town properties with small bay windows and absurd zinc spires, after a time he learned to appreciate the qualities of the place. It boasted a white-washed medieval church, where organ recitals were given in summer, flanked by a couple of half-timbered merchants' houses, at the end of the main street, and there were the woods, the seashore and a bird reserve at the end of a peninsula past an area of half-flooded meadowland. He liked to take a walk out there, surrounded by the huge vault of sky above the tufts of grass in the smooth calm water reflecting the cloud masses and the wedge formations of migrating birds.

Now and then he would visit one of the couples among his colleagues. They were all married and most had children. As a newly-arrived singleton he was met with friendliness and courtesy, but he always felt like a guest in their world, and he noticed that the women in particular confused his slightly reserved manner with arrogance. One woman had made a pass at him, she was a librarian and a few years younger than he was. He found her attractive and went out with her a few times, but when it came to the point he rebuffed her advances. It was not that he missed Monica. For the last year or two of their marriage they had lived silently side by side like two anonymous passengers, when the silence was not broken by sudden pointless quarrels.

Not that there was anything wrong with the librarian. She had a beautiful figure and a sense of humour. He actually made the initial moves himself when he went up to her one day to ask for a biography of Gustav Mahler. But he ended up by rejecting her. Naturally she was hurt, and since that episode he had stopped going to the library. It left him feeling chagrined, but he had been unable to explain either to her or himself why he had asked her to go, one evening after dinner when they had sat on his sofa listening to the adagio from Mahler's fifth symphony.

She was in a short low-necked dress and black stockings that night. She had taken off her shoes and drawn up her legs beneath her on the sofa, and she looked meaningfully at him out of her large, appealing eyes as they sipped their brandy. It was so obvious, everything seemed to have been arranged without a single word, and he lost the urge to have anything to do with her. After she had gone he told himself he could at least have gone to bed with her, as she had plainly offered, but when he woke up next morning, alone as usual, he was relieved. He ran into her in the street now and again, that was unavoidable in such a small town. They greeted each other politely and, as they passed each other, she tried to catch his eye.

Robert was responsible for Lucca Montale's treatment. It fell to him to tell her, a few days after the accident, that she was unlikely to see again. Her arms and legs were in plaster, and most of her head was covered with bandages, so only the lower part of her face was visible. She made no reply. For a moment he thought she had fallen asleep, then she moved her lips, but uttered no sound. He sat down on the edge of the bed and asked what she wanted to say. The words came slowly, with difficulty. Her voice was faint and uncertain, it threatened to crack the whole time, and he had to bend over her to hear what she said.

She asked what the weather was like. He told her the day was grey but promised to clear up. He said it had rained. Yes, she replied, she had heard it. Had it rained in the morning or during the night? In the night, he said. For a time neither of them spoke. He would have liked to say something encouraging to her, but could not think of anything. Everything that occurred to him seemed either foolish or blatantly unsuitable.

She asked whether Andreas was there. She used his first name, as if assuming Robert would realise who she meant. He told her Andreas would probably come later in the day. It felt odd to mention her husband like that, as if he knew him. He said Andreas had been there several times with their son, while she was unconscious. The boy's name was Lauritz. She wanted to see him. Then she corrected herself. He must come. Robert suggested she should arrange it with her husband. The next thing she said was very surprising. She did not want Andreas to visit her. Only Lauritz. Could she rely on that being respected?

Robert did not know what to answer. He said yes without thinking. If that was what she wanted. It sounded very formal, almost solemn. He looked at the trees, just coming into leaf. She did not want anything. He looked at her again. Her voice was expressionless, without bitterness or self-pity. He stood up to go, she asked him to stay a little longer. He stayed by the window, waiting for her to say something more. Was it certain? He asked what she meant, feeling foolish. That she would never see again? He hesitated. As good as certain, he replied. He said he was sorry, at once regretting it. She said she would like to be alone.

He relayed Lucca Montale's wishes to the sister-in-charge and asked her to arrange with the husband to let their son visit her. A few hours later Andreas Bark was sitting in Robert's office. He was pale and unshaven, his dark hair tousled. He slouched in his chair with exhaustion and asked if he could smoke. Robert assented with a wave of his hand, which he placed on the pile of case notes in front of him. Andreas Bark took a pack of cigarettes from his jacket pocket, he smoked Gitanes. There was something aggressive about the spicy smell of dark tobacco. Andreas Bark looked out the window. It really was clearing up. Robert gazed at the silhouette of a gypsy woman twirling in a dance with a hand on one hip and a tambourine held above her head, through the sinuous veil of cigarette smoke.

He must apologise. Robert looked up, met the other's eyes and said there was nothing to apologise for. He understood. It was really the wrong thing to say, but now he had said it, and the other held onto his calm gaze with his tired eyes behind the eddying cigarette smoke. It struck Robert they must be about the same age. There was something in the other's expression which in a mute, acquiescent way was trying to remind him of it. As if, in some transferred sense, they were old schoolmates, who could rely on each other's sympathetic insight.

Had she explained why she did not want to see him? Robert cleared his throat and brushed a hair from his white coat. Whether his patient had said anything about it or not, as a doctor he could not permit himself to pass it on. But in fact she had not said anything that could explain her decision. Why should she confide in him, anyway? Robert immediately regretted his question. That was making too much of the point. The other man sank into his chair still further and again looked out the window, where the pale sun created a chiaroscuro of shine and shade, then shine again on the grass and the wings of the hospital as clouds kept passing over it. He pressed down the loose tobacco at the end of his cigarette with his finger. He could bring Lauritz to see her during afternoon visiting hours. Robert said he would have to arrange that with the sister in charge. But would he . . . Silence fell, and he was obliged to look the unhappy man in the face again. Yes? When he spoke to her, wouldn't he say that . . . Andreas Bark broke off and said it didn't matter. They shook hands. Then he left.

Robert did not go straight home in the afternoon. Instead he drove out to the beach, as he did occasionally when he needed exercise. He parked in the fir plantation before the road got too sandy, and continued on foot through the dunes. The shore was deserted as usual. The sky was just as grey as the sand between the belts of dried seaweed with little air bubbles that Lea liked to crush between her fingers to make them crackle when they sat together on a Sunday looking out over the sea before he drove her to the station. The water was calm, it had a granulated surface in the offshore wind, and in the smooth, icy blue stretches the fishing stakes stood like trim markings from the coast and outwards towards the sharply defined horizon. Robert walked with long strides, head bent, absent-mindedly observing what passed through his field of vision, battered soaked herring boxes with rusty nails, crumpled starfish, milky jellyfish and empty white plastic bottles. Little waves lapped wearily at the edge of the water and made the silence seem deeper, more intimate.

He walked right out to the point where, in a gentle, indefinable transition, the beach gave way to sand spits, tussocks of grass, reed beds and narrow meadows stretching inland, everything separated by the bluish white mirror of the water. In one place a dinghy was moored to a pole in the midst of the folded calm of the water-mirror, merely a small silhouette against the emptiness of sea and sky. Robert had a definite objective, a rotting spar covered with little holes from ships' worms, where it was his habit to sit among the tall reeds to think, or just listen to birds' cries and the rhythmic, faintly whispering rush of wings, as he picked at the rotten wood.

He could well have been more sympathetic to the man in his office with his cigarette and his despair. He had felt really sorry for him. He caught sight of a bird sitting in among the reeds. It jerked its small head from side to side and forward and backwards with a mechanically ticking motion. He didn't know its name, he was not very good on birds. Several times he had thought of buying a bird book with coloured drawings which he could take on his walks, but the idea did seem a bit comical. Should he also get himself a pair of binoculars and some green wellies and tramp around like a typical enthusiast?

He remembered he was to have Lea the following weekend. If

it kept on raining they could always play table tennis and hire some videos. And they had been talking of making a kitchen garden. He had already bought garden tools from the hardware shop and been to the garden centre for seeds. The tools were in the scullery beside the washing machine, painted red, with beechwood handles. He hadn't even removed their stickers with bar codes. If the weather was reasonable they might get started. He hadn't wanted to do it on his own even though he had the time. The idea was for them to do it together.

The librarian had questioned him about Lea, he had even shown her some pictures. While he talked about his daughter she had smiled and looked at him with her nice eyes, and he could sense that the small anecdotes raised him in her feminine esteem. That embarrassed him, and he shied away from talking to her like that. Her encouraging gaze and understanding smile made him feel pathetically disarmed.

He lit a cigarette. Andreas Bark's masculine but painfully vulnerable face came to mind again. He didn't know what he should have said to him. After all, his wife was not dead. With a bit of luck and a few months' rehabilitation she would be able to go on, blind but alive. The untold marital drama being acted out behind the man's tragic mien and her refusal to see him was a far cry from his medical field of action.

Throughout his years as a doctor it had often occurred to him that it was the reverse side of life with which he was occupied, the side with the seam. Just like tailors of old who had only an indirect glimpse of the glittering world of fine ladies, it was the sad moments in people's lives that he shared with them, when some functional fault or accident prevented them from getting on with their dramatic or uneventful existence.

After he had moved to the provinces and by degrees accustomed himself to his new and quieter lifestyle, he had to admit that Monica had been right when she reproached him for not being more ambitious. Naturally he wanted to be proficient, and he did try to improve, but he never dreamed of being a virtuoso. The appointment at a provincial hospital was anything but progress in his career, and he discovered, to both his surprise and relief, that he didn't mind. The hospital was the innermost sphere in his world, it was there he spent most of his time, and it was from there that he looked out on the world where other people moved. Now and again they passed through his, but to them that was an unpleasant parenthesis, which they hastened to forget as soon as they escaped.

Their lives were not his concern, only their bodies, and he had grown used to working with the human body as a closed circuit separate from the life it lived. The organism was sufficient to itself and unaffected by the dreams and ideas raging within it. That was an idea he found encouraging. He liked his work, he liked vanishing into it, completely engrossed in finding out what was wrong with people, and what should be done about it. He liked observing how every aim for beauty and social status was irrelevant when it came to the body's own solitary life, the vegetation of the organs in time to the soft, meaningless rhythm of the pulse. In his eyes the anonymous innocence of the interior organs offset the broken illusions of the exterior, socialised body, its ugliness, obesity and wear and tear. But the anonymity of the organs was also a cunning commentary on the spoilt, exacting beauty of other and luckier bodies.

One day he had shown Lea an anatomical atlas with detailed colour plates. He described what she was looking at and carefully explained the function of the organs, but she wrinkled her nose and asked him to close the book. She thought the pictures were distasteful and protested when he reminded her that she herself looked like that inside, like everyone else, whether they were beautiful or ugly. It amazed him that the interior of the body could be as terrifying as its exterior seemed seductive. Perhaps it was not the organs that caused the disgust but the anatomical dissecting gaze that by revealing them so matter-of-factly also showed how vulnerable they were.

To the patients the hospital was an ominous place with its clinical atmosphere of linoleum, white coats, disinfectant and rust-free steel, and all of them had the same anxiety in their eyes, whether they tried to hide it or give it free rein. Hospital reminded them that whatever happened they would have to die sometime, regardless of how many wiles the doctors used to stave off the inevitable. When they relinquished themselves to his authority and placed all their hope in his white coat, he sometimes had to ask himself if it was the terror of being admitted that made them so meek rather than the hope of being discharged again.

But he knew very well that horror and hope walked together, and he had probably become hard to scare only because he had seen so many sick people and despite everything had cured a good many of them. He had even grown less horrified by incurable diseases simply by encountering them regularly. Sometimes he thought that one day it could be he himself lying there afraid of dying, but identifying with the dying did not make him more fearful than he would otherwise have been, rather the reverse.

Horror and hope. Perhaps you had to be really frightened to know what hope was. Perhaps. He didn't hope so much for his own sake, and Lea was the only person in his life more important than himself. The only thing which could terrify him was the thought that she might get meningitis or be run over by a truck.

The reeds whispered and swayed from side to side when a bird suddenly flew up with feverishly flapping wings. He threw away his cigarette stub and heard the glow fizz in the muddy water. Again he thought of the mutilated Lucca Montale, how he had patched her up to the best of his ability. She had driven along the dark side-roads, the road markings, the grass verges and the black trees had rushed past her long-distance lights, and a cat or a fox might have seen her, stiffened with phosphorescent eyes, with one forepaw raised. Not even at the utmost limits of her inflamed mind could she have imagined that twelve hours later she would wake up swaddled like a mummy to be told she had seen the sun shining on the grass and through the trees' foliage for the last time. She had been utterly electrified by the drama that had sent her out on the roads the worse for drink, and in her impassioned state she had ignored the fact that the most violent changes are brought about just as often by chance as by the violent travesties of the emotions.

She didn't want to see him, her unhappy, unshaven husband, who had waited for her ravaged body to decide whether to live or die. She insisted on this, throughout all the outward havoc her impulsive inebriated journey had occasioned. He must really have upset her. Again Robert visualised the silhouette of the dancing gypsy through the fog of tobacco, with her snaking hips, her tambourine raised in a fervent gesture, among the pile of case notes. He recalled the insistent gaze of the other man, the restrained desperation in his eyes. Andreas Bark had been sweating, and Robert had had to open the window when he left to get rid of the odour of his desperate body and his French cigarettes.

He heard voices from behind the reeds, a young woman's laugh. Robert stood up. He did not want to be seen hunched on his spar in the forest of reeds like some queer fish sitting there dreaming. His legs tingled and felt slightly stiff. He went out into the open along a narrow spit that divided the submerged meadowlands from the lake. There was no-one to be seen. Further along where the spit widened out there was a tall wooden shed, and when you walked past, the sky and the water on the other side glittered in the gaps between the perpendicular tarred planks of its walls. He could hear them in there, now the man laughed. The young woman said something in a fond, low voice. Then silence. Robert could make out their outlines in the narrow, bright spaces between the planks. He had stopped, but walked on hastily when he realised they might be keeping quiet because they had seen him out on the path.

Before his rounds the following morning the sister told him that Lucca Montale had had terrible nightmares in the night followed by long bouts of weeping. They had given her a sedative. Two large bouquets were on her bedside table. The previous day there had been only the one that Andreas Bark had asked them to take in to her. A thoughtless gesture, thought Robert. What use were flowers to her? Weren't they rather a signal to the people around her that others were thinking of her? The nurse asked how she was. She wrenched her mouth sideways in something meant to be a sarcastic smile. She really did look like a mummy, swathed as she was in plaster and bandages, reduced to a pale mouth that uttered brief answers when she was spoken to. Her condition had stabilised, now it was just a question of waiting.

For what? The nurse looked at him, perplexed, as he considered how to reply. He sat down on the edge of the bed and cautiously put a hand on her right shoulder, the only visible part of her body apart from her jaw which was not bandaged or plastered. Well, he couldn't say, he said, surprised at the gentleness in his voice. She made no answer, her mouth lay still in its folds, as if she were asleep. The nurse told her Lauritz would be coming in the afternoon. She spoke in an earnest, entreating voice. It was probably the best answer to give her. Lucca Montale asked her to take the flowers away, the stench was choking her. Robert and the nurse looked at each other.

As they walked along the corridor she told him the patient's mother had visited Lucca the previous day. She had not stayed in the room for more than a couple of minutes before coming out again, visibly shaken. The nurse had offered her a cup of coffee, but she had driven back to Copenhagen at once. She had looked surprisingly young, according to the nurse, who had recognised her voice but been unable to recall where she had heard it before, this beautiful, expressive female voice. Later in the day she had remembered. Lucca Montale's mother was a broadcaster. The nurse had asked Lucca if she was right, but the patient had been very curt and replied that she did not want visits from her mother or anyone else apart from her son.

Her decision did not need to be enforced, her mother did not come again, nor others. When Lauritz visited her, Andreas Bark waited outside the room, hunched in despair. Robert greeted him when he passed by and gave him brief reports of the patient's condition, controlling his impatience to continue along the corridor and escape the other's eyes. Andreas Bark must have registered his aversion and Robert was relieved to find he did not seek him out in his office again. Robert could not explain to himself what it was about the man that filled him with such revulsion. He did not try very hard to discover. There were other patients and their families to look after, and Lucca Montale took her place in the rows of prone figures in hospital gowns whose faces and sufferings changed at varying tempos, according to the seriousness of their cases and how soon they were discharged.

He only saw her for a few minutes during his daily rounds, and as a rule he was the one who spoke, when he repeated more or less what he had said to her the day before. Under the circumstances everything went on as it should do. He himself thought that sounded hypocritical, but why, in fact? If someone drank themselves senseless and drove at 150 km an hour along the wrong side of the motorway, there were limits to the miracles he could perform. She should be glad to be alive at all. Unless she had driven like a madwoman to get it over with once and for all. Get what over? Life, quite simply? Or whatever it had been in her life that had made her wish she were dead? She probably hadn't made any distinction.

Every time he thought about her he grew more convinced that Lucca Montale must have decided to kill herself that evening she quarrelled with her husband and got into their car to drive towards the motorway. But it made no difference what he thought. His task was to get her on her feet again so she could be discharged to whatever awaited her outside. He knew no more about her, on the whole, than he knew about his other patients. Besides, he only thought of her now and then, in the intervals when he paused for a moment's reflection in his office, dictaphone in hand, looking down on the hospital garden below. Otherwise not.

His days resembled each other. When he was at home he listened to music, Brahms, Mahler, Bruckner, Sibelius, the great symphonies that were like cathedrals, with the same shadowy heights, the same ribbed arches, and the same mysterious, coloured light divided into rays, cones and rosettes on the stone floor. Exactly like the real cathedrals in the south, which he and Monica had always visited in the days when everything was going well or at least seemed to be. She had not shared his taste in music, he had had to listen with earphones in the evenings when they were alone, and then she reproached him for isolating himself. At least it was some progress that now he could fill the empty house with one symphony orchestra after another without upsetting anyone. He did not think about anything when he listened to music. It poured through him like an impersonal energy, a huge, transforming power, and as long as it filled him it did not matter who or where he was. He watched the evening sky behind the birch trees in the garden, the grass in the wind, the children on cycles and the cars that occasionally passed along the road behind the fence, soundless as a silent film, while at the same time he felt both united and cut off from everything.

He went into Copenhagen once or twice a month and spent the afternoon and evening buying records, going to a concert or visiting some of his old friends. He had kept in touch only with friends from his life before he met Monica, and it was seldom he saw even those friends after he moved. Sometimes he went out to see his mother, she lived in a small flat in a block from the Thirties with a balcony where she could sit and look out over the harbour, the local heating station's row of slim chimneys and the railway lines with the express trains' shunting track.

His father had left her shortly after Robert was born and he had not seen him since; he had moved to Jutland and probably started another family there. He was a barber, thinking of him seemed quite abstract. He might already be dead. When Robert was fifteen he had decided to go in search of him. He succeeded in finding the address and telephone number. He could still remember the silence from the other end when he had told the strange man who he was. They arranged to meet in Århus, on neutral ground, as his father said in a tired voice that was hoarse and short of breath. He must be a chain-smoker. But when he was in the ferry crossing the Great Belt Robert began to lose heart, and he got off the train at Odense. What was the point of this?

Robert's mother did not marry again. She looked after him on her own, at first by cleaning, later by working in the canteen of a large firm, where in time she was promoted to catering officer. The best time for her had been when she worked in a home for children with behavioural problems. She rarely went out. When she retired, she resorted to the world of novels. Robert was not sure how clearly she could distinguish between their fictional life and the life going on around her. She herself was a spectator, terribly modest, content to be a witness of the world seen from the humble corner she allowed herself to occupy.

She loved Dickens and the Russians, Tolstoy and Dostoievski, and she had a weakness for Mark Twain, but her favourite book was Flaubert's *Madame Bovary*. When Robert saw the familiar volume open on the arm of the shabby easy chair beside the balcony door where she liked to sit, he always asked if it wasn't too sad. She smiled mysteriously, of course it was sad, but it was *so entertaining* too, and she said it as if in some secret way the one thing was a prerequisite for the other.

As a rule she hid her faded hair under a scarf. Time had made her stoop and she was very thin, but taller than most women of her generation, as tall as a man, and as long as he could remember she had worn the same kind of strong, mannish spectacle frames. She smoked about forty cigarettes a day, just as presumably her ex-husband had, thought Robert. That was the only thing they had in common apart from him. But they had come to a silent agreement that he should not comment on her smoking. He had almost come to the conclusion that she survived on a diet of cigarettes and novels.

She had always kept to a monotonous routine. The biggest event in her life had been the day he was admitted to university. Not when he finished but when he started, as the first one in the family. As far as he knew she had not been with a man since his father left her. But that couldn't be true, he thought, and one day he asked her. She did not reply, merely smiled her mysterious smile in a way that prevented him from seeing whether she smiled to protect her feminine pride or to shield him from stories he did not want to hear anyway.

Now and then she looked after Lea. Then she made her all the fatty and unhealthy dishes with thick gravy which Lea loved and Monica and Robert refused to make, and afterwards she read aloud to her from *Huckleberry Finn*, always that and nothing else. When Robert came alone she asked him worriedly how things were. He was not just her only child, he was also her only contact with the outside world, and for over forty years he had been the one who imparted deepest meaning to her life.

Her ceaseless questioning made him impatient and irritable and as a rule he snapped out brief answers, at the same time feeling guilty at being so grudging. But at other times she did not ask questions when he came, on the contrary she seemed distracted, as if he disturbed her reading. Not until he was on his way down the staircase with its terrazzo flooring and marble-patterned walls did it occur to him that she might only question him out of politeness and old habit. As someone trying to hide the fact that in reality she had lost interest in the noise and bother of daily life in order to devote herself to her daydreams at long last.

On Lea's twelfth birthday he was waiting in front of her school when she came out. She was surprised, it had not been arranged, he had gone into town on a sudden impulse. She stood there surrounded by her friends, who glanced at him shyly. She herself felt self-conscious. Her friends were going home with her, Monica was expecting them. He had bought her a pair of roller skates, and she tried them out at once there on the pavement, chiefly to please him, it seemed. He stood and waved as she went off to the bus stop with her friends, even though he was going the same way. He didn't want to embarrass them more than was strictly necessary, so he waited until their bus had left and took the next one. Twelve years. At that time they had really believed it was possible, he and Monica. They had both been tired of mucking around. They had more or less tried what there was to try, they thought. When she found herself pregnant they had already known each other a long time. They had jumped into it with their eyes open.

That was how they had put it to each other. Eyes open. But it was already hard to recall what he had thought then. Monica had become a stranger again. She was friendly, there was no longer anything to quarrel about, and her new husband was equally friendly. That was how it could turn out. As simply as that. She had stopped loving him and started to love someone else, and Robert had long ago stopped pondering over whether the one thing was the cause of the other or vice versa.

If he sometimes thought to himself that love was like music, it was not because he was feeling poetic. But love was just as invisible and hard to understand, perhaps because there was nothing to understand. An impersonal, transforming force, which found the way by itself according to its own interior laws, uncaring of who and what it pulled with it or left behind in its calm or restless flow. Music cared just as little about who played, the notes could not help it if they were played beautifully or clumsily, on finely tuned instruments or a miserable broken-down honky-tonk in which half the strings were missing.

He did not think in this vein every day. There was no one he could confide such thoughts to. When he was alone he could almost fall into a kind of trance, in which the thoughts landed and took off as randomly as the irresolute sparrows on the terrace. In the evening he read his professional journals, when he was not too tired. There was always a pile of them he had not got through. He merely riffled through the newspaper, and when he let it fall on the floor he had already forgotten the details of what he had read.

The only person outside the hospital he talked to regularly was Jacob, a young colleague who lived with his wife and their two small children in a house matching his own not far away. They played tennis once or twice a week, and sometimes Jacob invited him over on a Saturday. Jacob was very popular on account of his frank, uncomplicated manner. He was one of the doctors the young nurses flirted with, boyish in appearance, well-trained, with hair like yellow corn. Robert could feel Jacob looked up to him because he was older and came from a big hospital in Copenhagen, and this status compensated for the irritation at his heavier body and poor condition when Jacob beat him on the tennis court yet again.

Jacob's wife was dark-haired and had brown eyes, she was always well turned out in a relaxed way. She had an excellent figure, but there was something far too practical about her impeccable appearance which prevented Robert finding her attractive. Maybe that was why she did not like him, perhaps because as a divorced, single man he was a constant reminder of all the dangers threatening their domestic idyll. But it might also be that she had detected Robert's suppressed distaste for sitting in their garden chatting about everything and nothing, while the children rushed around and clambered all over their father. Or was it quite simply because he smoked? As a rule she asked him to stay and eat with them, and Robert did his best to seem house-trained, remembered to pick his stubs off the lawn and tried to keep up the flow of talk with her when Jacob in his apron was grilling steaks.

Jacob treated him as a friend, and the slight twinges of conscience Robert felt over his trusting openness made him behave as if they really were close friends. When Jacob confided in him, he responded with some confidential story about himself as an example for recognition, letting the younger man mirror himself in his experiences and see in them what he found useful to see. He had gradually developed a sincere liking for Jacob, although he never quite got over the feeling that Jacob's apparently uncomplicated and hygienic happiness was something separate from his own life. The games of tennis and the Saturdays in their garden became part of his routine, and neither Jacob nor his wife seemed surprised that he never worked up the energy to ask them back.

When Jacob once asked, Robert told him about his divorce and how he had discovered Monica was being unfaithful to him. It was a summer evening the previous year. They were in the garden, the children had been put to bed and Jacob's wife lay on the sofa in the living room watching television. Jacob listened with a solemn expression quite unsuitable to his boyish face. He was obviously showing his sympathy and respect for the confidence his discreet friend was placing in him, but Robert felt he could detect a touch of inquisitive curiosity in the other's attentive gaze. As he told his story he observed Jacob sitting under the garden umbrella in his trainers, his Bermuda shorts and the T-shirt from a Greek holiday island, as the glow from the barbecue died out. In the twilight, voices sounded from the gardens around them, and behind the hedges you could see the fleeting shadows of neighbours as they passed in and out through the lit terrace doorways.

While telling the story he felt it sounded like an episode from a Brazilian soap opera. He had been to a conference in Oslo, but when the last lecture was cancelled because of illness he decided to go home half a day earlier than planned. He did not know what to do with himself in Oslo on a raw Sunday in January. He called home from the hotel early in the morning before going to the airport. The answering machine was on. He asked himself later why he had not given a message instead of ringing off when he heard his own voice and the following long tone. When he let himself into the flat a few hours later Monica came out of the bedroom. She was naked, which surprised him, she always wore a nightgown in bed.

He asked where Lea was. She was staying over with a friend. He was going to go and kiss her but stopped when she looked at him with a stiff, almost hostile expression. It would be best if he went out again, just for fifteen minutes. At this stage of the story Robert made a point of describing in detail how he had stood in his own home in his overcoat, with snow in his hair, as his naked wife asked him to take a walk round the block, but Jacob held his serious expression. Monica remained standing there, fixing him with her unfamiliar gaze, and although it had begun to dawn on him that he had arrived at an inopportune moment, nevertheless he asked, almost as if to provoke her, why it was essential for him to go. For his own sake, she replied, and at that moment he heard through the door of the bedroom, which was slightly ajar, the jingling sound of a belt buckle.

What then? Robert smiled. Yes, what then? Jacob was becoming impatient. Did he go? No, he had gone into the kitchen and sat down at the table when Monica went back into the bedroom. He could hear their lowered voices in there. Shortly afterwards, steps sounded in the living room, they came nearer and he saw his hospital colleague pass the open door to the kitchen. And now came the wonderful moment in the story. Jacob leaned forward expectantly in his chair and quite forgot to look sorry for Robert, who paused before continuing.

It only lasted a moment, perhaps no more than a second, but his colleague, who had suddenly been in such a hurry to get away, still could not resist taking a look. Maybe he had imagined Robert would sit with his back to the door, broken by grief, or he wanted to make sure he was not ready to lunge at him with a bread knife. Anyway, the man did not lower his eyes, as you might have expected, when he passed the doorway and, when he met Robert's gaze, he was so disconcerted that he nodded politely. As he would have done if they had passed each other, both in their white coats, in one of the hospital corridors. Jacob sat back in his chair, crestfallen. Robert laughed. In fact it had been a relief. Jacob looked at him wonderingly. How? That was hard to explain.

Lea was to arrive late on Friday afternoon. As usual they had arranged that he would fetch her from the station. He left the hospital some hours before and drove to a supermarket on the edge of town for the weekend shopping. He was tired, he was always tired on a Friday, as if the whole week's fatigue had built up in him and weighed him down. As he pushed his trolley in and out among the others along the freezer counters he caught sight of Andreas Bark and his little son. They hadn't seen him. He pushed his trolley behind the shelf of bread and cakes and went over to the big freezers with dairy products, trying to remember whether he usually bought blackcurrant or strawberry yoghurt for Lea.

Again Lucca Montale came to mind, lying as she had done for almost a week, with arms and legs in plaster and head wrapped in bandages. One of the nurses had several times offered to bring her some headphones so she could listen to the radio, but she had refused every time. She just wanted to lie quietly, she said. She could not do anything else, blind and cut off from moving as much as a centimetre, reduced to being fed by a nurse and otherwise left to herself, as she had wanted.

Robert had prescribed plentiful painkillers for her, presumably she spent most of the day dozing.

With each day that passed she seemed more puzzling, not only because of her drastic action, but also her silence and self-chosen isolation. She seemed remarkably hardened, considering her condition. He could scarcely believe this was the same patient who, according to the nurse, had spent a night weeping heart-rendingly and inconsolably until the calming injection started to work.

When he visited her on his round he asked if she would like to talk to a psychologist. She waited a while before replying. What about? He couldn't help smiling. About her situation. Now she was the one who smiled or at least tried to with the twitch at the corner of her mouth he had learned to interpret as an expression of her hard-boiled sarcasm. Could a psychologist make her see again? He was about to reply with a pertinent affirmation, but stopped himself. It struck him that he didn't even know what she looked like. The only thing he had to help him was the recollection of the glimpse he'd had of the little picture on her driving licence. A narrow face framed by reddish-blonde hair, smiling confidently at the photographer as if nothing bad could touch her.

He decided on blackcurrant yoghurt and put the carton down in the trolley with the New Zealand leg of lamb, Moroccan potatoes and Chilean red wine. When he looked up again Andreas Bark stood in front of him holding Lauritz by the hand. They had seen him, he said, as if that was sufficient reason for accosting him. Andreas Bark smiled a bit sheepishly and looked as if he regretted stopping. Robert didn't know what to say. He felt unprotected faced with the other man's appealing gaze, now he was out of uniform and they stood there each with their trolley, outside his domain, on an equal footing. The silence embarrassed both of them, but then Andreas Bark clutched at a possibility. Robert had not yet been introduced to Lauritz. The boy stretched out his hand politely.

The feel of the small soft hand caught him by surprise. It awoke an unexpected and vivid memory of Lea's hand, when she was the same age. He had forgotten its weightless frailty and doll-like proportions. The recollection suddenly crossed his mind of how he had walked through streets and parks holding her slightly sticky little hand, alone or with Monica, when they were still a family. As Lea gradually grew bigger he had forgotten the various stages of her early childhood, until he had only snapshots to remind him, shiny and inconsequential, their colours already indistinct.

Robert resorted to the excuse of having to meet his daughter at the station, and at once regretted opening a door onto his private life. A white lie would almost have been better. Andreas Bark asked how old she was. The innocent question seemed like a far too intimate touch. Robert replied and smiled a goodbye, pushing his trolley off through the crowd with relief. Methodically and without looking from side to side he worked through his shopping list, past the cold counters with red meat and the shelves of brightly coloured packages, the displays of barbecues and flowered, folding garden furniture. All the time he had the feeling that Andreas Bark was watching his every movement.

Throughout the day the cloud cover had thickened. It hung low over the town and a cold wind tugged and tore at everything it could get hold of, making you think it was February instead of April. As Robert pushed his trolley through the check-out the car park was veiled in a shining mist of rain behind the fogged-up automatic glass doors, and each time they opened he felt cold air on his neck and around his ankles. He paid and pushed the trolley out under the porch roof where people stood waiting, hoping it was only a shower. A few plucked up courage, bent over and ran, the wheels of their piled-up trolleys rotating, sending them lurching over the asphalt, the men in shorts or jogging trousers, the women with bare legs under their summer dresses. Inveterate optimists, thought Robert.

A scarf of trickling water fell from the roof gutter and landed with small explosions at his feet. The wind turned the rain into a carpet rolling across the car park, and the dim light imparted a dull shine to the swells of rain-carpet. He glimpsed Andreas

Bark in the group waiting there. He stood leaning against an old-fashioned lady's bicycle looking out at the rain. The boy was seated on a child's seat on the luggage rack with his helmet askew. The bulging shopping bags hung heavily from the handle-bars. Robert thought of the picture of the totally wrecked car, which a local paper had printed on the front page, without naming the victim of the tragedy. A thirty-two-year-old woman. It might have been anyone, struck down by one of the countless accidents recorded daily in the press worldwide.

It looked like turning into an all-night show . . . Andreas Bark smiled gratefully as if he did not deserve Robert's taking pity on him, even speaking to him. His subdued, timorous expression seemed at odds with his pronounced features. That face seemed to characterise Andreas Bark as a man normally sure of himself. Now he was broken, and to add insult to injury he would have to cycle home in the rain like a Vietnamese rice-peasant, weighed down by his burdens. His gratitude had no end and several times he asked if Robert would be in time for his daughter's train, as they unloaded their bags side by side into the boot.

They left the bicycle where it stood. Robert adjusted the safety belt on the back seat to fit Lauritz's small body. As they set off Andreas Bark asked if Robert minded him smoking. Of course not . . . He opened the window a crack and lit one of his poisonous cigarettes, and Robert almost regretted his humanitarian impulse. He had no idea what they could talk about, but the rain on the roof made it easier to sit in silence. Andreas Bark's leather jacket creaked a bit, and the indicators ticked when Robert prepared to turn. Otherwise there was no sound except the drumming of the raindrops and the wipers' monotonous swishing on the windscreen. They drove over the railway line and on through the industrial district, Andreas Bark giving directions.

Suddenly he announced, out of the blue, Robert thought, that he had just had a première in Malmö. He was a playwright. Aha . . . Did he write in other genres as well? You had to ask about something. He had once written poetry. But that was long ago, he went on with a pawky grin. What was it about, his play? Oh, God, that was always hard to describe. The playwright smiled, and the smile seemed both shy and coy. That was why you wrote, wasn't it? To find out why. If Robert understood. He didn't, but he kept that to himself.

The tarmac shone as it ribboned through the black fields, and the ploughed furrows followed the gradual rise of the road towards the ridge ahead, where a brown-painted transformer station was outlined against the grey watercolour shades of the clouds. But now it was finished, anyway. So he must have some ideas about it, at least. Andreas paid no heed to Robert's teasing tone, or he had not caught on to it. It was a psychological play. That is, not psychological in the traditional, psychoanalytical sense. It was rather, what should he say . . . existential. A sharp smell of liquid manure wafted into the car. Andreas closed his window and stubbed out his cigarette.

You could say it was about evil, he went on. Now there was no stopping him. On the cannibalism of emotions, on the repressed darkness, what was mute and unadjusted in us, beyond the social and linguistic order. When all was said and done, like all stories, it was probably about death. He fell silent, almost exhausted, thought Robert. Like someone bidding at an auction who at length realises he isn't in a position to bid any higher. Then there was nothing but the sound of the screen wipers and the rain on the roof, while the farms and fields streamed past surrounded by trees, like islands in a black sea of earth with their grain silos and white-washed barns.

They turned off down a narrow gravel road leading towards the woods. A horse raised its head and watched them through the rain, its wet mane sticking to its neck. Robert glanced at the clock beside the speedometer. He had to be at the station in half an hour. It was tea-time. The nurse would give her a straw, and when she had gone away the playwright's wife would lie motionless in her darkness, listening to the rain on the aluminium blinds at the window. The same rain that was falling on her home.

It was an old farm labourer's house in red brick. Its thatched roof had been replaced with asbestos roofing. A clutter of toys was scattered around the courtyard and a tricycle lay on its side near a cement mixer and a pile of sacks covered with plastic. The woods lay close to the other side of the house, the wind rampaged in the sodden beech leaves. He helped Andreas in with his shopping. The kitchen and living room were painted white and could just as well have been part of a fashionable town apartment, with Italian furniture, art posters on the walls and rows of cast-iron pans.

On the kitchen wall hung a sheet of brushed steel with magnets from which hung shopping lists, recipes from magazines and a few photographs. It must be her, the auburn-haired woman with high cheekbones, pictured in several of them. Would he like a glass of red wine? He looked at his watch. Yes, please, just a quick one. Andreas sat down facing him under the notice-board and poured two glasses. They had finished furnishing the house a month ago. Andreas stopped talking and looked at the boy, he lay on the floor playing with Lego. Then he met Robert's eyes and smiled tentatively. A vase of dead tulips stood on the windowsill gaping at the pane, several dry withered petals had dropped.

The house had been a ruin when they moved in. They had done most of the work themselves, they had really slogged at it. And now . . . He didn't know. It was all so new. Robert said something about rehabilitation, where and how, shifting his gaze from Andreas to the notice-board behind him. Most of the photos had been taken around the house, which appeared at various stages of refurbishment. A sun-tanned Andreas mixing cement, in a mason's cap with a bare torso. Lucca painting window frames, in overalls, her hair tied carelessly at her neck and splotches of paint on her cheeks. In another picture she was in a light summer dress with the low sun behind her, giving Lauritz a swing, the boy hung horizontally in the air and her skirt flew out like a pale flower of folds around her long legs.

He kept on asking himself if she did it intentionally . . . Andreas observed him in the pause that followed, wondering if he had gone too far. There was a picture of Paris as well. Robert recognised the red awning above the café table and the peeling trunks of the plane trees in the background. He said he had asked himself the same thing. She was pale and dressed in a tailored grey jacket, with a petrol-blue silk scarf round her neck. Her hair was tied in a pony tail and she wore lipstick. Had she threatened to do it? The colour film enhanced the red that framed the narrow dark slit of her mouth, as if she was about to say something. No, not exactly threatened. She was looking into the camera with her green eyes. Robert told him she had been offered psychiatric help several times. Had she . . . Andreas hesitated. Had she said anything about . . . them?

No, he replied. She had not confided in him, as he had said. The boy came over to Andreas, who lifted him onto his lap and kissed his hair. He sat there with his nose buried in the boy's hair before looking up again. The terrible thing, he said, the terrible thing was that that very evening . . . He looked down into his glass before taking a mouthful. Robert looked at the picture of Lucca Montale in a Parisian café again. For a moment it seemed as if he met her gaze. He could not decide whether she looked surprised because she was unprepared for being photographed, or she had suddenly become aware of some connection he could know nothing about.

There was a large clock on the wall beside the notice-board. Lea's train would arrive in ten minutes. The boy let himself slide down on the floor and ran into the living room. That very evening . . . Andreas went on and turned away his face. Robert stood up. The other man looked at him in confusion.

Lea stood on the platform beside her large bag, shivering in the cold and looking down at the shining tracks. He thought she had grown although it was only a fortnight since they had been together. Monica had bought her some new clothes. She wore a thin jacket, white jeans, white socks and white trainers. She did not see him until he was almost in front of her, then she smiled with relief and hugged him, but he could feel her disappointment at his arriving late. He carried her bag through the vestibule, feeling ashamed at the excuse he had fabricated on the spot about a queue in the supermarket. Two down-and-outs stood near the exit drinking beer. Their washed-out denim jackets were spotted with rain, one of them had the usual dog on a lead. The owner of the dog raised his glass in a friendly toast to Robert as they passed. Lea wrinkled her nose, assailed by the reek of beer and wet fur. On the way to the car she told him a friend had invited her to stay with her parents in the country during the summer holidays. He turned in his seat as he reversed out of the parking place. Lea struggled with the safety belt before getting it out to click in place. She could come and stay with him during the holidays too, he said, changing gear. But Monica had plans for them to go to Lanzarote. Wasn't it too hot there in the summer? We'll hit on something, she said, smiling at him in the mirror. It was a very adult remark. It sounded like something Monica might say. Lea did not really resemble either of them, apart from having his hair colour, chestnut brown. She had been utterly herself from the start, a totally complete person who had merely used them as assistants in her advent. She asked him what was for dinner. Leg of lamb, he told her and asked after Monica and Jan. They used first names, had done so since their divorce. She was to give him their regards.

He had a meal with them sometimes when he was in town, it meant something to Lea. It was surprisingly easy, all three were very civilised, but he usually left after kissing Lea goodnight. Sometimes they referred to the divorce, but always in abstract terms and without mention of the little mishap that had brought about the change, when he arrived home too early one winter Sunday. Robert wondered occasionally whether he and Monica might still have been together if he had not caught her out. If he had just left a message on the answering machine when he called home from Oslo. Then his colleague might have had time to take himself off and everything would have seemed different. Perhaps she would have grown tired of her lover, tired of all the emotional turmoil, secrecy and practical lies. To exchange one doctor for another wasn't exactly revolutionary, anyway.

They did not seem passionately in love, she and Jan, but of course that might just be tactfulness, to make it look as if their relationship was already as much a matter of routine as his and Monica's marriage had become. They did not even refrain from kissing each other heartily when he was there, the way married people kiss, like siblings. Perhaps it was really some kind of sophisticated consideration, thought Robert, a blind to conceal their erotic hurricanes. Unless that was how you ended up in any case, like siblings, because in the end establishing a family was like returning to the family you thought you had left.

Lea sat on the sofa watching television while he unpacked the shopping in the kitchen. As usual he had bought too many things for lunch and too many biscuits, as if the larder had to overflow with abundance when Lea was coming. He could not find the leg of lamb. He went outside again and opened the boot, but there was nothing in it except the first aid box, the jack and the spanner for changing wheels. Andreas Bark must have taken the bag with the leg of lamb when they carried his things in. He could not face driving out to the house in the woods a second time that day, and he certainly could not face the other man's drama again.

He had forgotten to close the gate in the garden fence. Behind the wide panorama window onto the terrace he saw Lea's turned away figure and the television screen trembling like a drop of quicksilver, floating in the semi-darkness of the living room behind the grey hatching of the rain. She was watching *Flipper*. As a child he had also loved the plucky dolphin's adventures, and now the series was being repeated it was his growing daughter sitting there dreaming of Florida's blue lagoons. It had become a classic. What a cultural inheritance! He had cautiously tried to introduce her to such varied offerings as Vivaldi's *Seasons* and Debussy's *Children's Corner*, but they could not compete with the Spice Girls and Michael Jackson.

He stood there in the rain for a few moments reminiscing over the graceful dolphin and the sun-tanned, well-organised family it had rescued from so many criminal plots against their sun-warmed happiness. The bright technicolour of the films had faded with the years, and the whole thing seemed pretty naïve, but he clearly remembered how he had meditated over the wise playful dolphin Saturday after Saturday. Its feats of grace when it reared and turned somersaults over the coral-blue water expressed pure unsullied joy. Neither more nor less exhilarating and jubilant than Vivaldi's trilling, violin-shimmering springtime

He cooked the burgers they were to have had the next day. They would have to go and get a pizza when that time came. Lea was still watching television. He would really have liked to have her help in the kitchen. She did that sometimes, it was a pleasant way of spending time together, but there was something about her motionless and almost melancholy concentration that made him leave her alone. Perhaps she was tired.

She did not have much to say over dinner. If it stayed fine, he said, they could make a start on the kitchen garden, and he reeled off the list of seeds he had bought, but she didn't seem particularly keen on going out to dig. Last time she had been enthusiastic, it had actually been her idea. He asked her about school and what she had been doing since last time and she responded, slightly dutifully, he felt, but she did not volunteer anything herself. She had begun to go riding and almost made a little story out of her account of how a young horse had thrown off one of her friends, but the girl had not been hurt, and since then her horse had behaved perfectly. She ate nicely, that was something Monica considered important. Yes, she loved the roller skates, they were *ace*.

He couldn't help smiling at the word. It was like seeing her in nylon stockings for the first time when six months ago she had played the princess in the school play, with mascara on her eyes, dark red lips and a beauty spot on her cheek, when he didn't quite know what to think. And the trip to Lanzarote? Monica had said something about the beginning of July and when she came home, there was her friend with the summer cottage. He did not want to dig away at the subject too much, but he felt a stab of sadness at the prospect of not seeing her during the holidays. Or was it just as much the thought that Monica and Jan would have a monopoly on her? He asked if she would like some dessert, he had bought ice-cream and made a fruit salad. She chose the fruit salad. He wondered whether it was out of politeness, because he had taken the trouble.

She seemed sad, but perhaps he was merely over-interpreting her recurring silence and withdrawn expression. He was always afraid of being inattentive. After a while, as she sat pushing the last slice of banana around her plate with her spoon, he asked if anything was worrying her. She avoided his eye. No, nothing. He gently stroked the back of her hand with his index finger. Anything at school? At home?

She left his hand there, stroking cautiously. She looked away, into the twilight of the garden. Then she said it had stopped raining. She was right, the swishing of the rain had ceased and the evening sky brightened behind the silhouetted birches, a soft yellow under the hurrying frayed blue clouds. She helped him clear away and fill the dishwasher. He asked if she would like a game of table tennis. She looked at him for a moment. Okay, she said, smiling, and the smile seemed genuine. They played for twenty minutes, she was tough, he started sweating, out of breath. It was silly to play straight after dinner, but she seemed to enjoy it and he liked to watch her quick, lithe movements.

Afterwards he made himself some coffee. They sat down to

watch television. She leaned against him on the sofa as usual, covered with the rug. Neither said anything much, again her gaze was distant and abstracted. Now and then he raised some subject or other in an attempt to get a proper conversation going, but she just responded with brief comments as if to get it over with, apparently absorbed in what was happening on the screen. After she had gone to bed he poured himself a whisky and listened to one of Bach's cello suites in an old recording by Pablo Casals. He regretted being so direct in his questions over dinner. The old music wove its logical web around him and he followed every one of the crisp trembling threads in anticipation of their nodal point until he felt he was the spider.

When he went into the bathroom in the morning she had carefully hung her wet bath towel to dry on the bar above the heater. She was nowhere to be seen. She had made her bed as neatly as a housemaid would do. When they lived together she had always left towels crumpled up in a corner of the tiled floor, and her room looked as if it had suffered an earthquake, but of course she was older now. She was out in the garden with her fingers dug into the front pockets of her tight jeans, her face lifted to the trees. He couldn't see what she had caught sight of. A bird, maybe, or a cloud. He went into the kitchen to make coffee. When she came in by the scullery door soon afterwards she wiped her feet on the door mat as thoroughly as a guest.

It had cleared up during the night, the sun was drying the grass, and if not for the wind, it would almost have been warm. She spent the morning in the kitchen at her homework. He asked if there was anything he could help with. She looked up and smiled, there was nothing. After breakfast he took the new tools and the basket of seeds out to the small corner of the garden he had pegged off in a rectangle. To begin with she sat beside him watching him dig, absently plucking small handfuls of grass and dropping them again. He grew red in the face from slaving away bent over, and began to feel foolish. He certainly wasn't a gardener.

Then she got bored with just sitting there and soon she was

digging beside him until the sweat trickled down her forehead. She enjoyed it and made a mock grimace of disgust when she cut a worm in half and saw the two pink pieces wriggle off in different directions. He found an animal's skull, and they squatted down with their heads together as he brushed earth from the domed periosteum. They could not agree on the kind of animal it belonged to. A weasel, she said. He thought it might be a badger. She gave his shoulder a friendly shove. How stupid he was! He carried the skull carefully indoors on his outstretched palm, and they found a little box which she filled with cotton wool, so she could take it to school. And get the matter settled, as she said with a pedantic air which made him smile.

When they went into the garden again they found Andreas and Lauritz on the lawn. Andreas held out a supermarket bag and smiled apologetically, either because he had called unannounced or because he had taken Robert's leg of lamb. He had looked up the address in the directory, he explained, as if to account for his unexpected appearance. Lea looked expectantly from one to the other, Lauritz hid behind his father's legs.

Robert felt obliged to show some hospitality. He suggested a beer. Andreas didn't need a glass, thanks. The children had orange juice. They sat in the sun on the terrace, conversation hung fire. When Andreas leaned his head back to drink from the bottle Robert imagined he was taking in the whole property and the surrounding hedges and fence dividing it from the other houses and gardens. He who lived a free life in the woods, in his leather jacket, riding a rusty lady's bicycle, dramatist and pioneer in one and the same person. It must be good to live in a house like this, where everything worked. Yes, it was actually. Robert picked up the signal behind the smooth reply. The other man persisted. Did it have a sauna as well? No, replied Robert, looking down at his tennis shirt with the crocodile. There was in fact neither sauna nor jacuzzi, and he didn't have a parabolic reflector, either. Lea giggled and Andreas smiled fatuously. Robert loved her for that giggle.

Lea took the boy's hand to show him round the garden, and he went along with her trustfully. She seemed very grown-up as she entertained the child and encouraged him to work the newly dug soil with a hoe, taking care he did not hurt himself. She talked to the boy in a cheerful friendly voice, kneeled beside him to be at eye level, watching him and sometimes smiling as he made faces and clumsy movements. She had pulled her hair off her face and tied it in a pony tail. Now and again she brushed aside a lock from her cheek and pushed it behind her ear with a feminine gesture.

What a pretty daughter he had. Yes, said Robert. Andreas picked at the label of his beer bottle. Robert must excuse him for being a nuisance the day before, but he had no-one to talk to, not here, and it was all . . . he sighed. Robert waited. Lea made the boy chuckle down at the end of the garden. The whole thing was such a mess . . . how could he put it? That was what he had been about to tell Robert yesterday, when Robert had to go. The night Lucca crashed he had told her he wanted a divorce.

The shadows were lengthening. Lauritz came running over the grass. Andreas rose to his feet, lifted him up and swung him round in the air, as Robert had seen Lucca doing in the photograph in their kitchen. Lea went over to him and put a hand on his shoulder. How about asking them to stay for dinner? She smiled at him, her head on one side, as if she were his little wife. It would be nice, wouldn't it? She would help with the cooking. They could go on with the digging tomorrow. Andreas sounded surprised at Robert's suggestion. Now they had cycled all this way! But they didn't have to urge him, and he insisted on taking over the cooking. Inside he looked around at the design furniture and the prints on the walls and said admiringly what a lovely house it was. It was very Scandinavian and timeless, and the projectile-shaped Italian furniture in the farm labourer's house in the woods crossed Robert's mind. In the other's eyes he was obviously a true suburbanite.

Andreas turned out to be a practised cook, and he set Lea to preparing the vegetables while he stuffed the joint with garlic. There was nothing left for Robert to do, and suddenly the kitchen, where he usually ate alone, seemed small. Lauritz sat at the table drawing round-faced moon-men with shaven heads and matchstick bodies and he walked to and fro, poured out red wine, put some olives in a bowl to nibble and played extracts from Italian operas for them. Andreas sang along to several of the arias from *Cavalleria Rusticana*, wrinkling his eyebrows and shooting lightning glances that made Lea double up with laughter. Robert had to admit to himself it made him jealous, in the midst of his astonishment over Andreas's familiarity with Italian bel canto. With his untrimmed bristly hair, black T-shirt and unshaven charm he looked more like a bebop fan. Robert felt he had been invaded, but most of all he wondered at the easy, almost light-hearted atmosphere his guest had suddenly generated so soon after he had come out with his guilty revelation.

In the midst of it all the telephone rang. It was Jacob. Robert asked him to hold on and went into the living room, turned down the music and picked up the receiver. He could hear them chatting in the kitchen and called out to Lea to put the phone down. Had he got visitors? Robert said some friends had called. It sounded authentic, he thought, yet awkward, somehow defensive. He hardly ever had guests. Jacob was disappointed, he could hear. He was going to ask them over. It was about time he introduced them to his daughter. Robert said it would have to be another time, and felt pleased Andreas and Lauritz had turned up. Jacob asked if he would like to play tennis on Monday. There was something he wanted to talk to Robert about. What? Jacob lowered his voice, he would rather not mention it on the phone. Robert said Monday would be fine.

They laid dinner on the pingpong table, it was Andreas's idea. There wasn't enough room at the small kitchen one. They sat around one half of the table and while Lauritz dropped the contents of his plate into his lap with methodical concentration, Lea asked his father how you could become an actor. Obviously the role of princess in the school play had put ideas into her head. Andreas answered her naïve questions patiently and she listened with a grown-up smile and a hand under her chin, holding the stem of her wine glass of coke. After dinner she tried to teach

Lauritz to play table tennis. She stood him on a chair and didn't give up until to his own surprise he managed to serve.

Lauritz fell asleep on the sofa. Lea served coffee like a real housewife. It was too weak, but Robert didn't mention that. She listened while Andreas talked about Italy. He and Lucca had lived in Rome before Lauritz was born. He spoke of her as if nothing had happened. As if she hadn't practically driven herself into death one night the previous week because he had told her he wanted a divorce. They had had a little flat in Trastevere, and Lea swallowed his anecdotes about the quaint inhabitants of the working-class district who shuffled out shopping in slippers and dressing gown, about the winding alleyways with peeling walls and washing lines, about the baker's wife with her moustache and the blacksmith's chickens. Yes, chickens . . . imagine, in the middle of Rome! Robert thought it all sounded rather too authentic. Lea said Lucca was an odd name. Andreas explained that really Lucca was a boy's name. Her parents had been sure she would be a boy. But they had hung onto the name. Her father was Italian, she was named after the town in Tuscany where he was born. Lea thought it sounded beautiful and looked at Robert.

She began to yawn and reluctantly gave way to sleepiness. She kissed Robert on the cheek when she said goodnight, hesitated a bit and then gave their guest a kiss too. For a while the two men sat in silence over their coffee cups and Calvados. The easiness had disappeared with Lea. They could hear her gargling as she cleaned her teeth and soon afterwards the sound of her door being quietly closed. Lauritz turned over in his sleep, Robert put the rug over him. Again he felt surprised at how his guest could change expression from one moment to the next. Andreas lit a cigarette and flopped onto the sofa, blowing out smoke. The corners of his mouth drooped, a lock of hair fell over one eye and he fixed his vacant gaze on a point on the carpet beneath the sofa table.

Obviously, he said, he felt guilty, but . . . he was not to know she would . . . it couldn't have come as a complete surprise to her. Just after he'd said it he thought she had taken it with a strange composure. They were still at the table after dinner. Lauritz had been put to bed. To start with it seemed they would be able to talk sensibly about it. It wasn't hard for Robert to visualise, he had sat in the same kitchen, at the same table, and now he knew what she looked like. She had asked if there was someone else. He sighed deeply. He had said no . . .

Might he have another Calvados? Robert made a gesture. Andreas poured for both of them. Up to now everything had been so banal, the marital scene one night in the house beside the woods and the unfaithful husband sitting here on his sofa marinating his guilt in Calvados. He was not in the least sorry for him, though the banality of the other man's story made Robert despise him. He was just so tired suddenly. Andreas downed the contents of his glass in one gulp and looked at him through the billowing veil of smoke from his cigarette. He leaned his sorrowful face on one hand so his cheek half closed one eye and made him look like a grieving Caucasian. What sort of seductive silhouette was dancing behind his despondent gaze? Was she playing a tambourine?

He had attended the rehearsals of his play in Malmö. The set designer was ten years younger than him, from Stockholm, one of the new bright sparks. Much was expected of her. Andreas cast a glance out of the panorama window to the sheer deep-blue patch of sky over the dark outline of the treetops. He would never have believed it would happen to him again. He had thought he was too old to fall in love. He looked down at his empty glass. He had not slept with anyone else since meeting Lucca, although there had been plenty of chances. In his world . . . he smiled and looked at Robert again. Yes, people were always hopping into bed. But it was probably the same in hospital, too? Robert shrugged his shoulders and said nothing.

Ironically enough they had met each other in much the same way, he and Lucca. She was an actor. At the time she had been with a director, much older than herself. He had been to visit them at the director's house in Spain. The old guy was going to put on a play of his, he was a big shot, it was an honour.

And then suddenly she had been there, Lucca, and everything had become alarmingly complicated.

His eyes sought Robert's. Everything had gone so fast, and in a flash she was pregnant. He lit a fresh cigarette and picked a fleck of tobacco from his tongue. When he had jumped into it he hadn't dared to confront his doubts at first. Lucca just *had* to be the one, and so she was, at least for a time. As soon as they got to Rome they spoke of finding a house in the country. But how could he put it? It wasn't just the routine, the inevitable jogging along when you had a child. It was something else, something deeper. A lack he could not explain and so had been able to ignore for long periods at a time.

He felt he could not share his innermost self with Lucca. She didn't understand him, so she did not know how to bring out those depths in him he could hardly explain. He flung out his hand and almost upset the bottle. Robert threw a glance at the sleeping boy, covered by the blanket, the table tennis ball clutched in his small hand. Lucca had turned her back on the theatre after she had Lauritz, completely absorbed in the child and in building up their home with a trowel and great expectations. But what use was that, when she wasn't . . . their mutual attraction had been mainly physical. Bed had always been good, as a woman she was very . . . well . . . he inhaled and blew out the smoke with a deep sigh. But there was something lacking.

That was when Malmö came into the picture. It wasn't just a question of erotic fascination. Although she was very beautiful, he emphasised in passing. Her parents were Polish Jews, and she had that special blend of inky black hair, very white skin and ice-blue eyes. Robert couldn't help smiling. Gypsy or Jewess, it came to the same thing, a tambourine would be almost superfluous. But there was something else that made a difference, something more . . . Andreas did not know how to describe what it was she did to him, the Jewish production designer. It was as if she touched on something inside him, deep inside. As if she made some string vibrate, a string he didn't know he possessed. And each time he took the last hovercraft from Sweden he could feel his life's centre of gravity had moved so that he left it behind when he travelled home to Copenhagen through the night.

He hadn't even been to bed with her, in a way that was crazy, but it did convince him there was something different and more serious afoot. After the première she had gone back to Stockholm. He had called her on the quiet and they wrote to each other, he hadn't written that sort of letter for years. Several weeks had gone by like that. He had been on the verge of collapse, surrounded by bags of cement and ploughed fields and Lucca's anxious, searching eyes. Luckily he had planned a month's stay in Paris to work. She must have noticed there was something wrong, but she did not question him, neither then nor when she went to stay with him for a few days. And finally he had made up his mind. He had just come back from Paris on the night he told her. He stopped talking and poured himself another Calvados, this time he forgot Robert. The production designer knew nothing about his decision. He leaned back his head and drank. He had wanted to make a clean sweep first, he said, wiping his mouth on the back of his hand. And now . . . now he didn't know what to do.

Robert needed a pee. It wasn't because he did not want to listen, he said, going out to the bathroom. After he had flushed the pan and washed his hands he stood at the basin sceptically observing his own reflection. Why had he allowed this strange man to invade him, ingratiate himself with his daughter and keep him up late while he drank him out of the house? What were Andreas Bark's romantic chaos and pathetic attempts to justify himself to do with him? He felt like having a cold beer, but let it pass. If they started drinking beer he would never get rid of him.

When he went back to the living room Andreas had put on his leather jacket. He kneeled down in front of Lauritz, who sat sleepily with his bicycle helmet over his eyes as his father tried to get his feet into his shoes. Robert asked several times if he should drive them home. On no account! Besides, it was fine now, Andreas smiled, the moon would light their way. Robert grew quite alarmed at the idea and told him to ride carefully, almost fussing over them. They went outside. The moon was full. He stood looking at Andreas's silhouette as he bent over his bicycle. The playwright wobbled slightly as he disappeared into the shadows under the trees, until only his rear light could be seen. After a few moments he reappeared, still smaller on the silvery grey asphalt between the blacked-out houses.

As the train started to move he took a few steps alongside, continuing to wave to Lea through her window. Then she slid away from him, smiling and waving, and her face faded from his sight behind the reflection of the pale evening sky in the glass. He stood there under the station roof watching the train grow smaller and vanish at the end of the track, where the rails met, shining in the dusk. Everything around him seemed to stiffen. The nettles on the other side of the rails swayed slightly in the wind, but their rooted movement only emphasised all the surrounding immobility, the rusty goods wagons with unintelligible numbers and lettering in white, the empty platforms with their islands of bluish neon lights and advertisements for chocolate and life insurance picturing pretty women and resolute men. He walked back into the station, it was like a sleeping castle with its superfluous ornamentation and shining clock face beneath the comical spire on the roof ridge.

The station forecourt was deserted, but there were lights behind the windows of the red-brick apartment blocks dating from the early twentieth century, disappointingly uniform with their ground floors clad in sandstone or cement. A dairy had been replaced by a driving school, and in one corner there was a radio and television shop. The screens in the display window showed identical football players running around. The colours of the grass and the shirts varied slightly from screen to screen, and here and there he saw the blue light of other television screens behind the net curtains and tropical house plants with leathery leaves. The blue spots of light in the windows flickered in time with each other, according to who had the ball.

Maybe he had given in too quickly, too easily. He probably ought to have fought, tried to win Monica back, but he could not help smiling at the idea. He did not really believe you could bend others to your will once they had decided to love a new face or die behind the wheel, crushed beneath a Dutch truck. Moreover he would not have had the genuinely passionate conviction necessary to convince another person. His life had become simpler now he no longer had anyone to remind about unfinished business, and he had actually felt relieved when he left it behind him, all that bartering with meaningful caresses and vague promises. Nevertheless when he saw Lea in the train window, waving and smiling her all too brave, twelve-year-old smile, something seemed to wring his heart, an angry ownerless hand with white knuckles.

When he got home he made an omelette and ate it in the kitchen as usual. Afterwards he stretched out on the sofa and listened to the famous recording of Richard Strauss's *Metamorphoses* by Karajan and the Berliners. He closed his eyes and let the wide, vast expanses of the strings overwhelm him as they displaced each other in soft avalanches, brooding and impenetrable like layers of earth and darkness. He felt something hard against his back and felt for it with his hand. It was the table tennis ball Lauritz had been squeezing when he fell asleep there the night before. He went over and switched off the music, then opened the sliding door to the terrace. He sat down on the doorstep with a cigarette. It was chilly, but he stayed there.

They had slept late, he and Lea. In the afternoon they drove out to the beach as usual. She gathered seagull feathers, a whole bunch, and he pulled out his pen-knife and showed her how to cut the ends, on a slant, with a vertical slit from the point, so she could use them as quill pens. She was more talkative than the previous day, the unexpected guests had obviously cheered her up. She spoke of being an actor, and he encouraged her. She had done well as the princess. The sun shone, and although it was still windy the sand was warm to sit on. Lea collected bundles of dried seaweed and snapped the bubbles between her fingers. There was an offshore wind, and the calm surface of the sea sparkled where the little waves swelled up, at first as long lines that slowly grew bigger until they broke into a small comb of foam which made trickling tracks through the pebbles on the shoreline.

How long had he been friends with Andreas? She liked him, and Lauritz was sweet. Robert smiled and watched a gull swooping past. Suddenly it started to flap its wings and the movement was reflected as a white flicker on the water. Not very long . . . Were they separated, Andreas and the woman with the strange name? She asked the question lightly, casually. The parents of half her friends were divorced, that was how it was, and the children adapted themselves. Yes, he said.

They had told her one morning, he and Monica, while they were still in the kitchen over breakfast and the sheaves of Sunday papers. She had merely looked at them, first at one, then the other, before going into her room and closing the door. When he went in she was sitting on her bed drawing on the back of her hand with a felt pen. Sometimes she and her friends drew on each other's arms, but she was not drawing a flower, it was nothing, a growing, ever more complicated morass of turbulent lines crossing each other on her narrow hand. He sat down beside her and put his arm around her. She leaned away from him, looking down at the colourful duvet cover with an African pattern. He put his arm around her and sat there for a little while, trying to talk to her. Of course they both loved her. He looked at her, turned towards the stuffed animals leaning affectionately against each other. Both of them were still there. They just wouldn't be together. She asked him to go.

Suddenly they had stopped quarrelling or just snarling at each other, he and Monica. By catching her in the act he had unintentionally and at one blow made every quarrel superfluous. After her new man had sent him the nod of a colleague as he passed the kitchen door and gently closed the front door with a cautious little click, everything between them had been fittingly businesslike. She had slept on the sofa in the living room until she moved. She even took charge of all the paperwork. There was clearly not a lot to discuss, and they both showed goodwill in getting it over as painlessly as possible. For Lea's sake, as they said, almost conspiratorially, as if they suddenly had something in common.

He had had no suspicions, having assumed ups and downs were normal after ten years of marriage. He had not noticed that the downs had grown longer and longer, until everyday life was a treacherously calm sea in which shark fins shot up when you least expected them. An innocent exchange about cooking the dinner could suddenly end up in hair-raising accusations, and small oversights or chance errors mounted up like evidence in a long drawn-out trial before an imaginary judge. But who should condemn one and acquit the other? Crestfallen, they went back for a while to the everyday rhythm of trivialities until one of them again succumbed to accumulated boredom or despair and struck sparks at the slightest touch.

Afterwards he realised that her hypochondria and irritable outbursts had been a cover for her battered conscience, and he felt sorry for her with a backlash of sympathy. It must have been a nightmare, what for him was merely the numbed monotony of an extinguished cohabitation. When everything had fallen into place and they had adapted to their new reality, he was on the verge of telling her she had not needed to almost tear herself apart with tortures of conscience. He had had a secret as well, but that was an old story, and as he had never told her about it why do so now, when it could not possibly do anything to change things?

They went further along the beach towards the point. The wind sent fugitive cat's paws over the water. Lea took his hand as they walked, chatting at random. He felt wistful to think they had only now become close, a few hours before she would have to take the train home. For that had become home, the house Jan and Monica had bought, a bit flashy, Robert thought, out in one of the northern suburbs. With him she was only visiting. She said they should do more about that kitchen garden next time, they might plant an apple tree too, looking at him with a smile as if she could read his thoughts.

At the end, where the beach melted into an isthmus and lakes, he saw two figures approaching. A swarm of birds rose from the rushes and turned in the air, the flock spread out. When they came closer he recognised the librarian. She was with a man who looked younger, wearing a baseball cap. She had an old sweater on, and carried her shoes, walking with bare feet at the edge of the sea. She had nice legs. He recalled them beside him on the sofa, in black stockings. It had been completely up to him. He looked at Lea when they passed each other with a brief, formal smile and conventional nods on both parts. Lea asked who she was. Someone from the town, he replied.

When Robert arrived at work on Monday morning, the sister told him that Lucca Montale had suffered another breakdown during Saturday night. They had given her the same sedative as the first time. Robert recalled how Andreas had sat on his sofa interspersing one Calvados after another into the tale of his unfaithfulness. On Sunday she had complained of pain and asked for more Ketogan, but the doctor on duty had refused to increase the dose. She lay in the same position as usual when he visited her, legs raised in the air, shrouded in plaster and bandages. The lower part of her face was still disfigured by swelling and effusions of dark blood. He asked if she was in pain. Yes, she replied dully. He heard she had been distressed during the weekend. Distressed . . . that was some understatement. He didn't understand shit, was her scornful response.

As he lingered at the foot of the bed studying her battered face, he felt a twinge of guilt over the scraps of knowledge about her life he had unwillingly been made privy to. She was even more distressed than he'd thought, but he had no way of helping her. He sat down cautiously on the edge of the bed and asked if she was sure she did not need to talk to someone. She would have to accept her situation, he said, before she could make any headway. The words sounded meaningless. Make headway. He increased her daily dose of Ketogan as much as he felt was safe. The nurse sent him a brief sceptical glance as she noted it down. As he walked towards the door Lucca turned her face towards him. Thank you, she said. He hurried out.

Later in the day he was surprised not to see Andreas sitting in the foyer smoking his strong cigarettes as he usually did every day when Lauritz was visiting his mother. He asked the sister if she had seen anything of them. She had not, and the patient had asked for her son several times. When Robert was leaving later that afternoon they had still not turned up. He had an hour to spare before his tennis appointment with Jacob and didn't know what to do with himself. He drove out of town past the industrial district until he reached the gravel road where he had turned off the last time. The horse was grazing in the same place, the sunlight shone on its flank as it raised its head to look at him. He went on to the edge of the woods and parked in front of the house.

There were no toys in the yard and the cement mixer had gone, but the old bicycle with the child's seat was leaning against the house wall. He knocked several times. While he waited he caught sight of the electricity meter fixed into the wall beside the front door. The hand on the dial was not moving. He went over to the window and shaded it with his hand as he looked in. The kitchen was tidy, a shaft of sunlight shone on the floorboards and the table. The door of the fridge was wide open, the disconnected flex snaked across the floor in the sun, and the shelves were bare.

It had grown warmer, the sunlight sparkled in the green mesh of the net and made the air over the red gravel quiver. After their game Robert and Jacob sat getting their breath back on a bench by the wire fence that separated the tennis courts. Jacob gave him a chummy nudge, he must do something about his backhand. Robert just smiled and screwed up his eyes against the strong light. From behind came the repeated clunk, now to left, now to right, of ball against racket, followed by duller thumps when a ball struck the gravel. Play was in progress on several courts at once so the sounds came unevenly and only sometimes fell into a syncopated sequence that was at once broken again.

What was it then? Jacob looked at him, bewildered. What were they going to talk about? Oh, yes . . . He sat scratching the gravel with his racket for a few moments. It wasn't so easy. But he felt sure he could rely on it not going any further. Of course he could. He smiled shyly, he envied Robert sometimes. What for?

Jacob looked at him. Well, he had his freedom. Oh, that. Robert leaned back against the fence and stretched out his legs. Jacob bent over and looked at his racket. It was different when you had a wife and child, it was a bit . . . well, he knew all about that. Robert smiled. Was it someone he knew? Jacob looked scared, as if Robert had suddenly shown he was clairvoyant. She was his eldest child's gym teacher.

Robert was reminded of the young man in the baseball cap walking at the edge of the sea beside the librarian, and of the set designer in Stockholm with black hair and blue eyes who had unknowingly changed the course of Lucca Montale's life. Everyone went around falling in love. But what then, was Jacob going to get divorced? Again the younger man gave him a startled look. He hadn't thought of doing that. Surely it didn't have to be either or. Besides, she was married herself, he smiled, it was a real mess. But what could he do? He was mad about her, and she . . . it was the same. It had been instantaneous, the moment they saw each other.

She had just started teaching at the school as stand-in for a teacher on maternity leave. He had met her at a parents' meeting, he had gone along alone, she had a fantastic body. They had fallen on each other in the car when he drove her home. She had *such* boobs . . . Jacob gestured their size with his hands, but the word sounded unnatural, boobs, and his hands flopped down as if they were already exhausted by all the density they had tried to show. He got quite weak at the knees when he dropped the children at school. It was like being young again.

Robert looked at him. Jacob still looked very young with his fair hair and rosy cheeks. He reddened, both bashful and proud at the thought of the ungovernable and reckless passion inside him. And what he wanted to ask Robert now was whether he could take his rounds this evening. Her husband was away on a course. Robert hesitated a moment, not to tantalise the other man, rather not to disappoint him by making his willingness seem too trivial. It was no great sacrifice, he wasn't doing anything. Jacob looked really moved. He knew he could rely on him. Robert thought of his wife, who always smiled at him with her grudging, cool eyes. What was wrong with her attractive face and well-groomed outlines? Surely only their constant availability.

It was many years since as a young doctor he had had fixed duties but, because of staff shortages, Robert and his colleagues were sometimes obliged to take a night shift. He rather liked the nocturnal silence broken by sporadic sounds, when a telephone rang or a nurse walked along the corridor in her clogs. It was a different silence from the one at home, when he had eaten and sat alone in his sitting room, and it did not make him feel isolated in the same way. Alone, yes, but not isolated. When he was on night duty he sometimes let himself imagine he was on the bridge of a great passenger liner. The gigantic oil-burning boiler in the basement was the ship's engine room, the sleeping patients were passengers in their bunks, and the darkness outside was the darkness over an invisible sea. For some it was a journey to new adventures, for others the last voyage, but that did not alter the speed or the course of the ship.

He sat chatting to the night nurse, a slight woman in her late fifties. She talked about her son, who was travelling across the USA by car with a friend. Last time he called he had been in Las Vegas. She looked worried. She had two watches, one on each wrist. One showed what the time was in America. She had calculated how many miles her son covered every day, and synchronised the time on the American watch, at intervals putting the hour hand back one. She had never been to America, but could describe in detail what her son had experienced on his journey. As a rule he called home in the afternoon, local time, when it was night in Denmark and she was at work. He called collect. The nurse gave Robert a slightly scared look. He wouldn't tell anyone, would he?

Robert smiled and gave her a friendly caress on the back between the prominent shoulder blades, thinking of Jacob who was no doubt in his car now, heart beating, on the way to his tryst with the gym teacher. They were often on duty together. She had lived alone since her husband died of stomach cancer ten years ago. He had been a builder, she nursed him herself for his last months. It had not been a happy marriage, but she spoke of it without bitterness, as you speak of chance misfortune. She had merely been unlucky in the great lottery. But her children were doing well, her daughter was a doctor in Greenland, and the youngest was a student at the Veterinary and Agricultural High School in Copenhagen, when he was not hurtling across the USA.

When she was young she had worked as a volunteer in a children's clinic in the Sudan. He sometimes encouraged her to talk of her time in Africa, how she had been on the point of marrying an African when she discovered he had two wives already. She had believed she had met the real thing in the figure of a tall handsome Sudanese. Every time she told the story she smiled the same surprised, self-ironical smile, and Robert could suddenly see what she must have looked like as a young woman. A graceful, surprised young woman in the midst of black Africa. At other times she asked about Lea and gave advice on child-rearing in a slightly lecturing tone, but Robert listened without argument.

When she was called away to a patient he got out his walkman and played a tape of Haydn string quartets. He wound forward to the slow movement, misused as a national anthem long after Haydn's death. He hummed the introductory bars, *Deutschland, Deutschland über alles,* and smiled. Once again he had to admire the way the musicians, even as they played the first, lingering bars shrugged off the dead shell of ugly associations and liberated the music. He leaned back as Haydn whispered his civilised commentary through the earphones with the warm, crisp vibrato from instruments almost as old as the composer.

Jacob must have arrived by now. Robert pictured to himself how Jacob the naughty schoolboy with red cheeks lay in a strange house between a strange woman's legs groping her boobs. The house would no doubt have been a family home like his own, and the woman would not have differed so much from his own well-shaped wife. A woman's body like any other, in a bedroom probably furnished like most with pine and chipboard furniture covered with white laminate. And yet it was a drama that was nevertheless played out between them, forbidden in a completely irresistible way.

While the gym teacher spread her legs for Jacob, did he perhaps pause for a moment, on his knees as if in a sort of reverence, at the sight of her cunt. No doubt it resembled all other cunts, both the real ones and those in all the porno magazines and coloured diagrams in anatomical textbooks the world over. When he had been no more than a child Robert had felt there was something brutally prosaic about the female sexual organs compared with his vague daydreams of what awaited him when he grew up. On the other hand it was precisely their rather frightening reality that had made them so exciting to think about, the folds of the labia and their colour range of reddish brown and rose.

When he pictured Jacob gazing at the gym teacher's cunt, lying open to him surrounded by the functional, easy-care furnishings, the organic folds of its form were as anachronistic to think of as an antique would have been, a quaint art décor casket lined with red velvet. Oddly striking in the orderly, mass-produced common sense in low-cost materials of the suburban house. If you lived the regular life of a doctor or gym teacher in a medium-sized provincial town, the female sexual orifice was the last romantic cavern, the last refuge for your debilitated imagination.

Earlier, when Robert had gone to bed with a woman for the first time, he had not only desired her body but also its strangeness. When they lay together, he and a total stranger, it seemed as he touched her that he was fumbling his way into another, different world. Or rather, he found reality at last as his hands explored the warm unknown body beside him. As if he had been living in a dream from which he had finally woken. Until it was over and he sat on the edge of the bed gazing at his affectionate unknown lover asking himself if that was all. If it was the same body he was looking at now reality had resumed a depressing likeness to itself.

In a few hours Jacob would get up and dress in the strange

but not in the least exotic bedroom, before the beauty who lay regarding him tenderly, pink and sweaty. Perhaps she had been like a mystery he had tried to solve as he penetrated her, as far in as he could get. But afterwards she was again merely a gym teacher lying there with her big boobs asking when they could meet again. Perhaps Jacob was not the sort to let himself be worried by the fickleness of life, perhaps he would just lean back in his seat with a little smile, his body satisfied, and drive home to his sweet unsuspecting wife. Or would he too, like Robert, trawl through his memory to rediscover the precious reasons for his tension and dizzy expectation as he drove in the opposite direction?

You couldn't tell, and anyway what did it matter, thought Robert, as Haydn's emotional strings vibrated through his head. Desire was like music, just as abstract, just as meaningless and just as overwhelming. As soon as the old instruments were played again the music woke anew and made its impact on her. Far away in the darkness he could see a shining yellow ribbon which doubled up and disappeared behind the opposite wing of the hospital. It was the motorway to Copenhagen. The red and white pairs of lights passed each other along the bright curve, just as they did every night and had done on the night when Lucca Montale tried to take her life. Unless, being the worse for drink, she had merely made an error and by pure chance had gone down on to the wrong lane. In that case, where had she thought she was going? He heard the telephone through the graceful intricacies of the strings, switched off Haydn and picked up the receiver.

A woman's voice asked in English whether he would accept the call. She had an American accent. Robert assented and a moment later he heard a young man at the other end. Robert asked where he was. Arizona. What was it like there? The young man laughed, slightly delayed by the satellite connection. What it was like? He was calling from a truck-stop. There was a petrol station and a cafeteria, and outside were tall cactus and sharp red rock formations and a long straight road. Just like a film! Robert smiled. He could hear voices in the background, sounding as if their mouths were full of potatoes. He caught sight of the slight figure of the night nurse at the end of the corridor. He held up the phone and waved at her with it. She took off her clogs and ran holding them, eager as a girl. He felt a warm sensation in his stomach. Arizona, he said, grabbing one clog as he passed her the phone.

He put it on the floor, she smiled shyly and turned her back. He went out into the foyer and sat down on the sofa Andreas used. He lit a cigarette, and as he knocked his ash into the cement bowl he caught sight of some without filters among the stubs sticking out of the sand, they had dark shreds of tobacco on the ends. Andreas had probably gone to Stockholm to start a new life since his old one was now in ruins.

He glanced at his watch, it was a quarter past two. Jacob was quite likely not going home before night duty was ended as the gym teacher's husband had so conveniently gone on a course. Maybe they were sleeping in each other's arms as if in a trial marriage. Maybe he lay awake, maybe she snored. But would he stay in love with the gym teacher for her boobs' sake or out of sheer enthusiasm at the thought of starting again from the beginning? Robert pictured Jacob announcing the sad news to his wife, one evening on the terrace while the glow of the grill died down, after they had kissed the children goodnight. How he would, weighed down with guilt, but also with enjoyable reverence, bow to the laws of emotion and move from one family home to the other.

It was not very probable, though Jacob did not have the bent for drama of an Andreas, nor did Robert believe that his practical sporty wife had the imagination to drive herself to destruction on the wrong side of the Copenhagen motorway. Perhaps she too had her little secrets. Robert brushed ash from his white coat. The windows at the end of the foyer stretched from floor to ceiling, and a long way into the pallid mirror of the linoleum flooring, along the empty ranks of sofas where he dimly glimpsed his white figure and crossed legs. He could be any doctor on night duty, sitting enjoying a fag. What was that, Jacob had said? It probably didn't have to be one thing or the other. Again he visualised one particular face. It was a long time ago.

They had just bought a bigger apartment, where they lived until that winter day three years later when he came home too early. It had actually been somewhat beyond their means. It was large and needed a lot of decorating, but they could not afford to get it done professionally. It was in an old property just outside the city centre, near the harbour. There was a playground in the courtyard where some space had been made. Monica took Lea for a holiday with her parents while he did the painting. He joined them at weekends. Lea was to start in the first class at school after the summer holidays. He had installed himself in what was to be her room, with her mattress, a lamp, the stereo and a selection of tapes. The furniture and crates had been packed into one of the other rooms under plastic sheeting.

Monica called him every day. She had a bad conscience about lying in the sun while he was left in town slogging away, but in fact he enjoyed being alone. Most of the neighbouring flat dwellers were out travelling, and he could play music as loudly as he liked. He forgot the time, absorbed in the monotonous work while Verdi's *Requiem* blew through the empty rooms. Lying on Lea's mattress in the evenings reading the paper he felt like a nomad who had temporarily pitched camp in a chance spot. The feeling of a state of emergency had a cheering effect on him, and there were moments when he even wished it could go on, this pause between the daily life that had been packed up, and the one that would begin when he had finished painting.

Sometimes he said jokingly to Monica that when Lea had grown up they could leave the flat to her and move into a hotel. It was an old daydream, to live in a hotel room with only the most essential possessions, ready to move at a moment's warning, and while he was painting it was like bringing the dream to life. He ate at a restaurant every evening, alone or with a friend, and afterwards cycled through the town as he had done in student days. The nights were light, the walls and asphalt still held a little of the sun's warmth, and he sat in pavement cafés observing the passers-by, sunburned and lightly dressed, as if in a southern city.

One night, with one of his old student friends, he strayed into a discotheque. It was a long time since he had been in such a place, the music had changed, now it was even more fatuous and deafening, he thought. The girls wore the same kind of clothes as the big girls had at the beginning of the Seventies when he himself was still an adolescent schoolboy. Those fashions had become smart again but that only made him feel still more out of place. A new generation had taken over the town and he enjoyed standing at the bar wistfully thinking of the time he had lurched around himself with some unknown beauty, sweating and tipsy in the flickering lights, to Fleetwood Mac or The Eagles. He smiled, 'Hotel California', it was there, in the stupefied and weightless morning hours, that he had fantasised about moving in some day.

When the girls looked at him he could feel that in their eyes he was an oldish, slightly foozling guy on the wrong track. They were just as unapproachable and insecure, just as ingenuous and at the same time imperious as pretty girls always had been. They only had their dreams, their bright faces and their young bodies, but as long as the music played the lack of qualifications was a strength rather than a weakness. He threw them silent glances as he sat over his beer and soothed himself by thinking that luckily he no longer had anything to prove. He had never been unfaithful to Monica, the very thought seemed absurd.

He got together with her in his late twenties, while they were students. Up to then he had had four, perhaps five girlfriends, according to how strictly you interpret that definition, and apart from those there had been a handful of other episodes with no after-effects whatsoever. He could barely remember their names or distinguish one face from another. He had been shy when young, he had found it difficult to play the game, and he found it particularly hard to talk to completely strange girls when it was abundantly clear, at least to himself, that a conversation was the last thing he was trying to instigate. So he was all the more astonished when one of them offered her favours just like that and the Devil suddenly grabbed him as if he had never before done anything other than putting ladies down on their backs.

When he and Monica became an item they had already known each other for some years. They had been in the same circle of friends, and had themselves become friends, neither had believed they would ever be anything else. Maybe it was the reticent attitude in both that made them feel good in each other's company and at the same time stopped them falling in love. But it was also the dry sense of humour they shared. They were known as the ironic observers in the group, amusing themselves over the excesses of the others. Otherwise they were very different, Robert with his modesty and his eccentric penchant for classical music, Monica with her cool, sharp-edged manner and tough way of expressing things, with no mollifying circumlocutions.

Her contours were so clear and sharp that she was almost mysterious. In a discussion her arguments were as penetrating as chain-saws, she swam like a fish and at tennis served harder than the most formidable guys. No-one had ever seen her dance and she always went to parties or dinners alone. She left alone too, and rumour had it that she might be lesbian. She never used make-up and dressed like a boy in jeans and roll necks all the year round, but she was actually rather good-looking. She was blonde and her profile was almost classical with a prominent nose and small, square jaw. It just didn't occur to anyone to notice she was rather beautiful. You didn't think that far because her energetic, masculine movements and challenging grey-blue eyes stopped you observing her in peace.

Robert had been afraid of her until he discovered he could make her laugh. Since then they had been inseparable at parties in summer villas in the north of Sealand, late into the night when people began to filter in pairs into bedrooms or down on the beach. They were always the last ones to sit over the half-empty bottles and flickering garden lights, but they both brought such consideration or animation to their repartee that the idea of so much as touching each other would have seemed plain comic. Even though several people had in fact asked him whether anything was brewing. He himself didn't give it a thought.

At that time he was in a relationship with an architecture student who always dressed in black with make-up pale as a doll and blood-red lips. He never found out whether they were really a couple, she was unpredictable and disliked being shown off, as she called it. She insisted on his putting her in handcuffs when they made love, he hadn't tried that before. Otherwise she was hard to pin down, but although she was so elusive she could just as suddenly take it into her head to surrender to him. He went on putting up with her whims merely to hear her scream like a madwoman and feel her bore her long red nails into his shoulders once more when she came. He had grown dependent on her nervous, frail body and her need for ritual subjection, and when he heard the handcuffs clink around her delicate wrists he couldn't be sure who fettered whom. As a whole he was not sure of anything where she was concerned. He suspected her of continuing to see her former lover, an architect who in the end did not have the courage to leave his wife and children, but he never managed to find out for certain before she finally vanished from his life.

That had a depressing effect on him and he did not feel inclined to join the group of friends on their annual skiing trip to France. His relationship with the temperamental slave-girl had been so intense and hectic that he never had time to ask himself whether he felt anything for her beyond a passionate and confused desire. But after she had disappeared he plunged into melancholy and suddenly felt certain that the woman with her handcuffs held something profoundly inscrutable which he had not been man enough to elicit. Besides, he couldn't ski at all, though finally he let Monica persuade him, after he had entertained her with his disappointed ruminations, grateful to her for listening to him. She undertook to teach him and after a day or two he braved the ski lift with her. A few hours later he was in the local casualty department with a broken ankle.

Monica had thought he would learn to ski quite easily, and to begin with he thought it was just a bad conscience that made her devote so much time to him. She went skiing only in the mornings, and spent the afternoons with him at the holiday flat in the ugly concrete block where their friends slept in sleeping bags all over the place and wet ski socks steamed on every radiator. She rustled up lunches and made *vin chaud,* and he was surprised at her gentleness when she asked if he was in pain, or supported him when he hobbled out to the bathroom. He had noticed this gentleness when she sat beside him in hospital while his foot was put in plaster. She looked at him and smiled, and suddenly she put out a hand and stroked the hair from his forehead with a brief, easy movement.

She lit candles when it grew dark. They sat with their red wine, wrapped in blankets looking out at the snow-clad mountaintops between the concrete blocks of the skiing hotels. They talked about everything imaginable between heaven and earth, exchanged childhood memories and described the books they had read. They were not particularly profound but for once they dropped the safe ironical distance that had brought them together but held them in check. One afternoon, after a long pause during which neither had spoken, she asked if he would hate her to kiss him.

It was different, it was a world away from handcuffs and screaming and sharp red nails. The transitions were milder and less noticeable, from words to pauses, from pauses to caresses, and from their hands' indolent playful exchanges to the first time she straddled him and sank her blushing face to his under the blanket she pulled over them like a woollen Bedouin tent, with slightly narrowed eyes and a shy smile that he hadn't seen before.

To begin with they didn't let on, the others were too close and it was too delicate, too new. They gave nothing away, and he marvelled at the different faces she put on, and how good she was at keeping them separate. He went on wondering about it in the years that followed. When she showed him one face, the cool and distanced one, he was all the more attracted because he thought of the other one, and when she revealed her gentle, vulnerable side to him his tenderness increased at the thought that it was a face which showed itself only secretly, under cover, like that first time under the woollen blanket in the French Alps.

One warm Saturday morning he took a train north. The compartment was full of lightly dressed children and adults looking out impatiently at the glinting water and the little white triangles of pleasure boats leaning into the wind behind all the greenery racing past the windows. Monica had the car, she was meeting him at the station. She was in shorts and a bathing suit, leaning against the bonnet, absent-mindedly rattling the car keys. When he caught sight of her he realised he had been missing her. They were used to being together, a week was a long time. She smiled grimly and sent him an ominous glance as she started the car. He had something to look forward to, her father was in top form. But her little sister was home from New York, that should ease the situation. They got on so well together, said Monica with emphasis as if she was not quite sure. Robert had only met Sonia a couple of times.

Monica's father was a barrister, and she had inherited his hawk nose and jutting chin, although to a lesser degree. She had also inherited his cool, spiky sarcasm and a touch of his aristocratic diction. In town he always wore a grey suit and bow tie, but he was as distrait as he was elegant, and more than once he had appeared in the Supreme Court with bicycle clips on his trousers. When he was on holiday he reluctantly conformed to the rules of holiday wear and put on a pair of khaki shorts, but his white legs ended in a pair of brown leather shoes with a dazzling shine, and his shirt always looked newly ironed.

He could be extremely cantankerous and every day over lunch in the garden he made sarcastic comments on the undesirable sweetness of the herrings. Year after year they grew noticeably sweeter, as if they were turning into children's sweets! Apart from the sweet herrings he saw communists everywhere, and the fall of the Berlin wall had not cured his phobia. On the contrary, he ceaselessly complained about the reunification of Germany and the outrageous chaos apparent in his world picture. It almost sounded as if according to his view the Iron Curtain had existed to keep out the Asiatic hordes rather than fence them in. Robert had given up arguing with him, to his obvious disappointment.

Monica's mother was a plump but comely woman, always in pleated or tartan skirts and a silk blouse buttoned up to the neck. She was a shadow, every single movement and each word she spoke corresponded to what the barrister did or said. She put up with his malicious arrogance and choleric attacks, she anticipated his slightest wish with a sweet smile and calming, motherly tone, and her only defiance seemed to show itself in attacks of migraine that forced her to spend whole afternoons in her bedroom behind closed curtains. According to Monica she had taken her revenge by having an affair for years with a psychiatric consultant. Everyone knew about it but no one mentioned it, said Monica. A bit of a mystery, thought Robert. Surely someone must have whispered, at least. Moreover the consultant was the living image of her father, she told him, with silver-grey hair and unyielding opinions, only he wore a silk scarf round his neck instead of a bow tie.

When she heard the car in the drive Lea came running. She was only in underpants, with gawky sunburned arms and legs, and her navel protruded from her belly. She leaped into Robert's arms, almost knocking him over. The lunch table was laid under a parasol in the garden which sloped up to an undulating terrain covered with heather and juniper bushes. They sat down, and Monica's mother called several times in vain to the younger sister, carping and impatient, as you call to a child who will not break off her game. She did not appear until the barrister shouted her name in his deep voice with his head half-turned towards the house, bent over and expectant, with restrained irritation.

She must have been in her early twenties. When she sat down between Robert and Monica, he felt surprised they were sisters. Where Monica's movements were angular and effective, there was something indolent about Sonia. She moved at a slower tempo and lingered over each thing she did, as if she had to ask herself what she was actually engaged in, whether it was spreading cottage cheese on crispbread or pushing her untidy hair away from her soft, heart-shaped face. Her dark hair was a mass of curls and longer than Monica's, which was smooth and cut in a practical style. She wore a silver ring on one big toe and spoke with a slight drawl, pronouncing the s's like a schoolgirl in a way that irritated Robert. Her long batik dress had faded in the wash and hung loosely around her. Monica never wore dresses.

She was the wild one of the family. That's what they had called her when she was small, the little wild cat. They had been unable to control her, the barrister and his check-skirted wife, and she was sent to boarding school at fourteen. After leaving school she went to Israel, stayed in a kibbutz for six months and when she grew tired of picking oranges she went to Jerusalem where she attended dance school and fell in love with an American. She accompanied him when he flew back to New York, their relationship was probably at an end then, but to everyone's surprise she succeeded in getting admitted to Martha Graham's school. Her father paid up without protest. To make sure she didn't come back, Monica had said with a smile.

After lunch she pulled her dress over her head and started to do tai chi on the lawn dressed only in pants like Lea, who watched open-mouthed. The barrister changed his brown leather shoes for a pair of chunky clogs and began weeding the rose bed, his pipe clenched energetically between his teeth. Their hostess went indoors to lie down. Robert and Monica sat in deck-chairs reading. Now and then he stole a glance at Sonia, who went through her long drawn-out movements with a self-satisfied, contemplative expression. There was something frail about her torso, out of proportion with her strong arms and muscular legs. Her breasts were small and childish, as if not fully developed, and her hips were as narrow as a boy's.

Late in the day Robert and Monica drove down to the beach with Sonia and Lea. Sonia sat in the back playing mouse with a hand on Lea's back, tickling her neck and under her chin. They both giggled as if they were the sisters. When Sonia tickled Lea in the side she doubled up laughing and happened to kick the driver's seat, which was too much for Monica who asked sharply if they wanted to end up in the ditch. Robert turned round. They sat quite still in their corners peeping at each other, red in the face with suppressed laughter. Monica bit her under-lip and gazed stiffly at the road in front of her. He laid a placatory hand on her knee, she jerked it aside and he took his hand away.

She seldom mentioned Sonia. She had left home when her sister was five, but even though the little wild cat then had her parents to herself she had nourished an implacable jealousy of her sister. Once when Monica had brought a boyfriend home Sonia bit his finger so hard he had to go to casualty. At that time their father was in his mid-sixties and more remote than ever before, and their mother, who was fifteen years younger, seemed to wilt at the prospect of starting from the beginning again. She did have a life herself, as she said sometimes to her grown-up daughter. Monica asked why on earth she had had another child then, but her mother merely assumed a distant expression. It had been an accident.

Little by little Robert heard the stories of how Sonia had cut their mother's underclothes into small pieces with the kitchen scissors, poured ink over the case documents in her father's study and emptied a bag of sugar into the petrol tank of his new Volvo. The high point had come when at the age of fourteen she got one of the boys in her class to telephone a bomb threat to the Supreme Court one day when her father was appearing there. Monica could recall how her sister had sat, arms crossed with her eyes on the carpet while her father asked her why she hated them so much. She made no reply, but when he asked if she would rather not live with them, she had looked up and said yes.

She was taken at her word. According to her own account Monica tried to persuade their parents not to send her to boarding school. But what she had feared did happen. Sonia's hatred towards her had just grown formidably deeper. Her silence and enforced good behaviour when she was home on a visit was worse than all her terrorist whims. It was not until Sonia was at sixth-form college that they had come to an understanding, said Monica, yet Robert sensed a lack of genuineness in Sonia's smile when she finished her tai chi and flopped down smiling on the grass beside Monica's deck chair. At lunch-time he had noticed her sending brief, calculating glances at her elder sister, who listened intently to her father and replied to his questions in her higher and somehow diluted version of his antiquated diction.

The sun hung low above the pine trees behind the sand dunes and the orthopaedic hospital. It was an old seaside hotel from the Twenties, and Robert only had to look at the white-washed functionalist building to hear a distant echo of sentimental saxophones. More than once Monica's mother had described how her husband had proposed to her on the dance floor there, in his white dinner jacket. He corrected her every time, it was black, but she persisted with rare stubbornness. It *was* white. After all, it had been the only time anyone had actually proposed to her. The foaming crests of the waves sparkled in the low sunlight. The Sound was dark blue and melted into the misty sky behind the Swedish coast. The Kullen promontory over there was nothing but a frail grey finger pointing out into the blue. Robert held Lea's hands, she squealed when he pulled her through the surf. The sun cast a reddish glow on Sonia's and Monica's bare backs as they waded out. Monica was slightly taller than her sister but he thought they resembled each other seen from behind, sway-backed and slim. They laughed as they plunged in and vanished, each in a flower of foam and bubbles, to reappear a moment later a little farther out.

Sonia came out first, she thought it was too cold. Her lips were blue and trembling, she had goose-flesh on her thighs and breasts and her dark nipples stood on end with the cold. He handed her a towel. She smiled and turned her back while she dried herself. Monica crawled along the furthest reef with long, measured strokes. Her forehead and cheeks caught the sunlight when she turned her face towards them for a moment. He told Sonia she had changed since he last saw her. She certainly hoped so. She smiled again and wound the towel around herself and sat down beside him. He looked at their fluted shadows in the sand. Lea squatted a little way off, she had made a small hill of wet sand and was decorating it with mussel shells.

He offered Sonia a cigarette, she didn't smoke, he lit one for himself. How long was she staying? For a month, then she would go back. She talked about New York, where she shared an apartment in Little Italy with a Belgian girl. Actually there wasn't much Italian in Little Italy, the Chinese had taken over. Really . . . She asked if it wasn't a strain for Monica and him to work at the same hospital. A strain? Yes . . . She smiled at his uncomprehending expression. He said it was really very practical. But didn't they get on top of each other? He waved to Lea when she raised her head and looked at them. She had a shadow of wet sand on one cheek. You don't get much time to do that, he replied, and anyway they worked in different departments. She nodded in agreement and looked at him with feigned attention, as if she was not really listening.

He had changed as well. She dug her toes into the sand. He smiled and gazed at his cigarette. The wind lifted the flakes of ash from the glowing tip and bore them away. Maybe he was a bit fatter. She regarded him for a moment. Yes, but it suited him. He started to question her about her dancing in order to change the subject. Monica came out of the water and ran up to them, shining and wet. Sonia interrupted herself and looked at him again. Why did he ask about that? Surely it didn't interest him. She said it with a smile, seemingly not in the least put out. Monica groaned and pushed her wet hair off her forehead with both hands. She put on his bathing robe, tied it tightly around her waist and lit a cigarette, looking out over the water. The sleeves reached down to the tips of her fingers. She jutted her jaw and blew out smoke. Beautiful she looked, with wet plastered-back hair and sparkling drops in her eyelashes around the calm grey-blue eyes.

They had dinner on the terrace facing west, where there was a view over the hills. The last rays of sun shone through the grass and the glasses of white wine on the table. It sparkled on the cutlery and the barrister's unframed spectacles resting on the tip of his sunburned hawk nose. The talk was of weather and wine. It was South African, a bit of an experiment but there was not much choice at the local grocer's, and it was really quite drinkable. Monica yawned discreetly and Lea rocked her chair, ignoring frequent commands to stop. Sonia showed her how to turn her napkin into a white dove and a white rabbit by turns. They all had their own silver-plated napkin rings, including Robert. The napkins were not changed for several days, this was life in the country, of course.

After the others had gone to bed Robert remained sitting outside in the dusk with his host, chiefly out of politeness. They smoked small Italian cheroots, something they had in common. How about a whisky, then? He had a quite excellent single malt, a present from a client. He went inside. A purple glow lingered in the heather and the tall grass between the silhouetted pine trees and juniper bushes. He came back with the bottle and two glasses, stooping and tanned like old leather in the blue half-light. He really liked the Sibelius symphony Robert had given him for his birthday, the sixth, wasn't it? He sat on for a while with the cheroot between his fingers. Usually music was something that somehow passed one by with its themes and variations and whatever you call them. Robert would have to stop him if he got too muddled. But with Sibelius it was quite the opposite. Like moving around in a vast landscape. It wasn't that anything definite happened in the music, it just happened. He shook his head. That was probably a load of drivel. Robert smiled. Not at all. But he really liked it, indeed he did.

He replenished their glasses. Good stuff, eh? Not the usual meths rubbish. They sat for a while listening to the grasshoppers and the cuckoo. A silhouette detached itself from the shadows and came closer. The lights shining out from the living room fell on Sonia's round cheeks and pointed chin framed by her flowing hair. She had been for a walk. A little one to sleep on? She smiled indulgently. No, thanks. She turned on the threshold as she said goodnight. Robert could hear the floorboards creak and the dry sound of her bare feet on the stairs and far away a door being closed. His host sparked his lighter and sucked in his cheeks as he lit his cheroot again. Suddenly he looked very old.

Being a dancer didn't seem a very secure occupation. He held the cheroot vertically between two fingers watching the thin whirls of smoke. But still, he was glad she had at long last found out what she wanted to do. He paused for a moment. Sonia hadn't been easy. Robert could feel the other man looking at him in the dimness, but couldn't see his eyes. Well, they knew each other by now, he was sure he could rely on Robert not to let it go any further. He had never told anyone about it. He threw away the cheroot stub, a little red dot among the grass blades. Sonia was not his daughter. He had discovered it when she was small and their doctor, an old friend, had done a blood test on her for some reason. He had asked his friend to make the necessary analyses, confidentially. Neither of the girls nor their mother knew anything. But the tests had confirmed an old suspicion. And he *could* count on his fingers.

Robert undressed without putting on the light. Lea slept on a divan placed against the opposite wall. Monica was awake when he lay down beside her. She pressed against him and kissed his neck, while her hand slid under the elastic on his underpants. They lay quite still when they heard her father's heavy step on the stairs, like teenagers at a holiday camp, thought Robert. He felt burdened by the knowledge he had been laden with, and by having to lie here, constrained to keep it to himself. She pushed her tongue into his ear and took hold of his testicles. He really felt too tired but he knew what she was thinking. It was a week since they'd made love, and tomorrow night he would have left again. The longer their times apart were, the more important it became, as if they had something to prove. They didn't speak of it as such, it just lay in the air, the oftener the better, and if too long a time went by he could feel her getting worried.

There was so much he understood without her needing to spell it out. A glance was enough or a pause before she started tidying the living room or putting dirty washing in the machine, too energetically. But it could also be an ironic smile in the midst of the conversation and the partying faces if they were out amongst others. He knew immediately what she was thinking. They often laughed about their almost telepathic talents when one of them said something the other had been thinking the moment before, whether it was a reaction to what was going on around them or something they had talked about several days earlier.

If their mutual wordless understanding was what bound them together, in a way they had been destined for each other long before they themselves came to see it like that, under the blanket in the Alps. The irony that for so long had prevented them from being demonstrative and restrained their potential desire from erupting was simultaneously a secret code, a portent of later intimacy. But in all their trustful security they left just as much unsaid as they had when they were slowly edging towards each other without realising it.

They knew each other so well. He knew her excitability behind the cool façade and her reluctance to be the first one to stretch out a hand in reconciliation. She knew his awkward distraction and restraint, misinterpreted by those around him as arrogance. They made allowances for each other's foibles, outwardly they came close to being invincible, and reciprocally they made use of their knowledge to both please and punish each other. A few words about Lea needing shoes, or where you could find the best tomatoes, could cover an ocean of tenderness, and a remark that the oven needed cleaning could cause quivers of indignation over something quite different. And it was understood, the purchase of small white shoes or firm dark-red tomatoes was transformed into a loving act, and when the oven was cleansed of congealed fat, every affront was expiated.

It wasn't necessary to say everything, he had thought, happy at understanding and being understood, but as time went on he wondered if there were certain things that just couldn't be said. That was what he was thinking, with Monica lying at his side working away at him until he finally obeyed, almost by reflex, and began to grow hard in her practised hand. Now it was time, after a week of enforced abstinence. She sat on top of him, the bed creaked rhythmically as she started to glide up and down. Lea mumbled and turned over in her sleep, Monica stopped, giggling softly. She went on, more slowly, and the creaking sound gradually became a dry groaning each time he thrust against her cervix.

He tried to summon passion and cupped his hands under her breasts. They had started to droop a little, not much, just a little, she still had a nice body. But it seemed that she noticed his hands' hesitancy, the restraint in their light touch, for she took hold of his wrists and forced them down on the mattress on each side of the pillow moaning and pushing harder against him. That worked, he felt the blood vessels tensing to breaking point, and a tingling and trickling from below as she whispered to him encouragingly on its stiffness and hardness. For a fraction of a second he visualised Sonia, the drops of salt water on her pimpled, erect nipples as he passed her the towel. He jerked the image away as you brutally jerk a curtain, and finally they found release, soon after each other, she whimpered as she flopped down over him and buried her face between his neck and shoulder.

She moved close to him again with her face against his chest. He kissed her forehead and his fingers ran through her hair. She whispered how good it had been. He repeated her words. She couldn't know what he was thinking, yet he was worried she might notice. It was hot in the cramped room, he put one leg outside the duvet. Monica breathed in his face. Her breath was sweetish, a bit like hot milk. He kissed her again and turned over with his back to her. She put an arm around his stomach and pulled herself against his back. Intimacy – he thought of it again. At this moment it was no more than the feeling of being shut in together in a much too confined room. An enclosed space, he thought, in which the oxygen was gradually being used up. But that was only for now.

The next evening he and Sonia went into town together. Monica drove them to the station. He had brought the Sunday papers, but she didn't feel like reading. He sat wondering whether the golfing consultant in psychiatry was her biological father. As if that would matter to anyone except the barrister, who had been egoistic and self-pitying enough to initiate him into his small private hell. He tried to imagine her reaction if he were to tell her. Would she break down? Would she be relieved? She, who had accustomed herself to the role of the family's unwanted rebel. His secret knowledge increased the distance between them and strengthened his impression of sitting opposite a lonely neglected child.

They exchanged casual remarks interspersed with long pauses, looking out at the lit windows of residential suburbs, the trees bordering the paths beside the railway and the blue strip of the Sound disappearing and reappearing. The lamplight gleamed violet in the dusk and shone through the leaves of the trees. They did not know each other although she was his sister-in-law. The word seemed quite wrong, like a silly hat. She told him to feel free to read the paper if he didn't feel like talking. He unfolded a section and read haphazardly. He couldn't concentrate, and at one point when he looked up he found her watching him. She didn't look away, just smiled. He looked out at the station where the train happened to have stopped and stretched to read the sign above the platform as if he just wanted to see how far they had come.

He was annoyed with himself to have thought of her when he was in bed with Monica. It had only been an image, like one of the slides that sometimes gets into the wrong order in the projector so the series of glimpses of a summer day are suddenly broken by Lea in a yellow raincoat standing with her hand stretched out as if she is pushing at the leaning tower of Pisa. You don't know how it has got there and hurriedly switch to the next slide. Moreover, she wasn't in the least attractive, Sonia, sitting opposite him in loose denim trousers and a sweatshirt with a hood. Again he noticed her coltish features, her habit of pulling her sleeves down over her hands and childish way of pronunciation, as if the consonants were choking her. Besides, they had nothing to talk about.

The next day it started to rain. He left the windows open and breathed in the scent of fresh leaves and wet asphalt that blended into the smell of paint, with *La Traviata* echoing through the empty rooms of the apartment. When he thought about Monica it was not their routine intercourse in the creaking bed he visualised, but her profile in the afternoon sun, the remoteness in her grey eyes as she stood in his bath robe looking out over the Sound, as if contemplating her whole life. Their whole life. There was no difference, her life and theirs, they were one. Suddenly he missed her. He felt like getting up and going to her, untying the robe she had tied so tightly, pulling her to him and putting his hands on her hips. Even though it was merely an image.

He had to turn the music down, he wasn't sure whether he had really heard the doorbell. He stood motionless in the sudden stillness. The bell rang again. He went out and picked up the door telephone, it was Sonia. Shortly afterwards she was on the landing with wet hair and an uncertain testing smile. She was wearing high-heeled shoes, her thin silk skirt clung to her legs and her damp cardigan was a little too tight so her midriff was visible between the buttons. She carried a bottle of white wine. She had been close by and got caught in the rain, she thought he might be thirsty . . . The explanations poured out and fell over each other. He found her a towel and she rubbed her hair so it stood on end all over.

He took the bottle into the kitchen but then remembered the corkscrew was at the bottom of one of the boxes. There was a screwdriver on the kitchen table, he pushed down the cork. There weren't any glasses either, they would have to use mugs. When he went back to the corner room she was over by the window, clad only in bra and skirt. Her cardigan had been hung to dry over a floor sanding machine. She turned, he offered her a sweater. No need, it was quite warm. The black bra pushed up her breasts into two soft semi-domes so they looked larger than they were. He sat on the window sill, she on the top rung of the stepladder. They raised their mugs, slightly ceremonially, and both broke into a smile. The trees along the avenue threw their reflections on the shining asphalt. He had no idea what to say.

She said it was a lovely apartment. He described a few of their plans for it. She nodded, looking at him with a teasing smile, and again he suspected her of not listening. She put down her mug on one of the steps and took a walk around the room. Her high heels made her taller and her muscular legs seem more elegant. She turned round and walked slowly towards him, arms swinging, as she bent her head forward and fixed him with a cunning scowl under the curling threads of her damp, towelled hair.

The night nurse was still talking to her son in Arizona. He went for a stroll along the corridor, imagining a country highway in flickering sunlight, endlessly winging among the rocks. Made-up beds were ranged along the wall of the corridor, separated by windows overlooking the patches of light from the rows of street lamps nearing each other towards the city centre. The door to a sluice room stood ajar, a tap was dripping in there with a hollow, drumming pulse into the steel sink. He turned it off and went on.

He passed the room where Lucca lay. He hesitated before cautiously opening the door. She was crying softly, he went across to the bed. She asked who was there. Her voice was faint and worn out with weeping, and her nose was blocked, so she gasped after each sentence. She asked what time it was, he told her. He wasn't usually on duty at night, was he? Just occasionally, he said. He fetched a tissue from the shelf above the wash basin to help her blow her nose. Thank you, she said, moaning hoarsely. She couldn't get to sleep. He sat down on a chair beside the bed.

She asked why Lauritz hadn't come that afternoon as usual. She missed him. The last words trembled and dissolved into a pent-up whimper, her mouth twisted. The muscles of her neck protruded beneath the skin, trembling with tautness, and her shoulders shook as she alternately gasped for air and expelled it in cramped sighs until she gave in to tears. He placed a hand on her shoulder and stroked it cautiously as if he could stop the cramp. She wept for a long time, he kept hold of her. Sometimes the weeping seemed to quieten down, then it broke out from her throat again.

When she had stopped crying he told her Andreas and Lauritz

had gone away. Where? He didn't know. He told her he had been out to their house. She said they must have gone into Copenhagen to stay with some of his friends. Suddenly she was very composed and clear. He got a fresh tissue and again helped her blow her nose. That made her smile at herself a bit. Why had he gone to the house? He told her how he had met Andreas and Lauritz at the supermarket, about the rain and the mistake over the leg of lamb, about their evening with Lea and how surprised he had been when Andreas did not come to the hospital in the afternoon as usual. But he didn't mention what Andreas had told him about Malmö and Stockholm.

You have a nice voice, she said as he was talking. He thanked her. Then they both fell silent. He had not put on the light when he went in. The room was lit only by the dim light from the corridor falling through the half-open door. He could hear when she breathed through her nose, her breathing was calmer now. She asked him to put his hand on her shoulder again. Why hadn't he told her they had visited him? It had not been planned, he said, and he had been a bit surprised himself. Normally he didn't get involved in patients' lives, they were not his business. No, she said after a pause, of course they weren't.

He asked her why she didn't want Andreas to visit her. At first she made no reply. It was a long story, she said finally. But perhaps he already knew something of it? A little . . . he said. Again there was silence with neither speaking, before he finally managed to ask a question. Had she decided, that night of the accident . . . did she want to die? She did not reply at once, as if trying to remember. No, she hadn't wanted to die. She had mistaken the direction when she reached the bridge over the motorway. She wanted to drive into Copenhagen, to go there. She stopped. He went on sitting there with a hand on her shoulder, even though it forced him to hold his arm up in an awkward, tiring position. He asked if she was thirsty. She didn't answer, she had fallen asleep.

The sister in charge smiled at him when he arrived at work next morning. So *he* was Santa Claus, then! He looked at her, uncomprehending, and she pointed at his jaw. He put up his hand and felt the little tuft of cotton wool still sticking to the dried blood clot where he had cut himself shaving. He had felt dazed when he woke up after only two hours' sleep and almost collapsed when he got out of bed. It was strange to go back to hospital only a few hours after he had driven home early in the morning. The phone rang as he opened the door of his office, it was Jacob. His wife had just gone off with the children, he only wanted to say thank you, it had been amazing. When Robert went in to see Lucca on his rounds he asked her the usual questions, and she answered as usual in monosyllables, as if he had not been sitting beside her bed in the night wiping her nose and holding her shoulder.

He saw her again in the afternoon before going home. She lay with her face towards the window. The blinds divided up the sunlight into slanting strips, and one of them fell on her face. She must have felt its warmth on her skin. He sat down beside the bed. She asked what time it was. He told her. She thanked him. For what? For staying with her. He asked how she had known it was him when he came in just now. She smiled faintly, she had recognised his step. She had grown good at that sort of thing, lying here. He suppressed a yawn, but a small sound escaped him. She said he must be tired. He said yes. He didn't know what to say. Would she like to listen to the radio? No, she would only risk hearing her mother's voice. And she didn't dare run that risk? He observed the anonymous mouth and chin in the strip of sunlight, beneath the gauze that covered eyes, forehead and top of the head. Why? She turned her face away, it sank into the pillow.

He sat on, neither of them spoke. He was not sure if she was still awake. He sat listening to the snarling sound of the gardener's small tractor that was alternately distant and then louder when the tractor crossed beneath the window, up and down the lawn between the wings of the building. She turned her face to him again. Did he smoke? Yes, he replied, bewildered. Would he light a cigarette? She felt like smoking. He lit one and placed it carefully between her lips, which tightened around the filter. She inhaled deeply. The smoke caught the strip of sunlight in a pale mesh as it seeped out between her lips. He opened the window. Grass, she said. He looked through the slats of the blind to the lawn, divided by the mower into long, parallel tracks of cut grass blades. He himself could not smell the grass. He sat down on the edge of the bed. Now and then she made a sign with her mouth, he placed the cigarette between her lips again.

He fell asleep on the sofa when he got home, and did not wake again before the sun had disappeared behind the birch trees and the fence. He was hungry, but had not managed to do any shopping. It was half dark in the room already. On the terrace the garden chairs stood about casually just as he, Andreas and Lea had left them on Saturday. It seemed like several weeks ago. The chairs were white in the twilight, fatuous and mysterious at the same time. He considered going to get a pizza, but couldn't be bothered. He thought of Lucca. Would she lie awake again tonight, alone with her tears and her thoughts? She didn't even want to listen to radio. But she might like to hear music. She could borrow his walkman, he could make a tape for her. He decided on piano music and went to look out some records. He chose to start the tape with a couple of Glenn Gould's Bach recordings and to follow that with a programme of pieces by Debussy, Ravel and Satie. He enjoyed doing it and quite forgot to get something to eat. On the other side of the tape he recorded Chopin nocturnes, as many as it would take. The telephone rang in the middle of Chopin.

He hadn't spoken to Monica for several weeks. Lea was their only link now, and she had long ago learned for herself to pack her bag and catch a train out and back every other weekend. As usual Monica was matter-of-fact on the phone. She sounded friendly enough but there was not the least hint in her voice of their once having been together, neither bitterness nor placatory nostalgia. She was as practical and direct as ever, she had called to talk about the summer holidays. She and Jan had thought of taking Lea with them to Lanzarote, but perhaps Lea had already mentioned it? He asked when. The dates came promptly. It was at the same time he was on holiday himself. He tried to hide his disappointment, but she could hear it, after all she knew him. He could have Lea for the autumn holiday.

He made no protest, he had never done that. Ever since that winter morning when his successor nodded at him in confusion as he made his way out, in the most literal sense caught with his trousers down, Robert had been determined to avoid rows. Sometimes he suspected Monica had found his acquiescence frustrating. A spot of aggression on his part would probably have relieved her uneasy conscience. She had been allowed to keep all the furniture. On the whole she had everything she wanted, with Lea and everything else, and in her astonishment she chose to persist with her demands, always ready with some uncompromising argument or other. Nevertheless he went on giving way each time she trampled all over him, for Lea's sake as he would say to himself, but also, he had to admit, for his own. It eased his smouldering feeling of guilt and he could feel almost chagrined when she realised she had gone too far. As if she prevented him from paying off a debt she knew nothing about.

He was sure she had never discovered anything about his affair with Sonia, neither while it was going on nor later when it was over. He was convinced she would have asked, fearlessly direct as she was. It was of no consequence now, but through the years his secret had lain rotting in a corner of his consciousness along with the knowledge that had been forced upon him that she was only Monica's half-sister. No one seemed to notice anything when he went up to her parents' holiday cottage the weekend after he and Sonia had spent their first night together in the empty, newly painted apartment. So it was that easy, he had thought, visualising Sonia on Lea's mattress, naked in the glow from the candle he had thrust into the wine bottle.

When the barrister looked at him over his unframed spectacles he felt they had not one but two secrets between them. Otherwise all was as usual, the herrings were too sweet, and what had happened faded and grew transparent in his memory like something he had simply dreamed. He even succeeded in being sufficiently passionate at night so that the intimate tenderness in Monica's eyes the next day made her blind to his evasive, restless mood. He was amazed at how hard-boiled Sonia was when she lay on the beach chatting to Monica or played tag with Lea. Even if they happened to be alone together, she made no sign. She made small talk and replied indolently to what he said. Apparently she had forgotten everything, or else considered it of no importance.

It went on for a couple of weeks. Sometimes she spent the night with him, at other times she came in the afternoon and left late in the evening. When she stayed the night he always woke up lying half on the floor because the narrow mattress was too small. Once or twice they went for a walk together. They lay sunning themselves among the stripped-off people in the King's Garden, and sometimes she suddenly rolled over on him and kissed him just like the other lovers did. He was afraid of their meeting someone he and Monica knew, and pushed off her arm in embarrassment if she affectionately put it around him. She teased him about it and more than once he asked himself if she actually hoped someone would recognise them. It was odd to walk beside her as if they were a couple, and he was alternately delighted and irritated at her giddy impulses, such as balancing on a fence in the park or pouncing on a puppy and raving over it with the flattered owner looking on.

He went to the airport with her when she left to go back to New York. He was relieved when she went, but he grew quite intense in the departure lounge, even if it was mere politeness. He had not been in love with her for a second, but that had made his desire all the wilder, as if he was punishing her because he wanted her. When he watched her doing her self-important tai chi in her parents' country garden he couldn't understand how he could be having an affair with her, and when he waited for her in the empty apartment, he sometimes hoped she would not come. But every time he stood in the doorway watching her come up the stairs with her sly expression, he allowed himself to be overwhelmed by her body again, by its uncoordinated mixture of strength and frailty.

Maybe it was not her body in itself which fascinated him

so much. Perhaps it was simply its tangible and yet unlikely presence. The provocative and dizzy fact that it was possible, that he only needed to take the few steps over to Lea's mattress, where she lay naked waiting for him. Later, when he sat among the toy animals reading Lea her bedtime story, he sometimes recalled it was on that same mattress in that same room he and Sonia had lain together, sweating and groaning. It might just as well have been a dream.

They never had serious discussions, they talked nonsense and fantasised and he mumbled sweet nothings in her ear about how amazing and unique she was. He was aware that he lied. She was neither amazing nor unique, she was just there, and he could almost have been her father. He thought about it when he sat on the window-sill feeling the rain outside the open window like a cool breath on his back, while she came towards him, carelessly swinging her arms dressed only in skirt, bra and high-heeled shoes. He felt old when she stood between his knees and let him coax her young, slightly immature breasts out of the black, feminine garment. On the other hand he felt just as timid and impatient as he had been in his youth when, a little later, he lay between her thighs and she guided him inside her with an experienced hand. As if he didn't know the way himself.

His dammed-up passion changed into anger, and as he worked like an over-heated piston he felt strangely alone, dumped between his lost youth and his laid back self-assured maturity. Afterwards she sat cross-legged looking earnestly at him, hollow-backed with her decorative hair hanging over one breast. She asked if he loved Monica. He didn't know what to reply. She talked in a worldly-wise way about listening to your feelings and the other things you utter into the blue when you are young. He tried to smile like an adult, but the smile didn't really work, now he had given in so willingly to her seductive arts.

And maybe she was right. Maybe he had grown short-sighted and a bit deafened by easy-going mundane daily life. Had he come to live permanently under a local anaesthetic? Suddenly colours seemed faded, and he caught sight of the worn shiny spots, the insidious wear and tear and the battered, peeling corners of his relationship with Monica. He felt disheartened and inert at the thought of everything that had previously been so attractive about her, and he dreamed vague dreams of major changes.

But the dreams faded again just as fast, everything in him was just temporary and changeable. Like the weather, he thought, unsure of how he would feel in an hour or a week. It worried him. If he could fuck his wife's half-sister in his new home, and feel it meant so little, how much did it mean when he was together with Monica? But what was it he was questioning? After all, life was more than sex! Sonia must have infected him with her youthful fad for life philosophy, there was no need to make such a song and dance. He made light of it and the question stayed unanswered. Before long he thought no more about it. He quickly forgot her after she left, and when he did remember her he was amazed at how wild he had been about her. He recalled her childish way of talking and her school-girlish way of pulling her top down over her knees when she sat on the floor while he painted.

He was irritated with himself for having listened so devoutly, still sweaty after their amorous rigours, as she pretentiously analysed his emotional life. Not until afterwards did it strike him that he must have merely played the available supporting role in a domestic drama that had nothing to do with him. He felt ashamed on Monica's account, she who did not know why her little sister had become so affectionate when they sat on the beach and Sonia dreamily put her curly head on Monica's shoulder as they looked across at the blue strip of coast on the other side of the Sound.

He took his walkman with him when he visited Lucca on his round next morning. He put it on the duvet and placed the earphones outside the bandages on her head. She smiled expectantly. He carefully lifted the fingers sticking out from the plaster on her arms and showed her how to start and switch off the tape and move it forward or back. She was a quick learner. Thank you, she said, and again he noticed how she could accentuate the little words so they sounded either light or heavy. The nurse watched him, but he could not work out whether she was touched or merely surprised at his idea.

He saw her again in the afternoon before going home, as he had done the day before. She still had the earphones in place on her gauze turban. He could distinguish the faint, trembling sound of piano. He sat on the chair beside the bed, opened the window and lit a cigarette. Yes, please, she said. He placed the cigarette between her lips and she sucked at it greedily. Half past four, she said, and let the smoke trickle out between her lips. Half past four? Yes, it must be that time. How did she know? The sun, she said.

One of the strips of sunlight shining through the gaps in the blind sent a warm trail over the lower part of her face. Just like the previous day. She asked what she was listening to. He bent down to her face and put one ear to the earphone. Ravel, he said, *Tombeau de Couperin.* She smiled again. Paco Rabanne, she said. Is that right? Yes, he said, wondering if she was as knowledgeable about after-shave as she was ignorant of music. He felt his chin. The little tuft had fallen off during the day. There was only a rough spot of dried blood where he had cut himself shaving.

She switched off the tape and pushed out her lips. He gave her another drag at the cigarette and took one himself. She blew out the smoke with a long sigh. He put the hand holding the cigarette out of the window and tapped off the ash. The flakes of ash floated upwards and spread out. Her voice was little more than a whisper. Perhaps I did really love him, she said. He looked at her again. She turned her face towards him. Now she did not feel anything. Now it was merely a word. As if she had used up the words. He stubbed out the cigarette and threw it out the window. Used up, how? It was not just Andreas, she went on. Perhaps they had begun to run out long before she met him. Her fingers slid over the buttons on his walkman. They were the same old words, always the same. And every time she had thought that at last she understood what they meant.

When he rose to leave, the sun had disappeared behind the

opposite wing of the hospital. He said he would come again tomorrow afternoon. She asked if he was wearing his white coat. He looked down at himself as if uncertain. Yes, he said, slightly surprised. Would he mind taking it off before he came? He didn't come before he had finished work, did he? She smiled apologetically. He still stood at the foot of her bed. She didn't know what he looked like, she went on. She only knew he wore a white coat, but she'd rather not know anything at all. Okay, he said. No white coat. She smiled again. Half past four? Yes, half past four.

For once he didn't listen to music when he got home. He left the door to the terrace open and lay down on the sofa. He closed his eyes and recalled the picture of Lucca sitting at a pavement café in Paris looking into the camera with a surprised expression as if she wasn't expecting to be photographed or had a sudden flash of realisation.

He thought of what she had said and what Andreas had told him. He tried to envisage the story they had been involved in, from the scattered sentences he could call to mind. They were still as fleeting and disconnected as the sounds that reached him from outside and left their marks and traces in the silence, the blackbirds and the leaves of the trees, a passing car, children's shouts, a ball striking the asphalt. He lay like that for a long time, eyes closed. A bluebottle flew around the room hitting the panes with soft thuds until it finally found its way out through the open door and was gone. The second hand on his watch ticked faintly under its glass, close to his ear.

Part Two

Lucca hovered over the ribbed sand for a moment. She felt pressure in her ear drums and her head was buzzing. She let herself rise upwards and shot through the unresisting silver mirror gasping for breath. The sunlight flashed in the drops caught in her eyelashes and the little waves glittered as she swam towards the light. On shore, against the white sky, she could see the towers and high-rise blocks of the city, the slim chimneys of the heating station and the harbour gantries, all of them black and in miniature. She started to swim back. It was a Thursday afternoon at the beginning of June and there were only a few people on the swimming jetty. Otto sat leaning against the green wooden wall with his legs stretched out in front of him and a towel over his lap. He was too far away for her to see his face as anything but a blind spot. It looked as if he was watching her, but she couldn't be sure yet. She swam nearer. He watched her as she approached.

She swayed for a moment with exhaustion and a sudden feeling of lightness as she climbed out of the water. Otto was reading the paper. She sat down on the towel beside him and asked for a cigarette. He went on reading as he passed her the pack and the lighter. She enjoyed the slight dizziness when she inhaled. He asked if it was cold. She looked at him through the blue plastic of the lighter, it distorted his profile. Not once you're in. She rolled her swimsuit down to her navel, lay down and closed her eyes so the sun was dulled to an orange fog behind her eyelids.

The drops shrivelled up on her skin which tingled as they evaporated. She licked her under-lip to remove a shred of tobacco, and the taste of salt blended with the taste of smoke. The sun bit into her skin but the slight puffs of wind felt cooling.

She let her fingertips slide languidly along his flank under the edge of the towel and on down his thigh. Her fingers recognised his muscular contours and she imagined the faint tickling it gave him, the sensation of her nails among the tiny curled hairs. She smiled at the thought of what might be going on underneath the towel, as she went on casually caressing him.

Someone had seen her the other evening . . . his voice penetrated through the orange fog, the other voices and the cars further away, and the waves lapped around the stakes beneath them. The stakes she held onto, with slight distaste because they were slimy to the touch, as she let herself be rocked up and down by the waves. Yes? She visualised the stakes, they were black and covered with shells and green fringes of seaweed, which alternately stuck to them and streamed out in the water like loosened hair.

One of his friends had seen her with Harry Wiener, getting into his car. Otto's voice was as firm and supple as his body. It was at home with facts, everything that was firm and essential. It was a voice that handled words with the same matter-of-factness as when his broad hands took hold of objects or of her, opened a jar of capers with a single snap of compressed air or closed round her wrist when he bent over her in bed. He didn't know they knew each other, she and Wiener.

She pushed the stub between two planks. Nor did they. She saw it fall through the shade and hit the water with a brief hiss. Honestly, she said . . . that old poseur! She shaded her eyes with her hand, he leafed through the paper and bent over as he read a headline, as if he was short-sighted. Did he really think . . . ?

He didn't know what to think. The sun shone on the page and made her screw up her eyes. She couldn't see what it said. He turned towards her, she smiled. He lay down and closed his eyes. She turned onto her stomach and leaned over him, so that damp ends of hair brushed his chest. He put his hands round her neck and with his thumbs rubbed between the vertebrae of her neck. He just wondered why she hadn't said anything about it . . . that she had met him. She studied her fingers, they were still crinkled like the sand on the seabed. Otto's voice sounded different when he lay down, flatter, she thought and, putting on her sunglasses, she lay down beside him so his shoulder was against hers. She must have forgotten to.

She had almost forgotten. At least, until Otto reminded her, she had not thought about it for several days. Nothing had happened anyway, not like that. It was one of the last evenings of the run, and the theatre was half empty. The reviews had been positive, and she had been singled out for mention in several of them. But the weather was too good that spring, there were too many evenings when people just wanted to drift around town and sit in the twilight feeling summer was on the way. Only very few would feel like spending such evenings in a dusty cinema converted into an underground theatre, on a gloomy street away from the city centre. Besides, none of them was really well known, certainly not the dramatist, a big-headed Swede of their own age, in his mid-twenties, always in black, of course. They had spent all their time imitating his arrogant Stockholm accent.

She knew she had been good that night, better than ever before. The words had come of their own volition, as if they had formulated themselves, and they had left her mouth with no effort, without need of thought. She had forgotten herself and merely followed the movements of the role, yielded to them, given over to them, totally attentive. He talked about that, Harry Wiener, her presence on stage. She had caught sight of him during the performance, but strangely enough that had not made her nervous. She knew she could not do it any other way, and the feeling of exposing herself was not at all unnerving. It was like admitting something painful, while thinking that now one has nothing more to lose. The same strange calm.

She had never spoken to him before, only seen him in pictures and in the distance at a first night. His grey hair, combed back from his tanned forehead, was long and curly at the neck. There was something resigned about his face with its vertical lines and narrow lips, as if he looked upon the world through the bitter wisdom of a hard-won experience of life. But perhaps this was just how people came to look with the years, whether or not they grew wiser or more stupid. He was always elegant, wearing a camel-hair coat and Italian suit or letting himself be photographed during a rehearsal in a T-shirt and baggy chinos, with his spectacles on a cord round his neck and his narrow eyes on the stage. He was on his fourth marriage, but that did not prevent him from playing the part of seducer left and right. For a few months each year he retired to his house on a mountain in Andalucia, where he was said to be writing his memoirs.

The Gypsy King. It was Otto who had come up with that, and since then he had been called nothing else. It was not kindly meant, but king he certainly was. No one could surpass Harry Wiener. Otto had had a part in one of his Ibsen productions and could raise a laugh with his stories of brutal humiliations and hysterical attacks of weeping when the Gypsy King cracked his invisible whip. The actors feared him and dreamed of nothing else but getting a part with him. To be directed by Harry Wiener was like dipping your toes in eternity.

Otto was not impressed, it seemed as if he was determined not to be. In his opinion the Gypsy King's productions were no more than mundane theatrical gastronomy for the culturally hungry bourgeois, weighted with psychophile symbolism. That was yet another expression he had coined, *psychophile*. And why was it, in fact, that the Gypsy King only put on gilt-edged classics? When had he last stuck his neck out with a piece of new drama, where he could not automatically rely on his audience flocking in with reverently folded hands? Otto would much rather make films, he had already won several leading parts and come close to winning a Bodil award.

Lucca wasn't sure. She could see what he meant, yes, and she had once sprayed a whole mouthful of red wine over him laughing when he parodied the Gypsy King giving a demonstration of how to play Shylock. With all the drawers open at once, juggling with the whole of Judaism, as Otto had said. All the same, she had been gripped, almost secretly, when she and Otto had been to see one of the Gypsy King's shows. She was thinking of that on the spring evening when, after the performance, she was sitting at her mirror taking off her make-up, and caught sight of Harry Wiener in the dressing-room doorway.

He was different, that was the first thing she had thought, different from the person she had imagined. He seemed almost shy as he stood hesitantly on the threshold. He looked like an apology for himself and his colourful reputation. Might he interrupt? The other actors gaped like shepherds who had caught sight of their guiding star, and it had been Lucca who pulled herself together first, smiling and unconcerned, to offer him a chair. He just wanted to come and tell them how outstanding they had been. The word he used was *superb*. Lucca's cheeks burned when he looked at her and said a few things about her interpretation, words of a kind she had never heard anyone use before.

They sat listening in a semi-circle around Harry Wiener while he commented on their performance. Lucca thought it was only now she understood what she had been doing on stage during the past few weeks. He had a good deal of criticism of the text itself, but their production had not merely released the best aspects of it, they had managed to imbue a deeper psychological resonance into it as well. Harry Wiener's words sounded old-fashioned and stately, like old silver fish knives lying each in their perfectly demarcated space, wrapped in moss green baize. He had not taken off his camel-hair coat, perhaps because no one had asked him to. Underneath it he wore a dark blue T-shirt and black jeans, but he sported real crocodile moccasins. The right mix of elegance and something informal, now he had come to see what the young actors had to offer. She could just hear Otto.

She looked round at her colleagues. They were all ears. They barely managed to keep their mouths shut, and she was glad Otto was not there. He would have derided them for feeling so honoured by a visit from this illustrious guest and being the recipients of his gracious words of praise. Like a cub scout pack given an audience with Baden Powell himself. But what about Otto? How could it be that he was so horrified and sarcastic as soon as the conversation took on an emotional tone? Was he actually a bit ashamed of being an actor? Maybe that was why he always had to make a laughing stock of the old theatre chiefs and their silk scarves and gas lamp diction, which he could mimic to make you fall about with streaming eyes. In his heart he probably dreamed of appearing with a bare torso in some action-packed American gun-slinging film.

At a certain point Harry Wiener caught her eye in one of the mirrors, and she smiled a little ironic smile which was both lightly conspiratorial and sexily challenging in an aloof way. As if she wished to keep a certain distance and yet make herself known. Possibly she noticed a particular interest in his brief glance, which seemed to read her in a flash before he looked away again. Perhaps she was flirting a little. It was too fleeting to reflect on more closely, it was just a glance, and he removed it so quickly. There was something modest about him, and she tightened the belt of her dressing gown, suddenly conscious of having nothing on underneath. She had just come out of the shower when he turned up, but then he must be used to that.

He was downright clumsy, she discovered, when he looked around for an ashtray and happened to upset a box of powder over his elegant coat. He smiled and talked on while brushing it off with the back of his hand. There was not much of the gypsy king about him there in that messy dressing room. He spoke quietly and seriously in his deep, hoarse voice about the stage as a mental space in which we keep a tryst with our inner demons. Lucca took pleasure in listening to his voice and looking at him as he spoke. He sounded like someone who knew what he was talking about, someone who had paid for every single one of his insights.

Now she understood why all the actors he had worked with spoke about him as they did. With the exception of Otto. When Harry Wiener now and then looked at her she felt he saw something she was not aware of herself, as if there was more in her than she realised. He spoke meticulously and hesitantly, searching for words, almost as if he were thinking aloud, while he looked down at the toes of his shoes or the cigarette between his tanned fingers. His hands were surprisingly delicate. He interrupted himself in the middle of a sentence and smiled apologetically as he asked if they were thirsty.

They went to a nearby café, he ordered champagne, the exaggerated gesture embarrassed them. He regaled them with anecdotes about well-known actors, both living and dead. He made them laugh and was even ironic without seeming affected. He listened too, when they dared voice their own reflections and feelings, and gave good advice without being didactic, as if he just wanted to share his experiences with them and his wonder at all the questions for which even he had not found answers. The next day they asked each other why he had bothered to spend a whole evening with them. Maybe he had simply been relaxing, taking a break from the role of peripatetic myth. Maybe he took pleasure in their enthusiasm because it reminded him of the deeper reasons he himself had had for going on, year after year, instead of resting on his laurels.

When the café closed only Lucca, her friend Miriam and Harry Wiener were left. They stood for a few moments on the pavement talking, while a waiter piled chairs on tables. Miriam unlocked her bicycle and kissed Lucca on the cheek, fairly demonstratively, she thought, as her friend waved and disappeared round the corner. But suddenly she was standing with the Gypsy King in front of a closed café after midnight, in a square on the edge of the city centre. He turned up his coat collar and offered her a cigarette. She accepted it without considering whether she wanted to smoke or not, and he lit his silver lighter, looking curiously at her, as if now the initiative rested with her alone.

Later she had to admit to herself that his simple and direct way of handling things was impressive. There was no longer any constraint about him. He asked if she was hungry. He had a flat he used for work in town, they could go along there and have a snack. He said this with suitable innocence and yet with a droll look she couldn't help smiling at. She was tired, she said. But then the least he could do was drive her home! His car was a street or two away.

As they walked along the quiet side streets she wondered at

their walking there together, she and Harry Wiener. He said he had wanted to see her on stage for a long time. He had seen photographs of her. They had interested him, the photos, she had a distinctive face. He looked at her. She didn't need to be sorry about that! He spoke of photography, about how photographs reveal what we can never see with the naked eye because our eyes are always seeking a mirror of our ideas. How photography can reveal a reality that is otherwise inaccessible to us, how faces become visible in all their startling and fascinating strangeness. She had never thought about it like that before.

It was an old Mercedes cabriolet, silver-grey with a beige-coloured leather trim. She wondered if he might have chosen that colour because it matched his grey hair. Everything about Harry Wiener was tinged with silver. She sat with her hands between her thighs in the thin dress. Now and then he threw a glance at her knees in their black tights under the hem, beside his hand resting on the gear lever, but she felt it would be absurd to cover them. She listened to the hum of the motor and looked out at the illuminated town turning and turning around her. It seemed slightly foreign, the town, seen from his car. She told him where to turn off and asked him to stop a few doors from her own. He switched off the engine and turned towards her. Again she was astonished at his directness. He would like to kiss her, would she permit him? She smiled and shook her head. She was both very talented and very attractive, he said, and she was wrong if she thought the two things had nothing to do with each other.

After she got out she bent forward with another smile. He hoped they would meet again. She thanked him for the evening and slammed the door. His front lights threw a hard beam on the pavement slabs. The cats' eyes on the bicycles leaning against the wall shone red, and her long shadow rose abruptly and swung over the façade as he passed. She caught a brief glimpse of his silhouette in the back window before he turned and was out of sight. Otto had gone to bed. She took off her shoes in the hall and undressed without switching on the light. She imagined Harry Wiener thinking of her while he drove through the town. A strange thought. She lay down close to Otto's back, so they lay skin to skin beneath the duvet, pleased with herself.

In the morning Miriam called while Otto was in the bath. Had anything happened? Lucca was irritated. What did she mean, happened? Miriam laughed, that was obvious enough. Lucca protested, he had talked to the others just as much. Miriam laughed again. Lucca sat in an easy chair with a shiny, worn silk cover, pink flowers on a curry yellow background. They had found it in a skip. She was wearing one of Otto's creased shirts, nothing else, she had just woken up. She pulled her legs up in the chair and looked at herself in the tall mirror leaning against the wall beside the bed. She held the phone between her chin and shoulder as she gathered her hair into a loose knot. It had grown long, half of it fell down again around her cheeks. Otto liked her to put her hair up that way, casually. Miriam talked about her boyfriend, she wanted to have a baby, he was not keen. She was afraid he didn't love her any more. Lucca let her talk on. A child, that was almost impossible to imagine.

She looked at her legs. She had nice legs, they were long, and her thighs were narrow and firm. Her cunt was nice too. She had shaved it so only a little tuft was left. That was where the King of the Gypsies would have liked to make his way. It was comical to think of all the wiles he had made use of, with champagne and stories and sage advice drawn from the experience of a long life, all of it to no earthly use. Just because he had seen a picture of her and taken a fancy to such a young, talented cunt.

She spread her legs so they lay over the chair arm, listening to Miriam going on about the child she so much wanted. Now she looked like the front page of one of the porn magazines she sometimes saw Otto glance at sideways in the all-night kiosk. Imagine if the Gypsy King could see her now. He would go right out of his mind. Be jolted out of his old, flabby, wrinkled skin. It would almost have been worth letting him, just to be able to enjoy his crestfallen face afterwards. Was that all? Yes, your Majesty, that was the lot! She decided not to say anything to Otto. Even though she had been firm he might go on thinking about it all the same. Besides, it irritated her that she had stayed there listening to the Gypsy King and his profundities and allowed him to drive her home in his flash Mercedes.

When she had put down the receiver she rose and stood for a while in front of the mirror. She unbuttoned the shirt, she had lost weight, her stomach was perfectly flat. She didn't want any child, for the time being she would keep her stomach to herself. Otto had turned off the shower, she could hear him swishing water down the drain with the rubber swabber. She pushed the duvet on to the floor and lay down on the bed with closed eyes. She felt the air from the open window on her face, stomach and thighs. Music wafted down from one of the other floors, a monotonous thumping bass rhythm. A dog barked down in the street.

Otto opened the door of the bathroom. In a moment he would be with her. It was a game. She would lie there without moving, and he would walk to and fro as if he were searching for something and had not even noticed her. He would let her wait, the room would grow silent, and in the silence she would be completely exposed to his gazc, unmoving, in an extremity of tension, trying to guess where on her body she would feel his first touch.

Lucca met Otto eighteen months after she left drama school. She had heard about him and seen him at cafés and bars when out with her friends. He was already then a star in the making, an underground star if such exists. He had been interviewed in a woman's magazine as the rumbustious puppy of young film, and if he showed up at a party you could be sure of fireworks. He had been in a relationship with a well-known rock singer and in general was the type girls kept a watch on out of the corners of their eyes over their cappuccinos and looked away from with a chilly, unapproachable air. They always referred to him in ironical terms if one of their group lost her grip and naïvely gave way to her curiosity. In their opinion he was already established although according to the usual standards he was still only promising. And Lucca thought he seemed to fancy himself a bit too much when he swaggered around in a football shirt, knitted cap and flip-flops, or whatever he hit on, scanning the bar.

When she was offered a part in a television serial in which Otto was also appearing she felt surprised at first that he could be bothered with such a job, although she naturally accepted. He had just got out of prison, she was his girl, and while he was banged up she had naturally fallen for the cop who had run him in. It was a totally fatuous script, but Otto was good and that made her better than she would otherwise have been. He was kind to her, he calmed her down with a smile or made her laugh when she was nervous, and she was surprised at his discipline. He could sit and read the newspaper or tell stories until the moment before they had to go into action and then make his entry and throw himself into his part as if with a snap of the fingers he became one with it.

In fact, he did not act. He was always himself, a fictitious edition of himself, as he would have been if chance had shaped his life along the lines of the script. He summoned the aspects demanded of the role with ease and carried everything off with his drawling diction and adroit muscular physique. They sat chatting among the lamp stands and rolls of cable in a corner of the studio while the cameramen set up their lights. Otto had never been to drama school and wasn't planning to do so. He couldn't be bothered to spend three years lying on the floor touching people and breathing deeply. She might well have protested, but she didn't.

How did it start? As such things do start, as vague notions, playful fantasies, a special feeling aroused merely by sitting beside him, listening to his voice and feeling his eyes. His presence was reflected in all her words and movements, even when she turned her back on him and talked to someone else. One moment she could be really dissatisfied with herself, with her appearance, her voice and what she said, and the next she could have a sneaking feeling of not being quite what she thought she was. As if she hid a secret version of herself, so secret that she was unable to make out who she actually might be, the other woman behind her distrustful reflection.

He provoked her with his self-assurance and cool dispassion. She felt he could see through her ironic aloofness. When she tried out a sharp comment he quite simply appeared not to have heard her, unless he stared straight in her eyes so that his silence seemed a grosser insult than the most offensive reply. She admired his insolence, but kept her mask on. She waited for him to relax for a second, open up a chink.

One day when she arrived at the studio he was sitting outside in the sun studying his script. A toy-shop carrier bag lay beside him. She glanced inside it without asking leave and found a transparent box containing a red toy car. She asked him if he still played with cars. He said it was for his son. She sat down beside him, how old was his son? Six, he replied, putting down the script. He leaned his head back against the red-painted planking wall of the studio and closed his eyes. He must have been very young to be a dad. He shrugged his shoulders, she felt stupid. What was his name, then? Lester . . . that was an unusual name. He looked across the courtyard. He hadn't seen his son since he was born. He had met the mother when he was living in the States, she had fallen pregnant by accident. They hadn't been able to make a go of it. He said this dryly as if just describing what he had done on Sunday.

The following week Lucca and Otto were filming at night in a marina. It was the last scene they were acting together. They had a long wait before the lights were set up. He had to fall into the water during a fight in a speedboat, and he fell again and again, but she was the one who got cold, although it was the middle of July. He lent her his jacket. Later they shared a taxi into town. They spoke of the difference between making a film and acting in a theatre and about one of their older colleagues who behaved like a silent film star even when he was in close-up. He shook her hand, a bit formally, she thought, and said it had been good to work together. She agreed. Standing in the street when the taxi had gone she discovered she still had his jacket on. It was a motor cycle jacket with a zip, the sleeves were too short. That made her smile, as if it was touching. She had not even noticed she was taller than him. She put her nose under the collar and caught the scent of his strange smell.

She called him next day about the jacket. He sounded as if she had woken him up. She was sorry. She asked him to forgive her. He said she could just come round. His apartment was in a side street. She rang several times and was about to go when he finally opened the door. He wore a shabby bath robe with claret-coloured stripes like the ones old men wear for the beach. She couldn't help smiling and he smiled back. Smart, wasn't it? She didn't know if he meant the bath robe or the jacket he had let her keep. Then he pulled her inside, pushed the door to and kissed her. She closed her eyes and pressed herself against him with a sudden force that surprised her, as if she had to make haste not to be paralysed by the strangeness of the situation.

* * *

From the windows you looked down on a building site covered with weeds and rubble, haunted in winter by street girls and local pushers who warmed themselves at a fire in a rusty oil barrel. The flat was sparsely equipped with junk furniture which looked as if it had come from a house clearance. Some time in the Fifties it must have been in a working-class home with ambitions for higher things, and now it had been resurrected thanks to Otto's slightly perverse but extremely chic feeling for teak and moquette. On one of the walls hung a huge, hand-drawn poster for a Sergio Leone film, and in the window a reversed neon sign in fiery red letters announced *Fish is healthy*. She sometimes wondered whether the junkies down on the building site brushed back their greasy fringes and raised their heavy eyes to Otto's window. She pondered whether the message in their stoned brains seemed like a revelation or a studied insult.

The street offered a Turkish greengrocer, an Egyptian restaurant with belly dancers, a paraffin merchant, a Halal butcher and one or two massage salons. The entrance was dark and scruffy, it smelled of gas and cooking and wet dogs, and sometimes she surprised a bent figure on the stairs having a fix. She rather liked the atmosphere of kinky sex and shady dealings, the exotic scents, men with black moustaches and little knitted caps who spoke Turkish and Arabic, and women with their heads covered, wearing long coats. She had even grown used to the junkies and prostitutes. They knew her and scrounged cigarettes from her, and she had come to feel she belonged there as much as they did. But in their eyes she no doubt still seemed an upper-class git who had lost her way in town, strutting off with long steps and chin in the air.

When she wore high-heeled shoes she was almost a head taller than Otto, but he didn't seem to mind that. If he had they would hardly have been lovers. She was a tall woman, but always wore high heels. She liked glancing at her legs, reflected in shop windows as she strode along the pavement and could still feel like a little girl playing at being a lady, hardly realising she was supposed to be grown up, although she had long ago taught herself to walk on high heels without looking awkward. As a teenager she had been clumsy, hadn't known what to do with her long arms and legs, constantly tripping over furniture and knocking over glasses and china. She was still like a bean pole, her face was long and narrow, even her nose, and when she was in a bad mood she thought she looked like a horse. But that wasn't the worst thing to be. Her hair was coarse and as fair as straw, with a reddish tinge, her eyes were green and her lips were full and kissable. Anyway that was what Otto said when for once he was playing the gallant.

They couldn't have been more different. There was something compact and square about Otto. He had broad shoulders and broad hands, jaws and thighs, but his bottom was slight, and his eyes were a guileless blue which contradicted all the power he held within him. When he walked he put all his weight into each step he took. His movements were sure and precise and he always looked people straight in the eye without blinking. He had a dragon tattooed on one arm, he had been a sailor. Perhaps that was what had made him so meticulous about himself and his surroundings. He was always clean-shaven and his clothes newly laundered. He did all the housework, energetically with wide arm movements, as if it was the deck of a merchant ship he was scouring and swabbing.

When he embraced her it sometimes made her think of a drawing she had seen on a poster when she was small. She had forgotten what it advertised but could still remember the drawing of a naked man with legs apart holding a boa constrictor by its head and tail. The snake was much longer than the man, it wound itself around his muscular outline and hissed in his face with its cleft tongue, but it was held fast in his grip. She felt a bit like that snake. She liked teasing him and showing resistance and she quite enjoyed it when he got rough. When she finally gave in, reluctantly so he had to keep a tight hold on her, it seemed as if she was also enticing him to reveal who he really was. They had been together for almost two years now. She had never lived with anyone for so long, and she had not had other men since she moved in with him. Sometimes she wondered how long it would go on. She found it hard to imagine it just continuing, but still played with the idea.

It was not so much an idea, it was almost only an image, at a restaurant, for instance, when she saw a middle-aged man helping his wife on with her coat, lifting her hair over the collar and holding the door open for her with a smile. She calculated how long they might have been together, and for a second it was herself and Otto that her eyes followed through the window of the restaurant. Two slightly round, slightly wrinkled adults walking side by side looking at tempting kitchen equipment in the shop windows, chatting casually about everyday matters. Two who knew each other's habits, weak points and embarrassing little secrets. Maybe they were happy and serene, maybe it was a comfortable hell of mute resignation and an inexplicable bitterness. Maybe a bit of each.

She didn't talk to Otto about such things. That would have been out of order. She thought she knew him better as time went on, and they had more or less been through all they had to tell each other about previous lovers, and what else their lives had held. There were still closed doors and dark corners in him, she could feel that, but she would not have known what to ask about if she had dared. As far as she knew he had not been with anyone else since they met, but then she was there the whole time. It was easier to reach out for her than rush around town chasing strangers. Otto was not at all the lady-killer she had believed and everyone claimed he was. He was well aware of what he did to women, but didn't allow himself to be affected by it. On the contrary, he seemed shy and hadn't known anything like as many as she had believed. He had not pursued her, either, she came of her own choice.

Now when she was with her women friends she sensed she had crossed an invisible threshold. Their behaviour was unchanged, almost demonstratively the same, but she could see it in their eyes. If she casually mentioned Otto she had to take pains to make him sound like a perfectly ordinary guy. As if in reality he was a monster and not the unattainable object of their green-eyed jealousy. Everything was different, she had become visible at one blow. When she and Otto showed themselves in town people were gushingly friendly to her even when she had never met them before. The ones with stature even asked about her plans and responded with evasive half-promises. She mentioned it once to Otto but he didn't understand her. If people were nice it must be because they liked her. She thought he must be rather ingenuous to be able to appear so confident.

She was fascinated by his composure. He was the same whether they were alone or with others. She often had the feeling that it didn't make a lot of difference if she was there or not. Just as his body closed compactly around its perfect proportions, so his interior being was apparently self-sufficient. You could plant him on a desert island or in a foreign city whose language he did not speak, and the result would be the same. He seemed like someone who could get by anywhere, in any circumstances. He could spend hours without speaking, not because he was in a bad mood. It didn't prevent him from suddenly stroking her bum as he passed by, or bringing her a cup of coffee she hadn't asked for.

She had moved into his flat gradually, in a series of carriers and bags. They hadn't said much about it. Her cosmetics packed the bathroom shelves, her clothes crowded against his in the wardrobe and her paperback editions of English and American plays mounted up in piles on the floors among his thrillers and videos. It seemed neither to bother him nor make him reflect on what it was all about, where it might take them. Was it taking them anywhere, in fact? They went to London one spring and Morocco one winter, when he had a break between two films. It looked as if they belonged together.

When they were going out she occasionally asked him what he thought she should wear, but he didn't mind whether she pulled a sweater over her head or put on a short low-necked dress. He was never jealous, and although she gave him no reason to be, that did surprise her. There were plenty of men if she had been interested. There had never been a lack of those, for her. Several times she allowed herself to be talked into a corner by some stud who had the hots for her just to see if it provoked a reaction. But Otto went on calmly chatting to his friends without looking in her direction, and she had to disentangle herself from her experimental flirtation.

It wasn't that he was indifferent to her. For the most part he was considerate, at times downright affectionate, but just as often he left her in peace, and she could feel he expected the same from her. Now and then she asked if he would rather be alone, but he merely looked at her in amazement and smiled, as if she had said something odd. When he wanted to be alone, he went out. There was a pub round the corner where he played billiards, a rough gloomy place with tobacco-yellow crochet curtains, where none of her friends would dare set their feet.

He could make her feel invisible when he concentrated on washing up, watching television, polishing shoes or lifting weights. As if she wasn't there. At times she felt she was nothing more than a pair of hungry eyes that clung to his detached mien and perfect body. His attacks of introspective self-sufficiency had a titillating effect on her, like the maddening, pleasurable expectation when she lay in bed giving herself up to his circling, teasing caresses. His silence could fill the flat with an atmosphere that was as agonising as it was agitating, and it completely took possession of her until her body and gaze were a swollen, quivering receptivity.

If neither of them had anything to get up for they slept late. When she woke up one spring morning he was sitting in his underpants in front of the open window sunning himself and reading the paper. She called to him but he didn't answer. She lay watching him for a long time. The strong light glistened on the hairs on his chest and the dust motes hovering in the air. She crept over to him from behind, placed her hands on his chest and bent forward to kiss him, so her hair fell over his face. He moved his head and with a preoccupied air took hold of her chin while he went on reading, just as you pick up the loose skin on a puppy's jaws.

She sat down on the floor under the window and rested her feet on the edge of the chair seat between his knees. His face was hidden behind the paper. She let one big toe brush his inner thigh and massaged him softly in the crutch. He did not move but she could feel it worked. Then she bent forward and coaxed his cock out of the fly. It was violet in the spring sunshine, she took it into her mouth. He moved the paper and looked at her, neutral and interested, like a spectator. She met his eyes, trying to visualise what she looked like from up there with his cock in her mouth, like one of the whores in his daydreams.

The next moment she was lying underneath him on her stomach. He forced her down with all his weight so she could barely breathe and penetrated her, pressing her face against the dusty floorboards. She enjoyed his sudden violence, like a pent-up fury suddenly let loose. It hurt her, and he came before she had a chance herself, but soon afterwards when she was in the shower feeling his warm seed running down her thighs she couldn't help smiling at the thought that his sudden passion must express part of everything he obviously had no words for. All that was hidden behind his silence and remote gaze.

It was getting hot. Drops of sweat crawled slowly down from the roots of her hair over her nose. She lay on her stomach sniffing the smell of sweat and sun cream on her arms, the smell of summer. The little waves melted together in a winking field of reflections, and in the empty sky she saw the jet stream of a plane making its way like a needle glowing whitely. She turned and shaded her eyes with a hand. The tail of the white line spread out and dissolved into small clouds like the knobs on a backbone.

She closed her eyes. More people had arrived, children screamed when they jumped into the water, and the adult voices blended together so she couldn't hear what they said. The planks gave under her every time someone walked past. She stretched out her arm and let the back of her hand rest on Otto's belly. She looked at him. He lay motionless, as if asleep. She could perfectly well have told him about her meeting with Harry Wiener when they were at breakfast the next day. They could have laughed over the Gypsy King's unsuccessful attempt at seducing her. It was too stupid, and still more stupid of him to suspect something had happened.

Otto sat up, her hand slipped off his stomach. He looked out at the Sound. She wanted to say something, it didn't matter what. He stood up too quickly for her to be able to catch his eye. He walked to the end of the jetty and stood for a moment with his back to her before jumping in and vanishing. A few seconds later he emerged and began to swim off.

He had looked at her without interest when she described how Harry Wiener had turned up at the dressing room unannounced and invited them all for champagne. She plastered herself with sun block, slowly and thoroughly, so she didn't have to look straight at him all the time, as she reported what he had said about their performance. She described how happy that had made her, mostly to offset her astonishment when she came to his approaches in the car. She had taken it in good faith, she would never have dreamed that the Gypsy King could come to humble himself like that. She even exaggerated slightly and took pains to go into details about his old, rather feminine hands and how pathetically he had displayed his slobbering raunchiness. But the more she said the more she felt it sounded as if she was hiding something.

Smiling crookedly Otto said she would soon be getting an offer to play Ophelia or Juliet, it wouldn't be long. Couldn't she speak up for him and get him the part of Hamlet or Romeo? Or would that interfere with her plans? He said it lightly and she cuffed him on the shoulder, pretending annoyance in return for his ironical smile.

Rows of people were lying along the jetty and on the beach, so many by now it was impossible to see who was with whom. Quite close to her was a group of fragile-looking teenagers with budding breasts and bony shoulders. They whispered and giggled, now and then one of them raised herself a little and shaded her eyes as if looking for someone. At the edge of the sea a bald fat man carried a small boy in water wings. The man's stomach wore a mat of black hair and the boy's arms were so thin that the water wings kept sliding down to his wrists.

The wind was getting up and stirring the water into confused golden points. It whipped the sheets against the mast of a sailing dinghy keeled over on its side on the wet sand where the waves fell together and slid back. The sound reached right over to her, sharp and rhythmical, and the gusts of wind tore at the trunks of the tall beech trees in front of the sun. The top branches waved and their leaves glittered nervously in quivering sighs behind the intricate tape of smoke winding up from the cigarette between her fingers.

When she turned round Otto was on his way over to the jetty with long strokes. She lay down again. Soon she felt his heavy stride making the planks rock. He dripped over her and the cold drops woke her heated skin out of its trance. One drop fell on a lens of her shades as he sat down beside her with a sigh. The drop made the sky quiver and melt. He lit a cigarette and placed a hand on her knee. Her kneecap rested within it as in a cave. She asked if he was hungry. She sounded like a little housewife worrying about her spouse's nourishment. He took his hand away from her knee. Not specially . . . was she? He ate in a revolting manner, it was the only unpleasant thing about him. She had never thought much about it, merely noticed it. He smacked his lips and bent over with a protective arm round his plate as he shovelled in his food with his right hand and looked around scowling as if he was afraid someone might come and steal it.

He asked if she would like to go. Obviously he too was at a loss for something to talk about. As they cycled into town she asked herself whether she had invited the Gypsy King to try it on when she met his eyes in the dressing-room mirror. Maybe she had waited too long to look away or else she had taken her eyes off him too quickly as if feeling herself seen through. She bit her under-lip in irritation. Couldn't you look around as you liked? It might well be that she had wondered for a second what impression she had made on him, and so what? Surely her thoughts were her private property. Besides he had seemed to mean what he said about her performance. Could it all have been just a manoeuvre, a stage in the cunning strategy of seduction?

It was her first leading role and she had been dreadfully nervous. When Otto came home the afternoon before the première she had been standing in the living room doing voice exercises. He had bought a CD of Iggy Pop and played it at once, throwing himself on the sofa and starting to roll a joint. She caught his eye and narrowed her lips. He asked with false innocence if the music worried her. She went into the bedroom and slammed the door behind her. The drone of Iggy Pop's voice penetrated through the door with its monotonous bass and throbbing drums. On the other side of the narrow back yard she could look into a kitchen lit by an unshaded light bulb behind the dirty window. An old man in a net vest stood at the stove. His back was bent, it faced her so she saw only his bony shoulders and prominent shoulder blades in the vest, which was too big for him. He was frying bacon, she could smell it.

She took a deep breath and produced a low note that rose like a column from her diaphragm, as she had been taught. Then Iggy Pop started up again. She lay down on the bed, she couldn't remember a single line, and in three hours she had to be on stage. She turned and in surprise regarded the little dark spot spreading over the pillowcase, as if it was not hers, the tear sucked in by the finely woven cotton.

During the curtain calls Lucca couldn't understand how they had pulled it off so well. She didn't know whether she had been good or bad, she had merely followed the patterns laid down by the words and movements, mechanically like a toy train that rushes confidently around on its rails. But everybody talked of how she had lived the part, so full of genuine feeling. She was the centre of the first-night party, everyone wanted to kiss her and give her a big hug, even people she had only met once. She allowed herself to revel in it without holding back. Otto stayed in the background, he spent the evening in a corner with one of his friends. When she walked past them she could hear the sarcasm in his voice.

When they got home he did not spare her his outspoken opinion of the play, and when he read the reviews, which all emphasised her performance, he snorted and warned her not to let herself be flattered by such a pack of fawning poodles. She asked if he was jealous, but that was showing off, she didn't believe it herself. It was not a great success with audiences, and the flowers she had been given, gift-wrapped like the ones at the big theatres, withered after a day or two. Otto was the one who threw them out, the flat stank like a bloody brothel. He said it in his usual studiedly bragging tones, as he did when he wanted her to understand he didn't really mean it. But why couldn't he grant her a spot of success, when he wallowed in admiration like a happy pig in his mud?

She thought of the contrast between Harry Wiener's sympathetic, eloquent compliments and Otto's scornful comments. Who was she to believe? Maybe neither of them. Obviously the Gypsy King had had his demonstrable reasons for smothering her with his wit, but why couldn't Otto be generous about her success? Was he jealous, after all? In her scattered thoughts on the way home from swimming she confused the order of events, and saw Otto's scorn after the première as a reaction to the Gypsy King's erotic tricks three weeks later.

Maybe Otto had foreseen what might happen in the wake of her first outstanding reviews and the first newspaper interview she had ever given, in which she was presented with doe eyes, long legs and high acting ideals. Maybe he even felt that all the attention she was suddenly getting was a threat to his right of possession to what lay hidden behind those very eyes and between those very legs. If she had wanted to she could easily have stayed there in the Gypsy King's Mercedes. She could have gone up with him just like that into the legendary roof-top apartment where so many had gone before her, a little shy, a little girlish, with a coquettishly nervous hand constantly running through her hair, with her coat still on, as he mixed drinks and told stories about his meetings with Bergman and Strehler.

Otto cycled fast, as if trying to throw her off, and she had to tramp on the pedals to keep up. Sweat stung her forehead and her cheeks and made her blouse stick. When they had to stop at a red light she rode up beside him. She held on to his shoulder for support without putting her feet down, while the crossing traffic passed in a blue mist of exhaust and dazzling reflections.

She couldn't see his eyes behind all the shining movement in his shades. He smiled as he put out a hand and moved a lock of hair that had fallen in front of her eyes and stuck to her forehead. She felt like kissing him, but the lights changed to green.

She ought to be glad he had shown a touch of jealousy at the Gypsy King's come-on. It must be proof that after all she meant more to him than he cared to shout about. But that wasn't like him, it was more like Daniel. It was ironic, she hadn't thought of him for several months. Perhaps he was still sitting with his broken heart in his lap picking at the scabs.

She had never promised him anything. She broke it to him gently, at the same time safe-guarding herself. He sat on the piano stool staring down at the lid covering the keys. She could see herself, legs crossed, as a misty shining reflection in the curving instrument. The grand piano took up a third of the room, and his unmade mattress occupied another third. There was just room in between for the small table where he wrote out his scores. Here he spent most of his time bent over his bizarre music with its scattered, shrill notes and confused chords written for an orchestra he only heard in his own dark curly head. She had been fascinated by the invisible aura that spread around him when he played to her so that even the depressing surroundings took on a mystic air. He raised his head and looked at her through little steel spectacles. She stood up and walked to the window. He said he loved her. It was all very sad.

At the end of his street there was a damp-stained viaduct, and on the corner a run-down discount supermarket boasted garish posters advertising special offers. From the window she could look down on the street in front of an auto-repair shop. Splotches of bird mess shaped like flames covered the skylights and the cracked asphalt was blotched with oil. A tree stood in a corner of the yard, and even its roots were black with oil where they emerged from the asphalt. It was raining, the drops struck the window with a muffled sound and speckled the view with little pearl-shaped domes in which earth and sky changed places.

She turned round when she had taken in the scene's inventory of details. He asked who it was. He had been badgering her for a month at all hours of the day, at the Drama School, in cafés, on the telephone. He had burst in to pester her in the middle of the night in the crazed hope that she could be persuaded to love him. As if sheer dogged persistence could serve his cause. She conjured up Otto's secretive face, which she had been studying that very morning in bed while he was still asleep, to note each particular of it. The uneven arch of his brow beneath the long fair hair, strong eyebrows, broad nose and full lips.

Daniel had been jealous from the start, even when he had her to himself. On the other hand he could be happy in his ignorance, when she came straight from another man to visit him in his ascetic apartment. She felt like a dazzling guest from a differently callous and profligate world, and she marvelled at how abruptly reality could change in the space of a few hours. He gave her tea in the English faience cups he had inherited from his grandmother as he described the piece he was composing. She let him talk and studied the pictures on the tea cups of romantic lovers reclining in little rowing boats, rocked by tiny waves on a lake in the moonlight, surrounded by mountain peaks, tall trees and reeds swaying gently in the wind.

When they lay together on his mattress he could go into ecstasies over her high-heeled shoes and lace underclothes and the black stockings mingled with his biographies of composers and symphony scores like sexy meteorites come flying from space to land in the midst of his solitude. She had enjoyed closing her eyes and listening when he spoke of his music or read aloud to her from the *Bhagavad Gita* or Omar Khayyam. She had taken pleasure in playing with the idea of the oddness in the combination of him and her, but it had been only a game, an idea.

It had never occurred to her that it would be other than what it was. That he should be the man to exclude all other men. She had certainly not anticipated much. She had deferred all anticipations to some indefinite time, completely open to what might happen. The future had been white and untouched, and she had felt about it as you do when you open the door of a house in the country one morning when snow has fallen.

You hesitate on the threshold, hardly having the heart to go outside and leave tracks in the unbroken whiteness where only the blackbirds' claws have left simple dots and dashes that end as abruptly as they begin.

She had liked Daniel best when he sat at his piano and seemed to forget she was there. Something hard and decisive came over his mouth and eyes when he bent over the instrument, head slightly on one side. As if the music hid itself somewhere inside the black, varnished box, and he had to search for it with the keys, blindly, infinitely careful not to chase it away. There was a restrained strength in the touch of his hands on the chords, his fingers moving so swiftly and precisely. On the keys his hands displayed a disciplined confidence at odds with his clumsy, vague way of caressing her in bed.

As soon as he looked up his expression took on a short-sighted, otherworldly look. When she embraced him she could feel a sudden urge to protect him from colliding with hard reality. But she did not listen when he moved close to her and whispered tenderly in her ear. His adoring words and humble fondling were like a sticky web spun around her, and she wanted to provoke him into forcing a more dangerous, unfathomable music out of her than her conventional sighs rewarding his efforts. She did not believe him when, breathless and blissful, he told her how wonderful she was. He hadn't the least idea what he was talking about, she didn't deserve the words he took into his mouth.

But she did not properly understand that until she met Otto. Strangely enough, for Otto made her feel stupid and bungling, not because of anything he said but simply by letting his expressionless blue eyes rest on her unguarded face. In her thoughts she kept on returning to the morning she rang his doorbell with his jacket over her shoulder and a churning feeling in her stomach. He had just smiled and pulled her inside in a long, astonishing kiss. He could do what he liked, she had come of her own will.

She had been around a good deal, and men had passed through her life, young or slightly older, more or less briefly. She had been in love with some of them, until they submitted completely and reached out for her like shipwrecked sailors about to drown. Others had been more cautious, whether they were married and remorseful or just saw her as a gorgeous lay, available when the urge came over them. She had day-dreamed about them for months on end until her dreams were threadbare from being dreamed over and over again.

Otto was different, he didn't beg for love, and he didn't run away either, as she gradually stopped bothering to hide her feelings behind a mask of uncommitted ease. She was tired of throwing off emotional, snivelling guys who dreamed of nothing but tying her down. But she was equally exhausted from being a fuckable doll dreaming her sweet dreams of exciting, unattainable men who lay pumping between her legs like creatures possessed. When Otto embraced her she had no wish to flee or dream.

They had stayed in his bed that first day. She questioned him about the boy in America who had been sent a red car by post from his far away, unknown father. He didn't mind her asking, but when he replied, in a curt and matter-of-fact way, he made it sound like a kind of technical hiccup. A child clearly belonged to life's contingencies. All the same she couldn't help musing over the unknown areas in him no one had infiltrated before. Maybe he himself was unaware of them. While she lay in the twilight looking into his shadowy face, she fantasised about being the one who, like a traveller on a voyage of discovery, found and charted the blank spots in his interior and one day had them named after her.

One rainy day a few weeks later when she went to see Daniel she knew it was the last time. He played her a new piece he had just finished. She sipped the hot tea and gazed at the romantic pair on the cup in their rowing boat in moonlight. The black and white keys were reflected in his spectacles. His face was closed in concentration in a way that made her recall he was actually several years older than she was. It was only when he played that she thought of it. She hoped he would go on, that the music wouldn't come to an end, maybe because she knew what was coming, but also because that was how she liked to see him, buried in himself and his music.

She turned to the window again to avoid his suffering gaze and looked through the drops down at the yard of the car workshop. One of the branches swayed and spread a little silver cloud of drops around it when a bird flew up and vanished in an irregular lurching curve. A skinny tabby cat slunk along the fence with lithe steps and bent head. It stopped, lifted its head and sniffed, ears laid back. Cautiously it stretched out a paw, tested the cracked asphalt and drew the paw back again before sitting down with its tail curled round its forepaws, nonchalant and completely motionless as if it had sat there always.

She felt Daniel's hands on her hips and his breath against her neck. He loved her. Remorse struck her in the stomach with a hard, cold blow, but only one, immediately followed by a totally different feeling. It rushed through her with its warmth, as if guilt had released it. She visualised Otto. He could have her if he liked, whether he wanted her or not. That was how it had to be, and no one could help it. But if it hadn't been for Daniel, she might not have felt it so simply, so clearly.

Couldn't they be together one last time? She turned towards him. He looked at her with a strange expression, as if nothing mattered to him. He couldn't mean that. He blushed. Would she do that for him? He tried to kiss her, she turned her head away, he went on pestering. Then she gave in, as amazed as he was, and while it happened for the last time she looked into his ignominious, despairing face, but it was not so much contempt she felt, and in fact not pity either. Most of all it resembled gratitude.

She could still feel the heat from asphalt and walls even though the sun had disappeared behind the houses when they rode down their street. The sky over the roofs was yellow. Otto went on round the corner to get a pizza. She couldn't make out how the staircase could smell of wet dog when it had not rained for a fortnight. A pile of trash mail was on the floor inside the door and among it a couple of letters, one for Otto from the inspector of taxes, the other for her. The corner of the envelope bore the Royal Theatre logo. She registered that without thinking, maybe because she was tired after the cycle trip and the hours in the sun. Then she tore open the envelope, went over to the window and unfolded the letter.

It held just a few lines, signed by a secretary. In the coming season the theatre was putting on August Strindberg's *The Father,* directed by Harry Wiener. One of the women actors had fallen pregnant and would therefore not be able to play the part of Bertha, the daughter of the cavalry captain, as planned. Would Lucca consider taking her place? To further their planning, she was asked to respond within a week. She could feel she had caught the sun, her cheeks felt stretched and burning. A light was switched on behind a window on the other side of the building site and she saw a small figure walking up and down in the yellow square. She stuffed the letter back in its envelope and put it in the pocket of her jacket. She could hear Otto on the stairs.

They ate in front of the television and drank beer. Neither of them said anything special. Otto sat with his feet on the sofa table among the beer bottles and the empty pizza box, lazily watching a hit man in a dirty vest empty the magazine of his submachine gun with a resentful twitch of the jaw. She picked up a magazine and leafed through the pages of pretty girls showing off the summer fashions, strolling along with head on one side in the evening sunshine, now among slim palms in a Moroccan oasis, now beneath the wet laundry and drawn blinds above the balconies of an alleyway in Lisbon.

Later that evening they met up with some friends at a bar. Lucca fingered the folded letter in her pocket. She could have told him about it while they were at home, but Otto had been lost in his film. She felt irritated at having hidden it instead of leaving it out so he could find it for himself. As if she felt guilty. The place was packed and the crowd swayed back and forth every time someone pushed over to the bar counter. Standing beside Otto in the din of music and voices it dawned on her that she had been given the chance she had dreamed of ever since she hit on the idea of becoming an actor. Obviously Harry Wiener had meant what he said. She looked round at the clusters of faces. One day they would all know who she was. She felt a bit ashamed at the thought but couldn't help thinking it.

She caught sight of a tall man standing at the end of the bar bending over a beautiful girl. She was sure she had seen him before but could not remember where. He wore an elegant black jacket and his curly hair was cut short. The girl's face was thickly powdered and her breasts looked as if at any moment they might burst out of the bulging C cups. She smiled with her red lips and nodded assent to what the man was saying. Lucca recognised his self-effacing smile and awkward gesticulations. He seemed to have overcome the worst of his shyness, but where were his spectacles? Daniel had obviously taken to contact lenses.

She pushed her way over to them. When he caught sight of her she could see how he swallowed before smiling, but otherwise there was not much left of his old uncertainty. He introduced Lucca and the inflated beauty to each other. Her name was Barbara, and she widened her nostrils as she smilingly took Lucca's measure with her large dramatic eyes. They had just come back from a festival of new music in Munich, where he had conducted one of his works. He had even been interviewed by the *Süddeutsche Zeitung*. He managed to make quite a story of it. She said it was nice to see him and kissed his cheek before going on to the toilets.

She held her hands under the cold tap for a long time. The water splashed up on the mirror and she met her own eyes behind the trickling drops as she pressed her hands to her sore red cheeks. She shouldn't have stayed so long in the sun. Did Daniel also read Omar Khayyam's love poems to Barbara with the big breasts? Did she drink Chinese tea from a cup with romantic dreamers in the moonlight, while he entertained her with his twelve-tone serenades? And if he did? When she forced her way back through the crowd and the fog of cigarette smoke again, Daniel and Barbara had left. Otto followed her with his eyes from the end of the bar. Lucca smiled at him, but he didn't smile back, merely looked at her as if he had caught sight of something she was not aware of. She said she was tired. He could stay on if he liked.

It was warm, the window was open and she lay naked under a sheet, listening to the sounds of the city, the voices from other apartments, and the hollow rattling from the container in the yard when the chef of the Egyptian restaurant took the rubbish out. An Arabian song came from the restaurant kitchen, a woman's wailing voice accompanied by abrupt drums and strings. She pondered on Otto's calculating expression when she returned from the toilet. She lay absolutely still, listening. At last she heard the street door slam downstairs and recognised his quick step as he climbed. She closed her eyes. The sound of steps came closer and stopped suddenly. Then she heard the rattle of his keys, the lock clicked and the door opened. The floorboards in the hall creaked and a moment later she heard him peeing into the lavatory pan and the explosion of water when he flushed it away.

He came into the bedroom. She felt the soft air on her breasts, stomach and thighs when he lifted the edge of the sheet. She imagined his hands, their dry warmth and firm grip. She didn't move, holding her breath as she waited, tense and excited. Her nipples gathered into two small hard spikes and she felt her pores open wide like so many baby birds' gaping beaks, stretched in the air, hungrily piping.

Nothing happened. Afterwards she couldn't tell how long she had been lying there waiting before she felt the mattress give under him as he sat up on the edge of the bed. She heard the metallic click of his lighter and breathed in the smell of cigarette smoke. She opened her eyes. He was still in his jacket. He sat with his back to her looking out into the courtyard. She asked for a drag. He turned and passed her the cigarette. She could not see his face, he was just a dark outline against the open window. He took back the cigarette and knocked off the ash into the ashtray on the floor between his feet. There was something they needed to talk about.

It was quiet down in the courtyard. He inhaled deeply and blew out the smoke in rings that hovered like soft zeroes in front of the lavender blue sky. Yes? She tried to sound relaxed but was unsuccessful. Her stomach contracted. Maybe he had found the letter from the Royal Theatre in her pocket. But after all, it was only an offer of a job. Nothing had happened between her and the Gypsy King. She had told him all there was to tell, and as she spoke he had looked at her in a disinterested way that reassured her. They had even made a joke of it. How had it come to be a problem? Why hadn't she just shown him the letter?

She cleared her throat. What was it? Her voice was faint and dry. She propped herself on an elbow and looked at his dim silhouette. It was no good, he was sorry. She sat up in bed and pulled the sheet around her. What was no good? He turned towards the window. It would be best if they stopped here. The bluish light from outside fell on one side of his face. She could hardly recognise him. Was there someone else? He stubbed out his cigarette and stood up. If she really wanted to know . . . She looked up at him. Was it someone she knew? He went over to the door. He would spend the night somewhere else. It would probably be best if she moved out tomorrow.

The knife point had barely touched the white belly of the fish before it opened out in a long slit around the red and mauve entrails that gushed out onto the marble counter. She remembered how the sight had made her press her face against her father's stomach in the soft checked shirt he always wore when they were in the country. She hadn't seen him for years and sometimes was afraid of forgetting what he looked like, just as she had been when he went away. She lay in bed at night with a pocket torch, frightened of her mother surprising her with the faded black and white photograph she had eased out of the album from the desk in his study without her discovering. In the picture Giorgio was young, about her age. It had been taken on a square in his home town, the town she was named after. She had never been there. He had black hair and a smooth chin, he sat rocking on a café chair in front of a church wall where low-flying swallows cast their shadows.

Fascinated, she watched the fishmonger's knife severing the head of the fish, then discarding it, gaping with astonishment, among the blue veins of the counter. The knife scraped the slimy scales from the green and brown body covered with black freckles. She thought of the red neon sign in Otto's window. She had always hated fish. Outside she could hear the hollow thumping sound of a cutter's motor and the cars driving ashore from the little ferry with varnished wooden rails. She had leaned her cheek against them so as to feel the vibrations through the hull as she saw the fishing village disappear behind the fan of wake, as if they were sailing far away and never coming back. She's shot up all right, said the fishmonger, smiling knowingly. He said that every summer. His short nails were bloody at the roots.

They cycled through the plantation as usual. Lucca rode behind her mother on Giorgio's old bicycle. The plastic bag of fish dangled from the rusty handlebars, it kept almost sticking between the spokes of the front wheel. Else was still slim, but each summer the veins behind her knees stood out more, and her hair had gradually turned completely grey. You could hear the distant roar of the sea behind the rows of dark pine trees. The house, built of tarred planks, was the last one on a path with wooden fences around the small gardens of fir and birch. The sun only reached down for a few hours in late afternoon. For the rest of the day their garden was a shadowy morass of tree trunks, tall grass and raspberry bushes completely hid the stone wall dividing the garden from the woods.

The sun shone almost vertically on the planking wall. They lay in deck chairs, the smell of tar blended with the fusty odour from the damp-stained canvas. There was no telephone in the house, Otto would not be able to call even if he guessed where she was. Else lay with closed eyes, arms outstretched so the sun could shine on their paler undersides. The skin in the low neck of her dress was lobster-red and swollen, with deep lines between her flabby breasts. She did not talk much, perhaps she wanted to seem considerate, it was understandable for Lucca to be quiet. Although she should be glad it had happened now and not later, as Else had said when she met her off the ferry. Imagine if they had actually had a child! Lucca thought of Miriam, dreaming of having her own little baby.

She had called Miriam after Otto had left. Suddenly everything seemed very clear, and half an hour later she had finished packing her clothes and other things. It all went into two suitcases and four plastic bags, that was all she had contributed to Otto's life. She waited down on the corner to hail a taxi. A prostitute stood smoking, a little round-shouldered as if cold. She held the cigarette away from her body and bent first one leg in tight jeans, then the other. Lucca greeted her, they passed one another every day. Hey, was she off travelling? You could say that. Where? She didn't know yet. The prostitute nodded sympathetically. She knew all about that.

Miriam looked at her with a tragic face when she opened the door. She was a head shorter than Lucca, who had to bend down to let her friend embrace her. They stood there locked in each other's arms, rocking from side to side. Lucca began to cry, simultaneously asking herself why she had only begun to cry now. Was it Miriam's sympathy that had set her off, rather than grief at Otto ditching her? Miriam was alone at home, her boyfriend was a jazz musician and had a gig that night. They sat in the kitchen drinking vodka, turning the glowing ends of their cigarettes around in the ashtray so they grew as sharp as flaming spears. Miriam had always thought Otto was a shit, Lucca wasn't the first one to be dropped like that. But she couldn't well have said that while they were together. Incidentally, Miriam's boyfriend had seen him in town recently with a mulatto, a photographer's model, as far as she knew. Miriam hadn't wanted to say anything about that to Lucca, so as not to upset her.

She went on heaping scorn and condemnation over Otto until Lucca interrupted her. Were they going to have a child or what? Lucca was not really interested, but Otto had been slated enough for the time being. She felt battered by her friend's vicious words. Miriam changed channels promptly and lowered her voice, modest but also flattered at being able to share her dream of happiness with her sorrowing friend. Her beloved couldn't make up his mind, he had mumbled something about his freedom. What did he want that for? They had had a row. But Miriam herself was ready, it was a feeling in her body, she just wanted to have this child, besides, it would strengthen their relationship. If only he would understand. What else was there to look forward to? A gig and a cabaret here and there, like that comic one. She could actually sing very well, but no better than a lot of others. She was not the one Harry Wiener had invited to supper! She saw the little flicker in Lucca's eyes and laid a hand on her shoulder. The Royal Theatre, that was quite fantastic! She was really happy for Lucca.

Later they lay in bed with their arms around each other, the jazz man would have to sleep on the sofa, but Lucca could not fall asleep. She cautiously wriggled free of Miriam's heavy embrace and sat on the edge of the bed. The grey morning light was already penetrating the blind. Plastic baskets full of briefs, underpants and socks sat among the few books on the backless bookcase. Once they had been white but had faded into pale pink or pale blue shades after all the times they had been through the washing machine. The walls were adorned with photographs of sweaty, exhausted jazz musicians fastened with drawing pins, and ranged along the wainscot were Miriam and her boyfriend's trodden-down shoes in rows amidst the dust. On the bedside table a foot file and a pessary sat beside the alarm clock. It was only just past five.

Miriam turned over on her side, she had a heavy face, in sleep she almost resembled a man. None the less she always wore close-fitting tops that emphasised her full bosom, and leggings despite her hefty thighs. There was something brash about Miriam. When she made a real effort she could look quite good, but she was particularly noisy and coarse if she was in the company of women better looking than herself. As if she was secretly offended by their genes. Several times Lucca had been taken aback by the way she bossed her man about, the tall, skinny guy with a ring in his ear, only to sit the next moment on his lap and start tongue-kissing. She had told Lucca with a grin that she had practically had to rape him the first time they made love. Miriam used her initiative when things did not develop of their own accord. In her opinion to be desired was a simple human right.

Lucca felt a tickling sensation on one foot. A wood ant was on its way along the vein protruding under the thin skin of the arch. The deck chair creaked as she bent down. The mouldy canvas tore underneath her as the ant curled up and fell through her fingers. It was hot, she rose, and everything went black for a moment.

She retreated into the shade at the end of the garden, where the wild growth around the stone wall made a chaotic barrier facing the woods. In some places dusty broken rays of sunlight broke through the thicket and touched a reddish trunk or a tuft of dark green needles, disorientating the eyes in a confused web of golden light surrounded by soft formless shadows. Everything had been in movement, the heavy tree trunks and the shadows and beams of sunlight, when she clamped her legs around his neck. His beard tickled the sides of her knees as he walked over the domed forest floor covered by dead needles with a firm grip of her ankles. He stumbled and almost lost his balance every time she threw out her arms because she caught sight of a squirrel or a pigeon that flew up and flapped against the branches, but then the trees opened out and gave way to the sand dunes covered with marram grass waving smoothly in the wind, and there was the sea, vast and very, very blue.

She turned round and sat down on the grass. Else's deck chair was empty. She hadn't seen her get up. Her stomach tied itself into a knot and she lay down on the grass, thinking of Otto's eyes and his broad hands. The earth was cool and damp through her dress. Maybe he was lying looking at his hands right now as they explored a delicious mulatto girl's body, infatuated by the difference between his own pale skin and hers. The sizzling of butter in the frying pan blended with the grasshoppers' song. Lucca got to her feet. The top of the stable door to the kitchen was open. She stood watching Else coat the fish fillets in egg and breadcrumbs before putting them into the pan. She stood with one hand on her side as she turned them. Her grey hair was gathered into a careless, girlish knot and she had tied a pink sash round her waist as a skirt, indomitably feminine, thought Lucca.

There is more to life than love, she said, pouring out white wine. They sat at the garden table in the last golden light. You'll discover that sooner or later. She looked down into her glass and up again at Lucca. Work, for instance . . . Strindberg, wasn't it? They drank a toast to that. And children, what about children? Else thought about that as she parted flesh from bone. Children were a trap. Not you, she hastened to add with a reassuring pat on Lucca's hand. Lucca had been so easy. Else removed a tiny bone from the corner of her mouth and put it on the edge of her plate. But you look like a cow, she said, and you feel like a cow, and you *turn into* a cow. Lucca thought of Miriam.

What if they had had a child? He would definitely not have wanted that. She thought of the American boy who had been given a red car for his birthday. Otto never spoke of him, apparently he had said all there was to say. The boy existed, but they did not know each other and that's how it was. Otto didn't even have a picture of him. A letter from Lester enclosing a drawing had arrived in the autumn. The only sign of the mother's life was the neat, formal handwriting on the envelope. Lucca fixed the drawing to the fridge door with sticky tape. Otto accepted that, but when it fell down one windy day he left it on the floor. She got him to send the boy an advent calendar. She bought it herself. He looked at her as if he thought she was crazy, but he sent it.

She hadn't even contemplated the possibility of their having a child. Only now did she calculate how many potential children had spurted out of him every time to no purpose. A whole class, a whole school, a whole city of unborn babies. She had never seriously imagined them walking down the street one day with a buggy, on a Saturday morning shopping trip. Maybe because she hadn't dared. She visualised Otto's blue eyes. She didn't even know what they had seen, those eyes. Probably just a girl among so many others, a face in the line of faces blotting each other out on his sheet like transparencies projected on a screen. Click, and the world changed. But that can't have been how he saw it. His world was probably always the same, only it was full of girls.

Lucca turned to look at the woods. The shadows had grown thicker among the straight columns of spruce. She tried to recall the men she had been with, either for a night, a few months or longer. There were twenty-four altogether, if she counted her first sweethearts. She recalled the advent calendar she had bought for Otto's son. It pictured a crowd of children sledging and building snowmen and having snowball fights, all of them rosy-cheeked. She tried to reconstruct the sequence of the men she had known and visualised them with excited red cheeks and a number on their foreheads. When she kissed a new, strange face it had been like opening yet another lid, thrilled as a child with what might be hidden behind it. Had she really believed that Otto's face was the last one? Was she so naïve? Had she imagined it would be Christmas every night for ever?

It was still light when she went to bed, having told Else she had a headache. She closed the blind to darken the room, light nights had never appealed to her. As a child she had been afraid night would not come, she didn't know why, and she had been just as scared when Else drew down the black blind. She had insisted on keeping the bedside light on until she fell asleep. Else had draped one of her Indian scarves over the lamp and she had lain looking at the grey woollen petals and stems spreading over the ceiling and walls, where the embroidered flowers on the scarf threw their enlarged shadows. Now she lay open-eyed in the thick darkness of the room.

In the spring of 1965 Else and her first husband toured Italy by car. They were young and had only been married four years. She had married a successful young man, at least his parents were well-off, and Else's mother and father were more than pleased. She had played with the idea of being an actor and studied with one for a few months, but nothing came of it. In one of the photographs from that trip she sits smiling in a white open-top Aston Martin. She wears sunglasses and a light-coloured silk scarf tied under her chin, and the road snakes behind her through rows of black pines on the Tyrolean mountainsides. Else's first husband doesn't appear in any of the pictures. He was the one who took them.

In Lucca's opinion it was quite appropriate for him not to be in a single one of the snapshots. He was nothing but an eye in the camera he directed towards her mother, who did not yet know she was to be a mother the next year, standing in St Mark's Square and beneath the arches of the Colosseum, smiling the same delighted smile. Lucca smiled when she looked at those pictures. They made her feel she was the surprise itself in her own person. If Else had had a child with the invisible photographer, Lucca would never have been born.

On the way back from Rome the young couple spent a few days in Viareggio, where one evening the invisible photographer ate some oysters he should not have eaten. Who knows, thought Lucca. If his bourgeois upbringing had not equipped him with this fateful weakness for oysters, the world might have been different. It would have been a world without her, in other words a completely unthinkable world, since she was the one thinking about it. But no less real for that reason.

While Else's husband was lying ill she went for walks in the town and along the promenade. One afternoon a film was being shot, and she stood at the edge of the crowd of spectators behind the camera and the lamps shining whitely in the sun on a pale beautiful woman in sunglasses and a suit almost the same as Else's. The lovely woman walked along the promenade again and again with quick steps wearing a contemplative air. Else recognised Marcello Mastroianni as the anxious man in a black suit with a white shirt and tie who followed the woman, trying in vain to persuade her to stop. Only after the fourth or fifth shot did Else notice the young man in a striped sailing shirt walking alongside the camera rails with the boom held high above his sunburned head. He himself had been keeping an eye on the tall Nordic woman among the spectators for some time.

It turned out that the film crew were staying at the same hotel as Else and her husband, and the very next day Else got out of the lift on the wrong floor, astounded and delighted at her own faithlessness, while the invisible photographer sat chained to a lavatory pan on the floor below. She allowed him to recover a bit before she informed him of what she had decided in the meantime. He must drive home without her. She didn't love him any more, and she was bound to obey her feelings, she told him, and so the white Aston Martin had driven north with its lonely, rejected driver, out of the story. He left no more than a handful of holiday snaps of his lost beloved, which he sent her later without a covering letter, enclosed with the divorce papers so she could ponder whether it was a desperate or aloof, condoning gesture.

After he left, Else moved into the young sound engineer's room, but she soon grew tired of watching the filming. Instead she lay on the beach all day long, alone for the first time in weeks. For once in her life, she thought rebelliously. Later she went with Giorgio to his home town to be introduced to his mother, a black-clad grey-haired woman who lent them her bedroom and gave them breakfast in bed, secretly crossing herself. There, in a Tuscan widow's creaking bed, far too short and far too soft, Lucca had been conceived, according to her mother. In Lucca, with a view over the flat, tiled roofs and the hills with their olive groves and cypresses. It was Else's idea to give her that name, to remember the view from their room each time she uttered it. Giorgio had told her Lucca was a boy's name. What if it was a girl? Else didn't care. Boy or girl, the view over the roofs of Lucca was the same.

Later on she said that had been the happiest time of her life. They cavorted around Italy for three months. There was so much he wanted to show her, and in every place there were people he knew. To start with she didn't understand a word he said, but that didn't matter. His eyes and his hands and his laughter were expressive enough. It was a never-ending party, one long chain of light, shining hours and endless warm nights of hunting for yet another riotous moment's surrender to laughter and the craziest whims.

Giorgio went to Copenhagen with her. They were married at the town hall and spent the first year or two living in an attic flat with slanting walls and a loo in the courtyard. That was something Else always had to mention, the loo in the courtyard, as if it had been a special attraction. She gave up her dream of acting and became a presenter on the radio, while Giorgio knocked on the doors of the film studios in vain. But no one could use a sound engineer who did not understand the dialogue he recorded, and Else had to feed the family on her own. Lucca had no memories of that time. The first thing she remembered was the bedroom of the villa in Frederiksberg they moved into when her grandparents died, one soon after the other. The old mahogany bed where she snuggled up between Giorgio and Else in the mornings. She would creep in under his duvet, and he would bend one knee so the duvet made a cave with a narrow opening out to Else's soft body in the morning light. She curled up in there like a little Eskimo in her igloo, knees up to her chin so she could fit between his thigh and chest, sniffing up the safe smell of his body.

When she woke up one morning he was gone. Else sat on the edge of the bed stroking her hair, speaking calmly to her in the wonderful voice that could say anything to anyone in every radio set in the land. Lucca became accustomed to the strange *friends* who came to dinner. Sometimes they were still there in the morning when she had to go to school. Her father had been a dreamer, Else told her many years later, a spoiled slacker. But hadn't they been happy? Her mother fell silent for a long time before replying. Probably you were only happy a few moments at a time.

Lucca recalled the mornings in their bed when she pressed herself close to Giorgio's warm body, a summer day when she rode on his shoulders through the plantation and a New Year's Eve when she had been carried around the house by one strange guest after another, dressed as an Indian princess, wrapped up in silk with a red spot of lipstick on her forehead. She remembered Giorgio and Else dancing together, slowly and clasped close in the sweet, sickly smell of the funny pipes with no mouth-pieces that were passed round, and she remembered the music they danced to, Ravi Shankar, Carole King. Of course she had been in love with him, said Else, but they had been so young, it had been a young dream. There came a moment when you woke up.

Lucca thought about the morning she had woken up with Else sitting silently on the edge of the bed stroking her cheek. Lucca was afraid of forgetting Giorgio, and gradually did come to forget him. She saw no more of him during her childhood, but it never occurred to her to reproach him for that, and she did not ask Else why he never visited them. She did not want to hear her speaking ill of him, she would rather know nothing. So he became still more remote and indistinct. When she thought back to the morning when she awoke to the news that he had left, it was as if her father had been no more than a dream.

She found it hard to call up his face. It was his body she

remembered, his brown skin and black beard and the soft sound of his voice, not what he had said. She forgot the language they had spoken together. As time went on she pictured him only in isolated images. She could remember him recording sounds for her on his tape recorder. She had to guess what they were. The cooing of a pigeon, wet sheets flapping in the wind, a chamois leather rubbing a window pane or the thin tones of a guitar from an egg slicer.

He had taught her to make spaghetti with butter and grated nutmeg. She recalled the sweet scent of nutmeg and sitting in the kitchen watching him eat while they listened to Else's cool, precise voice on the radio. Neither of them understood perfectly what she said. It was the voice itself they listened to, both familiar and strange as she spoke to all and sundry. Suddenly he wasn't there any more. She was in class one. She had her meals by herself in the kitchen, looked after by a nanny, when Else was on the radio at night. When she grew older, she made herself *pasta al burro* with nutmeg while listening to her mother speaking through the transistor's vibrating plastic trellis, far away and yet so close she could hear the saliva between the consonants in her mouth.

There had been quarrels behind closed doors, and once while she was listening to them shouting at each other, she stole into his room with its bookcase filled with tapes of the sounds of rain and thunder and crackling fire, of dogs and birds, telephones and slamming doors. She found the album with photographs of him when young, the pictures from the town of her name. Cautiously she picked off the old glue that fixed her favourite pictures to the thick cardboard page, fearful as a thief. As if she were not merely taking what belonged to her. For it was her own story which began with the black and white photographs she was hiding. The one of Else in an open Aston Martin on the way through the Tyrol, unaware that she was on the way to her meeting with Lucca's father. The one of Giorgio on a square in his home town, rocking a café chair in front of a church wall, brushed by the arrow-shaped shadows of the swallows, waiting for Else without himself being aware of it.

Else's loneliness had acquired a purposeful character. All those men, thought Lucca, only to end up sitting alone in her childhood home surrounded by the wreckage of three marriages in the shape of furniture in various styles, according to the differing taste of the men and what had been in fashion at the time. Lucca was fascinated by her mother's transformations as they came to light in the pictures of her.

With her first husband she had been a coquettish high-heeled blonde with narrow sunglasses and projectile breasts, undulating along in one checked suit after the other. Lucca couldn't remember his name. With Giorgio Else had become a hennaed hippie in loosely fitting Indian cotton, and when Ivan came on the scene she turned into an authoritative career woman in dark, tailored jackets. Else laughed at herself, how could she have fallen for that Jacqueline Kennedy hat or that *djellaba* with embroidery around the collar. She did not seem surprised at the actual transformations, times changed, she had merely gone along with them.

Ivan ran an advertising agency. He had a square, brutal face and was always tanned, but Lucca wasn't sure whether that was sun or whisky. His voice was very deep and she could hear how he loved it. He always sounded authoritative and effective, rather like pilots when they announce the cruising height and calculated flying time, so a feeling of shaving lotion and optimism fills the cabin. When he came back from one of his numerous business trips he always brought Lucca a gigantic box of chocolates. She felt suffocated by all that chocolate and the shame of accepting his bribes.

At first she didn't believe it when Else told her he had moved in. She could not imagine a man more different from

Giorgio and the other men who had lived with them for a short or longer spell. They had all been actors, journalists or architects, and Ivan didn't suit the vegetating jumble of shabby heirlooms, palsied cane furniture and wilting pot plants. Oceans of newspapers, magazines and books flowed everywhere, and housework was done only when strictly necessary once a month when Else made a trip through the rooms with the vacuum cleaner in one hand and a cigarette in the other. But in a trice everything was transfigured. The cane furniture was replaced by bent-wood chairs, an opulent leather sofa made its entrance in company with a sofa table made of marble, and the walls of the damp-stained hovel were painted so white they made Lucca's eyes hurt.

Else herself underwent a gradual transformation. She started to shave her armpits and cut her long hair. She was a different woman in her new buckled shoes, lipstick and eye shadow, and pale stripes. Previously lazy and untidy, she now radiated energy when she got home from broadcasting and served up a beautifully prepared dinner in no time. Formerly she had not been slow to put her changing lovers in their place with a sharp, cynical remark. Now she smiled in a feminine way as she listened to Ivan's boring, self-satisfied accounts of the brilliant *concept* he had proposed for some campaign or other for a bank or a travel firm or a new kind of toffee. She was quite simply in love.

Lucca had to ask herself how this same woman could have fallen in love with her father. At dinner she mentioned Giorgio several times, but Ivan did not allow himself to be affected. He questioned them with interest about his predecessor, and although his cold-bloodedness irritated Lucca, she managed to enjoy seeing Else squirm as she answered his questions in subdued tones. No, they had no contact with him apart from an occasional postcard and a present every few years when he remembered Lucca's birthday. That's very strange, Ivan thought, giving Lucca a sympathetic glance that infuriated her.

Else laughed a lot when she was with Ivan, and it was no longer the ironical, at times scornful laughter as when she and her women friends sat in the kitchen drinking white wine and telling stories about the stupidity of men. It was open, unrestrained laughter, as if above all she was laughing at herself. Her laughter often left her smiling unconsciously, lost in wonder at what had happened to her. Ivan made her laugh, as Lucca faintly remembered her laughing when Giorgio picked her up and carried her out into the cold waves, kicking and flinging out her arms and legs.

She was thoughtful when she came down to the kitchen in the mornings. Previously she had talked like a machine-gun. Now she was the one who, distrait and delayed, looked up from her mug of coffee and asked Lucca to repeat what she had just said. Lucca thought that perhaps it didn't matter who made her mother happy, and the thought confused her. Over the years Else had known so many men, one face had succeeded another like the numbers on a wheel of fortune clicking past the little peg that always reminded Lucca of the fuse on a huge firecracker. As if the whole tombola and its contents of gigantic teddy bears would explode in crackling fireworks if the wheel of fortune revolved too fast and started to shoot out sparks. But the wheel didn't bolt, it stopped at Ivan. He was to be the lucky teddy bear Else could hug at night.

They were married, in church, the year after Lucca's matriculation. She felt that she had landed up in the middle of a film under production and was forced to stay in the pew because the camera kept running. Incredulously she watched her mother in the low-cut, slit wedding dress of cream Thai silk as she walked alone up the aisle, with Ivan waiting at the altar, shining with sweat in his dress-suit. In the past, when she sat in the kitchen with her hennaed friends, Else always had a ruthless comment at the ready on bourgeois marriage as disguised prostitution. Now she herself had taken to it like another prize cunt in gift-wrap.

At the reception Lucca was surprised to find she knew so few of the guests. Most of them were Ivan's friends, but many seemed more like business contacts than what one understands as friends. At Lucca's table the talk was of *segments* and *communications strategy*. She slipped away during the bridal waltz and didn't come home until late. Else sat on the kitchen table with a cigarette in one hand and a sausage sandwich in the other, in her white corsage and white silk stockings and suspender belt. Her thighs bulged out in the bare patch above the stockings and her bra was so tight it looked as if she had four breasts. Laughter bubbled up in Lucca's throat, she could not stop it. Else looked stiffly at her for a moment, deathly pale, then she put the sandwich down on the worktop, jumped off the table and slapped her.

Lucca couldn't remember ever having been beaten. Wordlessly she left the kitchen and went up to her room. Her cheek still burned and she regretted her cruel laughter. The next morning she apologised to Else. Ivan had gone to work and they sat over their coffee mugs as usual. Else stroked her cheek, the same cheek. She must try to understand, even if it might be hard. Else looked at her with tired, sorrowful eyes. She wanted this. She was going to try for happiness, and no-one, not even Lucca, would stop her.

That summer Lucca stayed at the villa as little as possible, she often slept with a girlfriend. She took a job as an assistant at a nursery school. None of her friends were in town, she was on her own, Else and Ivan spent most of the time at the holiday cottage. They drove into town together every day and Ivan fetched her from Radio House in the evening. Lucca hardly ever saw them. The school holidays had begun and there were only a few children left at the nursery school. It was an easy job, she spent most of the time at the playground sitting in the sun smoking with the teaching staff, while the children took care of themselves.

One afternoon it was her turn to lock up. One of the children was still waiting to be fetched, a boy of three. He anxiously asked where his father was. She took out a puzzle for him. In the end he started to cry. She sat cuddling the sniffing child until finally his father turned up, red in the face and full of excuses. He had been at an important meeting.

She had not seen him before. Usually the mother fetched the boy. He might be any age between thirty and forty, his short hair was grizzled, but his face looked young. He picked up the boy and stretched out his free hand. Apparently he thought they should say goodbye properly now he had let her wait so long. He fetched the boy on the following days as well, and every time he went out of his way to ask if it had been a good day, smiling shyly.

He was good-looking, broad-shouldered with a narrow waist, and there was something lithe about his movements, but she did not give much thought to that before she met him one Saturday afternoon, cycling. His hair was wet and stood on end and he wore a sleeveless vest so you could see his brown, sinewy upper arms. A badminton racket stuck out of a bag on his luggage carrier. He had been playing, he said needlessly, awkward because of the unexpected meeting, then plucked up courage and invited her for a beer.

His shyness reassured her, although he was twice as old as she was. He seemed like a contemporary who had happened to be born much earlier. He turned out to be easy to talk to, and he smiled boyishly at nothing. Later on she remembered him for his restrained strength, as if he was afraid of hurting her. It was the first time she had had an affair with a man who was so much older than herself.

It lasted a month. He visited her in the evening once or twice a week, and he always remembered to have a shower before cycling home. They had the villa to themselves, but the risk of Else or Ivan happening to turn up only made her nervous and still more impatient when she was waiting for him. They used the mahogany bed in Else and Ivan's room, where Else and Giorgio had slept in their time and where she had crept into her father's warmth under the duvet on Sunday mornings. She liked thinking of that when she looked at herself in the mirror on the wardrobe door, infatuated and marvelling as she sat there astride a strange, married man in the selfsame bed.

In the days that passed between their meetings she felt she was moving in a different world. The dangerous and dramatic world where each of them carried the secret of the other. She thought of him practically all the time, both when she was alone and in the playground listening with half an ear to what the teachers were saying. She watched his son running around among the other children, knowing nothing of what his father got up to with her in a strange house when he had kissed him goodnight and cycled off with his racket. Was she in love? She did not know. She always remembered him somewhat differently from what he was when they were once again in Else's bed. She felt more in love with him when they were not together and she cycled through town alone, surrounded by the invisible aura of their secret.

He did not come for his son so often any more, but the few times he did she was surprised at how good he was at seeming natural. Her legs started to tremble when she caught sight of him. He even looked into her eyes as he bade her a smiling farewell with the boy on his arm, as if they had never been closer than that. Usually his wife came. She had short hair and looked like a mouse with her pointed nose and receding chin. It seemed a bit strange to greet her, but not as strange as she had feared. The trysts with her husband took place in a world where the mouse-faced woman did not exist. Just as Lucca did not exist either in the safe, everyday world in which she was only the assistant who looked after the woman's child.

The mahogany bed in the quiet villa was a white island in the twilight, an enchanted island where you forgot what you had left behind. A secret island where you could live a whole life without becoming a day older than you were when you went ashore. He was only a dark figure on the white sheet in the dusk, and she felt she put everything she had known behind her when she slowly undressed before him and felt the air from the open window on her skin. She closed her eyes and he caressed her cautiously until she could wait no longer. When at last he penetrated her it felt as if she split in two lengthways and her limbs and bones parted from each other, light and delicate as birds' bones. She imagined they were held together by his hard sinewy arms, that she would float away on the wind if he let go, and she clung to him so that he should hold her still tighter and pierce still deeper inside her and split her into even smaller, even more splintered and vanishing fragments.

One evening when she lay listening to the water running onto the bathroom tiles, she heard a muted sobbing from in there. She went into the corridor and opened the door. He was crouching under the shower with his head between his knees and his hands folded around his neck. The water trickled down his back, which shuddered rhythmically in time with his sobs. She squatted down beside him and was about to put her arm round his shoulders, but something made her stop, she didn't know what. Maybe it was the sight of a grown man sitting on the tiled floor weeping. He stood up, found a towel and went into the bedroom. She sat on the bed watching him dress. When he had laced up his shoes he said they would have to stop meeting. He was suddenly very calm. He couldn't. He couldn't do it. What? He glanced at her briefly. Nothing . . . She followed him with her eyes from the window as he disappeared on his bicycle with his badminton racket sticking out of the sports bag on his luggage carrier. The next day she called the nursery school and handed in her notice.

She went up to the holiday cottage that afternoon. Ivan sat reading in the garden. He had on a faded T-shirt and sandals, almost playing the part of an ageing hippie with a haircut, and not the dynamic advertising chief who talked like an energetic pilot. She had never seen him with a book before. He got to his feet when she went into the garden, not specially surprised, it seemed. He explained, almost apologetically, that Else was working late and would probably come the next day. But she would stay? He had bought a large steak, there would be enough for two. Actually he was one of those people who could get a bit sick of fish. Lucca smiled, and he looked inquiringly at her, awkwardly waving the book he still held in his hand. It was a yellowing paperback, he had found it on the book shelf, *The Outsider* by Camus. He hadn't read it for years. He had read a lot when he was young, he added, as if frightened she might not believe him.

He was different, more subdued than usual, friendly without seeming to launch a charm offensive. It struck her that he behaved like someone at home with himself. They were both at home, but they behaved very politely, as if they were also each other's guest. He opened a bottle of white wine, she brought glasses. They sat in the garden talking of Camus. The best thing in the book was the beginning, he thought. The descriptions of an oddly stupefied life, the heat and the sea, the women, the monotony. The feeling of being anonymous, as if everything was at one and the same time very close and yet distant. That was how he had felt for years, until he met her mother.

He had worked and worked, he hadn't really done much else, there hadn't been time for private life, nor had it interested him. In fact nothing had interested him. Maybe his work, when he was immersed in it, but otherwise . . . He had known various women, but each time he had let it fall apart. He had had the feeling of being adrift, as if in a boat without oars, taken by the current, just on and on, he had no idea where.

He had never believed he was suited to living in a permanent relationship. Perhaps he wasn't, he added with a smile, time would tell. He looked down at his glass, embarrassed. It wasn't always easy, he went on after a pause. Her mother was demanding, but she knew everything about that, of course. And when you both had a past . . . they weren't so young any more. Enthusiasm alone . . . he smiled again and left the sentence hanging in the air.

Lucca looked at him, attentive to every single word and gesture. She felt her gaze made him shy, he dared only respond to it for a second at a time. The rest of the time he looked ahead or studied the creases in his trousers, smoothing them thoughtfully with his palm. For the first time she glimpsed what Else must have seen in him behind the façade of self-confidence, shaving lotion and expensive habits. Something lonely and unguarded which at moments came in sight on his face, almost innocent in his appeal for understanding or at least acceptance.

He opened another bottle at dinner time. They ate outside as they did when Else was there. He asked her what she was going to do. She didn't know what to say. Travel, she said. Maybe she wanted to be an actor. It sounded naïve. She had not really thought through the idea herself, and Else had not been particularly encouraging when she heard that her daughter was thinking of repeating the foundered ambitions of her own youth. She did not consider it the right thing for Lucca and asked what made her think she had any acting talent? But Ivan seemed to take her seriously.

She had radiance, anyway. He didn't know anything about drama, but he knew something about radiance, about *presence*. She seemed very mature, he felt, older than she was. But luckily she was still too young to mind being told that. He smiled and winked at her. Lucca was about to get irritated at his wink and the way he pronounced the word *presence* when he asked why she didn't go and look for her father. She said she didn't even know where he lived. But she could probably find out! It was important for her, more so than she might realise. He had eyes in his head . . .

He looked at her, and now it was Lucca's turn to look down. But who was he to sit here and talk twaddle, he went on reassuringly and started to talk about his childhood. His parents had sent him to boarding school when they were divorced. His mother was said to have found someone else. His father prevented him from seeing her but he didn't discover that until he had grown up and it was too late. Imagine living in hatred of your mother, he said, and then finding you had been wrong. Again she caught a glimpse of something vulnerable in his eyes, as if a boarding-school boy stood on tiptoe inside him, in shorts and with grass on his knees, squinting through the cracks in the hardened mask his face had turned into with the years.

He had bought strawberries. He opened the third bottle of wine, although she protested. Had their wedding been ghastly? She shrugged her shoulders and let him fill her glass. It had been Else's idea. She put her feet up on the chair and leaned back, supporting her glass against her knees. She felt drowsy in a pleasant way. To have a white wedding, he went on, lifting his glass. She thought of Else's thighs, bulging out in the bare patch between her stockings and suspender belt when they met in the kitchen on her wedding night. He looked over at the edge of the woods before drinking.

He could well have done without such an exhibition, himself. He sought her eyes again. She looked at him over the rim of her glass, sipping her wine. He perfectly understood why she had made herself scarce. He himself had felt like heading off just then, he smiled, that is, if it hadn't been for Else. But she had been so happy that day. Lucca nodded. The strawberries were big and dark red, she ate them with her fingers and bit them off at the stalk. The juice made her lips sting slightly. He asked if she would like coffee. She said she felt like an early night. It had been nice, he went on. Yes, she replied, and met his eyes. He thought they understood each other better.

Not until she lay down did she realise how drunk she was. The air was hot and stuffy in the little room. She opened the window and threw off the duvet, felt the coolness on her naked body, curled up with her knees under her chin as she had done when as a little girl she had crept up close to Giorgio in the mornings. The wine made her dizzy although she lay quite still. She felt the room turning slowly around her, if she herself wasn't turning, as if she was in a boat without oars, adrift on the whirling currents that carried her along in circles, on and on through the half-dark summer night.

She thought of the weeping badminton player under the shower and of his strong arms that had crushed her and at the same time held her together so she should not break apart and be blown away like the almost weightless remains of a disintegrated bird. It already seemed so remote, something she had long since left behind. She turned and turned, floating unceasingly on the current, and with a little, strangely happy pain it came to her that she had felt his hands for the last time when she lay like this curled around herself, as he lay beside her with his tensed stomach against her spine and pressed his warm, hard cock between her thighs.

But it was neither his hands nor his cock she felt and it was not like gliding from a doze into a dream. It was like awakening, not to reality, but from a misty dream to one that was crude and sharp, when, as if struck by an electric shock, she turned round and kicked. Ivan fell on the floor with a crash, pale in the dim light and with an erection that looked both comical and macabre in the midst of his flaccid nakedness. She had pushed herself into the furthest corner of the bed and pressed against the wooden wall with the duvet held tightly around her. *Out,* she screamed, *out, get out!* He rose, swayed and looked at her in despair before going out and closing the door behind him. She remained in her corner, shaking all over. Soon afterwards she heard his car start and the gravel on the road crunch beneath the tyres as he drove away. When she began to breathe calmly she got out of bed and dressed.

She walked along the cycle path through the plantation although it was a detour, shivering among the spruce trees in the dim light. When she came down to the harbour she looked anxiously around her, but could not see Ivan's car anywhere. No one was about. She sat on a bench near the ferry quay and looked across at the fishmongers' empty window-panes, where a crooked little moon shone above the marble counter and the posts along the quay and their floating shadows on the undulations of the calm water. The last ferry had sailed. She was afraid of falling asleep while she waited, and it was like a cut in a film, dreamless and without transition when the sun roused her and she rose, dazed, from the bench and saw the cars boarding the ferry, clattering over the steel ramp.

She put her hands on the varnished rail and felt the faint quivering of the engine's vibrations drumming through the hull. Slowly the wake opened its fan of foam in the increasing distance from the wharf beneath the little red lighthouse that had always made her think of a clown in a red jersey, with a white stripe on his stomach and his clown's nose in the clouds. She recalled how she had stood between Giorgio and Else screwing up her eyes against the reflections on the water, like needles in a chaos of flashes. She remembered that it had been like travelling for real, far away from everything she knew.

Her mother never found out what had happened. Lucca waited before going home to the villa until she was sure Else was at work. She was thinking of the last postcard she had received from Giorgio a few days after her birthday. It was as brief as ever and written in the usual careless handwriting. The card showed an early Renaissance painting, an altarpiece with the Madonna and child, blue-white and with set features, slim, with narrow eyes, against a golden background. The card had been stamped in Florence like the others he had sent in recent years. He probably lived there. Anyway, it was all she had to go on.

She packed a bag with essentials and left a note to Else saying she was going away for a week with a friend. Then she found her passport, went to the bank and withdrew all her money. That evening she was in a train travelling south. She changed in Hamburg and slept through most of Germany, leaning on her bag. In the morning she arrived at Munich where she changed again. A few hours later she was gazing out at the spruce-clad slopes of the Tyrol.

The brakes squealed underneath her, the train stopped abruptly and she was jerked forwards. There was blood all over her thighs. A droning voice from the loudspeakers drowned out her sobs with its list of town names. The sun shone horizontally through the frosted window glass of the toilet, golden like the background to the stiff-necked Virgin Mary and her chubby child on Giorgio's postcard. In her haste she had forgotten her period was due. She had put down the leaden feeling in her stomach to the shock, the delayed anger and sense of being left completely on her own. She had woken up in a tunnel through the Alps feeling a stickiness in her crotch, and cursed herself when the train emerged into the light and she saw blood trickling down her legs under her skirt. She placed her jacket over the dark patch on the seat and rummaged feverishly in her bag for a pair of clean briefs.

The toilet stank and the floor was soiled around the lavatory pan where male passengers had stood swaying in time to the movements of the train. She threw the blood-soaked briefs in the refuse bin, pulled a handful of tissues from the holder on the wall and stuffed them into the clean briefs, but she bled through them at once. She had sat there bleeding for the best part of an hour when the train stopped. Several times impatient hands had rattled the door handle. For the past twenty-four hours she had eaten nothing but a dry ham sandwich in Munich station, and had thrown half of that away because the bread swelled like a sponge in her mouth. Hunger, pains and loss of blood made her tremble, and her forehead was covered with cold drops of sweat.

The train did not arrive in Milan until the evening. Her legs buckled under her when she tried to stand up. She took off the long-sleeved blouse she wore under her denim jacket, and tied it like a loin cloth under her skirt, buttoned the jacket over her bare torso and looked at herself in the mirror. She resembled a pregnant drug addict, pale and sweating, with red circles round her eyes and a swollen stomach. Her head swam as if she was doped when she climbed down to the platform clutching her bag.

She found the way to the ladies' cloakroom with a bag from the station pharmacy. A bent old woman in a blue overall was washing the floor with a gigantic mop. Her face was dark and wrinkled and her eyes were big and black beneath the headscarf she had pulled right over her forehead. She looked Lucca up and down and shook her head, smiling. Half her teeth were missing and her cooing voice sounded more like that of an infant than an old woman.

She put down her mop, took Lucca by the wrist and led her out of the door. Her hand was crippled with rheumatism. Maybe she was a real witch, thought Lucca, letting herself be led along a dark passage and further on down a corridor with dirty walls. The witch went on mumbling to herself in her cooing baby's voice without letting go of Lucca's wrist for a moment, rocking from side to side like a little tugboat.

The last door along the corridor led into a whitewashed room with a shower and a basin. Lucca started to undress and the witch clapped her small crooked hands. She picked up the bloody clothes and went out. Lucca gasped when the streams of icy water struck her. She turned on the hot tap and closed her eyes as the heat went through her, into her flesh.

She wondered how Else would have reacted if she had told her what had happened. She wasn't sure her mother would have sided with her as a matter of course, remembering what Else had said the night of the wedding when she found her sitting on the kitchen table in her corset and silk stockings. She was going to try to be happy, and Lucca was not going to stop her. Maybe she would even have looked at her sceptically, in the way she briefly and secretly glanced at her firm, slim body and taut breasts.

She might even have asked whether Lucca had not herself played up to Ivan, possibly without realising it. She was still so young that she probably did not fully understand the extent of the impression she made on an adult man. Lucca recalled the glances Ivan had given her now and then, if he went into the kitchen as she bent over the dishwasher, her breasts visible in the neck of her blouse, or when they met in the corridor on their way to the bathroom, he in a dressing gown, she in briefs and a T-shirt. Veiled glances he felt ashamed to acknowledge. She had not allowed herself to take any notice of those glances, and when she thought of them she felt sticky. She tried to remember whether she had made any wrong moves as they sat in the garden drinking white wine. Whether she had looked into his eyes in an ambiguous way or allowed a smile to stay on her lips a second or two longer than necessary, marvelling as she did that he could talk so sensitively about himself.

She wasn't ignorant of the impression she made on adult men. She provoked them, she felt that, whether because of her long-limbed slenderness or her courageous eyes that dared to meet and hold a stranger's gaze. Perhaps it was the contrast between her young fragility and the fearlessness in her eyes that was so provocative. Sometimes it amused her, at others she was alarmed at how little was needed for the sight of her to make cracks in their armour of even-tempered maturity. It might be a chance exchange of glances on the street, it might be the father of a friend or one of Else's acquaintances she chatted to with a girlish smile, but it was only a game, as when you pick up a knife and feel how sharp it is, with a cautious finger along the edge of the blade. She herself felt a thrill, but also a touch of fright, when mature men opened the door to give a glimpse of their experienced, slightly superior façade. In fact there was something distasteful in their betrayal of themselves as they interviewed her about her future plans, as if that could interest them. She was only attracted to those men who did not allow themselves to be provoked by her youth. Serene men resting confidently in their ageing skins.

When she met the badminton player she knew at once it would

not last long. They walked through Frederiksberg Gardens on that Saturday when they met by chance. They passed several newly-weds being photographed by the lake with its swans and the island with the Chinese pavilion. So many couples were coming to the garden, he said, they would have to take care not to get into each other's pictures. He stopped to tie his shoelace. She held his cycle for him as he bent down, balancing on one leg. There was a big black patch of sweat on his vest between the shoulder blades, and suddenly, without thinking, she laid her hand on his back. Maybe it was only because she wanted to feel the thin damp cotton sticking to his spine. He put his foot back on the ground and looked at her with a sorrowful expression, as if her touch had inflicted him with an unexpected pain. They stood opposite each other, he raised one hand, then stopped and held the hand in front of him as if he was about to change his mind, before cautiously brushing her cheek with the back of his hand. He knew himself it was meaningless, but all the same he did it.

When she had dried herself and put on clean clothes she went out into the corridor again. She found the witch behind a half-open door, sitting at a small table covered with oil cloth. The walls were filled with metal shelves full of cleaning materials, and an army of mops was deployed in a corner. Her clothes were in a bucket of soapy water. The witch nodded and cooed something, as she poured out coffee in a bowl, put some sugar in it and set it before her on the oil-cloth. Lucca sipped the hot coffee. The witch's wrinkled mouth worked like a hamster's as she observed Lucca with her black eyes, that made her haggard face seem still smaller. The coffee was strong and very sweet and Lucca felt the sugar and caffeine spreading through her starved body.

Suddenly the witch struck the table as if seized by an idea, and started rummaging in a shabby mock leather handbag. She put a photograph in front of Lucca, bent at the corners from the numerous times it had been fished out of the worn bag. The three smiling people had red eyes in the flashlight. A hefty, balding man in a loose shirt held a cigar in one hand and had an arm round the shoulders of an equally stout woman with a child in her arms. They stood on a pavement and on the other side of the street behind a basketball court surrounded by wire fencing could be glimpsed a square, brown brick building. A car was on its way out of the picture, only the tailboard was left, and Lucca recognised its yellow colour from films. *Mio figlio,* cooed the witch, drumming the smiling man in the face with a bent forefinger. *America, America,* she went on and looked at Lucca encouragingly.

As they sat silently opposite each other she heard someone turning on the tap in the bathroom. Soon afterwards a tall African joined them. He nodded politely and went over to the far end of the room where the mops were ranged. He wore a blue overall like the witch, he was tonsured and very thin, and his bare feet left wet prints on the dusty floor. His feet were very large. He rolled a small carpet out in front of him on the floor and stood facing one of the shelves of scouring powder and chlorine in big plastic cans. The witch looked down at the picture of her son, daughter-in-law and grandchild, lost in her own thoughts while the man in the corner raised his hands to his face and spoke out hoarsely in a subdued, chanting tone. Lucca wanted to leave, but couldn't raise the energy. The man kneeled on the carpet and rose again, he repeated this several times. He kneeled again and bent over with his forehead to the floor, so she saw only his bent back in the blue overall and the pale skin on the soles of his feet, etched with dark lines.

It was evening when she was in a train again, freshly washed, all in clean clothes with a fresh sanitary towel in her briefs. She watched the dreary tenements beside the railway, where lights had already been lit behind the half-closed blinds, sometimes catching a glimpse of garishly lit rooms or along monotonous side-streets with parked cars and flashing neon lights. A pine tree stood on a little hill in front of the evening sky. The trunk was crooked and bent, and the spidery crown's ramifications were stretched out under the dense clusters of needles. She leaned her forehead against the dark, vibrating pane, feeling an increasing tension in her body, as if she were a clock being wound up.

She arrived in Florence after midnight and found a cheap *pensione* in a side street. A bald man with liver spots on his pate showed her the way along a murky corridor. She opened the shutters, the window looked onto a narrow courtyard. She put her head out and looked up to the small section of dark sky. When she had undressed and was lying under the blanket between the worn sheets, it seemed completely absurd that she should be in the same town as Giorgio, that he was in another bed somewhere, alone or with an unknown woman. Maybe she would never find him, maybe he would have no wish to see her. Maybe he had moved to another town.

In the morning when she went out to the little reception desk at the end of the corridor the bald man had been replaced by a pregnant woman in a large apron. Behind her the door to the kitchen stood open, pots were already steaming on the stove. An elderly black-clad woman sat in a corner of the kitchen watching television. The television voices almost drowned out Lucca's and she had to gesture furiously before managing to convey to the woman that she needed a telephone directory. There were four people with the name of Giorgio Montale. She wrote down the addresses and phone numbers. The pregnant woman stood at the stove stirring the pot with one hand pressed to her side. Lucca asked to borrow the telephone and held a clenched fist to one ear. The pregnant woman smilingly shook her head without ceasing the mechanical circular movement of her ladle in the steaming pot.

There was a bar at the end of the street. Lucca asked for an espresso and poured in three bags of sugar. She had never drunk black coffee before. That was something the witch in Milan had taught her. There was a pay-phone at the end of the bar. She dialled the top number on her list and pressed a finger in her ear to muffle the loud voices and the hiss of the coffee machine. The first Giorgio Montale was an old man with a cracked, piping voice. A woman's voice answered to the next number. Lucca asked for Giorgio Montale, and the woman's voice repeated the same incomprehensible question in an insistent tone until she finally gave up. Lucca thought the woman had cut her off, but the next moment she heard a soft man's voice. She asked in English if he was Giorgio Montale. He was. The man with the soft voice spoke a little German.

Lucca started to shake at the knees as she introduced herself and explained why she was calling. The man was very friendly. No, unfortunately he didn't have a daughter in Denmark, but he and his wife had always wanted to go to Stockholm. He had two sons, but she was a girl, why was she called Lucca? She explained that she was named after her father's home town. It was a beautiful town, he said, she must be a beautiful girl. He himself came from Palermo. Lucca could hear his wife talking to him in the background. He was sorry, he would have to hang up. He was sure she would find her father.

Neither the third nor the fourth Giorgio Montale answered the telephone. Lucca found her way to the station and bought a street plan at a kiosk. She found the addresses in the index, unfolded the map on the floor and bent down over the crooked web of streets, surrounded by the shoes and suitcases on wheels of passers-by. One of the Giorgios lived in a suburb, the other in the city centre, on the other side of the river. She decided to walk across there. It was hot, and the narrow streets were crowded with tourists, trudging sluggishly along in groups. She walked map in hand so as not to lose her way and only fleetingly noticed the façades of green and white marble of the churches she passed en route. The river was yellowish brown like the house walls, and from the bridge where she crossed she could see another bridge with small houses built on it, at a distance they looked like birds' nesting-boxes. Behind the flat, tiled roofs beside the river rose the dome of the cathedral, it too was covered with red tiles, slightly pointed in its vast curvature.

Soon afterwards she was on the second floor of an old building ringing the doorbell. The marble floor of the landing was checked like a chess board, and the wooden panels of the staircase were dark and shone with varnish. She rang again and was about to go when she heard a bolt being drawn. She jumped, she had not heard steps inside the apartment. The man who opened the door must have been in his early thirties. His short hair was fair and stood on end, but his skin was dark and his eyes brown. He was very muscular, and there was a marked contrast between his broad hairy arms and the soft movement he used to smooth the collar of his kimono, as if he was caressing himself. He smiled and put his head on one side, giving her an inquiring look.

She asked if he was Giorgio Montale. He shook his head, still smiling, negatively waving his index finger to and fro as if she was a child who had done something wrong. She asked if Giorgio Montale lived there. He nodded but she could not understand what he said in his lazy, melodious voice, which was surprisingly high. The man looked at her expectantly. A large blue-grey cat appeared in the doorway. It laid back its ears and pressed its head lovingly against the man's powerful legs. She couldn't find anything to say. He held up a flat hand as a sign for her to wait, pushed the door partly closed and came back soon afterwards with a notebook and pen. She wrote her name and the name of the pensione.

Walking back to the river she realised she hadn't eaten anything yet. Everything seemed pretty hopeless. She felt sure it was not her Giorgio who lived with the blue cat and the man with yellow hair. The idea made her smile. The list of addresses was already crumpled from being clutched in her hand. When she caught sight of a taxi she signalled. She gave the driver the last address and leaned back in the seat. Gradually the historic buildings came to an end, and the town looked like any other city with straight streets and modern houses. They drove for a long way before the taxi suddenly stopped in front of a big housing block. She paid and stood looking around her. A group of boys were kicking a football around on the bare ground between the blocks of damp-stained concrete with covered balconies where washing hung in layers. The sun was already low in the sky. In the distance a water tower loomed over the row of cypresses beside a motorway. On the other side she saw the silhouette of the big arched roof over the rows of seats in a stadium.

She rang several times when she had finally found the right door. No one was in. She sat down on the stairs and leaned against the cool wall. Voices sounded from the surrounding flats, a child cried, and a television blared a high-pitched fanfare. She bent her knees and pushed against the wall when a woman passed her on her way up with her bulging bags of shopping. Shortly afterwards an old man came down, slowly, his back was bent. He stopped a few steps further down and looked at her curiously with his runny eyes. His shirt stuck out of the fly on his shiny worn trousers and he had forgotten to shave his throat. Lucca smiled at him. He didn't seem to notice or else did not take in her friendly expression. He merely stared at her vacantly before going on downstairs.

Half an hour passed before Lucca heard steps approaching again. A woman came in sight and stopped where the old man had stood. She must have been in her late forties, fifty perhaps. Her thick hair was a grey and black bird's nest around her pale, worn features. She had narrow eyes which fixed Lucca with a hard glance as she slowly came on up the stairs. Lucca stood up and introduced herself. The woman brushed the hair from her eyes with a bony hand before hesitantly extending it towards Lucca. She spoke English with a strong accent, in a hoarse voice. As she unlocked the door she explained that Giorgio would be in later. She turned in the open door. Her name was Stella, by the way. She looked at Lucca and gave her a delayed smile.

She apologised for the mess. Lucca glanced round. It looked as if no housework or tidying up had been done for a long time. The furnishings were so anonymous that they said nothing about the inhabitants of the flat, other than their total lack of interest in its appearance. There was a dining table at one end of the living room, still adorned with cups and plates from breakfast. At the other end were a shabby sofa and two assorted armchairs. There were no curtains and the walls were bare. In one corner were a television and an ironing board in front of a pile of cardboard boxes full of clothes. Stella asked if she was hungry and started to clear away the cups and plates.

The door to the bedroom was open, Lucca glimpsed an unmade bed. It is a small flat, said Stella behind her back, putting a plate of cheese and salami on the table. Did she have somewhere to stay? Lucca nodded and sat down. When had she arrived? Stella lit a cigarette as Lucca ate and explained how she had found them. Stella would have to go out again soon, but she could just wait for Giorgio. They both worked in the evenings, actually he should be home by now. But she should have something to drink as well! She shook her head at her own vagueness and went back into the kitchen. Lucca looked out at the covered balcony. Three man's shirts hung on the line floppily waving their sleeves.

Stella came back with a bottle of mineral water and a glass. Unfortunately that was all she had. She should have known Lucca was coming. Lucca said she had tried to telephone. Stella lit another cigarette and inhaled, looking at Lucca with her hard narrow eyes. She had expected her to turn up one day. Suddenly she got to her feet, Giorgio would be sure to come soon. She went into the bedroom. When she came back she had on a white shirt with a black bow tie, a black, thigh-length skirt and black stockings. There was something inappropriate about the tie, and Stella looked as if she could see what Lucca was thinking. Her hair was combed back from her forehead and gathered with a clasp. Her face seemed still more angular and wasted without the bird's nest of unkempt hair to frame it. She put out her hand in farewell. Lucca would probably have left when she came back. She hoped she would have a pleasant stay in Italy.

Lucca heard her steps fade out of hearing down the stairs. She rose and opened the bedroom door. Their clothes were jumbled together in heaps on the bed, the floor and over a chair. A low bookcase held books in close-packed piles and on top of it was a framed photograph. She recognised Stella, a younger, sunburned Stella in a flowered dress. Beside her stood a man with dark curly hair and a full beard. He wore a checked shirt hanging loose over his trousers. The same old shirt he had worn when they were at the summer cottage. Lucca recalled the feeling of the soft, washed-out material when she pressed her face against his stomach. She put a hand over his jaw. The eyes were the same too, the creases around them when he smiled.

She lay down on the sofa in the living room. Now it was just a question of waiting and she would hear the steps coming up the stairs and a key inserted in the lock. She thought of Stella's hard, inquiring scrutiny before she took the last steps up and stretched out her hand.

She awoke in semi-darkness. At first she did not know where she was. She could feel there was someone in the room and sat up in confusion. He sat astride a chair over at the table with his arms resting on its back. He looked at her, supporting his chin on his crossed arms. His beard had gone and his unruly hair looked as if someone had emptied an ashtray over his head. Slowly she recognised his features from the youthful black and white picture, behind the furrows carved into his face. He had been observing her while she slept. It's me, she said in Danish, in a muted voice. It's me, Lucca . . .

He nodded and smiled faintly, and only then did she notice the tears that had gathered at the corners of his eyes. She rose and went over to him, but stopped when he turned his face away. She stood still for a moment before cautiously laying a hand on his shoulder. He looked up at her, dried his cheeks with his palms and got up from the chair. Then he suddenly smiled and flung out his arms like a clown, as if to excuse his tears. He embraced her. She didn't cry. She would have liked to cry, she had pictured herself weeping.

She was surprised he was not taller. He smelled slightly of sweat, but his smell was not as she remembered. While they stood there embracing he said something she did not understand. He held her away from him and smiled again. He spoke Italian to her. Apparently he had forgotten the scraps of Danish he had learned while he lived with Else. She hadn't imagined they might not be able to talk together. It made them shy. He pointed to his watch and smiled again. *Andiamo,* he said and nodded towards the door.

She had no idea where he was taking her. Now and then he looked at her with his sad eyes and smiled mysteriously. He asked her to wait outside a shop and soon returned with a bottle of wine and a bag smelling of grilled chicken. He waved the wine and the bag and smiled, indicating they should go on. He put on speed, occasionally glancing at his watch. They had walked for a quarter of an hour when they came to a cinema. Was he going to invite her to the movies? Giorgio went first up a steep staircase on the side of the building. The steps led to a door in the middle of the bare wall. He unlocked it, switched on the light inside and held open the door for her with a gallant gesture.

While she watched he took a big reel of film from a round box and fixed it with practised movements on one of the projectors. He called her over with a cunning look and pointed to a little window. Down in the auditorium the audience were taking their places. He pressed a button and the lights dimmed in the hall. Then he started the machine and the spool began to rotate with a ticking sound while the film ran past the bright ray of light that penetrated the darkness of the cinema. Giorgio pointed to his watch again and shook his wrist as if he had burned himself. Lucca had to smile.

He took plates, cutlery and glasses from a cupboard and laid a small table between the projectors. The grilled chicken was still warm and Giorgio watched her gleefully as she gnawed the meat from her half and sucked her fingers. He took a sip of wine and washed it around his mouth with the air of a discriminating connoisseur which brought the smile to her face again. They drank a silent toast, Giorgio assumed a ceremonial expression, and it all made her feel she was in a silent film, partly because of the ticking sound of the machine, partly Giorgio's comic gestures. He wanted to amuse her, but the melancholy look did not leave his eyes. The wine relaxed her, and the tension that had held her in its hard grip for two days was replaced by a crestfallen flatness. There was so much she would have liked to ask him about, so much she had wanted to tell him.

He rose, put a reel of film on the other machine and told her by signs to look out of the little window. Lucca viewed the distant picture floating in the dark. A man and a woman lay in a four-poster bed making love in the golden light of an open fire, and suddenly she saw a little white flash in the right hand corner of the picture. Immediately Giorgio set the other projector going and the next moment the couple in bed were succeeded by a group of riders in fluttering cloaks galloping beside a wood at dawn. He stopped the first projector, took the reel off and carried it over to a table with two steel plates on which he rewound the film. He went to the window and absent-mindedly watched what was happening on the screen.

When they were in the street after the show he took her arm and led her to a bus stop. Fishing a crumpled packet of cigarettes out of his breast pocket he offered her one. She accepted it, although she didn't feel like smoking. There was hardly any traffic. Long rows of cars were parked beside the closed shutters of the shops. A little further on they heard the shrill yelp of a burglar alarm. Giorgio stooped slightly, one hand in his pocket, now and then taking a drag at his cigarette. He looked at her and shook his head as if he still couldn't believe his eyes. Lucca . . . he said softly. She smiled back, but it was a slow smile, her mouth felt sluggish and stiff.

There were only a few people on the bus. A girl of her own age sat looking blankly out at the shuttered façades. The thick layer of powder on her cheeks made her look like a doll in the dull light. She cautiously pulled at the nylon stocking on one knee where a stitch had run and moved her head from side to side, she must have had a stiff neck from sitting on an office chair all day. Behind her sat a young man in soldier's uniform with a rucksack between his legs. He had his earphones on and sat with closed eyes, nodding mechanically. Lucca could hear a faintly pulsing whisper from his ears.

Giorgio patted her arm and pointed at the window pane reflecting their transparent faces. He straightened her profile like any street photographer and rearranged his own face in profile, alternately pointing at her nose and his own, glancing at her out of the corner of his eye in a way that made her laugh. He laughed himself. It was true, she had his nose. He looked down at the hands on her lap, laughed again and let his shoulders drop as he shook his head wonderingly. Lucca, he mumbled, Lucca . . . she laid a cautious hand over his and stroked the prominent veins on its back. He regarded her fingers attentively.

They left the bus in front of a big modern hotel. The porter glanced disapprovingly at Giorgio's crumpled shirt hanging outside the faded jeans. When they had passed him Giorgio turned and put out his tongue at the figure, back turned, in top hat and tails. He winked at Lucca with a cheeky expression that made him look like a schoolboy, soliciting her admiration for his pranks. She followed him into the empty bar. It was furnished like an English club with dark panels and deep leather sofas. A tall woman in a white shirt with a bow tie stood behind the bar. Stella looked neither surprised nor glad when she caught sight of them. Giorgio went to introduce them to each other, but she interrupted him with a quick remark. He flung out his arms and sat on a bar stool. Stella asked what she would like to drink. Lucca asked for orange juice, Giorgio had a beer.

Stella translated what he said in a neutral tone, like a professional interpreter, but Lucca could hear she did not translate everything, and not precisely as it was said. He had been very surprised. If he had known she was coming he would have taken time off so they could go out to eat. He was very glad to see her. Lucca replied to the questions Stella translated, and watched Giorgio as he listened intently to Stella's rendering of her replies. He asked about ordinary things, whether she was still at school and what plans she had for further education. She told him she might be going to act. He looked at her seriously, it was an insecure way of life.

She asked why he did not work in films any more. Stella hesitated a moment before translating. He smiled and gesticulated with fingertips together. He did still work with films! Then he cast a long look into the mirror behind the bar. It wasn't so easy. Besides, they didn't make real films any more. They only made stories of car chases and bare breasts! Stella gave a crooked smile as she translated. And he didn't want to do it just for the money. He looked at her like a teacher. You had to believe in what you did or it wouldn't be any good. There was always a way to survive. He wagged his chin rebelliously. He survived . . . Lucca nodded, he looked at her warmly. Maybe she would become a great actress. Maybe one day she would play the leading part in one of the films he showed at the cinema! He laughed at the thought.

They sat in silence for a while. Stella served a German couple who came to sit at the end of the bar. For the first time Lucca was aware of the synthetic music for strings that seemed to come from all around them. Giorgio put his head on one side with a dreaming air as he played on an invisible violin. Stella came back. Lucca cleared her throat. Why had he never been to visit them? Stella gave her a brief glance before translating. He looked away and took the last cigarette in the pack and patted his pockets, he couldn't find his lighter. Stella handed him a box of matches. He burned his fingers when he lit the match and sucked greedily at the cigarette. It was a long story. He didn't know how much her mother had told her. They had been so different . . . he sent her an appealing look. He had once suggested coming, but her mother had thought it wasn't a good idea. Lucca couldn't tell whether he was lying. He slid off the bar stool and looked at her apologetically as he nodded in the direction of the toilet.

Stella removed the ashtray by his place and put down a fresh one. When he was out of sight she looked at Lucca and held her eyes with her own narrow ones. She seemed very tired suddenly, her cheeks drooped around the corners of her mouth. Lucca didn't know whether it was fear or anger she saw in the other woman's gaze. Stella spoke in such a low voice that it was hard to hear what she said. *Leave him alone* . . . she whispered . . . *please* . . . Lucca turned her face away. The German made a sign to Stella, holding out a note in his fingers. Giorgio came back. He clapped his hands together and said something loudly to Stella, who turned round and threw him a stern glance, as the astonished German picked up his change from the counter. Giorgio looked at Lucca with raised eyebrows and an expression that seemed to say something like: What a right shrew he had to live with.

When the Germans had left he repeated what he had said. Stella translated in a weary voice. He would take her out to see the town tomorrow, if she could come. Did she know where the cathedral was? They could meet there. Twelve o'clock? Giorgio nodded questioningly. Lucca nodded back. Stella asked how long she was staying. She didn't translate that. Lucca replied that she hadn't decided yet. She said she wanted to go back to her pensione. Giorgio offered to walk back with her, but she said she would take a taxi. Stella went to ring for one. He walked out of the hotel with her, neither of them said anything while they waited. When at last the taxi came he smiled brightly, almost as if relieved, she thought, as he hugged her close.

She hesitated when she saw him waiting outside the Baptistery next day, behind the dense traffic. He had on a brown velvet suit, even though it was very hot, and a white, newly ironed shirt. She had wept in the taxi on the way back to the *pensione*, soundlessly so the driver wouldn't notice. She had lain awake a long time, listening to the sounds of the town that reached into the courtyard. But what had she expected, in fact? He had changed into someone else after all these years, his life was different now. To him she was a distant, painful memory.

Had Else prevented him from seeing her? She didn't believe that. She would like to, but she couldn't. Neither could she decide whether he looked touching or simply pitiful as he stood in front of the Baptistery's green and white-striped marble façade in his best suit, nervously watching out for her. She hesitated as he caught sight of her and waved exaggeratedly, as if she was ashamed, either of him or of herself. He looked quite good with his pronounced features and unruly, grizzled hair, but his stooping shoulders and perpetual clowning left the impression of a man life had cowed. A man who had resigned himself to its blindly banal necessities.

He showed her the cathedral and the Galleria dell'Accademia with Michelangelo's David and the slaves fighting to release themselves from the marble they have only half escaped from. He led her through the Uffizi galleries and she walked beside him among the Japanese and American tourists and only caught disconnected glimpses of faces, bodies and landscapes in the old paintings. He talked incessantly as if believing she would understand in the end if he just kept on, as he had done when she was little. He was tireless, but the sights of Florence were all they had to keep them there together. Luckily there was plenty to see. She recalled Stella's timid, threatening face when she asked her to leave him alone.

They ate at a restaurant in a side street, a simple place with sawdust on the floor, frequented by workmen. He was obviously a regular customer. The owner smiled at her and shook his head in acknowledgement of life's singularity when Giorgio introduced his grown-up daughter from Denmark. No, she didn't speak Italian. What a shame! She understood that much. After lunch, as they were having their espresso, Giorgio pulled a photograph out of his pocket with a secretive look on his face. Was it a picture of them together? Maybe there was still a trace of the years when he had after all been there. A fleeting impression of a New Year's Eve when she sat in his arms dressed as an Indian princess. A proof that it was true that he had once run with her on his shoulders among the spruce trees of the plantation, with laughter bubbling and rising inside her like waves.

She looked at the black and white photograph and recognised the young Giorgio. He stood with a boom in one hand, the other resting on the shoulder of a man she also thought she had seen before. A handsome man, more handsome than Giorgio, with tired, screwed up eyes and a prominent chin. He placed a finger on the picture and she remembered the witch in Milan and her portrait of her son and daughter-in-law with red eyes. He looked at her in triumph. *Mastroianni!* he said, smiling nostalgically as he emptied his coffee cup. She gave him back the picture.

He looked out at the street through the coloured fly curtain. Suddenly he pointed at his watch, as he had done the previous day. She visualised the projecting room where they had sat eating chicken and smiled, embarrassed.

They went back to the cathedral. Now it was time to say goodbye. She knew it, and she could see he knew it too. They embraced. She had decided to leave him alone, but only now did she realise what it meant. He stood looking at her, hands at his sides, for a moment without the clown's conciliatory grimaces, which swore by laughter because the last freedom in the world was obviously that of being voluntarily comical, ridiculous at one's own expense. But she did not think of that until long afterwards, many years later. She would remember his face framed by the Baptistery's limpid uncluttered Renaissance geometry, his face devoid of waggishness. He too knew their parting was behind them, that it was only a matter of seconds, and so he could allow himself to stay a little longer.

She noted his untidy grey hair, the furrows on his forehead and cheeks, his mouth's natural expression of mute regret and the eyes with the smile lines deeply scored into the thin skin. He must have smiled so much in his life. He raised his hand, hesitated a second and gently brushed the tip of her nose with the knuckle of his index finger. His nose. The only trace of himself he had left apart from her name and a few blurred pictures. Then he slowly took a step backwards, and another. His eyes turned dark as tunnels and he raised his arms a little way, hands open, as he turned and walked away with quick steps.

Everything inside her clenched into a hard breathless knot, and for a moment she clung to the iron railing between the traffic and the marble wall of the Baptistery, until the knot loosened and the cobbles beneath her melted and flowed out of sight. She let the tears run at will down her cheeks, indifferent to the worried or curious glances of passers-by. It was easier to breathe when she walked with long steps and a salty smarting at the corners of her mouth. When she reached the station her eyes had dried. Only the dried-up traces of tears made her cheeks feel slightly taut.

The sky above the walls encircling the courtyard had taken on a deeper blue when she was woken by a knock on her door. She got up and opened it. The pregnant woman in the apron signed for Lucca to follow her. When they came to the desk at the end of the corridor she caught sight of a tall man dressed entirely in white. He was probably in his mid-thirties, his long, chestnut-brown hair fell over his forehead and his green eyes looked straight into hers as he stretched out his hand with a smile. He spoke fluent English, his name was Giorgio Montale.

He had got her message. She looked at him, uncomprehending. He showed her the note with her name and that of the boarding-house and she recognised her own handwriting. She explained that she had thought he might be her father. He looked at her attentively, apparently he understood everything straight away. He had no children. He smiled again, more carefully now. He had thought she might be one of his unknown cousins. He had come back to Italy a year or two ago, had been living in England. But had she found her father, then? She nodded. The pregnant woman observed them curiously from the kitchen, stirring her eternal pot. Couldn't he at least offer her a drink? Now they had established the fact that they had absolutely no connection with each other . . . she smiled. Why not?

His car was parked at the door, a black Ferrari. As she leaned back in the soft leather seat she came to think of the little white dot, like a visual disturbance in a corner of the picture, which had told her father to start the second projector so that the cinema audience did not notice the reel-change. But this was not just another reel, it was quite a different film. The white-clad Giorgio drove along the narrow streets completely at home. He taught English at the university, he had studied at Cambridge.

She told him about her journey, about the reunion with Giorgio and about Stella, surprised that she could talk so easily to him. It was like hearing someone else telling the story. It had been an illusion, she said, astonished at the word. She had believed the reunion would be a revelation, but he was nothing more than the man who happened to be her father. How could they have anything to say to each other after all those years? Giorgio contemplated her with his green eyes, and his serious face made her feel she was discovering something about life as she spoke, something hard and adult.

They had a glass of white wine on a terrace from where they could look over the town's misty silhouette with the irregular tiled roofs and the dome of the cathedral in the evening light among the gentle wooded slopes of the mountains. During a pause he suddenly smiled. Listen, he said, and she heard the bells, some faint and distant, others closer, linked in a pealing perspective of high and low resonant strokes. He asked if she had any plans for the evening. She shrugged her shoulders and shook her head with a smile. He rose and went inside to telephone. She saw him standing at the pay phone, a fabulous white figure in the semi-darkness of the bar. Soon he returned. Did she like lobster? Carlo had gone out shopping.

The whole property belonged to Carlo's family, it was a seventeenth-century *palazzo*. He was not boastful about it, rather apologetic as he led the way through the gateway with its large, iron-framed lantern. The gateway led to a courtyard garden which had a little fountain surrounded by dark foliage. The bleached Carlo met them at the door, in a kimono as before, of dark red shiny silk. Later she thought Carlo must have at least as many kimonos as there were rooms in Giorgio's apartment. She was not sure she got to see all of them, either the rooms or the kimonos. The apartment seemed endless and all the rooms were high-ceilinged and square, with chess-board marble floors, heavy velvet curtains and imposing, formal antiques.

It all happened without noticeable transition, in one gentle movement that resembled Carlo's way of moving in his smooth kimonos, as muscular and lithe as the big blue cat that followed him everywhere. While they ate Lucca kept laughing at his exaggerated theatrical attitudes and melodious voice, which lingered over the words. He didn't mind her laughing, almost caricatured himself to amuse her, and meanwhile Giorgio observed them slyly with his shining eyes. He translated what Carlo said and talked of the English writers he was writing a thesis on. Gays, the lot of them, as he said with one of his unexpected smiles.

Lucca had never heard of Forster or Isherwood, but she enjoyed listening to his Cambridge accent and being looked at by his green eyes. Giorgio talked at length of the homeless Isherwood, who had cast off the chains of his bourgeois English childhood in favour of the decadent Berlin of the Twenties and later, when the Nazis took power, had fled to California where he flirted with Hinduism. His identity had no solid foundation, said Giorgio, because he had cut off one anchorage after the other, as he gradually realised in his life the sentence which commenced his Berlin novel: *I am a Camera*.

When he spoke to her it was as if an ancient eccentric world had bred this charming, grown-up boy to open itself to her through his words and his wise eyes. He spoke to her as you speak to someone you have known for a long time. He listened attentively to her account of the course of her young life, and gently, so that she should not be embarrassed, he showed her how to eat a lobster without cracking it into a thousand orange pieces. She felt she had found a friend. She had never felt like this with a man, certainly not with the boys of her own age, but she felt safe, for Carlo was always there to remind her that Giorgio could not possibly intend anything but simply sitting together chatting and listening and laughing.

Why didn't she stay the night? They were all lounging on separate sofas drinking green tea, which Carlo prepared on a charcoal pan on the huge stove. Yes, why not? Carlo showed her the way to a room with a four-poster bed similar to the one she had seen in the film the previous afternoon, in the suburban cinema where her father worked. A towel, a toothbrush and a kimono were laid out, as if it had always been intended that she should stay. When he waved goodnight she laughed at the affected waving movement he made with his fingers, and he smiled back companionably and closed the door behind him.

She slept until late into the morning. When she opened the shutters she looked out over a jumble of tiled roofs, a sea of stiff, terracotta waves. Her bag was on a stool beside the window. She heard a faint chinking behind her back and turned round in a fright, as Carlo put a tray with a cup of coffee on the bedside table. Today his kimono was mint green with yellow flowers. The blue cat jumped onto the bed. He picked it up by the scruff of the neck and carried it out. She found Giorgio in the kitchen. He had been to fetch her bag in the morning and paid for her room at the boarding-house. She asked if he had kidnapped her. He smiled. Had he? The green eyes looked at her inquiringly.

That day they took her with them to the Uffizi. She didn't like to say she had been there the previous day. And it was completely different from when she visited the museum with her father. She had felt almost choked by all the pictures she hadn't looked at properly. Giorgio reassured her, they would only do one floor. You could spend a lifetime at the Uffizi, he said. So you had to choose what to miss, he went on with a smile, art or life outside. He was dressed in white again, and Carlo wore black silk pyjamas. She took pleasure in noticing how the tourists stared at the tall slim girl laughing with the white-clad aristocrat and their bleached muscular friend.

Giorgio wanted to show her one of the rooms with altar pieces from the early Renaissance. He spoke of the pure, stylised severity in the presentation of the faces, the figures and the folds of the clothing, and he told her of the Byzantine influence. Carlo went on ahead. She stopped before one of the numerous paintings of the Madonna and Child. She was not sure but she felt she recognised the picture from the postcard she had been staring at in the train, the only clue she had in the search for her father. She gazed for a long time at the pale young woman's face with its faintly blue tinge, introspectively dreaming as if she had forgotten the child in her arms, surrounded by the faded and mottled gilding that was cracked into finely branching lines. The gold melted before her eyes and flowed over the woman's face. She made haste to dry her eyes with the back of her hand, but Giorgio had seen. He laid a hand lightly on her shoulder and smiled, fixing her eyes with his. It's nothing, she said.

He took her arm and led her out into the gallery that ran the whole length of the building. She caught sight of Carlo at the end, in silhouette against a high window, he stopped and turned towards them. Giorgio let go of her arm. It's strange, he said, as they went on. He looked up from the tiled floor and lowered his voice. You look like my sister . . . When they came up to Carlo she noticed he avoided her eyes. He put his head on one side and said something in a querulous voice that made Giorgio laugh. The poor man is about to pass out with hunger, he said. But they had probably had enough pre-Renaissance for one day.

They went into an expensive restaurant, an old-fashioned, formal place where the white cloths swam like ice floes in the quiet semi-darkness. When they had ordered Carlo got up and left the table with a remark that sounded ironical, almost taunting. Lucca asked what he had said. He says he's jealous, smiled Giorgio. But she wasn't to believe it. Carlo was wild about her, and he feigned jealousy purely for his own enjoyment. He gave her a long look and suddenly stretched out a hand, stroked her loose hair back from her forehead and gathered it into a knot in his hand at her neck. There really was a faint likeness, even though she was fairer. He shook his head in wonder and let go of her hair. Of course it was just an idea, but he couldn't help thinking she might have grown to resemble Lucca.

She asked him to tell her about his sister. He fidgeted with the heavy cutlery. There had only been a couple of years between them, they had been like twins. They had always been together and told each other all their thoughts. When they were in the country they found hiding places in the trees so the grown-ups could not find them, and at night they crept into each other's rooms. The first to wake up had to wake the other one so they were not found out. The wine waiter brought them a bottle. Giorgio looked dubiously at the label and asked the waiter a question or two, then with a resigned expression let him open it.

It had been like being cut in two, he went on, when their parents sent him to England. Carlo came back. He put his head on one side, rested his elbows on the table and laid his fingertips together as if he was listening with interest, but Lucca could see he did not understand anything Giorgio said. Giorgio took no notice of him. He had not only lost part of himself, he had also torn his sister apart and gone away with one half of her. He paused and pushed the foot of the wine-glass back and forth on the cloth. She had drowned during a holiday on Elba when she was fourteen. If only he had been there . . . It was an accident, but he had never forgiven their parents. After the funeral he went back to England and stayed there. He interrupted himself as he raised his glass and smiled at them.

It really was like being kidnapped, a fairy-tale flight from everything she knew. Every day they went out in the black Ferrari, driving along winding roads between terraces of vines and olive trees up to mountain villages surrounded by high walls. She was shown round medieval monasteries with cool vaulted ceilings, where water dripped in the gloom, and they sat over lunch for hours on sun-dappled terraces with views over the mountains. She drew her hair back from her forehead and tied it in a pony-tail. She had not worn a pony-tail since she was a child, she usually let it hang free. She could see Giorgio noticed it, but he made no comment.

She thought about what he had said when he lifted the hair from her face, that she resembled his little sister, his idea of what his sister might have looked like. If she had lived she would have been about Giorgio's age now, a grown woman. Lucca could not visualise her own face in ten or twenty years. As a child she had often asked Else what she would look like when she was grown up, but Else had merely shrugged her shoulders. Time would tell, but she would probably look like herself. Lucca hadn't believed her. After all, Else had changed over the years, since she was young, driving through Italy in an open sports car unaware of what the future would bring.

Was it just age that made the difference, or was it something else?

When they drove home in the evening from yet another excursion she sat curled up under a rug on the back seat, listening to Giorgio and Carlo chatting casually to each other. Like a married couple, it occurred to her, a couple who had lived together a long time. But she still couldn't understand how Giorgio lived with Carlo as if he were a woman. In contrast to Carlo there was nothing in the least feminine about Giorgio, and when she met his exploring gaze she had to remind herself that he did not look at her as other men did.

He did not mention his sister again, but she was sure he thought about her. She played with the idea that she was a living memory for him, or rather, a living reflection of his fantasy about the face and the figure his dead sister had never been able to develop. A smiling ghost walking beside him through the quiet villages with the unaccustomed tight feeling of her hair, which she had combed back and tied with an elastic band. When they walked beside the ruined ramparts facing the mountain slopes, surrounded by invisible cicadas, she fancied he was her brother, who had brought her back to the future she had been denied.

One hot afternoon they all lay on the big Persian carpet in front of the fireplace smoking a joint, lazily passing it around to each other. Sunlight smouldered through the cracks in the closed shutters and diffused a golden light through the semi-darkness. They had come home early and lay slouched in their kimonos, as if they had sought refuge from the midday heat in a shady oriental garden. Lucca had had a bath, her hair was still wet and the kimono stuck to her damp skin. Carlo was lying on his side with his head resting on his bent arm and half-open mouth. He had fallen asleep. She rose and the carpet's wine-red and moss-green arabesques twisted and turned around her. She stood still for a moment, waiting for the rocking feeling beneath her feet to pass off. Giorgio sent her a muzzy smile and threw the end of the joint into the stove. A spidery wisp of smoke wavered upwards in the darkness there. She smiled back. She knew he was watching her as she walked across the cool marble floor.

She went into her room and lay down on her back in bed, feeling all her muscles relax. On a high, she felt as if her head, body and limbs drifted apart from each other so that each began floating out in different directions from an increasing vacuum without gravity. She didn't know how long she lay like that. At first it was like being brushed by a warm draught from the open window, then she felt his breath on her feet, then his lips. She hadn't heard him come into the room. To start with they merely brushed her, then he kissed her, his mouth finding its way up her legs and thighs. He clasped her buttocks and pulled her to him. She kept her eyes closed and lay completely limp as his tongue slid between her labia, totally concentrated on the pulses of sensation that streamed through her, again and again, ever stronger until she began to shudder in a long, convulsive release. The walls resounded with a hard, sharp clapping. *Bravo!* She recognised Carlo's melodious, feminine voice.

Giorgio was still on his knees by the bed, between her thighs. Carlo stood in the doorway clapping his hands demonstratively with his head on one side, smiling sarcastically. Giorgio stood up and turned towards him. Carlo took his face between his hands in a hard grip and kissed him with his tongue. Then he let go of him and sent Lucca a triumphant glance, licking his lips and walking out of the door backwards. Giorgio stood with his back to her, head bent, facing the wall. It might be best if she left them, he said. He went out and closed the door behind him.

She dressed and packed her bag. She never saw either Giorgio or Carlo again. When she opened her door the apartment was utterly silent. Only the blue cat sat in a corner regarding her, calmly waving its tail back and forth over the tiles. She cautiously eased the bolt back and slipped out of the front door, like a thief, she thought. As she walked she took off the elastic band that held her hair in a pony tail and shook her head so the hair fell around her shoulders. When she drew near the railway station she passed the bus terminal and caught sight of a bus with her name above the windscreen. Without another thought she bought a ticket and took a seat at the very back of the bus. She still had no idea of where she was going.

As she sat looking out at the hills in the low sunlight she realised that from the beginning and up to now her journey had been directed by her name, her father's name and her own. But she had not herself chosen her name, and she had not herself decided who was to be her father. She thought of the one Giorgio Montale, of the darkness in his eyes when he had embraced her in farewell and taken a step or two backwards alongside the façade of the Baptistery, raising his hands a little to the side in a gesture of regret. And she thought of the other Giorgio Montale, who an hour before had stood with his back to her and his face locked in Carlo's hands, allowing himself to be kissed and hesitantly, with the same resigned movement, lifted his hands and placed them on Carlo's hips. She thought of what he had said about homelessness, about severing all moorings. Hadn't hers been severed long ago? Lucca was merely a name, a sound, no more. What was she going to do there? Was Lucca anything more than yet another tediously beautiful town, where she could walk around feeling sorry for herself among the flocks of Japanese tourists taking photographs of each other?

The bus stopped at a place where the road turned. A man made his way along the gangway with a suitcase and a cardboard box tied up with string. She seized her bag and got out just as the doors were closing. She stood on the roadside as the bus disappeared round the bend skirting a slope of cypresses. The man went down a path beside a high stone wall, rocking from side to side with his suitcase and his cardboard box until he disappeared among the crooked olive trees. She caught sight of a slim lizard sitting motionless on one of the rough, sunlit stones above the path. A drop of sweat crept down one eyelid and made her blink. When she opened her eyes again the lizard had vanished. She shouldered her bag and crossed over to the shade on the opposite side of the road.

She did not get up when the telephone rang downstairs, far away, so far it seemed nothing to do with her. It must be someone wanting to talk to Else. She had still not told anyone she had moved back to the villa. Even Miriam thought she was still staying with Else in the country, but she had only stayed at the cottage a couple of days. Perhaps it was Else phoning. She didn't want to speak to her, anyway. She couldn't stand her sympathy, constantly mixed with bitter advice and censorious analyses of Otto's blunted emotional life. They were not kindred spirits, and she had no use for her mother's comfort or that Else had known the whole time how it would end.

She had just woken up. She lay looking out of the French window that had been open through the night. It had rained and she listened to the whipping summer rain until she dozed off in a long, imperceptible transition in which the rain kept on foaming and whispering. The telephone rang again. The air was warm and damp, the sunlight filtered palely through the mist over the garden of the Agricultural College, and the wet crowns of the trees glittered softly. It kept on ringing.

How indomitable, Lucca thought and suddenly remembered walking hand in hand with Else beside the roses with their name plates, bearing their extravagant names in a neat hand. She remembered the Japanese trees with delicate, curling branches, which bloomed in spring and lost their white petals to the wind, disguised as snowflakes. In winter only the names of the roses stayed above the snow on their brave little name plates. They had laughed at that, Lucca and Else, the empty white beds where the names, undaunted, went on blooming. Whether it was summer or winter the walk always ended on the narrow path out to the lake, to the little island with an old tree which had a bench around its great trunk. They sat there watching the ducks and the walls of the college, and she remembered feeling lost, sitting beside her mother on their desert island, where nobody knew they were.

Only Else knew she was back in her old room. It had not changed in all the years that had passed since she left home a few days after she came back from Italy. Where had she been, by the way? She remembered her mother's worried, accusing face. Luckily Ivan was on one of his business trips. Lucca described her meeting with Giorgio, and she told her about Stella, but she didn't say anything about the other Giorgio, nor did she say anything about Ivan entering her bedroom the night before she left. Else asked a few questions about Stella, what she was like. Lucca could feel she was slightly interested, and she willingly told her about Stella's hard-edged features, about her bar-tender's costume and about the bar in the suburban hotel furnished in the English style.

It probably had to happen sometime, said Else. Of course she had had to go and find her father. The words sounded strange in her mouth, your father. Else regarded her with an expression that was both tender and exhausted. So it had been a disappointment? Lucca took her hand. It doesn't matter now, she said, and as she said it she felt for the first time that she and her mother were equally adult. Else was just older, that was the only difference. She soon realised that Else knew nothing about what had happened at the cottage when she was alone with Ivan. How could she have known? She didn't even know Lucca had been there that night.

At that time one of her friends from school shared a flat with another girl, and they needed a third tenant. That was how she met Miriam. She got a job in a café and earned just enough to manage. After she moved she avoided visiting Else and Ivan for several weeks, until she could no longer make excuses without it seeming strange and perhaps in itself suspicious. Ivan behaved normally when she went to Sunday lunch, but after the first course while Else was in the kitchen he smiled in a way that told her he did not feel threatened and even regarded her as a kind of fellow conspirator.

Miriam was taking lessons from an actor, she planned to apply for entrance to Drama School, and when she heard Lucca had been playing with the same idea she kept on urging her to go to an audition with her. Lucca was accepted, Miriam failed and was not admitted until the next year. Lucca could not understand why it had all gone so easily for her. She had only done what she was asked, but perhaps she succeeded because she was not quite so anxious to get in as her friend. She had just been herself, her teachers told her later. She had to smile. Just herself . . . who could that be, then?

She discussed it with one of the other students, a loud-voiced fellow already going bald, whom she befriended because he could always make her laugh. Herself! he giggled. How could you know yourself? If you knew yourself, you must be different from yourself. This was a linguistic misunderstanding, a logical deadlock. You could only get to know yourself if you could observe from somewhere outside yourself. But then you would no longer be yourself! On the contrary, you were always a second or a third or a fourth, all according to whom you were with. He had read philosophy for some years before deciding to become an actor, because after all everything was just one big comedy.

In reality she did not at all mind being a mystery to herself. When she was in the train on her way back from Italy she felt glad not to have been to Lucca. She pictured Giorgio, her own Giorgio, in front of the Baptistery. His gesture, at once ashamed and relieved, as he turned round and walked away without looking back. She was no longer his daughter, nor Else's for that matter. She was her own, no one else's. She thought of Ivan's pale erect cock in the semi-darkness of the cottage and his dismayed expression when she had kicked him onto the floor. She would not try to stop Else being happy. When the train arrived in Munich she tore up Giorgio's postcard. She gazed for a while at the Virgin Mary's face, the child's foot, the folds of the garments and the faded gold before throwing the pieces into the ashtray and getting her bag down from the luggage rack.

As time went on and she learned to work at a role and build up her characters with the aid of meticulous detail, it seemed to her that she herself held something of every single role she played. The playwrights also showed her how people resemble each other more than they care to admit. She had long talks with her sparse-haired friend about *Peer Gynt* and about the comparison of selfhood with an onion whose innermost core, when one peels it, turns out to be empty. He said that was what it had been like with the Jewish temple in Jerusalem. The holiest of holies, where none might enter, had been nothing but an empty room deep inside the temple. He laughed savagely so she could see his sharp canine teeth, and for a moment she wasn't sure whether it was his wolfish grin or the thought of the innermost emptiness of the onion and the temple, that made her shudder.

She thought again of the town of Lucca which at the last moment she had decided not to visit. One day she would go there. Maybe she would go with her lover. She fantasised sitting in a car approaching the curve where she had got off the bus, between the olive grove and the slope of cypresses. She could see no further than where the road made a bend, just as she could not see who was behind the wheel. She replied to her cynical friend that all his emptiness was probably nothing in itself without what was outside, whether it was rings of onion or temple courtyards. That frightful emptiness was nothing more than an opening onto what you could not know. He looked at her sluggishly, putting his head back as he drank his beer, but she thought that was actually not a bad answer. Perhaps she was no more than a frame around the secret hollow space where something would one day show its face.

The telephone was still ringing. Maybe it was Otto . . . she sat up with a start, leapt out of bed and ran naked onto the landing and downstairs, two steps at a time so she nearly stumbled. Maybe he had guessed she had moved back home. It wasn't so hard to guess. Who would call Else apart from him? Everyone knew she went to the country on holiday and stayed there the whole time. Maybe he regretted the brutal way he had dropped her. Maybe he just regretted . . . she forbade herself to think the thought to the end. But they ought to be able to talk about it. After all, they had lived together for two years.

As she rushed through the house she thought of his lazy voice. She could hear it already, maybe he would suggest they met for a chat. The loss overwhelmed her again. She had believed they belonged together. He was still the first man who had made her feel like that, whether he wanted her or not. She had felt he saw her as she was, and she had no longer dreamed of being anyone other than the one his eyes had lit on. His hard blue eyes had penetrated into her innermost place, and it had not been empty. She had been there the whole time, invisible in the darkness as she had been when she hid in Else and Giorgio's wardrobe and spied through the keyhole's little dot of light, until the light was extinguished because he had guessed where she was. Next second the door was torn open with a thrilling creak, so the light and his merry eyes fell on her simultaneously, and it made her jump as if she could already feel his hands under her arms picking her up.

She tried to quieten her breathing before picking up the receiver. It was Harry Wiener. Did he disturb her in the middle of her morning gymnastics? She said she had been out in the garden when she heard the telephone. She thought the garden sounded better than bed. She could hear him smile as he talked to her in his old-fashioned, well-articulated voice. Had she received her script? Yes, thank you. She thought of the script bound in red card that was on the floor beside her bed. She had not opened it yet, she had not been able to concentrate. Every time she picked it up she thought of Otto and how he had seemed jealous, no doubt to make it easier for himself.

She recalled his silence the day they swam and her own misgivings because she had not told him Harry Wiener had visited the dressing room after the performance to praise her empathetic presentation so fulsomely. Would everything have looked different if she had woken him when she got home and told him about the Gypsy King's unsuccessful efforts? Was there actually no unknown mulatto model somewhere in the background as Miriam had imagined? Did Otto really think she had started something with the old drama guru? That she had fallen for his camel-hair coat and his unruly silver-grey locks? Had she herself ruined everything?

Although rehearsals were not due to begin for another few months, Harry Wiener said, it was his habit to meet the actors in good time so they could chat for a bit. He sounded as if he had forgotten his familiarity in the car when he drove her home. Asking if he might kiss her. What did she think of the role, then? She grew hot and bothered. It was hard to talk on the telephone. Exactly, replied the Gypsy King with another invisible smile. That was why he was phoning. That is, he was phoning to suggest they met over a cup of tea. Lucca suddenly felt he sounded a touch flustered beneath the self-assured, cultivated varnish. As if after all he had not quite been able to repress how he had compromised himself. Was she doing anything that afternoon? Lucca said she would just look at her diary.

She stood with the receiver in her hand and looked down at herself. She had got a tan, the mahogany colour stopped in a curve between her hips and stomach, where her own paler colour disappeared under the tuft of curly hair. She raised the receiver again. No, she wasn't doing anything. Right, then, how about five o'clock? She thanked him. For the role, she added. He was the one to say thank you. It has been yours for a long time, he replied. It was a strange reply, she thought, when she had hung up. She was just about to pick up the receiver again and dial Otto's number, but held back, like all the other times she had been about to give in to her need to hear his voice, regardless of what it would have to say, hear he still existed. She made coffee and took it upstairs, pulled a T-shirt over her head and sat in bed with the red script.

She had spent most of the week in bed or in the garden, she didn't feel like seeing anyone. She had lain weeping or staring at the grass and the clouds and the square of sunshine that crossed her wall in the course of the day. She kept to her room if she was not in the garden. When she walked through the downstairs rooms, Else's furniture and things seemed like silent witnesses waiting only to gossip about her. But what would they have gossiped about if they could? Her attacks of weeping? Her stony immobility when she lay prone, as if waiting for someone to come and find her?

She had eaten nothing but pot noodles and frozen pizzas for a week. She had lost weight, she had to tighten the belt of her jeans two holes more than usual. Her hair hung loose and greasy from the loose knot at the neck, she had not bothered to wash it, and she had pimples on her forehead and chin. She had not had pimples since she was fourteen, and when she pressed them out they left big pink scars. As a whole she did not look exactly ravishing as she cycled off in Else's old Faroese sweater with the script in a plastic bag on her luggage carrier. But she looked as she ought to, she thought, as she caught sight of herself in the mirror on her way through the hall. She wasn't going to make an impression on anyone and certainly not on the Gypsy King. Then she would see if she really had deserved her part.

She had collected her cycle from Otto's entrance the day after she took a taxi to Miriam's with her things. She had stood for a long time on the corner opposite the Egyptian restaurant before plucking up courage, afraid he might suddenly turn up and at the same time hoping he would. Suddenly the street seemed a strange, hostile place, the same street she had cycled along the evening before when they came back from swimming. She had looked at the golden evening sky between the buildings and felt at home. It was already in the past, another life. It took no more, a single sentence was enough. It will be best if we stop now . . . She knew she would not get him back, and yet she could not go on. It was like standing on the edge of an abyss knowing that the next step is a step out into the blue.

That was how it must have been for Daniel two years earlier when she stood in his apartment looking out at the rain as she said what she had to say. Daniel, with his stoop and his short sight. He had sat staring down at his black and white keys as if they could tell him what music to play now. But he had found it, obviously, when she ran into him that evening at a bar, cheerful and wearing black like a real artist and with a large-bosomed lady. Lucca asked herself whether they were real, his loving muse's splendid breasts. She smiled at the thought of Daniel's unhappy face. You survived, she knew that, but she didn't want to know it. Who would be the next number in the series? What kind of face would she kiss now, fantasising about what was hidden behind the unknown eyes? Any old pleasant face with an invisible number on its forehead. It was probably never Christmas on grown-up calendars.

She thought of Else, who had entrenched herself behind her work and her women friends, because there was more to life than love, as she said. The problem was just that she did not start to question what was really interesting until love came to an end. The something more in life, was it anything but a substitute? One evening she had called in a strange voice and said she was going to swallow all the pills in the medicine cupboard. When Lucca arrived at the villa she had filled herself with, not pills, but Ivan's whisky. He had gone off to New York with a girl of twenty-three. He too had come out with it plainly. Well, not quite. He had said he couldn't feel whole-hearted about her, Else brought out, with a mouth quivering with wounded pride and held-back tears. He had said they had slipped away from each other, although what he probably meant was that his new girlfriend had a tighter cunt. Lucca held her mother's head on her lap and stroked her hair as she wept. What she could have told her there was no point in telling now. Else could have asked about it herself. It must at least have occurred to her that something like that could have happened. Not least now when Ivan had hopped off with a girl her daughter's age. She must have noticed Ivan's discreet glances at Lucca's long legs. But she didn't ask. Poor old, flabby cunt, mumbled Lucca, and Else's weeping changed into hollow, grating laughter. The next day she ordered a removal van and had Ivan's furniture taken to the tip. He never even complained.

The sky had turned a hard blue and the sun glittered in the puddles after the downpour of the night. The water splashed around her spokes, it was windy and the air was full of whirling dust and flashing reflections which made it seem the wind was making the light gleam in everything that moved. As Lucca cycled through town she thought of the years which had passed since her trip to Florence. The years before she met Otto and believed that at last here was someone who saw into the depths of her, right in where she herself could not reach. She remembered the men she had known and remembered her hesitation, always the same whenever she was about to surrender, when for a fleeting second she already saw the end of the story that was just starting.

A second which came every time, while everything was still only circling movement and significant glances. A disconnected second where it became so strange, so hazardous, this game that was always played blindly, with bodies as pawns. But then she had closed her eyes in a hurry and kissed them, amazed at her own haste. She had hastened to kiss them before she began to doubt too much. She had hurried on into a fresh beginning, for there was no point in hesitating. There had to be more beginnings, all the time, if something more was to come of it one day, and she had begun and begun, sometimes for sheer fun, at others with a secret plan to sound out luck.

But all too soon once more it had been nothing but two bodies in a room going over the usual phrases surrounded by the usual furnishings with a view over the usual streets and days. It had turned out in the usual way. The usual slight lassitude during the same sweet assurances. The same excitement, the same brief dizzy dive from the usual feverish peaks of desire. For a time it was wildly thrilling again to meet a strange man at strange secret places and launch into new bold methods, screaming and yelling, hair unleashed. But either they grew too busy talking about the future, or they were suddenly too busy to meet, if she ventured to say something about tomorrow or next year. Some of them were married and dreamed of being divorced, while others wouldn't dream of getting divorced even though they were bored with their spouse. Then there were those who were not married and became overwhelmed with claustrophobia at the mere thought of it, and finally those who had just split up and needed time, as they said. As if they had anything else.

When she met Daniel she was certainly not looking for yet another love affair. She had just dropped a film cameraman who had left his wife, convinced he was going to begin on a new and completely different life with Lucca. At that time she was in love with a lawyer who had no intention of leaving his wife but who nevertheless called her at intervals of weeks and months to ask her to meet him at some hotel or other. She knew there was no future in it, but she kept seeing him even though Miriam scolded her for allowing herself to be used, as she said. He had caught sight of her without her knowledge. Craftily, discreetly, he had found out who she was, what she did and where she lived. He had kept watch on her from a distance, until finally one day he made himself known with a brief anonymous letter in which he suggested they met at a café. She gave in to her curiosity and went along. The moment when she entered the café without knowing who she was going to meet was perhaps the most intense in their whole relationship.

She did something to him, he had said. That was the closest he came to expressing his feelings. She had been practically obsessed, she told Miriam later, by his remarkable ability to transform himself. When they met at a restaurant he was the cool arrogant solicitor in a distinguished suit, but as soon as they were in the hotel room he turned into a ferocious beast who threw himself over her with sudden violent rage. He always blindfolded her when she had undressed. That was how he wanted her. She never saw him naked and it fascinated her, when she lay in the hotel bed with her eyes covered, delivered over to his gaze and his ferocity.

After six months he stopped calling her, and every time she phoned his office, his secretary said he was in a meeting. Lucca pondered on the expression, but meetings were obviously something you could get stuck in. She waited for weeks until one day she happened to pass him in the street, coming out of a restaurant with another suit. Her beloved gave her a blank look as he passed, as if they had never met. She was shattered, until one evening Miriam asked if she might only be in love with him because she couldn't have him.

She met Daniel at a party. Miriam had dragged her along, she didn't know anyone there. She and Daniel left at the same time and walked through the town together. He suddenly started to talk about twelve-tone music, just as he had done while they were in the kitchen because neither of them felt like dancing. He was intelligent but very innocent as well, and she was charmed by his unworldly decency and suffering face. She sensed he had no idea of how to go about moving from words to action, so to speak. When he paused she kissed him and asked where he lived.

He fell in love without reservation, and his sincerity made her feel depraved, whereas with the lawyer she felt as young as a seduced maiden, defenceless against his raging lust. For a while she rather enjoyed her own cynicism, when she went straight from an assignation with the lawyer to Daniel in his comfortless suburb, to sit on his bed and drink tea out of his grandmother's porcelain china cups while he played his strange music. There he sat at his piano, ignorant of where she had come from, and her secret made her feel free in a treacherous and homeless way. Like a double agent crossing frontiers in disguise so no-one knows who she really is, and wondering about that herself.

Perhaps Miriam was right, perhaps her passion for the lawyer was an illusion she could only maintain because the affair was never a reality outside the anonymous hotel rooms. But with Daniel, who wanted her so much, she was never in love. She was just fascinated, especially by oscillating between the two men who knew nothing about each other, between the roles of sacrificial lamb to desire and faithless fallen woman. Until at long last she met Otto and felt all her masks fall off.

As she cycled along to her appointment with Harry Wiener something came to mind which she had often thought of when she was with Otto. One day long before they met, she might have cycled past him, perhaps she had even seen him for a second and then forgotten him the next moment. At once she feared he might come walking across a pedestrian area with his arm round the waist of Miriam's notorious mulatto, who had been haunting her tortured imagination for over a week. She made a detour to avoid the streets where she risked meeting him, which made her think that in a little while she might pass the man who would be able to love her. He must be somewhere, but maybe they had already crossed each other's path. She came to think of Else, who must be sunning herself in the country in one of the deckchairs with their mouldy seats, red as a lobster, eyes closed and mouth sagging.

It was getting cloudy again. The wind urged the ragged grey clouds so fast over the town that the roofs were lit and quickly darkened again in waves of shadow. On one side she could see the arched zinc roof of The Royal Theatre, on the other the gilded onion domes of the Russian church, and behind them the harbour, alternately blue and grey in the movement of the clouds. The sky was slate grey behind the cranes of the naval dockyard and the broad drum-shaped tanks on the fuel island further out. If she leaned over the railing shc could look down into the street, a horizontal beam peopled by wood-lice and ants walking on their hind legs in the bird's eye perspective.

Better take care, said Harry Wiener as he came out on the balcony with teapot and cups on a tray. The sugar bowl was missing and he went inside again. As she waited, lightning made a crack in the cloud cover over the airport. It's going to be a great show, he said, smiling cheerfully as he came back with the sugar bowl in one hand and his script in the other. He bent his head a little and looked at the thunder cloud over the spectacles on the tip of his curved, sun-tanned nose. His checked shirt hung half out of his trousers, his long grey locks curled around his ears like wings, and his feet were bare in the worn-down espadrilles.

It was obvious he had forgotten she was coming, when he opened the door and looked at her in confusion, as if with no idea of who she was. He admitted it at once and apologised politely. He had fallen asleep on the sofa. That calmed her as she stepped inside the rectangular room, the only one in the apartment apart from the kitchen-diner and the bedroom, which she glimpsed before he closed the sliding doors. A glass door between two wide panorama windows opened on to the balcony, the three other walls were occupied by bookcases from floor to ceiling. The place was smaller than she had imagined, more intimate, furnished with design pieces from the Sixties with worn, beige leather covers, faded Kelim carpets and the inevitable Poul Henningsen lamps.

When she was in the lift staring at herself in the narrow mirror she regretted not having done something about her appearance. She couldn't decide whether she looked like a hanged cat or something the cat had dragged in, as Else used to say about herself when she stood in front of the hall mirror. Maybe she looked like something in between. A half-strangled cat dragging itself up to the renowned and awe-inspiring Gypsy King. In her melancholy state she had forgotten what it meant to her to be going to tea with Harry Wiener. She had forgotten to look forward to it and fear it, and when she sat in bed with the duvet around her reading *The Father,* she quite forgot why she was reading the play at all, completely engrossed in the story. Only in the lift did it strike her that the step onto the top floor would also be a decisive step in her career. That word usually made her smile ironically.

Harry Wiener poured out the tea and asked if she took sugar. No, thank you, she replied politely, but maybe a spot of milk. He beat his brow with an exaggerated gesture and rose again. It doesn't matter, she hastened to say. He stopped and looked at her over his spectacles. Why did she say that when she had just said she liked milk in her tea? He smiled amiably as he said it and she smiled too. If you want milk you shall have it, he said, going inside. She looked at his script, it was already tattered and dog-eared even though rehearsals would not start for another three months.

He made her relax, she didn't know how, and she couldn't understand this was the very same feared and admired Harry Wiener she had heard so many stories about. The same Harry

Wiener who had made a pass at her in his Mercedes. Good, now we're about there, he said, placing a small silver jug on the tray. He really seemed to have forgotten everything that evening, but she was glad she had put on Else's Faroese sweater. It had turned cooler, too. They sat silently listening to the distant rumbling and watching the purple flashes and white forks of lightning over the harbour. Lucca did not know what to say and she was surprised it was not difficult to sit, each in their bamboo chair, saying nothing. Harry Wiener slurped when he drank. That surprised her, considering how cultivated he was. He was at home in himself, and she almost thought he had forgotten her.

I went to see my wife today, he said suddenly in a low voice. She is in hospital, he added. Lucca looked at him expectantly. He looked over at the harbour entrance. I hope she's awake, he said. She loves thunderstorms . . . He lit a cigarette. She is dying, he went on. Lucca looked at the script in her lap. It has spread, he added, there's nothing to be done. Lucca said she was sorry. He looked at her. He hadn't told her to appeal to her sympathy. He just thought she should know, now they were going to work together. If he should seem distrait. He regarded her for a moment before going on. She asked me to sell the house, he said. He had not thought of doing that before she died. It was a house north of town, he hadn't been there for months. Yes, it is strange, he said, as if replying to something she had asked him. He looked at his cigarette. But enough of that. What did she think of the play?

She hesitated, then said Strindberg must have had problems with women. He smiled, but not patronisingly. That was true enough, but it was not true to say he hated them. He was afraid of them, which was something else. If anything it was a particularly virulent case of unhappy love, he smiled. Strindberg was a deserted child who as an adult cursed the mother's womb that had exiled him. Incidentally, all artists were deserted children. He looked at her. 'Your mother was your friend, but the woman was your enemy . . .' he said slowly, as if to emphasise every word. He smiled again. Yes, it was banal, of course, but that's how it was. That was why the Captain was so bewitched by the power of motherhood. And that is why, said Harry Wiener, he breaks down, because he doesn't know for certain that he is your father.

Lucca jumped. She had forgotten she was sitting on his balcony only because she was going to play the cavalry captain's daughter. Harry Wiener took a mouthful of tea. This time he did not slurp. Doubt over paternity is the oppressed woman's only possible revenge in a patriarchal universe, he said, putting down his cup. But it was not the only cause of the captain's suffering. He also suffered because, in Strindberg's universe, life and the ability to pass it on belonged to the women and to them alone. Why do you think he paraphrases Shylock? he asked. For a moment she forgot who Shylock was, but he did not expect her to answer.

'Hath not a man eyes?' He leaned forwards in his chair, the bamboo creaked as he stretched out his hands in an appealing gesture. 'Is he not warmed and cooled by the same winter and summer as a woman? If you prick us do we not bleed? If you tickle us do we not laugh?' He let his hands drop into his lap and leaned back. Shylock had to argue for his humanity because he was a Jew, an outcast, and the Captain had to do likewise. You could go so far as to say that to Strindberg men were biology's Jews, its wandering homeless. 'In the midst of the moonlight . . .' he added softly, holding her eyes, '. . . surrounded by ruins on all sides.'

A drop fell on the balcony floor, followed by another. The next moment the whole balcony was spotted with raindrops. The gilding on the Russian church's onion dome sent a mysterious light on the background of the dark grey sky. Harry Wiener rose and picked up the tray, she carried in the cups, he let her enter before him. She sat down on the sofa, he settled in an armchair. The low lamps in the corners of the room surrounded them with a warm, subdued light. The view was already dim in the misty rain. He had left the door to the balcony open, and Lucca felt the rain like a cool breath in the warm damp air.

While the thunderstorm passed over the city he questioned her about the roles she had played and how she had interpreted them, and he listened to her with the same intensity he had shown in the dressing room after the performance a few weeks previously. While she had been paralysed with shyness when she arrived, now she suddenly noticed she had plenty to say, and heard herself voicing ideas she had never shared with anyone before. She told him how working on the roles had made her feel that the innermost core of her personality was a hollow space in which she could be anyone at all, and how the feeling sometimes terrified her and at other times overwhelmed her with its freedom. Harry Wiener smiled, almost wistfully, she thought. Yes, he said, we are separate, but not so different. That is why we both understand and misunderstand each other.

Again they were silent, looking out at the white vapour of rain above the glinting rooftops. He glanced at his watch and dispelled the enchantment when he rose and said he would have to ask her to leave. She was struck by how direct he could be without seeming rude. Maybe it was simply because he was used to getting his own way. He had an appointment soon with a young dramatist, they were going to discuss his manuscript. But perhaps she knew him? He must bc about her age, perhaps slightly older. Andreas Bark was his name. Very promising, one of the really big talents. She had heard of him. Did she have a car? She said she was cycling. Oh, well, we must get hold of a taxi. Of course he would pay. She said that was too much. There you go again, he smiled and handed her a hundred kroner note. He really couldn't have her catching a cold from sheer modesty.

The bell rang while he was phoning, and he motioned to her to press the door button. Then he came into the hall and shook hands with her. See you in the autumn, he said, and closed the door behind her. She walked down the stairs that wound around the bars of the lift shaft. The lift passed her when she was one floor down and through the window in the door she saw a dark, averted figure slide past.

Part Three

So far it had been a miserable summer. Every time you thought it was getting warm at last, it began to rain and blow again. Monica and Jan had had the right idea, to book a holiday in Lanzarote as early as April, but Robert still felt disappointed over not spending time with Lea when he was on holiday. She said nothing about it on her visits to him, not even when the end of term was approaching, and he suspected she was avoiding the subject to spare his feelings. That made him more dispirited than the thought of being without her. When she came they worked together on the kitchen garden, and one Sunday afternoon, when the sun shone for a change and the temperature climbed to a tolerable minimum of summertime, they went out to the beach to swim.

The water was icy cold and he only took a quick dip. Lea was a good swimmer now. He stood at the water's edge shivering and watching her swim along the sandbank with sure, regular strokes. She swam over to one of the fishing stakes which were set in a straight row at right angles to the shore, forming an interrupted perspective against the calm expanses of sea and sky. As she held onto the post with one arm and waved to him with the other he felt both happy and sad, and when she came out of the water and waded towards him, tall and shining in her swimsuit, he realised why. It would not be long before he had to part with her, not because she would be catching the train as usual and going back to her mother, but because she would have no more use for either mother or father. It was only a question of a few years before she began to live her own life. They would still see each other, but she would be a guest, when she came. It would no longer be her second home, if in fact it ever had been, his overlarge house in the suburb on the edge of the quiet provincial town in which he had ended up after the divorce, by chance as it seemed to him now.

If there had been a meaning in his life during the many years that had passed it had existed in this girl coming towards him, wading through the cold water and wiping her eyes with her knuckles as she pulled down the corners of her mouth in a comical, troubled grimace. She had been the meaning of it all, anything else had come to seem pale and complicated compared with her. He stood waiting, holding her towel and then wrapping it round her and rubbing her back. She teased him for only having a dip and saucily grabbed at the loose skin on his hips. Hadn't he better do something about those handles? He put out a hand to tickle her. She leaped away and ran off. He ran after her, but her legs had grown too long for him to catch up with her, and suddenly he felt a stabbing pain in one foot as he tripped and fell. He heard her laugh. She couldn't go on being the meaning in his life, she would soon be busy enough with her own.

His heel was bleeding and he caught sight of a rotten plank with a bent rusty nail in it. A siding, he thought, as she came towards him. He had driven himself onto a siding. He thought of the quiet house where he sat listening to music every night the whole year round when he got home from the hospital. Should it be Brahms or Bruckner tonight, after he had driven Lea to the station, or Bartók for once? She put a supporting hand under his arm as they went back to the car. He asked her to fetch the first aid box from the boot. She insisted on helping him, and he let her clean the wound with iodine and showed her how to put on a bandage, secretly enjoying her sympathy.

They had brought her bag so they could drive straight from the beach to the station. His heel smarted and throbbed. She sat beside him looking out at the fields and the clouds. The weather was worsening, the light was grey and metallic over the restless corn. Silence fell between them, as it usually did before they parted. The first drops appeared on the windscreen followed by more until he had to switch on the wipers. When he stopped in front of the station she said he didn't need to go in with her. She sat on for a moment. See you after the holidays, then, she said. Yes, he said, smiling. Take good care of Mum and Jan! She looked at him. Take good care of yourself, she said seriously and kissed his cheek. He watched her as she ran through the rain with her bag over her shoulder. She turned and waved, and he signalled with his headlights. Then she was gone. He could hear the train approaching and started the car again.

He had been to see Lucca every afternoon before going home, and he had remembered to take off his white coat before going into her room, as she had asked him to. What was it she had said? It seemed a strange notion. That she would rather be completely ignorant of what he looked like than have to content herself with knowing he had a white coat on. But she did ask when he went in to her the day after he had lent her his walkman. She asked what he was wearing, and he replied, slightly flurried. Blue shirt, beige trousers. But what kind of blue? He had to think about that. Twilight blue, he said finally, surprising himself at the comparison. Twilight blue, she repeated and smiled. He had made a new tape for her. He had enjoyed choosing the pieces of music and deciding on their order, and it had given him the chance of hearing music he had not listened to in years. Ravel, Fauré, Debussy, he kept to French music and Chopin. She had asked for more Chopin. He spent most of the evening on it.

He always came at the agreed time, when the ray of sunlight shone on her face through the blinds outside the window. He did not switch on the light when it began to rain, she asked him not to, as if it made a difference to her. Then she lay in the semi-darkness listening to the whipping of the drops on the aluminium blinds. He sat down on a chair beside the bed. Her arms and legs were still encapsulated in plaster, but her head was no longer bound up in bandages. It looked almost normal, apart from the stitches in her forehead and the yellow-green bruising that was wearing off, and her glass eyes. He recognised her from the photographs he had seen in the kitchen the day he drove Andreas and Lauritz home in the rain, but she had lost weight, her features had grown sharper.

She seldom mentioned Andreas and Lauritz. He did not ask

why she stuck to her decision not to let Andreas visit her, but he could feel she missed her son and suffered because of her own obstinacy. The weeks went by with no word from Andreas, but she did not ask if he had called. Robert assumed he was still in Copenhagen, unless he had gone to Stockholm to try his luck with the exotic designer. He considered asking Lucca if he should contact Andreas, but never got around to it. Something about her silence held him back. She was remarkably silent about the drama that had ended when, drunk and beside herself, she had got into their car to drive to Copenhagen on the wrong side of the motorway.

She did not talk about the life she had lived with Andreas in the house by the woods, which they had transformed from a ruin into the home that now, in a different and more comprehensive sense, lay in ruins. It seemed as if she had completely repressed the fact that she was married and had a child, totally engrossed in the years that had gone before. Robert thought of old people who cannot recollect the immediate past and instead remember details and events from their early years which they thought they had forgotten. But he was not witnessing a loss of memory. She just no longer knew precisely where she was, surrounded by sounds and voices, an indeterminate space where hearing was the only sense by which she could distinguish what was close from what was far off.

She had suddenly been thrown into herself, without her eyes' firm grip on reality, delivered over to the evasive images of memory. She seemed like someone who is obliged to tell the story from the beginning, try to describe herself as she had once been, ignorant of what awaited her later. Someone who attempts to return to the start and from there follows her own steps, as you do when you have dropped something on a walk and retrace your steps with your eyes fixed on the ground. Without her explaining it he understood, at first with only a vague apprehension, that this was how she had to approach the night when everything in her life crashed into sudden darkness.

Perhaps it helped to tell her story to a stranger who knew only the ending but had no idea how she had arrived there.

He knew what it was she was slowly trying to isolate, this event which wrenched the words out of her mouth with its irresistible force. She approached it day by day, the thing she still could not talk about, but she held back, dwelling on each stage of her story and losing herself in tortuous digressions. Only by detours could she approach what she still did not understand. She took her time. Her words were like her hands, hesitantly reading the objects passed to her. With the words she touched each face that entered her story and traced the physiognomy of events, as if she could find the sudden turn, the unexpected gulf into which she had fallen.

She had just about got to Andreas, although she had not yet met him, when she was discharged and transferred to a rehabilitation centre. Her plaster had been removed a few days before. Robert and a nurse supported her when she attempted her first steps on the floor in front of her bed. Her long legs seemed even longer, thin and white after the lengthy confinement to bed, with protruding kneecaps. She was dizzy and her legs gave way, so he had to carry her back to bed. She wept and asked to be left alone. When he visited her in the afternoon she was asleep with the earphones on. The tape was still playing. He bent down with his head close to hers and heard Chopin's *Nocturne* No. 4, the peaceful yet rhythmically changing chords, the strangely reckless melancholy. Twilight blue, he thought and smiled involuntarily as he crept towards the door and closed it carefully so as not to wake her.

When he told her about the rehabilitation centre, she realised she had no clothes to wear. She asked him to go out to the house and fill a suitcase. How could he do that? You'll have to break in, she said. Was that such a good idea? She smiled as if she could see the worried look on his face. There was a key under a stone on the left of the door. The old lady's bicycle had fallen over, and little piles of seeds and dust had gathered in the folds of the plastic cover over the pile of cement sacks. He picked up the bicycle and found the key. He still felt like a burglar as he walked through the quiet rooms where a grey transparent film of dust already covered the floors. She had said there was a suitcase on top of the bedroom wardrobe, but there was nothing there. Andreas must have taken it with him. He found a black plastic sack in the kitchen and took it back to the bedroom. He opened the wardrobe. Even though he was alone, and even though she had asked him to do it, he felt as if he was spying on her and pawing her as he began to select garments from the piles of blouses and lace underclothes and hangers with dresses and jackets. He avoided the brighter things without thinking why, and reminded himself she would need shoes as well. Most of her shoes had high heels, it would probably be better to avoid those at first. He chose a pair with moderately high heels and also found some trainers at the bottom of the wardrobe.

He stopped in front of the notice-board in the kitchen and studied the photographs he had kept glancing at when the unhappy Andreas invited him in for a glass of red wine. Lucca in overalls painting window frames with paint on her cheek. Lucca in the drive with the low sun behind her, the little boy hanging horizontally in the air at the end of her outstretched arms and her dress whirling around her brown legs like an open, illuminated fan. Lucca at a pavement café in Paris, under the plane trees, cool and elegant in her grey tailored jacket, hair combed back from her forehead and red lips parted in the middle of a thought or a word as her eyes seemed to meet his gaze, at once confidential and surprised.

They said goodbye in the hospital foyer. She was in a wheelchair. She turned her face towards him, so his white coat was reflected in her dark glasses. I haven't told you everything, she said, stretching out her hand. He pressed it, after a slight pause because he was not prepared for her formal gesture. But he must be tired of listening to her going on about herself. He said he would be coming to see her. He stood and watched as she was pushed through the glass doors. As the wheelchair stood on the ramp and was lifted up to the level of the minibus rear doors, she was in profile with her red-blonde hair gathered into a pony tail, masked behind the big sun glasses, pale and unmoving as a photograph.

* * *

It rained all evening. Lea had left her wet swimsuit in the car. It was pink, almost cyclamen, but it looked good with her thick dark brown hair. She had inherited his hair, but she had Monica's prominent chin and energetic way of moving. He hung up the swimsuit to dry on a hanger in the bathroom and stood there looking at the feminine object turning limblessly around itself as it dripped onto the tiles. It struck him as almost incredible that Lea was the only female who had been in the house since that night barely a year before when the librarian had sat on his sofa listening to Mahler. She had looked at him with her dark eyes just waiting for him to lean towards her and place a hand on one of her inviting knees in their black stockings. All too ready. That had probably been the problem. That he could visualise it, all too readily.

His foot hurt every time he walked on it. He cursed and again heard Lea's teasing laughter when he stumbled on the beach. There was always a rusty nail somewhere when you felt at ease and carefree for a moment. He sat down on the lavatory seat cover and examined the wound. She had looked quite remorseful when she went up to him and saw the blood. As if it was her fault that he couldn't look where he was going. She stroked his hair consolingly, and he glimpsed in her gesture the young woman she was slowly turning into. The night before she had told him about a boy at school. He was the tallest in her class. He was quite different from the other boys, she said, more mature. The word made him smile. The tall boy wasn't keen on playing football like the others, and he generally kept to himself. He had brown eyes. They had chatted, one day at the bus stop, but otherwise he did not seem to notice her at all. She had written a letter and slipped it into his bag during the lunch break, but he had not replied. Robert said he was most probably just shy and found himself worrying about everything she would have to go through.

He put a plaster on his heel and limped into the kitchen. A bowl of cornflakes from the morning was still on the table. He did not clear it away. He liked to see the tracks she left behind, a swimsuit here, a plate there, an unmade bed or a comic among the newspapers. The rain pattered on the leaves of the trees outside, and behind the veil of drops on the kitchen window he could see the blurred glow of the lamps in the neighbours' living room. He made an omelette although he wasn't really hungry. When he had eaten he switched on the television and sat down. He did not usually watch, he had lost interest when he left Monica, and he had only bought a television set on Lea's account. The idea of sitting watching television alone had seemed as depressing to him as the idea of drinking alone. He poured himself a double whisky and stretched out his legs in front of him on the sofa. He didn't feel like listening to music, he only wanted to sit there with the pictures passing before him. News he only caught half of, episodes of serials he had not followed, guessing games whose rules were a mystery to him and pop videos of surly young men in disused factories. Whatever.

He zapped between channels. Two films were being shown simultaneously and at one point both of them showed a sex scene. He hopped back and forth between the two, both were filmed in subdued golden light, and the close-ups of distorted faccs and hands on skin melted into each other until he could no longer determine which of the films they belonged to. There was an interesting contrast, thought Robert, between the pictures of naked body parts and the pictures of the lovers' transported faces. One type of picture showed, or at least tried to indicate, what was happening. The other type showed, or tried to show, what it meant. The bodies slavishly followed their own agenda, but the faces were not content to reflect the purely physical excitement, they also witnessed something different, something more. The moist glances and pathetic expressions said that this was love, or rather that the rhythmical palpability on the screen was the urgent consequence of love, if not its urgent confirmation, which perhaps, came to the same thing.

Robert debated whether he might be getting slightly drunk. He switched off the television, poured yet another whisky and went to open the sliding door to the terrace. His foot did not hurt so much now. The rain splashed onto the paving stones, drummed against the white plastic furniture and soughed further off in the twilight, outside the semi-circle of yellow light from the room behind him. He breathed in deeply through his nose. Grass, she had said, when he opened the window that first afternoon when he sat with her and the scent of newly mown grass rose up to them from the lawn between the wings of the hospital. He looked out into the hissing garden. Grass and twilight blue. Lea must have got home long ago. She would have been fetched at the central station by Monica or Jan, they had probably finished eating by now. No doubt she was in bed dreaming of a boy with brown eyes.

He sat down on the step, lit a cigarette and tried to find out why the sex scenes on television had put him in a bad mood. Was it only because it had been so long since he himself had been to bed with someone? He clinked the ice cubes in his glass. Well, he could just have seized the opportunity when it was offered. He felt annoyed about that sometimes, and once almost called the librarian. She was certainly a charming woman, and they might have made a go of it. They might even have suited each other when they had been through the introductory manoeuvres. But when he and Lea were walking along the beach one Sunday and passed the librarian with a younger man in a baseball cap, he had been just as relieved as he had been when he put down his brandy glass on the sofa table and told her kindly that he would prefer to spend the night alone.

He had felt tired already at the prospect of having to begin all over again. The librarian's pretty eyes had cornered him, full to the brim so they almost overflowed with expectation. Her dark gaze had tried to convince him there was so much significance in their meeting, the librarian and the doctor from the city hospital. She had presumably been in love, it was honest enough, but he had not been able to free himself of the suspicion that all she needed was a man, because she was pretty starved where men were concerned, and had wrapped up the elementary and entirely respectable needs of her body in a daydream in which the divorced doctor from Copenhagen was something unique. After all, a provincial town didn't have all that much on offer.

But wasn't he the one who was incurably romantic, since he

was so disheartened by her slightly affected infatuation? Wasn't it the best reason in the world for falling in love, that she was quite simply lonely in the good old-fashioned sense? Wasn't there a secret, immature dream of the great revelation lurking beneath his cynical exploration of motive? Perhaps he had merely been piqued because her situation reminded him of his own, suddenly making him think of scruffy widows' hen parties, where lonely hearts gather for mutual comfort. She had made him feel exposed and available, and he could not tolerate being recognised.

He remembered his shyness as a boy before his voice began to break, and he recalled the letter Lea had written to the boy with brown eyes. He thought of the times some girl or other had made her coltish approaches, and how he had rejected or simply ignored her brusquely, although she made his legs shake. Naturally he had been flattered, but at the same time he had been abashed by the girls' looks and giggles and little folded notes with squares where he was supposed to put crosses. Actually quite a practical system, those little voting cards, he thought now, but then he couldn't bear for a girl to anticipate his clumsy interest like that. He felt she recognised something in him which he had barely come to know, and that she put her fingerprints on this something, already all too familiar, as if it belonged to her merely because she had caught sight of it.

At other times a girl could make him feel guilty for no reason. Like the time his mother had got the idea of sending him to dancing class. It was held in a hall with stucco and red velvet curtains. The boys stood in a row along one wall and the girls sat on gilt rococo chairs along the opposite wall. The boys wore white shirts and bow ties and hair combed back with water. The girls were in dresses with stiffened skirts in soft colours, pale blue, pale yellow and white. At a given sign the boys had to cross the endless parquet floor, choose a girl and bow, and one day when he had trotted across the floor as usual and bowed to the first girl he came to, she looked expectantly into his eyes and asked an unexpected question which made him blush with shame and irritation. Had he chosen her because of her dress?

The feeling of shame stayed with him when he first ventured

into the whispering, fumbling darkness of teenage years. When he had courted a girl long enough and she finally allowed him to kiss her with his tongue and explore her with his hands, she also beseeched him with her doe eyes to behave as if she alone out of all the girls had managed to set his heart on fire. He felt like a deceiver, although his aims were as artless as anything could be. It was then he first discovered the remarkable gap so-called erotic scenes on television had made him think of again. The gap between bodily sensations and the feelings those sensations were so cunningly named after, making it easier and more decent to confuse them.

He learned to lie both to himself and to the girls he wanted to go to bed with, but each time he was in bed with a strange body, he wondered again why it is called 'being in love', although you still only know each other as bodies. Lovely, strange bodies, which, it is true, do utter words, but words you can't attach to anything because you haven't in fact any idea of what those words mean, or who she is. It was ironic, he felt, but sad as well, for when you finally found out who it was you had been in love with, usually you were not in love any more because she had become so familiar. The promising strangeness that had aroused your fantasies was like a downy, shining surface that quickly wore away. Then all you could do was hope that before then you managed to become really good friends.

Monica had become his friend, and yes, he had loved her. It must have been love, the joy of seeing her again if they had been apart for a few days. The tenderness that could trickle out of him when he raised his nose from the grindstone and suddenly caught sight of her in the midst of the laborious daily routine that was so safe and boring. All the same, he had thrown himself at Sonia when she offered herself. Even though the previous day he had sat on the beach in the low sunlight watching Monica as she stood smoking a cigarette and looking out over the Sound, as if he understood in a flash why they were together. He had obviously forgotten it again as quickly, anyway there was no connection between his impulses. One day he fell in love afresh with his wife, and the next he went to bed with her little sister.

He could not get close to Sonia and be on intimate terms with her because she did not know the barrister was not her father, and his own secret cast him out of the intimate sphere where Monica and he had lived together. He was only half there, his other half stayed outside, and all the time he had to show himself to her sideways on so that she should not discover his unknown side, obscured by lies and dissimulation. The strange thing was that she was not surprised. Obviously she had grown used to not seeing him in full figure because they had gradually come to see each other in their fixed roles as colleagues, sexual partners and financial allies.

They started to talk less, more superficially on his part, since he felt the necessity for censorship. And on hers? He didn't know. He never discovered when she started to distance herself, engaged as he was in covering his own remoteness with conventional demonstrations of tenderness and the usual chat about everyday matters. In time he forgot what it was she must not get to know. It stopped meaning anything. It didn't matter who Sonia's father was, and he grew indifferent to Sonia herself, a chance passing delusion, but then Monica and he had already grown used to the unnoticeable distance that had arisen. It had already made them less to each other, more indistinct.

Only in bed was he completely surrendered to her. That is, his body was, and their bodies' commerce became a test of what things were like between them, when afterwards she cuddled up to him with a satisfied sigh and said it was good, or asked anxiously if it had been good for him. The question made it sound as if their bodies were no more than tools for the other's satisfaction, and that was how it seemed now and then. When she straddled him and rode at a furious gallop on the spot, he sometimes thought of the little painted horses mounted on a plunger that children can ride on when you put a coin in the slot. It seemed to him that they were alone with their separate desire and satisfaction. He felt lonely in spite of their being as close as anyone can be. He felt he was seeing her body and his own from another place, but where was that?

It was raining harder. Every gust of wind threw rain at his face.

It had grown cold. He rose from the threshold with stiff legs and threw his cigarette stub onto the lawn before closing the sliding door. It kept glowing on in the dark blades, surprisingly long. Then it went out. His eyes fell on the grey television screen, with the sofa and a standard lamp reflected in it. He took his glass and the whisky bottle into the bathroom. A bath, that was the thing. He put the plug into its hole and turned on the hot water until steam arose. Then he turned the cold tap on slowly, but only enough to stop him from being scalded.

As he undressed he pondered whether it was really the affair with Sonia that had ruined his marriage, and in that case whether the guilt or the memory of her young body had been the deciding factor. His clearest memory of her was the moment before they kissed each other for the first time, when she had hung up her jumper to dry on the floor-planing machine and strutted around among the paint-pots in the empty corner room clad only in bra, skirt and high-heeled shoes. As she went over to him and bent down her head to meet his eyes through her wet hair, there was a second when the well-known world raised a flap to reveal something quite different, so briefly that he could not make out what it was. The rest was less clear, his treachery and the wildness, her body beneath his on Lea's mattress in what was to be the nursery. She had disappeared from him behind the grimaces of delirium.

He dropped his clothes in a heap on the floor and looked at himself in the mirror. He had grown heavier in recent years. He considered masturbating, but couldn't be bothered. He could barely achieve a proper erection on his own, and it was a long time since he had had the opportunity of discovering whether a woman could do a better job. He remembered a nurse after a Christmas dinner when he had just moved to this town, but she had left shortly afterwards. He turned off the taps and got into the bath. Slowly he sank down into the hot water and leaned back with a sigh as the heat penetrated his flesh right to the bones. He had forgotten to take off the plaster, it loosened itself from his heel. Delicate winding threads of iodine spread like smoke in the greenish water.

He had been just as alone when he was in bed with Sonia as when he was with Monica again later. Alone some place far inside his body as it did what the two women and he himself expected of it, mechanical and obedient as a willing little horse. The difference was that with Sonia it had been sex from beginning to end. Other relationships had started with sex and had gradually come to include something more, friendship, tenderness, confidence. The particular thing about his relationship with Monica had been that it began with friendship, with an innocent, ironical agreement, when they had met in the circle of young friends who went skiing together. Whereas in the end it was about less and less until it ended in nothing but sex, food, washing and pay-cheques.

Not until long after becoming friends and much to their surprise had they found themselves together under a woollen blanket in a holiday apartment in the French Alps. If he had not broken his ankle and if she had not felt obliged to entertain him while the others were out in the snow, it might never have come to anything. But there had been a shy and unexpected gentleness in her otherwise ironic, authoritative or matter-of-fact face when she lowered it to his and pulled the blanket over their heads like a tent. That made him love her without warning, without transition, and he really experienced their bodies' first, tentative approaches as the result of love, not as its confirmation, for neither had as yet asked anything or demanded an answer.

It was still raining in the morning, and it went on raining until midday. When Robert went into Lucca's single room on his rounds, an old man was in there. Everything was as usual, apart from the old man the patients were the same as the day before, but he suddenly realised he felt bored. Since Lucca was brought into hospital he had grown used to seeing her twice a day, on his morning rounds and in the afternoon before going home, when he sat by the window listening to her story. Sometimes she did not say anything special, or she asked questions about the music he had recorded. At other times he stayed just for a quarter of an hour silently sharing a cigarette with her until she fell asleep.

To start with she had been an interesting interruption in his orderly life. When she had gone he discovered he had grown accustomed to her being there. Something was lacking without her, although her bed was quickly filled by another patient. He had not felt this with any other patient, and it disturbed him a little, although not until now. He suddenly saw that his afternoons with Lucca had been a breach of his medical professionalism. He had not given a thought to the possibility of his colleagues and the nursing staff finding it strange, but when he was on his rounds on Monday morning he felt he was being watched. He took pains to behave as if everything was normal, which in fact it was. That was the boring thing about that Monday. Everything was normal again after an interruption that had been so long that he had forgotten the everyday routine that had been broken.

It cleared up a little at midday and the sun shone cautiously on the wet grass of the lawns. He was in his office when Jacob put his head round the door. He smiled boyishly. It looked as if they might be able to play after all. If it didn't start to rain again the court would have time to dry. Robert had forgotten they had arranged to play tennis that day, but Jacob didn't seem to notice his confused expression. He smiled secretively. His wife had been away visiting her parents all Sunday. With the children. He made a fist and moved it to and fro beside his hip before closing the door behind him.

Several times Jacob had entertained him in the canteen with stories of his breathless trysts with the gym teacher, until one day Robert cut him short by snapping at him that he should be more discreet. Jacob looked quite scared and he was himself taken aback at his snarling tone. One evening when the weather was reasonable he had been persuaded to come over for dinner. While Jacob in his apron stood at the barbecue grilling steaks his wife walked past him, and he suddenly grabbed her round the waist, making her squeal, throwing a laddish glance at Robert. The man-to-man signal seemed repellent to Robert, but he was amazed at Jacob's cold-bloodedness. Had he himself been as cold-blooded? He must have been.

A few years after their affair Sonia had married a young Danish solicitor she had met in New York. The barrister and his wife were extremely pleased. The young couple were married in Holmens Church in Copenhagen, and the wedding breakfast was held at the Langelinie Pavilion restaurant on the Lakes. Robert had not seen Sonia since he had gone to the airport with her and kissed her goodbye with assumed intensity, as if their shared afternoons had really meant a lot to him. He had to admit that she looked disturbingly good in the fussy wedding gown, her hair artificially piled. Her coltish air had gone, and although she still talked like a child with strongly voiced s's and a lazy, clumsily articulated diction, nothing was left of the Bohemian slut he had allowed to seduce him.

It was a wearing feast, and the speeches were too long, full of jokes meant to give a thorough or moving portrayal of the bride or bridegroom. In between he conversed with his neighbour at table without paying attention to his own words. She was a stewardess and interested in tarot cards. Meanwhile he kept his eye on Sonia, pluming herself like a beautiful bird in a nest of white. He fantasised that at any moment she might take off from the table and fly away over the heads of the amazed, well-behaved guests, out the window and on over the harbour until she was only a white fluttering spot that could be taken for any roving seagull.

During the meal he drank a good deal to relieve his boredom as the stewardess explained the significance of the tarot cards to him. When he glanced now and again at Sonia he felt surprised over having tumbled around with his wife's half-sister on his daughter's mattress. As she sat there beside her husband, radiant and feminine in a completely grown-up manner, she was certainly very attractive, rather like the beautiful women in fashion magazines you offer a fleeting glance before leafing on, because they are after all only pictures.

He had been relieved when she went back to New York and he was just as relieved to see her married. Everything that took her further out of reach seemed to affirm that their affair had been a misunderstanding. They had had nothing to say to each other, all they had in common was their familial relationship, and even if their meeting had been a chance encounter, it still resembled a kind of traffic accident. The wrong woman in the wrong arms, that was the sort of thing that happened when the head lost control of the body. How was it to know the difference of its own accord?

He came on her after coffee in the cloakroom in front of the lavatories. She was alone. He said he was glad to see her. She said she had missed him. He didn't believe that, but he smiled, nevertheless. She took a step forward, her white skirt meeting the creases of his trousers, and put a hand on his shoulder. It was an obvious invitation, and he kissed her, wondering how to escape. She took his hand and led him through the door of the women's toilet. Luckily no one was in there. She pulled him into one of the cubicles, locked the door behind them and laughed softly as she half closed her eyes. He kissed the bride, what else could he do when they were standing there in the cramped cubicle? She unbuttoned her dress and pulled out her breasts, smiling and looking at him earnestly. They were bigger and more taut than he remembered them. I'm pregnant, she whispered. He could not decide whether her tone was triumphant or sarcastic. He kissed her breasts, she sighed. Her wide skirt whispered drily against the walls. He heard someone come into the toilet and the lock turned in one of the other cubicles. They stood quite still, as Sonia, with a hand on the hard bulge behind his fly, held his gaze.

He walked out to the point. The sand crackled in thin flakes beneath his feet. On it there were still traces of the rain, myriads of small craters. There was a smell of rotting seaweed. The cloud masses shifted slowly as they swelled and bulged, grey-blue with white edges where the sun touched them. The sea was blue-black under the horizon, closer to land the surface turned into a pale, milky blue. It resembled a bare wide floor, dull and granulated with small ruffles except where a current change left its smooth trace. Big seagulls landed on the beach and stalked off with arrogant, black eyes. Chief gulls, he thought, feeling intrusive when he obliged them to take off with indolent wing beats as he approached.

He looked at his watch. Jacob would be waiting in the changing room. There would not be any tennis that day. Robert couldn't stand the challenging, self-satisfied expression when his eyebrows spoke meaningfully, merely waiting for Robert to pump him, duly impressed, about the passionate gym teacher with big boobs. This was the first time he had stood him up. In general it was a long time since he had stood anyone up. He was always there, ready and willing in his sparkling white coat, prepared to deal with the functional break-downs of his fellow beings when they were wheeled in, anxious or mistrustful. Mostly they came to trust him, patient, professional Robert with his cultured weakness for romantic symphonies. He stopped to light a cigarette, bent his head and shielded the lighter flame with his jacket. Like a sleeping bird, it occurred to him, with its beak buried in its wing.

Had he quite simply been unlucky? A player among players, who place their bets, win or lose? Was that how he had ended up on his siding, on a deserted shore, in a white coat at a provincial hospital, on a sofa in front of a panorama window looking out on his designed plot of landscaped, hedged-in nature? Was it merely one of the unpredictable results of love, a fortuitous outcome of its meaningless and inevitable power to change bodies and faces about and distribute them further. Once more he meditated on how far, how immeasurably far he was from Monica's blushing tenderness under the blanket in the Alps when she called him about Lea's arrangements in a practical, measured tone. As if Lea was not their daughter but merely a mutual task to be undertaken with suitable care and efficiency. It was clearly of no importance that she was their joint flesh and blood, as they say. It was just a trick their bodies had played on them, his microscopic tadpole that had turned into a little folded frog in her womb, a complete little person in embryo.

Once they had been close. They had known each other so well, but with the passage of time he had come to confuse his knowledge of her, crystallised by habit, with the particular moments when he felt her face loosen up and reveal what she was like inside. He knew more about her than anyone else, but it had still not been her, he thought now, walking by himself on the heavy sand, heading for the point. She had shown herself to him in the way she had grown to be, but it was not really herself he had seen and heard. Only the outward echo of her being, the reflections in her tone of voice and her manner, all the little quirks and habits of behaviour. Only rarely had he caught a glimpse of the person she was behind everything she had become.

He visualised her standing on the beach in his bath robe, her back to the low sun, gazing at the waves' shining foam. Or at home by the window, pausing with the hot iron raised over a flat blouse sleeve with sharp folds, looking at something outside. That was how he remembered her, halted in her movement on her way through the days, self-forgetful, as if he had suddenly become invisible and free to spy. He had almost had to sneak up on her at unguarded moments to track down what had originally aroused his feelings.

He also watched her when they were with other people. Her

laughter or attentive gaze suddenly showed him a different Monica, one he imagined as truer than the woman he knew, whether it was her laughter that sounded more inviting, or her expression that was warmer than he was used to. It made him jealous, but it was not so much the man she happened to be talking to who aroused his jealousy. It was the unknown, non-existent person he himself should have been to call out this bold, almost frivolous smile which he did not seem to have seen before. This moist, lingering glance he could not remember she had ever bestowed on him.

At other times he felt he saw her in a more authentic, genuine form, rather as she must have been when a child. He recalled one summer morning when he awoke in her parents' house in the country. It was early, but she was not lying beside him. Lea was still asleep in her cot at the foot of the bed. He opened the window to let in fresh air and heard her subdued voice down in the garden. She was sitting with her father at the table where they had their meals when the weather was fine. They did not sit opposite each other as usual, she was beside him pouring out tea. Robert could not hear what they said.

The barrister was wearing only shorts. He sat with head bent, looking down in his tea cup as he spoke, resting his elbows on his knees with hands folded in front of him. Although the skin of his torso hung flabbily around his chest and stomach there was something youthful in the way he sat. Now and then he stopped talking and screwed up his eyes as if pondering over his own narrative. Monica sat in the same pose, bent forward with her elbows on her knees, supporting her cheeks in her hands and glancing at him. Suddenly he looked at her and laughed, jerking his chin slightly upwards, as Robert had so often seen her do.

It was the same movement, a cheerful, arrogant little salute to the irony of fate, as if to put himself on eye level with the unpredictability of life. She laughed too, and as they laughed they leaned against each other. Her eyes turned into two narrowed cracks and her face arranged itself into rays of smile lines. For a moment Robert saw precisely how she must have looked when she was a little girl. He felt like going down and joining them to hear what they were laughing at, but he didn't. Most probably he would not have understood what was so funny.

He felt that Monica was the one he had known best of all. She had told him things about herself she had not told anyone before. Now he did not know her any more, now it was Jan she confided in. When they talked on the phone or occasionally met he could not understand they had once been nearest and dearest to each other. So fleeting was closeness, vanishing without trace, he thought, going on between the calm sea and the pine trees of the plantation. He turned towards land, the windswept trees were replaced by scrub and marram grass. On the other side the beach gave way to a flat expanse of lakes and strips of ground.

When she had let him into her confidence, her words had been like telegrams from a distant place, about remote events he had to try and picture to himself at random. There she lay in bed before him talking about her childhood and the men she had known, about the times she had been in despair or happy, what she feared and what she hoped for, but he could not get at the story itself, just as he could not see behind her face. She had probably not told him everything. She must have deliberately withheld some things, while other things just didn't sit with her words, and he did not know what questions to ask. In time they stopped asking most questions.

The sky grew lighter above the rushes and the inundated meadowland. The grass blades resembled hatchings thinning out where the hand had tired of drawing, the last strokes of the pen resembled hesitant commas in the void of air and reflections. The ground squelched beneath his feet as he went out on to the isthmus between the meadows and the lake. Out there the beach was merely a narrow sand bank fronting the sea. Only the tall reeds rose above the surface as he approached the wooden shed and its tarred planks with cracks the light shone through.

When he came to the reeds he caught sight of something blue among the pale yellow stems, a small flat piece of light blue cardboard. He went closer and recognised the silhouette of the mettlesome gypsy dancer with her raised tambourine. Had Andreas thrown away his empty cigarette pack? There couldn't be many people in the small town, or among the visiting ornithologists, who smoked Gitanes. Perhaps he had taken the same route as Robert before he packed his suitcase one day, took his little boy's hand and went to Stockholm to try his luck with the black-haired production designer's astonishing blue eyes. The wisps of smoke around the gypsy girl's curvaceous waist had blended with the blue colour, faded by sun and rain so there was no longer twilight around her but broad daylight. She had gone on dancing all night with undiminished fervour, long after the invisible guitars had been put away in the invisible guitar cases and the invisible chairs piled up on the invisible tables. She had danced till dawn, long after the invisible cigarette smokers had gone home, hoarse with fatigue, tobacco and unrequited desire.

He seated himself on his usual worm-eaten post among the reeds, hidden from the world, he thought and again visualised Jacob. Now he must be waiting with his racket on the tennis court, rocking impatiently on his feet because he had to hold back all the erotic titbits he had intended Robert to drag out of him one by one. He studied the faded Gitanes pack. A voluptuous female silhouette like that probably danced in the mind's eye of every man, without the light ever falling on her face. You might call her anything that appealed, but there would always be the same provocative hand on her hip, the same sway of the waist, the same dizzy swishing of skirt and hair and the same jingling tambourine above her head.

It was banal, of course, but all the more effective. The darker the silhouette was, the more it came to resemble a key-hole in the shape of a woman, which made the observer believe he was the key to her mystery and she the door that would eventually open on to an unknown world. But the black outline of the dancing beauty did not indicate a particular woman. The artist had omitted individual features and all that was left were the titillating basic forms of femininity, the wasp waist, swelling skirt and billowing hair. The silhouette of the beautiful gypsy lass was a darkened hole, carefully cut out, into which any attractive woman might fit, lay a hand on her hip, bang the tambourine and play the role of a dream on the verge of fulfilment.

That was how the gym teacher twirled around in Jacob's thoughts, how she showed off her fabulous breasts in the dark corners of his daily life as husband and father. That was how Sonia, scented with summer rain, showed herself to him in the empty apartment smelling of paint. And that was how the Jewish designer lured Andreas to puncture the idyllic soap bubble that had surrounded the refurbished house by the wood. Robert dropped the cigarette pack among the reeds. There she would lie, the unknown gypsy, among the birds' nests and rustling stems, until she rotted away in the brackish water. An increasingly blurred silhouette dancing bravely on day and night, forgotten by all, with upheld tambourine and swaying hips.

She too probably had her dreams as she danced for everyone and no one. Like the other lonely dancers she must dream that someone would catch sight of her. A strange guest in the smoky tavern, who would come in one evening and direct his gaze on her like a sudden projector lighting up her face. For each dancing silhouette there would be a masculine silhouette in the doorway of the tavern, and just as she danced in men's thoughts, so the figure on the threshold lingered in her thoughts as she shook her hair and called to him with her tambourine. Had he finally come?

Perhaps she had already visualised his outline, sure that she would be able to recognise it through the rolling fog of cigarette smoke, for it was the outline of someone she had once known. And maybe the stranger in the doorway felt the same way. Maybe he had been going from tavern to tavern all night, standing in the doorway watching one gypsy after another in the hope of finally recognising the contours of his first love, or the genesis of his love, which perhaps, perhaps not, was one and the same thing.

The radio was made of dark wood, shining with varnish, and the subdued light of the lamps was reflected in its rounded corners. The switch buttons were shiny too, yellowish white, and one of them clicked when the girl's hand reached out lazily to push at it with the ends of two fingers. It was a long hand, pale, almost white, but a different, cooler white than the buttons and the smaller press buttons between them, in a row like the flat, rounded teeth in the lower jaw of a herbivore. A coppery light shone from the dark green glass plate around a dull pupil, and Robert could remember how the bright narrow eye had reminded him of the air bubble in a spirit level, blinking just as restlessly as the girl's hand moved the red needle past the names of towns printed in slanting columns. There was a boiling, rushing sound behind the woven panel covering the loudspeaker, and disconnected words and sounds escaped the storm and the close-knit covering, but they did not correspond to the town names, Tallinn, Sofia, Berlin, they were Danish and Swedish voices, there were none from further away although the needle traversed quite different distances, now between Warsaw and Leningrad, now between Vienna, Prague and Budapest.

Apart from a suitcase each for their clothes, the radio and her father's clarinet were all the girl's parents had brought with them after they left their country the year before her birth. Almost twenty years had passed to make it familiar with the new words and sounds, yet Robert thought everything sounded slightly strange, as if heard from the distant city they had left behind them while they were still young. To start with they must have wondered at the sounds produced by their old radio in the new surroundings where they slowly learned to speak again and like their small daughter mixed up the words from their old language and the new one.

The green pupil stopped flickering, apparently its eye had settled on something. The white hand let go of the button, the red needle stopped midway between Belgrade and Trieste, and a different kind of crackle sounded through the panel, the breakers from a hall full of clapping hands. That too subsided, silence followed and the first notes sounded in a breaking wave of gathered, released and re-accumulated power, Brahms's third symphony. A sea of clanging tones from instruments that Robert felt flowed together, so he could not distinguish one from another, possibly because the varnished wooden box was too small for all that music, the wooden frame creaked like an old dinghy, but no doubt also because he had only just started to distinguish the surface ripples of music from its under-current.

He was seventeen, she was almost two years older, the girl in the armchair watching the snowflakes in the violet light from the street lamp as if in a trance. From the beginning he had marvelled at her eyes, so far apart. She had pulled her legs up under her in a mermaid pose, and the space between her eyes made her face seem open, but her gaze was remote as she sat opposite him listening to Brahms. Her cheekbones were broad, her hair brown, and the side parting made it fall over one eye. At intervals she pushed it behind her ear with a weary hand.

She wore flesh-coloured nylon stockings, she was the only girl he knew who had that kind, old-fashioned look, just like the armchair she sat on. Everything in the apartment was bleak and shabby, and he had had to remind himself several times that it was only the radio her parents had brought with them and not the other furnishings. When he went to see her in the quiet street with its pompous tenements from the turn of the century, it was almost like visiting her in the distant town they had been obliged to leave. The apartment looked like those he imagined belonged to people in her parents' home town, and the father had not changed anything in the twenty years that had passed, even after the girl's mother left them and went back. She had never settled down in the foreign, western city. They had not fled because of her.

The girl had only told him snatches of the story, which he had to piece together himself, at intervals. When her mother decided to go home the idea had been for her daughter to join her later. Robert didn't understand how the mother could have left without her, she was only six at the time. But the child stayed with her father, and although it was pure guesswork, Robert had the feeling that a promise had been broken. Something in their silence confirmed his assumption. A year or two later they heard the mother had died. She had been ill, the girl had told him, without explaining the cause, and Robert had the impression that it was not the name of the disease she kept to herself. Her silence seemed rather a pact which she and the bald man with horn-rimmed glasses had made, whether it was a secret they guarded, or the mother's death itself they shielded each other against. There were no pictures of her in the apartment, only some of the girl at various stages of her growth, in silver frames with a leather flap behind so they could stand up on the sideboard. It looked as if the man with horn-rimmed spectacles and his deceased wife had managed to have a whole crowd of children.

Now she sat like a mermaid in flesh-coloured nylons looking into the darkness through the veil of snowflakes. Behind the yellowed panelling her father played his clarinet with its shining silver keys. They could not hear him, they just knew he was there, in evening dress, like an inseparable part of the music, a foaming whirl in its breaking wave. Robert had seen his evening suit hanging on the dining-room door. She brushed it for him before he put it on and straightened the white tie, as he impatiently squirmed at her care, perhaps embarrassed to let Robert see his daughter in the role of deputy for a solicitous wife. She was a head taller than her father, but he was a small man, anyway.

Robert had been embarrassed himself when her father opened the front door for the first time in a smoking jacket and checked slippers. The man gave him a suspicious look through his thick spectacles. Although he felt slightly guilty Robert couldn't help comparing his stumpy figure with the dismal interior, moss-green and brown, with heavy wine-coloured curtains and table centres askew and antimacassars on the backs of the armchairs. There was no television, only the old radio. He felt like a guest in another time, but he corrected himself later. It was not another time but another world. The girl had been embarrassed too, the first time he sat at the table under the chandelier with unshaded bulbs. She served while her father questioned him in his tortuous accent. She was embarrassed, Robert could see, at having so much of her life suddenly laid bare in the garish glare of the chandelier. She had been embarrassed because her father received him in slippers. She said it in their own language, but Robert guessed what she said. When they sat down to dinner her father had changed his shoes for a pair of black ones. Surprisingly small shoes, impeccably polished and shining.

Ana was the most beautiful girl he had ever seen. Later on Robert asked himself if she had really been so beautiful, but in vain, his scepticism failed when he brushed her face clear of oblivion. Nor could he set her young face against a middle-aged woman's to compare them and observe the results of time's revenge on the innocent arrogance of any young beauty. For all he knew, age had made her still more beautiful, but he could not be sure. He had not seen her since she graduated. But she had certainly been arrogant, and her haughty manner, with her unfashionable blouses and skirts, made her still more unusual.

At that time most of their contemporaries, boys as well as girls, had started wearing hand-made shoes, flared corduroy trousers and blue Chinese denim shirts. Clumping footwear and denim shirts had even sneaked into the sixth form college they attended, where she was a year ahead of him. It was a private school with a glorious past, teachers in ties and sea-green walls. The spherical lamps and plaster cast of a Greek hero in the vestibule, the nationalistic sentiments and the smell of wax polish held sway while the world outside grew ever more rebellious and shoddy. By an unpredictable coincidence Ana, with her old-fashioned, well-brought-up air, was better suited than many other pupils to the school's atmosphere of discipline and good manners.

Seen from the street the heavy red-brick façade with its deep window recesses resembled a fortress intended to shield and sound-proof the classrooms from the subversive slogans blaring from megaphones and fluttering from banners above the processions of protesters marching past outside. Robert had bought himself a pair of sloppy shoes and a blue denim shirt and had just finished reading Chairman Mao's selected works. He had not only read them as an antidote to the head's admonitions at morning assembly, he had also, it later occurred to him, made himself familiar with the chairman's ideas in unconscious solidarity with his mother, who slaved in a factory canteen until her hands were rough and cracked. In contrast to the mothers of his school friends whose hands were smooth, cared-for and indolent when they were stretched out to bid the polite plebeian boy into their warmth.

She smiled at him absently, his hard-working mother, when he tried, over the rissoles or fried plaice fillets, to make her understand why thc dictatorship of the proletariat was inevitable, or talked about The Long March as if he had walked the whole way himself. She was too tired to follow his train of thought, her feet hurt, and when he made the coffee she was already ensconced on the sofa with Dostoievski or Flaubert. Once he made an attempt at Ana's dinner table. He depicted the liberation of intellectual resources in the classless society and did not notice until it was too late that she cleared her throat and tried to catch his eye, as the clarinettist just looked at him out of his horn-rimmed spectacles. The thick lenses made his eyes seem smaller, simultaneously defenceless and resigned, as they regarded the young man sitting there eagerly proclaiming. He seemed to be looking at him from some far-off place. Later, when his revolutionary fervour had burned itself out, he always saw that distant look behind the clarinettist's spectacles when the conversation centred on class war.

For a long time he had watched Ana's serious face during morning assembly or going up or downstairs past the dusty plaster hero. He thought about her when he lay awake at night. She was often by herself, which made things more difficult for him, because her solitude increased her air of inviolable aloofness. He did not know how to approach her, nor what he would hit on to say. She did not seem to notice him. To her, no doubt, he was merely an overgrown child.

It was Ana who spoke first, one day after school. She caught him up on the pavement and passed him a newspaper. He had dropped it. It was a Trotskyist pamphlet with a red star in the heading. He had walked along with the red star sticking out of his pocket, for the effect. She held it out in front of her between two fingers and he asked if she was afraid it was infectious. It flew out of him, to his own astonishment. Maybe it was to compensate for all the times he had followed her at a distance and thought about her when he was alone, without her knowledge. She smiled. He had never seen her smile before.

They took walks together after school, in the parks, and she lent him books, mostly poetry. She wanted to know what he thought of them. Gradually the poetry collections replaced the subversive material on his shelves, not because he had suddenly exchanged his revolutionary world view for a lyrical one but because he was interested in everything that could tell him something more about her and bring them into closer contact. If she had guessed he was in love with her she made no sign, nor did she apparently notice how others gossiped about the odd couple they made, the fiery agitator and the eastern European loner from their respective forms. He only pretended to be bothered by the gossip. It was to be the two of them against the rest of the world.

She looked at him attentively when he dutifully explained what he had got out of reading some poet or other. He felt stupid, he wanted to kiss her, he suffered and rejoiced at the same time when they sat on a park bench watching the swans and talking about life. She drew him into a serious, intense atmosphere where the shadows were darker and the colours glowed more deeply. If Robert thought he was a fierce social critic, in Ana he found a still more implacable and uncompromising spirit. On the whole, everything that issued from the radio and the television or was shown on cinema screens, in Ana's opinion was just pop. She could not have hit on a more derogatory expression, and when she pronounced the word she wrinkled her nose which creased the skin around her nose and nostrils into little folds, making her look like a fastidious rabbit.

It looked sweet and Robert couldn't wait for her to say the word. He provoked her to utter it by talking about films he knew she would hate. But she did not think, like Robert, that everything labelled pop betokened false consciousness, capitalist society's calculated method of brain-washing the working class and preventing it from developing a necessary class consciousness. Deep down she felt the populace was pop-minded, and she tacitly let him understand that she herself belonged to a persecuted but superior elite of intellectual aristocrats, of *artistic* people, as she said. That was her favourite word and it signified the absolute opposite of pop. It brought them to the verge of quarrelling, but it was obvious that she enjoyed their discussions, and while he argued in favour of the proletarian view, secretly he dreamed of getting a place in the select circles of artistic people, preferably a place beside hers.

She began to invite him home. He took it as a promising sign, but nothing happened. They sat in the living room, never in her room, sometimes her father was with them. They drank tea. Robert had not imagined there could be people who sat drinking tea in the afternoon like that, talking of poets or composers, as if the world revolution was not smouldering just round the corner, ready to burst into flames any day. He sat there in his denim shirt listening to records with Ana and her father, different recordings of the same pieces, and the father conducted with both hands as the music played. He gave a commentary on how various conductors interpreted the same score. That was how Robert became captured by music, like a detour to Ana, to the moment he was waiting for. He continued to love the great symphonies long after his love for her had died out along with his faith in the permanent revolution. The works of Brahms and Mahler were the inadvertent remains she left behind her when she vanished from his life, but at least that was something. Trotsky left no more in his memory than the unsuccessful attempt to picture what it must be like to have an ice pick in the head.

One afternoon when they were alone his eyes fell on a little gold star of David hanging in a chain around her neck. He had not noticed it before and asked if he could look at it, stretching out his hand so his fingertips almost brushed her collar bone. They had never been so close to touching each other. She took off the chain and let it fall onto his palm with the star uppermost, observing him with her dark eyes as he weighed it in his hand. Was she Jewish? Her paternal grandmother had been. The star of David had belonged to her, so her father was Jewish too, according to tradition at least, although her grandfather had been a Christian and her father was an atheist. She herself must be half Jewish, she said, taking back the star.

She bent forward so her hair hung down in front of her forehead as she fastened the chain round her neck. He recalled the red star on the newspaper she had given back to him when they talked together for the first time. Was the golden star to be the route to their first caress? Her neck was slimmer and more delicate than he had thought, and he was about to bend forward and kiss it when she raised her head again, so her hair flopped freely around her. She smoothed it, pink in the face, and he didn't know whether it was bending down that had brought the blood to her cheeks or his intention, which must have been written in large letters on his forehead.

Nonplussed, he grabbed at the first subject that came to mind and asked her to tell him about her grandmother. She had disappeared during the war, in one of the camps. Ana paused, looking at him to see the effect of her words on him and judge if he was worthy of hearing the story. Again she made him feel stupid and boorish. There was a sombre tone in her voice as she spoke and he shuddered as tourists do when, in shorts and T-shirts, they come in out of the sun to the cool vaults of a sanctuary, not so much because they feel like it but because they think they should. Her grandmother had left her small son with a farming family in the country. They saved him, but they also became his only family. Several months before he left them her father had decided to join the partisans. No one knew where or when he died, or how. Ana's grandmother was deported a few weeks after she had kissed her son goodbye and hidden the gold chain with the little star of David under a loose paving stone in the pigsty.

Ana often went back to the story or talked in more general terms about her Jewish background. She had read everything she knew. Apparently her father had repressed his origins or lost any interest in them. He did not like Ana wearing the star of David although he had given it to her himself when she was a little girl. But the more he evaded her questions the more she questioned him and read from the piles of books in her room on Judaism and Jewish history. Robert discovered that she had cultivated her identity as half-Jewish or quarter-Jewish, according to how exact she wanted to be, for a long time. By his interest in the star on her neck he had unintentionally led their conversations onto a track they could not get away from again. When she held her monologues on the cabbalists and the Talmud, on the diaspora and the twelve tribes of Israel and how many great artists had been Jews, he cursed himself because he had not had the courage to kiss her bare neck.

Her passion for everything Jewish was quite different from the passion for music she shared with her father. It did not make him feel any closer to her, on the contrary it made him feel she removed herself to a world from which he was excluded. A world where he had no chance because measured against it he must seem so ordinary and anonymous. He suffered more than ever from his secret love, sure it could not stay hidden any longer, and that in her thoughts she mocked him for his cowardice. He dreamed of assailing her with a sudden embrace, literally pulling her down to earth and waking her to life away from what he came to see as a ghostly passion. When he attentively listened to her stories of the intellectual superiority of the Jews, he tried to suppress the anger that welled up in him and also made him feel ashamed. Sometimes he was about to forget that it was she and not the Jews he was angry with. But he was jealous of her Jews, both living and dead, and when she dwelt on her grandmother's death yet again, he felt paralysed.

It was not only that he had to stop on the threshold of something neither of them would ever come to comprehend. It was also because he dared not say what he was thinking. For in contrast to him she did not allow herself to be paralysed, she persisted in entering the forbidden darkness of history, as if it was not only the story of her grandparents she told, but her own as well. He felt he began to understand why her father creased his brow every time he saw the little star on her neck. In fact she wore it not as a symbol but as an ornament. She had surfeited on the tragedy of her unknown grandmother, and on her father's, although she had had no part in them, born as she had been in safety on the right side of the war and the Iron Curtain that separated her father from his homeland, where she had never set foot.

One evening at the beginning of winter he sat in their kitchen while she cooked, and as usual he was the one who listened, bursting with lust as she spoke of the Jewish respect for the written word. She described how it was forbidden to throw away old Torah scrolls, and how the worn-out scrolls were kept in the synagogue attics. Suddenly he interrupted her and asked if she regretted that her mother had not been Jewish so she could regard herself as a valid member of the chosen people. He did not know if it was the sarcasm in his tone or the reference to her mother that made her fall silent. He felt immediately he had broken a tacit agreement, but he had only become aware at the moment he violated it. He tried to continue the conversation and asked, peaceably he thought, how there could be room for all those Torah scrolls in the attics of the synagogues, and how you could stop the mice eating them. She did not reply, merely went on peeling potatoes with unrelenting accuracy.

At the table her father asked her why she was so quiet. It's nothing, she said, avoiding his glance, painfully distressed at being so directly confronted in the presence of Robert. Her eyes settled on a distant point between them, and she sat like that, withdrawn and unmoving, with her head raised a little, so Robert could see the full length of her throat, that throat he should have kissed long ago. She had taken off the star of David. Robert was sure she had been wearing it when he arrived, but he didn't feel he could put that down to a victory. She stayed unconquered with her dreaming eyes and her way of holding her face, as if weighed down by the luxuriant hair, absorbed in a secret thought. Her arrogant expression made him forget his remorse in the kitchen when she stood staring silently down at the peel sliding off the yellow potatoes in curved strips and falling into the sink with a soft sound like heavy drops. He felt she obliterated him with her silence and her absent gaze, and he felt the urge to wound her still more.

He thought of an article he had read in the newspaper about the Israeli expropriation of Palestinian property. He started to describe what he had read, and the clarinettist listened, interested. He agreed with Robert, the Jewish treatment of the Palestinians showed that Zionism was not a whit better than any other form of nationalism, on the contrary it was serious treachery against the Jewish people's experience as a persecuted minority. Robert watched Ana as her father spoke. Her eyes were still distant, but slightly softer and darker, he felt, as if they grew larger. He was surprised at his luck, but was not allowed to enjoy it, before Ana dropped her cutlery with a crash. The clarinettist gave her a surprised look through his horn-rimmed spectacles as she left the dining room. The door of her own room slammed. He put down his napkin on the cloth and rose. Robert stayed at the table, listening to him as he talked quietly to her through the door in their foreign language.

She had glanced at him as she stood up, and it was not anger he read in her shining eyes, nor was it self-pity. She had merely looked at him through her tears as if to make quite sure. She looked at him as if she had known all the time that he would betray her, and had only herself to blame for letting herself be carried away by his sympathetic air. As he sat alone at the table, he felt the treachery burn his cheeks, but many years would pass before he completely understood what had happened. In fact he had not wounded her. That at least would have been a warmer gesture. Instead he had revealed the coldness in his young, fumbling desire. He had held a hard mirror up to her and shown her what she already knew.

He could have shielded her from the sight, but he did not. Without seeing it he had confirmed to her that she was alone. By reminding her that she was not the one she dreamed of being, he had simultaneously come to reveal that he himself had only dreamed about her. You dream the dreams you need to, he thought later. He had been too young to understand why she dreamed as she did. On the other hand, she had immediately realised that he still only needed his dreams. Where she had adorned herself in her Jews, he had adorned himself with his love instead of letting it elicit a scrap of mercy.

She did not speak to him for almost a week, and he dared not approach when he caught a glimpse of her in the corridors or on the way up or down the staircase, past the plaster Greek. He was in despair, he couldn't concentrate in class, and he felt assaulted by scornful eyes, while his stomach clenched in fear and hope at the thought that they might pass each other in break. One afternoon he rang her doorbell, with shaking knees. Her father opened the door, she was not at home. He invited Robert in. He didn't like to say no when the clarinettist asked if he would like a cup of tea. Ana might well turn up, he said, smiling in a way that made Robert feel he was made of glass. She was a sensitive girl, but he must have discovered that. No more was said on the subject.

It had snowed all day and Robert's shoes were soaked. The clarinettist asked if he didn't want to take them off to get dry. He kept on even though Robert said politely it wasn't important. Surely he didn't want to get pneumonia? Ana's father was about to take off his shoes by force when Robert gave in and shyly watched the bald man crushing up newspaper and stuffing the wet shoes with it. He leaned the shoes against the radiator and stood there looking at Robert for a while before sitting down again. They had not been alone together before. Now he was caught, without shoes and without Ana. Her father put sugar in his cup and stirred it thoroughly. How was the world revolution going, then? Robert's face flamed. It would take a bit of time . . . The other looked at him over the edge of his horn-rimmed spectacles and smiled, but not maliciously, almost kindly. It must be nice, he said, to have something to look forward to.

He questioned him about his mother, and Robert said more than he meant to. The clarinettist regarded him attentively. He kept his eyes on him even when he lifted his cup to his mouth, which was a mere slit in his short-sighted face. To his astonishment Robert discovered that he no longer felt shy, and before he could stop himself he was recounting how he had found his father's telephone number, how strange it had been to call up the gentlemen's hairdresser in a provincial Jutland town and present himself as his son, and how at the last moment he had changed his mind and left the train on the way to their arranged meeting. He stopped and to avoid the other's eyes looked around the room. He caught sight of the black suit hanging on the door. You can hear me play this evening, said Ana's father. Robert looked at him, the clarinettist smiled again. They would be playing Brahms.

They heard the sound of a key in the front door. When Ana came into the room she stopped abruptly before coming over and sitting down with them, then taking a gulp of her father's tea. They sat in the kitchen eating sandwiches after her father had gone. They didn't talk about what had happened the last time he came to visit. Nor did they talk about Jews. He told her about his English teacher, who had been furious because hardly anyone had handed in their essays. I have turned a blind eye to a lot, the teacher had said, but now I've seen enough of you! Ana laughed. He asked if she skated. She did. Perhaps they could go skating one day. If the cold spell lasted the ice on the lake would soon be thick enough. It had grown dark outside and snow was falling again. He asked when the concert would begin. She looked at him in surprise. Now . . . Would he like to hear it? They rose and went into the living room. She pulled up her legs in the armchair and he thought she probably always did that when she was alone. She bent over the radio so her hair fell over one eye, and lazily stretched out a hand.

A clattering of flapping wings broke the silence a little way off. A flock of birds rose in concert from the reeds and fell into a triangular formation with an equal distance between each. The triangle of beating wings made a turn in the air, dwindling into the perspective towards the axis where swollen clouds were reflected in the quiet water. Robert rose from his crumbling post and saw the flock and its flapping reflection approach each other. He threw a last glance at the silhouette of the dancing gypsy woman on the cigarette packet's blue square, no longer twilight blue but pale blue like the sky and the folded surface of the water behind the reed-bed.

He began to walk back, again visualising Ana one winter evening in their early youth, beside the darkly varnished radio where her father was playing among the other musicians, the instruments flowing together in one great movement. He sat in the armchair opposite her, right on the edge, while the waves of music struck the densely woven panel of the wireless set. Ana sat looking out at the falling snowflakes outside. Cautiously he rose and went over to her, squatted down and laid a hand on one of her ankles in the flesh-coloured stockings. She slowly turned her face towards him, not surprised, almost in a kind of dawning recognition, and with a strangely soft, lithe movement slipped down to him on the carpet. Afterwards he couldn't work out how she had disengaged herself from her folded mermaid position and down into his embrace.

He had not forgotten her face in the warm, slanting light of the lamp, surrounded by her fan of hair on the wine-red and withered green vine leaves. It stayed with him even after it ceased to make him heavy at heart. Her face was still clearer than a photograph after he had grown up and other women had succeeded her. It kept on breathing. He remembered not only her broad cheekbones and the distance between her dark eyes, but also the feeling of being wide open, the second before he bent down and his own shadow covered what he had seen.

It was the same feeling many years later when Monica pulled a woollen blanket over her head to guard their first kiss against the cold and the raw winter light and the ugliness of the holiday flat. And perhaps he had just been waiting, it occurred to him that afternoon in the French Alps, for a face with the same almost painful gentleness to sink down over him and wipe out the image of Ana.

But he had been mistaken, his last love had not eclipsed the first one. Instead, his relationship with Monica had made him doubt his capacity to love. If there was a hidden connection between Ana and Monica it seemed more likely that his first delusion had been pregnant with all the succeeding ones. But he did not think like that in the Alps, and later when he was with Sonia in his and Monica's newly painted home, he sometimes pictured Ana afresh, her expectant face framed in flowing hair, and he felt she signified a promise that had never been fulfilled.

They lay rolling about among the threadbare arabesques of the carpet, their hands under each other's clothes, tongues enmeshed, until she tore herself free. He looked at her, crest-fallen, thinking she did not want it after all. She wiped saliva from her mouth and started to unbutton her blouse. Take off your clothes, she said quietly. He obeyed. Everything suddenly took on a very practical tone. He kissed her neck as her fingers searched for the hooks of her bra. How skinny you are, she said and made him feel like a skeleton. Her breasts were smaller than he had imagined and her hips broader, thighs stronger. This is what I look like, she said, as if she had read a slight hesitation in his eyes, and he kissed her passionately and frenetically like a drunkard afraid of getting sober. She fell backwards and started to laugh. His hands went roving all over her. He didn't like her laughter. Not so fast, she whispered and showed him how, with a light hold of his wrist. She seemed a little too expert.

He had a condom in his pocket. It had been there a long time. He took it out, bashful, and broke the seal. She didn't say anything but he could see what she was thinking. He was prepared all right. Licentiously considerate. She watched him roll it on, curious. This was it, then. The smell of rubber made him feel coarse and still more undressed. She guided him and after a couple of attempts he made his way in. She smiled and squeezed up her eyes, her hair stuck to her damp forehead, she groaned. He ejaculated almost at once. He could see that was a disappointment, but she was sweet. They lay close to each other, listening to Brahms. She gave him a far away look and stroked from his forehead down over his nose with one finger. He said he loved her. She made no reply.

For a week or two he really thought they were a couple. He thought of it with ecstasy when he waited for her outside the school. They strolled together in the snow-white parks and went skating when the ice on the lake grew thick enough. He took her home and introduced her to his mother. He wondered nervously what Ana would see in her, and on the way upstairs in the modest block he puffed up his mother's love of Tolstoy and Dostoievski. Afterwards he felt foolish for having been over-enthusiastic in crediting his mannish mother and her red, cracked hands with a love of the arts. When they were alone in his room Ana said that his mother seemed a fine person. It sounded far too studied. They lay on his bed, he kissed her and pressed a hand between her nylon thighs. She pushed it away.

She seemed to have got over her rapture for Jewishness, and he never saw the star of David again. All that was left was poetry, but she did not talk about it as enthusiastically as before, and he soon grew bored when they adjudicated between what was pop and what was art. He wanted to talk about *them*. They often just lay on his bed or hers, when they were alone at home, without saying anything as they caressed each other, she slightly absentminded, he insistent and expectant. After they had made love she always covered herself with the duvet. She didn't like him looking at her body. Sometimes she fell asleep. When he realised they were not sweethearts any longer and maybe never had been, it was not her broad hips and small breasts he visualised when he lay sleepless at night cultivating his broken heart. It was always her face beneath him on the carpet the moment the whole thing began.

It did not end, it ebbed out, until with one blow it became clear to him that it had been over for some time already. She started to have things to do in the afternoon, and when he arrived at her home unexpectedly it was quite often her father who opened the door. He had tea with the clarinettist as the thawing snow slid off the roofs outside. They listened to records and talked about music. Robert learned a lot about music that winter, and in the midst of his unease he discovered that he liked sitting in the gloomy apartment talking to the bald man.

The clarinettist never seemed surprised when Robert rang the doorbell. Nor when he turned up one afternoon even though Ana had said she would not be home until late that night. There was a music stand by the living room window, the clarinet lay on a chair beside it. Robert asked if he was interrupting. Not at all, but now he was there he might as well make himself useful and get them a pot of tea. He went into the kitchen and put the kettle on, and as he waited for it to boil he listened to the cool, melancholy notes from the living room. Ana's father went on playing when Robert carefully put the tray on the sofa table and sat down in his usual place. The man by the window seemed not to notice him. He played as if he was alone, lightly rocking to and fro in time to the melody with his small, short-sighted eyes glued to the score and his mouth locked in a downward curving, somehow regretful grimace around the mouthpiece of the clarinet.

He continued to play when the front door banged. Robert turned round, and through the half open door he saw Ana in the passage with a man. They had their backs to him and didn't see him. They hung up their coats on the row of hooks and disappeared out of sight along the corridor to her room. Robert sat on until the clarinettist put his instrument down on his lap and looked at him over his horn-rimmed spectacles. Bartók, he smiled and took off his glasses. He held them up to the window, lowered them again and polished the lenses on his shirt. His eyes were brown like Ana's and bigger than usual. He put on his glasses and looked out of the window. There was a rubber plant on the window-sill. He stretched out a hand and picked at the outside, withered edge of one of the leathery leaves. Brown dust fell on the sill. Bartók, Béla, he said slowly, looking out at the wintry light.

Robert was at the kitchen sink when he heard a car in the drive. The engine stopped, a car door slammed, and soon afterwards the doorbell rang. He hesitated for a moment before going out to open the door. No one was there, but he recognised Jacob's car behind his own. The telephone rang in the living room. He stopped on the threshold. Jacob was out on the lawn looking in at the panorama window. It was dim in the room, presumably he could only see his reflection and the clouds and trees by the fence at the end of the garden. Robert had forgotten to switch off the answering machine when he came in. The telephone was beside the window. If Robert answered it Jacob would see him. If he ignored it, it would still look as if he had just gone for a walk.

He heard his own voice saying he was not in and asking the caller to leave a message after the tone. The volume was turned up so high that Jacob must be able to hear it. He stayed on the grass. Robert was almost certain he had not seen him, but still it seemed as if their eyes met through the wide window. After the tone there was silence, and in the silence he heard someone breathing. When he recognised Lucca's voice he could not decide whether he felt a bad conscience or annoyance at the idea of not talking to her. He went over and picked up the receiver, turning his back on the window. When he looked out into the garden a few moments later, Jacob had vanished. He heard the car start and drive away.

Her voice was muted, almost confidential, but maybe she only lowered it because there were other people in the room she was calling from. She had learned to dial for herself. Wasn't she clever? He apologised for not having been to see her yet, and asked how she was doing. It sounded tame. She replied with a question. Had he spoken to Andreas? Robert thought of Stockholm. No, Andreas had not contacted him. Why didn't she just call him? Surely she must have an idea where he was. She said nothing. Robert asked if he should try to call Andreas for her and at once felt cross with himself for voluntarily allowing himself to get entangled in their private complications. He had only asked to break her silence. She hesitated. Would he do it? He said yes. She wanted to see Lauritz. Maybe, if it was not asking too much, could he take the boy to see her? On a Saturday or Sunday, when he was not working? He must promise to say no if it didn't suit him. He smiled at the small hypocrisy.

She gave him the name and address of some friends Andreas used to stay with when he was in Copenhagen. He would have to find out their number, she couldn't remember it. He got the number from directory enquiries and called. It was engaged. He pushed open the sliding door and went outside. The sun shone through the busy clouds and made the white plastic chairs on the terrace shine so he had to narrow his eyes. He went to stand in the middle of the lawn where Jacob had been. The shining reflections of the chairs swam in the panorama window in front of the dimness of the room and the more distant, indistinct picture of his lone figure on the grass. How had he ended up here? Even if he strained his memory to the utmost, and really succeeded in tracing the order of events down to their smallest links, he had a suspicion that it would not bring him closer to an answer.

The following days were warm, the clouds dispersed, and the high pressure transformed the sky into a pale blue desert stretching all the way into town. The heat made the air quiver over the asphalt of the motorway. The wind blew in through the open windows and pulled at his shirt sleeves, and he felt light and empty-headed as the road signs increased in perspective and abruptly flew over the windscreen. He listened to *The Magic Flute* and quite forgot why he had set off. It was a long time since he had been in Copenhagen, and when he passed the south harbour he recalled all the times in the past when he had returned after a trip in the country, relieved to see the city towers again, the sparkling water of the harbour and the cranes above the goods trains' marshalling yard. He could leave his job, sell the house and move back into town. He could do whatever he liked. What was he waiting for?

Noisy pop music issued from behind the door. He knocked loudly. She was as brown as cocoa and unnaturally blonde, the woman in the black slip who opened the door. Her dyed hair was short and stuck out untidily around her pinched, sun-tanned face. She looked at him enquiringly as she squeezed up her eyes to avoid the smoke from the cigarette between her lips. She had a small artificial pearl on one nostril. The apartment was at the rear of a block in the city centre and consisted of one large room with vertical wooden beams in the centre. Piles of clothes were scattered on the furniture and the unmade double bed, and the confusion of fashion garments, empty pizza boxes, used coffee cups and randomly dropped objects seemed to go with the drumming rhythm pumping out of the loudspeakers. She must have been the same age as Lucca. The bangles on her wrists jingled when she removed the cigarette and threw out a hand to show the way. She apologised for the mess and shouted to Lauritz, who was on the sofa watching television. It didn't occur to her to turn down the music. A sun-tanned man stood at one of the windows wearing nothing but briefs, talking on a mobile. He threw a glance at Robert and nodded curtly before turning his back on them. He was athletically built and absent-mindedly caressed the muscles on one upper arm as he spoke.

Lauritz did not react, totally hypnotised by Tom and Jerry chasing each other across the screen. The woman with dyed hair looked Robert over as she called the boy. On the telephone he had introduced himself as a friend, but he could feel she was wondering if he was something else and more, this respectable substitute uncle from the provinces in his checked shirt and moccasins. He had asked for Andreas when he phoned. The woman had said he was away travelling. At last Lauritz raised his head and caught sight of them. Robert was not sure the boy recognised him, but on the other hand he did not seem shy, rather resigned, as he slid off the sofa and came to shake his hand. The woman with dyed hair walked in front of them back to the door. The man in briefs was still talking with his back turned. Robert said he would bring Lauritz back in the early evening. She turned round in the open doorway. Was it true that Lucca would never see again? How dreadful . . . She smiled at the boy and ruffled his hair before closing the door after them. Lauritz smoothed his hair as they walked downstairs.

Robert asked him if he could remember the day he and his father had driven home from the supermarket in Robert's car. The day it rained. Lauritz thought about it. Then he asked where his father was. Hadn't his father told him where he had gone? He couldn't remember. As Robert drove north he glanced at the boy now and then in the rear mirror. He could only see his forehead and eyes watching him expectantly. He wished Lea had been there. He remembered how she had led the boy round the garden as if he was her little brother, when Andreas had come to deliver the leg of lamb that had been left in the car.

She had called the previous day. He was mowing the lawn and the noise of the mower almost drowned out the telephone. She laughed at his breathless voice when he answered at last. She was calling from the airport on the way to Lanzarote. He was sweating, his T-shirt stuck to his shoulder blades. Her laugh was the same as the week before when he ran after her on the beach and stumbled. He looked down at his trainers as he listened to her voice. The toes were covered with grass clippings. He wanted to say something to her but couldn't think what. He asked her to send a postcard. She said she would and kissed the mouthpiece at the other end. It sounded funny.

Lauritz had fallen asleep when they drove into the parking place in front of the orthopaedic hospital. Robert called to him softly until he woke with a start and looked around him, rosy-cheeked and confused. As they walked towards the entrance he let go of Robert's hand and started gathering pine cones from under the pine trees. Lucca smiled when he gave her the hard, prickly cones. Robert stood where he had stopped at the end of the terrace a nurse had directed them to. She sat in the sun on one of the deckchairs. Seen from a distance she might have been any woman smiling at her son, looking at him through her sunglasses. Lauritz climbed onto her lap and pushed his head under her chin. Robert walked up to them and the sound of his steps on the terrace floor made her lift her face. The boy looked at him watchfully. Thank you, she said. It was kind of you. She was suddenly formal, she had not been like that on the telephone. It was nothing, he said. No, was all she replied. He said he would go for a walk on the beach.

There were a lot of people there, and he felt much too dressed up and conspicuous among the anonymous bodies lying in rows in the sun. He sat down some way up the beach and took off his shoes and socks. The shrill cries of children rang out and then were swallowed by the deep sound of the breakers. The light dazzled him, reflected in the water that ran back before another wave gathered itself and slumped down on the wet sand. Kullen's low cliffs were blue and misty, and now and again he saw a little flash over the Sound when the sun struck a passing car window in Sweden.

Robert lit a cigarette. He had not been here since Monica and he were divorced. This was the view she had stood gazing at as she smoked, one late afternoon when the other beach visitors had gone home. Yet it seemed quite a different place. There was nothing left but disconnected impressions, and he was not even sure he remembered them precisely, those fleeting moments of closeness, like coming suddenly out of the shade and meeting the sunlight. He had believed you could build on that kind of thing, and now they were in Lanzarote.

He sat there for half an hour. Occasionally he looked at the hospital's white functionalist building, formerly a fashionable seaside hotel. He recalled the story Monica's mother had always told when she'd had something to drink, about how the barrister had proposed to her one evening there on the dance floor, between two dances, poised and romantic in his white dinner jacket. Might he have chosen her for her dress? And if so, why not? Just as love had its consequences, so love itself was a consequence of every possible and impossible thing, small or large. He brushed the sand from his feet and stood up, put on his shoes and pushed his socks into his pocket. Small things holding some mysterious transformative power often proved surprisingly influential on one's imagination. The luxurious way a skirt swung around a girl's legs in time to the tunes of the age. A modestly blushing smile beneath a woollen blanket in the Alps. A white hand lazily pushing the button on an old radio and a dreamy gaze at the snow under the lamps. No more was needed.

Lucca was still on the terrace. Lauritz lay on the floor rolling his pine cones. Her long face with its high cheek-bones and straight nose seemed both melancholy and arrogant, as if shaped by an old, indomitable yet never satisfied hunger. She sat with her face lifted to the sun and a faint smile around her mouth. He did not know if the heat was making her smile or the sound of his step and the deck chair giving way beneath him.

They were silent, you could hear the sea, but only as a muted soughing beneath the staccato, clicking sound of the bristly scales on the cones Lauritz was rolling over the terrace floor. One of them landed at her feet, she bent forward and picked it up. Her fingertips investigated the hard shells along the edges. What had Andreas had to say? He has gone away, said Robert and paused. I think he is in Stockholm, he went on. Stockholm, she repeated. Yes, he probably was . . . Lauritz came up to her, she passed him the cone. He asked when she was coming home. She brushed the hair back from her forehead and pushed the unruly lock behind her ear. I don't know, she said, stretching out her hand. The boy bent his face so her fingers could brush his cheek. He kneeled on the floor again and threw down the pine cones one after the other.

Had he got a cigarette? He offered her one and noticed how surely her hand, after a moment's fumbling, found the pack and coaxed out a cigarette. She took hold of his wrist when she heard him ignite his lighter and bent her face so her hair fell in front of her forehead again and came dangerously close to the flame. He lifted up the lock with his free hand as she lit her cigarette. She leaned back quickly and blew out smoke, and he noticed her cheeks were slightly flushed, but that might be owing to the sun. It had reached the tops of the pine trees around the parking place, and the shadow of the terrace parapet formed a bluish triangle on the blinding white end wall. The wind made the needles of the pine trees sway in unison and moved the ash from the cigarettes over the floor tiles so it spread and took off in whirls of grey flakes. She didn't really know where she was, he thought. Lauritz had climbed into a deckchair a little way off. He had a pine cone in his hand and looked out in front of him, it wasn't clear what he was watching.

You haven't told me anything about yourself, she said. I am always the one who talks. Always, he thought. Had they spent so much time together already? He brushed ash from his knee. Where should he begin? She turned towards him. Wherever he liked . . . He looked into her dark lenses, duplicating two identical twins each in his check shirt, both bent forwards, each with a cigarette in his fingers.

He knocked several times, but no one came. He knocked again, harder. There was complete silence from behind the door. Lauritz had sat down on the top step. One by one he let his pine cones tumble down the stairs. Robert tried to remember what he had said to the woman with dyed hair. He was sure he had arranged to bring the boy back in the early evening, but as the minutes went by he began to doubt. He sat down on the step beside Lauritz. Maybe she had forgotten, maybe the music had drowned out his voice. Lauritz dug him in the side with a finger. He said he was hungry. Robert looked at him. The boy's eyes seemed older than their soft, downy surroundings. They waited patiently to know what he was planning.

They went to an Indian restaurant in the same street. Lauritz only wanted rice. As he ate he gazed around him, fascinated by the gold-painted, oriental arches of the interior, cut out of plywood and lit with mauve bulbs. Did India look like that? More or less, replied Robert and to pass the time began to tell him Kipling's story about the civet cat. When Lauritz had finished with his rice it looked as if it had snowed on the cloth around his plate. Robert went out to call the woman with dyed hair and the muscle man. A well-educated woman's voice answered. No contact with the mobile at present. It was nearly half past eight. He thought of what he had told Lucca about himself, about Monica and Lea. He felt he had said too much. He stood gazing blankly at the mosaic of numbers on the telephone, considering what to do with Lauritz. Then he lifted the receiver again and called his mother. She sounded surprised, he had not spoken to her for several weeks. He asked if he might call in and explained the situation to her as briefly as he could. It sounded muddled to him. When they were in the car Lauritz asked where the big girl was. Robert told him she was his daughter. Were there any civet cats in Lanzarote? Robert didn't think there were.

The boy fell asleep on the sofa where Robert's mother had lain reading every evening for decades. They sat on her little balcony looking out over the railway lines and the marina further away, beneath the heating station's red-brick colossus. Did he usually drive his patients' children around? He smiled wryly. The sky was violet blue over the Sound, and the remains of daylight glowed pale on the rails and the forest of masts and tall thin chimneys. She asked about Lea. When he replied, she fell silent. She had never said what she really thought about the divorce. She had liked Monica, they had had good talks, but she had not been all that sympathetic when he told her Monica wanted a divorce. Nor had she condemned her daughter-in-law when he told her about the morning he arrived back too early from his trip to Oslo and almost surprised her in Jan's arms. In her opinion the episode belonged to those chance misfortunes which should not in themselves be given too much weight, and she was probably right. But her silence had had the effect of a reproach. Did she think it was all his fault? She couldn't possibly know about his affair with Sonia. What had she seen? He had never asked her.

She looked old now, her face hung from her cheekbones and her chin in wrinkled bags, and the masculine spectacle frames seemed larger than ever. She picked up her coffee cup with a slow, slightly shaky hand and steadied the edge with her upper lip while she drank. Her eternal coffee. He had made coffee for her every morning from the time he was ten until he left home. On Sunday he had even brought it to her in bed, black as tar with masses of sugar. It was her only extravagance apart from her insatiable consumption of nineteenth-century novels. I don't feel human until I get a cup of coffee, she would groan when she went into the kitchen in the morning, drunk with sleep she towered in the doorway, rubbing her face with her big red hands. A man's hands, cracked, with short nails and prominent veins.

He had to make his sandwiches himself, and from early on he learned to do his own washing. She was too tired when she got home from the canteen. They shared the housework on Sunday afternoons when the others were playing football in the courtyard. She frequently sighed but otherwise she did not complain. He did what he could to avoid being a nuisance, and he never complained about the clothes she bought him once or twice a year when the sales were on. She bought summer clothes for him in the autumn and winter clothes when summer was approaching, always the cheapest you could get, they were really ghastly, of course. He was ashamed of his clothes and he was ashamed of her, and he was ashamed of being ashamed.

When he grew tired of lying in bed in the afternoons grieving over the loss of Ana, he gradually began to realise that it was not only love that had made him suffer so, but self-disgust as well. And still later, after he had married Monica, it struck him that there had been an almost tangible connection between the two emotions. With her aristocratic airs and exotic beauty Ana had made him feel a pariah. He who had writhed when he had to go to school wearing the wrong kind of trousers. It had been as clear as it was futile that she was the very one to deliver him from the curse.

But her eastern European home had not only been the gloomy background that emphasised her aristocratic and wonderful pallor when finally, one evening with snow falling outside, he was permitted to hold her face between his hands. He had continued going there long after he should have realised it was hopeless. One afternoon after another he had tea with the clarinettist while he waited for her. He accepted the humiliation merely for the sake of listening to classical records with the kind man with horn-rimmed spectacles and a quaint accent. It had been a more inviting place to be, and he had preferred it to his mother's two-and-a-half room apartment with its view of the heating station and passing trains.

A train glided through the twilight in an arc. He looked at his mother. Neither of them had said anything for a while. They had never talked to each other a lot, not even when he lived at home. They mostly spoke of practical things and in the evenings both sat reading. Now and then she would laugh and read a snatch aloud to him, which he listened to with only half an ear. Not until he grew up did he realise that she had never really known how to get in touch with him, exhausted and remote from the world as she was. He had misunderstood her awkwardness and taken it as coldness.

The row of lit carriage windows passed across her thick, curved lenses and hid her eyes. She put a hand on the parapet and stroked the painted cement with her palm. It's still warm, she said, smiling. From the sun . . . He touched it for himself. She was right, the cement was still quite warm. It left a fine layer of grey dust in his palm. He wiped it off on his trousers. She would have called him one of these days if he hadn't come. Perhaps it didn't mean so much to him to hear it, but his father was dead, she had seen the announcement in the newspaper. Again that phrase, *your father*, as if she herself had had nothing to do with him.

She had never mentioned him in any other way. She had hardly ever mentioned him at all, the gentlemen's hairdresser in a distant provincial town he had once been on the point of visiting. He didn't know what to say. He tried to realise it but could not feel anything. She tried to read his silence. She did not feel upset about it, she said, it was all so long ago. Her tone was unusually hard, almost blunt. The death announcement had been signed by the children. So he had had more than one since he left them. The funeral had taken place. She smiled briefly and looked at him as if to catch him feeling moved. Still, it was strange, he finally got out.

The strange thing was that she had ever married the man. But of course, she went on, if I hadn't, you wouldn't have been born. He lowered his eyes and lit a cigarette. Now he mustn't think she had gone around snivelling over his father all these years. It had been a misunderstanding that they had ever got together, and it had only been an instance of the irony of fate that he was the one to take his leave . . . She stopped and drank the rest of her coffee. For a moment her face was nothing but spectacles and cup. She probably hadn't ever told him about it. Her voice was different now, softer.

She had been the cloakroom attendant at a restaurant where there was dancing. A musician who played the bass worked there. She'd been secretly in love with him for months, and finally he caught sight of her. One early morning when the restaurant closed he went home with her to her room. The landlady was always asleep when she got home from work, but all the same she asked him to take his shoes off on the stairs. He still had his orchestra dinner jacket on, a sparkly one, and patent shoes. When he took off the shoes she saw he had a hole in one sock. His big toe stuck out. She smiled at the thought and pushed at the handle of her coffee cup so the cup turned half round.

When she saw his pale big toe poking out of the sock and his expression when he realised she had seen it she knew she loved him. She smiled again and looked into the empty cup. If he hadn't had that hole in his sock she probably wouldn't have let him. Everything else about him had been perfect. He had been so well groomed it made her frightened, but that morning she was no longer frightened. She had always hated being so tall and broad-shouldered, she had felt like a lighthouse, but he was just as tall and he made her feel they matched each other. He had had such a nice voice, and he had said some nice things to her. No one had spoken to her like that before.

She stopped and looked up. He should have been your father, she said. They had been together for a couple of months, she and the handsome bass player. She had been in seventh heaven until summer arrived and he met someone else. She looked out over the parapet towards the brick mass of the heating station that still kept a faint reddish glow in the midst of all the blue. Then she had come across the gentlemen's hairdresser. Robert gave her a long look. She felt it and met his eyes. But he was not to sit there feeling sorry for her, it was long ago. She had been so young. Things didn't always come up to expectations, he knew that himself, it was nothing to snivel over. She rose and piled up the cups to carry them out. Hadn't he better call those people?

He rang and again heard the well-modulated woman's voice. Still no contact with the mobile. He had already come to a decision. Carefully he picked Lauritz up and put his pine cones in his pocket. The boy raised his head, half asleep, and then laid it back against Robert's shoulder. His mother stroked him kindly on the back when they said goodbye in the doorway. She didn't usually do that, she had never been very demonstrative. On the way downstairs the light went out. He went slowly down the stairs towards the little glowing orange point where the switch was, afraid of stumbling with the sleeping child in his arms.

He laid him on the back seat, covered him with his jacket and drove through the town and southwards along the motorway. As the blue road signs approached and rushed past, he thought of the unknown bass player with the nice voice, who should have been his father. Who would he have been then? Had his mother occasionally put the same question to herself when she sat on her balcony or lay on the sofa and looked up from her book for a moment? Had he been a reminder that just grew and grew all through his childhood, that nothing turned out according to plan? It wasn't anything to snivel over, she had said, and instead of snivelling she had stuck to her job and sacrificed herself for her son. She had sought flight in novels and, compared with their more dramatic and tragic fates, she had doubtless thought her own was too trivial and average ever to be called a fate. It had just turned out as it had. Nothing to write home about.

There were a lot of lorries on the motorway, German, Italian, Spanish lorries, and Dutch ones. He stayed in the inside lane although that made him slower. He felt like listening to music but did not switch on for fear of waking Lauritz. It was really a kind of kidnapping, but what could he do? It was a real mess. He had stumbled straight into the chaos and confusion of perfect strangers as if they were his concern. He recalled an expression he had often heard his mother use when she commented on something she had witnessed or heard about. As if it was anything special. That was her judgement when someone complained of their troubles or protested at life's injustice. Only war, natural catastrophes and mortal illness could produce a sympathetic remark. Was it her own privations that had made her so scornful towards others' woes? He did not believe that, for she had never seemed bitter, only extremely remote. It was more likely that her contempt for her own pain had made her unfeeling about others', until she stopped distinguishing.

When she sighed it was not because she was sorry for herself. Her nose and throat had just developed into a kind of ventilator from which disappointment, regret and sorrow were ejected now and then, quietly and without fuss. That was all she allowed herself, a minor character, as in her own opinion she was, in the great novel of the world, whose chief action in any case took place somewhere else, far out of range. Her frugality was not only dictated by her scant means, she practised it on principle and maybe it was a way of compensating for her unusual height, which had embarrassed her so when she was young. She apparently thought she took up more space than was right, and so ought to restrict her existence in every way possible. She had never thought of herself and as a whole had spent everything she earned on her son. Once she had bought a bicycle for his birthday, a shining, brand-new blue cycle with white tyres. He had wished for one for a whole year without ever really believing he would get it, but when he woke in the morning and saw it standing beside his bed, his rejoicing was dulled by the thought of what it had cost.

While Robert drove down the motorway with the sleeping Lauritz on the back seat he asked himself whether his mother with her pinching and scraping had actually wanted to punish herself because she had a child with the wrong man, when the right one had thrown her over. It was nothing special, nor did she feel that she herself was, and looking back he suspected that in her heart, with all her frugality she had intended to economise herself into extinction. Her total lack of egoism had not prevented her becoming slightly misanthropic. In her view no human being was anything very special. But she had also found a strange, anonymous freedom when she sat on her balcony and now and then raised her eyes from one of her novels to watch the trains go by.

Luckily Lea had left some cornflakes at the bottom of the packet. There were enough for one portion, and the boy looked on approvingly as Robert gave him breakfast on the terrace. He had slept in Lea's room. When Robert went to wake him in the morning he was lying with an arm around one of her old teddy bears, kept for sentimental reasons. Could he remember being here before? Lauritz looked around and thought. He could remember playing table tennis with Lea and digging in the garden. He asked when he was going home. Later on today, Robert replied without knowing what he was talking about. He went to get Lea's Tintin books and brought one of the white plastic chairs onto the lawn where the sun was shining. He took off his bath robe, his body was quite white. Lea was right, he ought to do something about those handles. The problem was he couldn't really be bothered. He sipped his coffee, looking at the strange boy bending over the table, absorbed in interpreting the little pictures where Tintin and Captain Haddock escaped from one scrape after another with a mixture of chance, optimism and adroitness.

He closed his eyes. It was hot already and he enjoyed feeling the grass under his bare feet and the sunrays warming his pale skin. He really should go in and call the woman with dyed hair and the muscle man to tell them where Lauritz was, but he didn't feel like moving. It was so long since he had sat in the sun, and he defended his laziness by working up some indignation over their irresponsibility and the recklessness Andreas had shown in leaving his son with such superficial friends. He was sure he had told them when he would bring the boy back.

Andreas called later in the morning. He would come and fetch Lauritz. Robert was about to say something about the woman with dyed hair having forgotten their arrangement, but didn't, amazed the other man apparently took it for granted that he had taken the boy home with him. Andreas would come at once. Where was he calling from? The house, he replied curtly. He had arrived yesterday evening on the last train, he hadn't wanted to call so late. How considerate, thought Robert, and offered to drive. He had a car, after all.

When they turned off the main road and drove beside the meadow towards the wood they saw the horse in the same place as it had been two months earlier, on the rainy day when Robert took Lauritz and Andreas home. The sun shone on its flanks, which quivered as if from a shock when the flies pestered it. Andreas came out into the yard and squatted down with open arms as Lauritz ran towards him. They sat in the garden on a bench by the house wall. Lauritz was on a swing hanging from a big plum tree. Andreas had set a bowl of plums between them on the bench, violet blue, with a matt skin like dew. The grass had not been mown for a long time and was almost as long as the corn in the field at the end of the garden. The wind made the cobs rock from side to side in snaking tracks, and poppies glowed restlessly, scattered amidst the corn. Andreas offered him a cigarette, they smoked and ate plums. Robert tried to think of something to talk about.

How had the première in Malmö gone? Andreas squinted in the sunshine. It had come off very well, the Swedish reviewers had been quite over the moon. But that didn't matter now. Pensively, he lowered his eyes and dug his nail into the circle of loose tobacco at the end of his cigarette, then abruptly started to talk. Robert was surprised they seemed to be on such familiar terms. On the telephone Andreas had been very short, almost formal, maybe because he thought Robert might be cross. Look at me! called Lauritz. They looked. He was standing up, his hands on the ropes, swinging high. They waved, the boy laughed.

Andreas had come back from Stockholm the previous day. He was no longer quite sure what he had been thinking on his way up there. When he had read the scenographer's letters or written to her he had felt that here at last was someone who touched his innermost soul, more than anyone had done before. Now he didn't know. They had arranged to meet at an outdoor café on Strandvägen. He was surprised she had asked him to meet her there and not at her home in Söder. He was given the explanation when she arrived, twenty minutes late, as beautiful as he remembered, pale, black-haired and with blue eyes. She did not live alone. It sounded complicated. For about six months she had been about to leave the man she lived with, but she had not yet brought herself to do it. They sat silently watching the glinting water and the ferries plying up and down. Neither of them could find anything to say, strangely enough after all the letters, all the confidences and tender words that had gone to his heart so deeply.

When she finally came walking towards him smiling in the sunshine it had seemed as if all his hopes were coming with her, no longer in the form of vague thoughts hard to pin down, about how his life could change and take on a new direction, but in the shape of a living body appearing to hold all possibilities in store for him, stepping lightly among the café tables. She went to his hotel with him, now he had come, after all. That was how it seemed, precisely as dispiriting and dull as that, when they lay side by side on the hotel bed afterwards. It had not been exactly passionate. He was not even sure she had had an orgasm. He called her in the evening. She was not alone, she said, it was difficult to talk properly. He called again the next day in the morning. Her husband had just gone. Were they actually married? She laughed down the telephone. No, not exactly.

She had read the new play he had sent her. She made some comments, and again he felt it was there, the special understanding between them. She had hit on things in the play no one else had understood. He said he was coming round to see her. She didn't think that was such a good idea. He took a taxi. She seemed different when he saw her in her own surroundings, somehow more ordinary. They drank herb tea and she showed him her sketches for an exhibition she was working on. She resisted when he went to kiss her. He threw her down on a sofa, she twisted free. She couldn't do it here, she said and asked him to leave.

Maybe there had been something hyped up, something rather too stilted about those letters, both hers and his own. They had been scaffolding for each other's castles in the air, he said, smiling bitterly, as he sank his teeth into a plum and wiped juice off his chin with the back of his hand. Lauritz was lying in the tall grass, the swing swayed back and forth under the tree. Andreas had kept on phoning her. The more he doubted his precious and all-consuming passion, the more he persisted, until one afternoon a man's voice answered from the apartment in Söder. He slammed down the receiver. In the morning a letter awaited him at the hotel reception. She had gone to Gotland with her husband. It was no good. She hoped he would understand.

He had not told the scenographer what had happened to Lucca, and he hardly thought of her at all during his stay in Stockholm. When she did cross his mind it was in the guise of an evil spirit who had constantly threatened his attempts to release his innermost self. At first in the form of her all too unconditional, indeed her frankly parasitic love, later with the deadly, bourgeois daily routine and finally his own bad conscience. Robert recalled what Andreas had said when he called on him one evening and drank his Calvados, tortured by guilt and the urge to rebel. How he had long been in doubt about his relationship with Lucca, and how he had felt a lack of challenge when she turned her back on the theatre and had Lauritz, then focused all her energies on the boy and on creating their home. But in the plane from Stockholm he saw it in quite a different light. She was his victim, he thought, as the pine forests and blue lakes passed beneath him, and he had almost killed her. Although she was the most important thing that had ever happened to him. She and the boy. To think it was only now he realised that . . .

He lit a fresh cigarette and looked at Lauritz, who was trying to make a ladybird crawl up his hand. Robert cleared his throat. What if the scenographer left her husband? Andreas turned to him, apparently floored by the idea. He shook his head, she would never do that. In reality they were too alike, they were equally introspective, it would never work. That was probably why he had once fallen in love with Lucca. Because she was so different from him. No, as he said, he had deceived both himself and the set designer in Stockholm. Besides, she was too young, too immature, the illusion of one of them had nourished the other, it had been a dream that could not stand the light of day. Yes, it seemed rather like waking from a dream. As if he had slept through all those years with Lucca and Lauritz right in front of him, the only people who had ever seriously meant anything. The only ones he might ever mean something to, something real. He owed her that . . . he owed it to all three of them, he corrected himself. He rose, went over to Lauritz and kneeled beside him in the grass, stroking his cheek. The boy seemed not to notice him, totally absorbed in the ladybird. Andreas walked slowly back to the bench.

When something goes up the spout, we call it a mistake, thought Robert, because it is hard to get your head round the thought that it is not only ourselves but just as much luck and circumstance which form our lives. Then it's better to admit we were foolish. He thought of his mother and his father, the deceased gentlemen's hairdresser he had never known. If the barber had stayed with her, wouldn't he perhaps not have been a mistake? He might even have turned out to be a nice man.

What had Lucca told him? Robert looked at him. Told him? Andreas sat down beside him again. Yes, surely she had said something, given a message or request. He faltered. How was she? Robert said he could not tell. He met Andreas's eyes. He didn't know her well enough, he went on, to know, but in the circumstances she seemed to be managing. Andreas sat looking in front of him, either at Lauritz or the poppies in the swaying corn or the swing hanging motionless beneath the plum tree's crown. Of course it would be different, he said quietly, now she was blind. But it was a question of will. He had realised that. One must exert will on one's life, it would not live itself. And was there any life other than the one to be lived every day? The intimate things he had despised so much, daily life, the child . . . you had to take them on, stand up and face them . . .

Robert asked what he meant. Andreas looked at him in surprise. Lauritz called from inside the house, Robert had not seen him go in. Andreas shouted that he must wait. Lauritz called again. We're talking! shouted Andreas, half turning towards the open door. Lauritz went on calling. His father rose with an irritated expression and went inside. Robert walked round the house. Andreas caught him up in the drive. If he saw her . . . well, he didn't know. Was he going to see her? Robert replied that so far they had not arranged anything. Andreas looked down at his shoes and nudged a small stone with one toe. If he saw her would he tell her what they had talked about? Robert promised he would. He went over to his car. As he got into the driving seat the other man was still standing there. He started the engine and moved off. Andreas raised his hand, but Robert did not manage to wave.

He was in a bad mood when he turned into the suburban road. The sun was high in the sky. It shone whitely on the asphalt and the polished cars in the drives and the leaves of the dense shrubberies along the pavements. He sat on in the car when he had parked in the entrance and switched off the engine. He thought of the picture of Lucca he had seen on the notice-board in their kitchen, sitting at a pavement café in Paris, elegantly dressed in a grey jacket, with her hair in a pony tail. Lucca looking into the camera as if she had just turned round, apparently surprised at being snapped. He visualised the picture clearly, the plane trees in the background, her green eyes, painted lips slightly parted, possibly because she had been about to say something. Her gaze seemed to pierce the shining membrane of the photograph. It reminded him of something, he didn't know what. Something forgotten, something never quite understood or completed, a missed opportunity perhaps.

It was quiet around him. He could hear the whispering, pinging sound of a sprinkler in one of the adjoining gardens. He looked at the lath fencing alongside the drive. In some places the bark was peeling off the laths and hung in loose slivers. The gate was open. He could see a portion of the newly mown lawn and the terrace with its white plastic chairs and their transparent reflections in the panorama window's repetition of everything within range. Chairs, grass and small white clouds. He turned the key again, put the car into gear and backed out onto the road. Soon afterwards he reached the outskirts of town. He drove through the industrial district, passed the hospital and came to the viaduct leading to the motorway.

It didn't matter what he thought about Andreas. They had a son, the fool was still her husband, after all, and it didn't matter if his newly won and rather tacky insight into life's true values had been induced by being forced to leave Stockholm with shattered hopes. Something or other had to induce it and one cause could be as good as another. His sudden piety was of course merely an attitude, but he was clearly unable to explain things without sounding pathetic and pompous. You had to ignore that, as you considerately ignore people's handicap or speech impediment, an embarrassing limp or lisp. His sticky chatter about the important things and standing up for them sounded like another of his splendidly illuminating self-deceits, but in the long run it didn't make a lot of difference what you thought. Maybe illusions had roughly the same function as your skin. You could breathe through them. If they were stripped off, the contact with reality would doubtless be too raw. They should be allowed to dry and crackle and peel off in their own good time allowing new, fresh layers of illusion to form in their place.

The only thing that mattered was whether you were together or not, whether you were alone or had someone to be with. Whether there was a scrap of kindness and sympathy, a scrap of patience with your weak, unaccomplished sides. Then you could always think your own thoughts, tinker with your self-portrait and dream great or modest dreams. On the whole life lasted longer than your dreams, thought Robert, and when they stopped it ought to be bearable. Lucca would never regain her sight, but maybe some sort of life did await her, even if everything had crashed into darkness and solitude. Perhaps the months and years could do for them what they themselves could not envisage just now, and if he was the one who could give her the chance of considering a future with the repentant Andreas, he might well afford the time to play the role of messenger.

He waited for a long time on the terrace where she had sat with Lauritz, until he heard the slight tick from the point of her thin white stick. It made him think of the sound of Lauritz's pine cones rolling over the tiles the previous day, the prickly sound of the hard seeds. A nurse led her by the arm. She had been surprised when they told her he had come, not expecting him to visit her again so soon. Actually she had not been sure he would come at all.

She was wearing a long black dress with many little buttons, one of the dresses he had brought her from the empty house. Her hair was combed back and held in a pony tail just as in the picture from Paris, and she had put on lipstick. Someone had helped her. The nurse left them alone. Lucca put a hand on the parapet. Maybe they could go for a walk on the beach, if he felt like it. He took her hand and laid it on his arm, and thus they walked, in an old-fashioned way, he thought. She said it. Now we're walking like two old people . . .

The shadows had grown long and gathered in small, bluish puddles on the trodden sand. The foam of the waves shone in the low sunlight. Only a few holiday-makers remained on the beach. Up in one of the dunes he saw a white-haired man putting on his bathing robe. He resembled the barrister, but Robert could not decide whether it was really him. They walked at the edge of the beach where the sand was damp and firm. They walked slowly but he could see she was regaining the use of her limbs. It was the first time she had been down on the beach. Her white stick left little holes in the sand, a wavering track. She breathed in through her nose. Seaweed, she said. It was true. A salty, slightly rotten odour hung over the intertwined belts of dried kelp between the edge of the sea and the dunes. It was better than the smell of cleaning materials . . . She paused. Her hand slipped from his arm when she stopped. She couldn't bear being in hospital. She said it quietly, like a statement. No, he said.

They sat down on the sand, close to the sea. She bent her knees and pulled her dress down around her legs. The waves were small, and there was a silence after one had fallen before the next arched itself and collapsed. Fans of water and foam reached right up to the shadows of their heads and shoulders. He told her Andreas was back at the house, and what he had said that afternoon. That he was sorry. That he wanted to try again. He said nothing about what had happened in Stockholm. She picked up a handful of sand, closed her fist and let the sand filter down again in a fine stream like the sand in an hourglass. Was that why he had come? To tell her this? Robert was silent for a moment. Yes, he said.

The last grains sifted out of her hand, and she laid it flat on the sand. He looked at her, waiting for her to say something. She sat with her face directed at the breaking waves. She was no longer the person who could return. Her tone was hard and clear. She was no longer the one who could decide for that, she went on. She said no more. They fell silent. He took his cigarettes from his breast pocket, there were two left. Would she like to smoke? No, thanks. He lit a cigarette and looked across at Kullen. She didn't know . . . Now her voice was so low that half the sentence was lost when a wave broke. He asked her to repeat it. She cleared her throat. She didn't know anything any more. She drew a deep breath and put her head back, and he saw the tears running down under her big sunglasses. She wiped them away with her fingertips so the knuckles pushed up the edge of the sunglasses and he caught a glimpse of her glass eyes. She sniffed and breathed out through her mouth. It was like living in a waiting room, she said. Without knowing what she was waiting for.

He invited her to come and stay. That would make it easier to be with Lauritz while she thought over what to do next. She turned her face to him, and he looked out at the waves to avoid his reflection in her dark glasses. He had not thought of it before, but as soon as he had said it, it seemed the obvious thing. She could have his room, he could sleep in Lea's. After a week or two she might change her mind. When she had spoken to Andreas. At some point they would need to talk.

She did not reply. Neither of them said anything as they walked back. She stopped in the foyer and let go of his arm. Had he meant it? He sounded more offended than he meant to when he replied. What did she think? She smiled apologetically and reached out for his arm again. It was just . . . unexpected. They went on across the foyer. Why should he care about all her problems? She directed the dark glasses towards him as if regarding him with an expectant look. Let's say I am someone with too much room, he went on at last. Too much room? Yes, he said. Too much room, too much time. She stopped again and tapped her stick on the floor, raising it and letting it go. And how did he intend to get her out of here?

He asked her to wait on a sofa in the foyer and went into the office to ask for the doctor on duty. He had gone home. Robert told the secretary he was taking Lucca with him. She looked at him incredulously over her reading glasses. They couldn't discharge a patient just like that. I am her doctor, said Robert. He took full responsibility. It sounded rash. The secretary pushed her glasses up her nose. It was against the rules. Don't you worry about that, replied Robert and promised her she could rely on him to witness that she had protested.

He went back to the foyer and took Lucca up to her room. She sat on the bed while he packed her bag. You must be crazy, she said. Not exactly, he replied. The secretary and a nurse came in sight at the door. Was he next of kin? Not really, he said. Lucca turned away, picked up the pillow and lowered her face. The secretary pulled the corners of her mouth down in an offended grimace and handed him a ball pen and a document. Would he kindly sign this? He did so without reading it through. When they had gone, Lucca collapsed over the pillow. It was the first time he had heard her laugh.

The sun had set and the sky was pink and lilac when they came out onto the motorway. He put on a tape, they sat listening to the music. After they had passed Copenhagen she felt hungry. He drove into a lay-by with a McDonalds. They ate in the car.

She got ketchup on her chin and one cheek, but he didn't say anything. In the end she discovered it herself. You must tell me when I mess myself up, for God's sake, she said, wiping her face with the serviette. There was still some ketchup on her cheek. He took her serviette and removed the red streak, started the car again and glided in to join the column of red rear lights between the pale yellow fields in the twilight.

Part Four

It was snowing again. They had thought winter was finally over. It was late March and there had been cloudless days with bright sunshine when they could sit outside in their coats. Lucca stretched out a hand and switched off the alarm clock. She pressed herself close to Andreas's back, he was still asleep, and snoring. As a rule that did not bother her, and when it did she just held his nose between two fingers. She snored too now and then, he said, and she barely stirred when he gently turned her onto her side. They knew each other, they were not shy about anything any more. They had even stopped locking the bathroom door. She had never thought she would be so much at ease with anyone that she could leave all the doors open. Only the door of his study was always closed. When he came out at the end of the afternoon the air in there was thick with cigarette smoke. She and Lauritz had grown used to him being in the house and yet miles away behind the closed door, inaccessible until he emerged late in the afternoon, pale and distrait.

He never spoke of what he was writing when he was engaged in it. He couldn't, he said. He was afraid of losing the scent of what he was trying to pursue with his words. What could not really be said at all. But when he finished a new play he couldn't wait for her to read it. He felt actually wounded, although he tried to conceal his disappointment, if she did not read it quickly enough and say something about it at once. She had plenty to do with Lauritz and the house, but he would gladly look after everything if she would only sit down and read his script. She dropped everything and took the sheaf of pages to bed. It irritated him, she could feel, but she had always preferred to read in bed, sitting cross-legged, with the duvet around her like a lined nest.

Sometimes she found it hard to understand what he wrote, but perhaps it was not necessary to understand everything. He had said so himself in an interview with a Sunday newspaper. That what was immediately understandable in fact stunted one's perception, whereas seeming obscurity put one on the track of something only glimpsed. Something silent and more profound that could not be contained and pinned down with simple concepts. He was so clever that people were sometimes quite frightened of him, but he didn't like her to remind him of that. He had made his mark, he was one of those who counted, and she was proud of him. She was not even ashamed of being proud of her husband when they attended a première. Why should she be?

As a rule she had a few critical comments on his scripts, it might be a dramaturgical ambiguity or something in the development of a character which felt contradictory, and he listened to her even though she only had her intuition as an actor to guide her. It made her happy when she persuaded him to alter or omit something, not because he acknowledged her to be right but because she felt that brought her into contact with what he was doing, with him. The part of him she could not reach because it expressed itself only in writing, and because he had to protect this secret side to be able to write at all.

She had always wanted to play a role in one of his plays, but Lauritz was born soon after they moved back from Rome, and in the years that followed she had only done a few radio plays. She had concentrated on the child and the house. She coped almost single-handedly in the periods when he was working on something new. Miriam scolded her for letting her career run to seed and slouching around like a country housewife in apron and wellingtons. Miriam almost gave her a bad conscience, and she didn't know what to say in her own defence, but that only lasted until they had put down the receiver or waved goodbye at the station. Afterwards she did wonder why she felt neither frustrated nor unhappy or oppressed, as Miriam obviously felt she should. It was rather the opposite feeling. A leisurely happiness to which she didn't give much thought, related to the clouds that unnoticeably changed shape on their journey between the edge of the woods and the horizon. In the course of the day, while her hands were busy with all manner of practical things, her thoughts circled on their own like the swallows, now low around the house, now high up among the drifting cloud formations.

Lauritz had changed her. She had been ready, when she met Andreas, without herself being aware of it. He saw it before she did, and he had not been frightened by what he saw. He had gone on unremittingly, further than anyone else had dared. Right into her secret empty core, open to the way things might happen. He had turned out to be the one she had waited for, and so it had been Lauritz and not another man's child who had grown inside her until there was no longer any room for him. She had screamed so hard she thought she would die. She had felt as if she was being ripped open and turned inside out. Nothing had ever hurt so much, and no one had made her as happy as the small, creased, purple-blue child who was placed on her stomach so she could see his cross face and squinting little eyes and the heart hammering wildly in his frog-like body, covered with foetal grease, still linked to her by the twisted cord. Andreas wept, she had not seen him weep before, and she loved him more than ever, but she herself did not weep. She groaned and trembled and smiled all the time at this brutal, naked, screaming and bloody joy.

To Lauritz it didn't matter who she was, and yet he had never been in doubt. He could smell and taste who she was long before he learned to focus his eyes on her and recognise her face. People asked if it wasn't hard having to get up in the middle of the night and adjust her whole life to the boy's needs. They clearly did not understand it was a relief. She was relieved when she realised she had ceased to care about her own bungled ambitions and egocentric dreams. She forgot time, it was no longer divided into hours and days. The child had become her clock, time did not pass any more, it grew before her eyes.

Else was worried and Miriam almost indignant. They let her understand, each in her own way, that in their opinion she was exaggerating her newly acquired maternal feelings all too willingly, indeed, almost fanatically, subjecting herself to the child and to Andreas. They almost despised her because she allowed him, the great sensitive artist, to withdraw to his study and go to Copenhagen to tend his career or travel about Europe in search of inspiration, while she trotted around with the buggy out there in the country. She did not respond, merely smiled infuriatingly. Miriam did not begin to understand her until she herself became pregnant. She was eight months gone now.

Else had fallen silent on the telephone when Lucca called from Rome and told her mother she was pregnant. Wasn't it a bit soon? After all, they had only known each other for a few months. She felt hurt at her mother's cautious reaction. How long was she to wait? How reluctant and choosy did you have to be when life finally offered the simplest and most basic of all questions? Her entire life had gathered into a single moment when she lay beside Andreas one morning behind the closed shutters and told him she was pregnant. The future had begun just there, when he asked if she wanted a child, and she replied by asking if he did. He said yes without hesitation. Yes, with her.

Else asked if she realised that at best it would put a brake on her career and at worst put a stop to it. Just when she was about to make it. Lucca remembered what her mother had said when Otto dropped her. That there was more to life than love – work, for example. She remembered Else's bitter mouth and sunken face when she sat, eyes shut, sunning herself. Later on, as her stomach began to expand and her legs and face swelled up, she thought several times of their conversation that time at the cottage. In fact, she resembled a cow, a pale cow who looked questioningly at her in the mirror with her amiable eyes. When Andreas took her heavy breasts in his hands, milk seeped from her nipples, and he kissed them and let her taste the milk on his lips. She would never have believed it, but she felt a secret pleasure in seeing and feeling how the unknown child quietly and laboriously ruined her figure. Men had clutched it so often, but now they no longer looked at her, and soon she too forgot to note whether they did or not.

Andreas mumbled in his sleep when she kissed his throat. Your train, she said. He shot up in bed and looked at her in confusion. She stroked his cheek and smiled. He would still be in time if they got up now. He sat for a while on the edge of the bed, looking like a child in the morning, hair on end and narrowed eyes, a sulky child. She put on her bath-robe and looked out of the window. The snow whirled in spirals around the dark branches of the plum tree. It had settled already in white strips along the furrows arching over the roof ridge of the neighbouring barn. The sky was as uniformly white as paper.

Lauritz lay on his stomach, his rump in the air. His cheek was rosy and swollen with sleep, and a little patch of saliva had fallen onto the pillow beneath his soft mouth. His toy elephant stood in place with its trunk stuck between the bars of the bed-head, staring intensely at him out of its button eyes. She called to him softly and took his hand as he woke up. She made the coffee while he ate his porridge, Andreas had a shower, and she read the paper. As she leafed through the film and theatre supplement she recognised Otto. He was kneeling on a railway track, in breeches, check shirt and a sleeveless woollen slipover. His hair was cropped and he had a watchful expression in his eyes, tense as a hunted beast of prey.

She sipped the scalding coffee. The caption said he was playing the lead in a film about a resistance group in World War Two. She had to look at the picture for a long time before she could connect the watchful partisan with the face she had once kissed and the eyes she had once looked into as if they held the answer to every question. She had been so sure he was the one she was to love, and be loved by, and yet he had merely been the latest on the list. She had known there would be others after him when it was over, but had not believed it. She remembered how hard-headed she had been, completely unreceptive to what everyone could see for themselves. Was it just because he had dumped her? Perhaps, but surprisingly soon it had opened up again, that vacant spot within her, her secret openness to whatever might appear, though still not present.

Andreas had time only for half a cup when he finally emerged from the bathroom. They would have to leave at once if he was to catch his train. He stood fidgeting at the door while she struggled to get Lauritz's coat on. She asked if he had remembered his ticket. He sighed impatiently. When they went into the drive the boy put his head back and opened his mouth to let snowflakes melt on his tongue. She drove. Neither of them said anything much, they were too tired. Andreas drummed on the lid of the glove box. The snow blew across the asphalt and along the ditches and the black fields faded on both sides into the falling snow. He said he had left his address on his desk. He had borrowed an apartment in Paris, he would be there for just over a month. They had arranged for her to join him at Easter. Else had promised to come and look after Lauritz.

The lights of the train were already in sight behind the snow. The rails seemed to end in nothing but whirling drifts. He lifted Lauritz up and kissed him. See you at Easter, she said, looking into his eyes. At Easter, he smiled, picking up his suitcase, as the rows of carriages stopped behind him. He would call when he arrived. They kissed. Doors opened and people got in and out. As he was turning round, I love you, she said. He hesitated and looked at her again. She smiled and he regarded her for a moment as if taking a photograph with his eyes. Perhaps to take the picture with him, of her standing on the platform holding Lauritz by the hand, with snow in her hair. He stroked her cheek. He loved her too, he said, and hurried into the train a second before the doors closed with an automatic slam.

He often went away to work. He needed to be alone when he was finishing something or starting something new. He had been working on his new play for six months and at the same time attending rehearsals of one of his earlier pieces. Since the new year he had been in Malmö several times a week. He had made almost no progress on his script, which he had promised to deliver at the beginning of April.

She was glad he was leaving. He had been withdrawn and irritable for the final weeks before the première in Malmö. He had grumbled about unimportant trifles and generally been impossible to be with. She knew his awkward times and had herself suggested he went away. Else had a woman friend in Paris who was going to Mexico for a month, he was staying at her apartment. He had worked in Paris several times before, in cheap hotel rooms. He liked being alone in a big city where he didn't know anyone. She looked forward to going down there to disturb his solitude. She visualised how they would surrender to their pent-up hunger for each other, as they usually did when they had been apart for a while.

Lauritz went on waving until the train had disappeared into the snow. When he was sitting on the bench in front of his locker in the nursery-school cloakroom he asked if Andreas would be in Paris now. She kissed him goodbye, and a pretty young woman took him by the hand and led him off. Lucca recalled the time when she had worked at a nursery and lay on her mother's bed in the afternoons with a grown man who played badminton. The snow melted at once in the streets among the drab houses, but outside the city the landscape was white, and as she drove along the side-road, the dark edge of the woods resembled a cave opening up in the whiteness into a night filled with falling stars.

She switched on the radio and started to tidy the kitchen. Last night's dishes had not been washed up. She filled the dishwasher, scoured the pots and pans, made coffee and sat down to smoke a cigarette. The noise of the dishwasher blended with the music from the radio. The floor of the living room was covered with piles of books. They'd had a bookcase made to cover one wall, she planned to paint it while Andreas was away. They had agreed on grey, white would be too difficult to maintain. Lauritz left his fingerprints everywhere on the newly painted doors and sills. The door of Andreas's study was open. She looked at the cleared desk where his portable computer usually stood. She missed him already, although she was used to being alone, whether for a day or a month. Up to now there had always been something in the house that needed finishing off, leaving her something to get going on when he was away. To her surprise she had discovered she was quite competent at do-it-yourself, and she had enjoyed setting the house in order. It had come to interest her more than acting, and it gave her satisfaction in a quite primitive way when she looked at a wall or door panel she had repaired and painted herself.

It had taken longer than expected, and sometimes they had been about to give up, but she was stubborn, and now only details needed seeing to here and there. That might have been why she was already missing Andreas. She had forgotten herself while there was still enough to do, and the days passed like hours whether he was away or at his computer. When she was acting she had forgotten herself too, but only to become someone else. While she slogged away in her dirty overalls with the cement mixer and trowel she was no more than a hard-working body, and that was a release.

To start with it had been a mere dream, finding a house in the country. They had both grown up in the city. They started to talk about it in Rome, during the six months they lived in Andreas's cramped apartment. She suggested it mostly for fun. It was the kind of thing you cooked up crazy stories about when you had fallen in love, a place in the country. She came out with it one late summer morning when they had stayed in bed because it was too hot to do anything but lie in the shade behind the shutters and caress each other very slowly. He took her at her word just as he did a few months later when she told him she was pregnant. How could he be so sure? He ran his hand lightly over her stomach, which would soon swell up and weigh her down to earth, making her break out in a sweat at the least exertion. Sometimes you must believe your own eyes, he said. Otherwise it would all come to dust and blow away while you looked at it. No one had talked to her before like that.

The apartment in Trastevere had only one room, and when he was working she went out walking. He worked a lot, and after a few months she knew every single street in that part of the city. She admired his gift for concentrating and keeping at it for hours on end. Apparently he could always write if he wanted to. At that time he used a portable typewriter, and when she went upstairs late in the afternoon and heard the keys still tapping on the keyboard she went down to the bar around the corner and waited another half hour. It was almost like sitting in a living room, and she started to talk a bit of Italian. It seemed there was still something left in her of the language she had spoken with her father, hidden away in a fold of her brain or rolled up at the bottom of her spine. Soon she could talk to people in the street, in contrast to Andreas who never learned more than the most necessary phrases and was completely uninterested in talking to anyone but her.

She never thought of visiting Giorgio again, although now and then it did cross her mind that she was in the same country as he was, only a few hours away by train. Florence, the city where she had found him and then lost sight of him, was a different world from Rome, the city where her passion for Andreas slowly turned into something tougher, more durable, as an unknown being started to grow a nose, a mouth and eyes inside her. In the evening he read aloud what he had written during the day, and although she admired his arbitrary, stylised dialogue, she often forgot to listen. The sound of his soft voice was enough for her, feeling it like a quiver in her cheek when she rested her head against his chest. The voice spoke to her from a place she could not reach, where he had to be alone, but it was from in there that he had seen her come along and decided not to let her disappear from sight. His voice echoed within her when she walked alone in the shadows among the crumbling walls or sat in the sunshine on the Campo di Fiori. Only his voice was real, not the words, not his theatre. His voice and the unknown child filled her completely. He had believed his own eyes, and she believed in what he had seen.

The wind made the snowflakes circle in spirals over the yard. She suddenly realised it was Else she was listening to. Her mother was announcing the radio programme for the day in the cultivated voice Lucca had listened to since she was a child, alone at home with some nanny. It was the kind of voice that could say whatever you wanted it to. Every word sounded the same in Else's mouth, as if tongue, lips and teeth were tools intended for breaking up the words and separating them from what they actually meant. Else had been sceptical when Lucca told her they were moving into the country. The poet and his mummy-nurse, she called them for almost a year, until she grew tired of smiling at her own mordant wit. She visited them occasionally in their cave, as she termed it, and Lucca was quite encouraged every time she saw her mother raise her eyebrows and suppress all the pointed comments jostling behind her tight, pinched lips. She had forgotten how to look at herself from outside and she enjoyed Else's distaste for the dirty and chaotic building site where Lauritz tumbled around with a bare bottom and mud plastering his face.

Lucca had never imagined she would come to live out of town. When they moved in the house was barely habitable, and everyone said it was mad to settle with a child in a place which didn't even have electricity. As if Lauritz wasn't completely unplugged. At first they made do with paraffin lamps. They washed outdoors under a garden hose while the bathroom floor was being laid, and cooked on an open fire in the garden. In general they lived in a way the prairie settlers must have done. It was a point of no return. Everything they owned had been invested in the house and the building materials stacked up in the yard.

She had put the city behind her, the streets she had roamed, just a face among the shifting faces, always hunting for another pair of eyes to mirror her. She had put the city and the men behind her, those she had known and those she might have come to know. All the men she had doted on or left, all the grand or petty stories that had been so many blind alleys, wrecked beginnings and failed attempts to attain the life that was to be hers.

She had painted just one and a half shelves when the telephone rang. It was on the window sill. She had to stride over the piles of books on the floor, brush held aloft so it did not drip. It was

Miriam, her voice thick and stifled with sobs, she had to talk to someone. Lucca asked what had happened. Miriam started to weep. While Lucca waited for her to calm down she caught sight of a grey streak of paint running down from the brush onto her hand. She held it vertically, but it kept on running like a melting, soft ice-cream. Miriam's sobs subsided. Her partner had left her. He'd said he didn't love her any more, and that it was a misunderstanding, the child they were to have. He'd been under pressure. She sniffed and moaned. He'd packed a bag with clothes and gone off in a taxi, she didn't know where.

Lucca thought of the lanky jazz musician. He had always seemed feeble to her when Miriam bossed him around or plonked herself down on his lap demanding tongue kisses with everyone looking on, as if he owed her proof of his fiery passion for all the world to see. But he'd had the courage after all to back out, but why so late? Miriam had no idea. She had really believed the child would bring them closer together. He had even accompanied her to childbirth class. She began to weep again. Lucca pictured the skinny jazz lover sitting in stockinged feet on the linoleum floor with the bloated Miriam between his knees, surrounded by the other men and their wives, snorting in chorus, while he pondered on how to escape from the fix he had got himself into.

She recalled the night Otto threw her out and she sat drinking vodka at Miriam's. She remembered her friend's dreamy chat about having a child, and how outraged she had looked as she told her that her partner was afraid of losing his freedom. What did he want to use that for?! The way Miriam had imposed her pregnancy on him had been just as pigheaded and discordant as when she broke into his conversation and stuck her tongue down his throat. But they could not talk about that, especially not now. All Lucca could do was listen to the unhappy Miriam and explain that she was unable to go into town because she was alone with Lauritz.

After putting down the receiver she stayed by the window. The snow covered the garden and the field. It lay like white shadows along the dark ramifications of the plum branches and framed the little blue tractor Lauritz had left on the lawn. The sky was like granite. She studied the streaks of paint that had split into a branching delta over her hand and lower arm, like blood, she thought, if blood was grey. She would like to have shown more sympathy and her conscience nagged her because she had not invited Miriam to come and stay.

She laid the brush on the newspaper beside the paint pot, wiped her hand and sat down at the desk in Andreas's study. On it were only some paper clips and the note of his address in Paris in his angular, slightly untidy handwriting. The room stank of old cigarette smoke. He smoked too much, especially when he worked, and always the same strong Gitanes. He coughed in the mornings, but paid no heed to her comments. Sometimes she could hear him trying to suppress his coughing in the bathroom so she wouldn't notice it. She opened the window and breathed in the cold, raw air. The view was different from his room, you could just see the ends of the plum tree branches. She picked up one of the paper clips and straightened it out, gazing at the white slope of field partly hiding the roof of the neighbouring barn.

She felt she had let Miriam down on the phone, but had not known what to say, and couldn't say what she thought. That probably what had happened was Miriam's own fault, because she had obstinately pushed her pregnancy, deaf and blind to all warning signs. Miriam who always took what she wanted, and wore tight trousers even though her thighs were too fat. Lucca had never believed their relationship would last, and perhaps Miriam had doubted it too. Had she thought she could hold onto him by having a child? Naturally she would never admit that, not even to herself. And now a child was coming into the world, a child like all the others with the same demands for affection, the same urge to feel itself a genuine fruit of love and not merely the result of a mistake made by two confused people.

She could have said all that to Miriam if she had dared, but she had no right to say it. Who could distinguish between genuine feelings and illusions? Perhaps Miriam really did want a child, partner or no. Lucca recalled how soberly her friend had assessed her own future possibilities as an actor. A bit of cabaret here and there, as a comic. And what about herself, Lucca? She had been furious when Else comforted her by saying that Otto hadn't been right for her anyway, and that it was a good thing they had parted. Think, if they'd had a child! Now Lucca had to admit she was right. Her passion had been blind and immature. When she looked back on herself then it was like thinking of another person. As if she had been different from the woman she had become with Andreas and Lauritz. But if she really had changed, she could do so again. The idea sickened her, the idea that changes could just go on and on. And what if she was the same, after all? How could she be so sure that her love for Andreas was more real than her love for Otto had been? Was she so sure now, because Otto and Andreas, each in their respective order, had just been the latest man in the row? Did she feel sure because it only happened to be Andreas she had a child with?

She looked at the note with the address and telephone number in Paris. She felt the urge to call him, just to hear his voice, but it was too early. He would not arrive until late afternoon. It was a long time since they'd had a proper talk, she felt. There was always something in the way. She had so much to do, and he was always working. Besides, for the past two weeks he had been away most of the time, in Malmö. It worried her if they grew distant from each other for a while, on friendly terms but busy and slightly conventional when they kissed good morning or goodnight. She felt he had been distant recently. In Paris it would be different, surely. She longed for Easter.

She leaned over the table and closed the window. Suddenly she was hungry and decided to make some lunch before continuing to paint. As she negotiated the piles of books again on her way through the living room her eyes fell on a bundle of old scripts. The top one was bound in red card. The title was printed on it, *The Father*, by August Strindberg. She picked it up and leafed through the dog-eared pages with pencilled notes half obliterated. She took the script into the kitchen and put it beside the cooker while she heated water for pasta. Indirectly, Strindberg had been the beginning of her relationship with Andreas, but of course she had not known that then. Not even when they passed each other, he in the lift on his way up, she on her way down the stairs after she'd had tea with Harry and looked out at the thunderstorm over the town.

She felt like *pasta al burro* with grated nutmeg, the way Giorgio had taught her to make it. It was the only thing she had learned from him, her sad clown of a father, who had merely flung out his arms as if there was no more to say as he walked backwards beside the baptistery in Florence before turning and vanishing from sight. 'In the midst of the moonlight,' she thought, 'surrounded by ruins on all sides.' She looked at the torn script and began to smile. So she did remember something. But there had been no moonlight, it had been broad daylight, and the baptistery stood just as when it had been built, dazzlingly beautiful and geometric in its green and white marble. It was only that it hadn't gone as expected, she thought, as the steaming water in the pan began to bubble and shake.

The room was in total darkness. She could hear the cicadas behind the shutter of the small window. They kept the shutters closed all day to retain as much as possible of the night's coolness. She pushed off the sheet and stretched out a hand. He was not there. The hands of the alarm clock shone green, floating in the dark. It was only just past seven. He couldn't sleep late any more. He had told her with a wry, apologetic smile, as if it was one of the things he had lost. She summoned her energy and swung her legs over the edge of the bed. The tiles were smooth and cool. She reached for the kimono hanging over a chair, and fumbled her way through the darkness with a finger brushing the rough, white-washed wall until she found the door.

Daylight fell in a sharp triangle from the doorway to the roof terrace. She climbed the stairs and stopped at the top. He had not noticed her yet. His hearing was not too good, but he did not like to admit it. She stood still. He sat cross-legged under the canopy of woven bamboo. He was reading a book, his tea cup raised in his hand as if he'd forgotten the cup and left it in mid air. The bamboo wickerwork splintered the sharp sunlight into a frayed pattern on the stone table and the tiles, and splinters of light waved over his combed-back grey hair and lined brow, his face with its crooked nose and his brown torso with folds of loose skin around the stomach and below the chest cage. He was wearing the white linen trousers she had bought him in Madrid.

She waited. He had to discover her. It had become a game she played, more with herself than with him. Coffee's ready, he said in his hoarse voice, without looking up from his book. But he had seen her. She went and sat down opposite him. He smiled, leaning his head back to look at her through the glasses on the tip of his nose. There you are, he said. Here I am, she answered, stretching out a hand to stroke his knee. She poured herself a cup of coffee, put in plenty of sugar and sipped it as she gazed over at the range of mountains lit by the slanting sunlight, which emphasised the folds and grooves with long, blue-grey shadows among the shades of rusty red and rose.

The houses looked alike, all white-washed with flat roofs and small barred windows, like scattered sugar lumps up the mountain-side. It sounded beautiful when you described it, and when you saw the village from a distance it did resemble a picture postcard, with orange trees and olive groves and everything you could expect, but as soon as you got up there the place had a depressing air. The cement road was broken up into craters lying in wait to trip you up, the electricity cables hung in untidy garlands, and the houses were either crumbling, on the verge of collapse, or being restored, with dreary concrete walls. During the day there was never a soul about except now and then a pale weary woman in a dressing-gown behind a kitchen window. The place seemed to be inhabited by housewives and scrawny cats lying in the dust, and the only other sign of life was the smell of frying oil and the noise of television sets churning out their advert jingles from the resounding semi-darkness of the dwellings.

Harry's house was the last one in that part of the village, it faced east and from the roof terrace there was a view over a dried up river-bed with steep sides. The river-bed was cracked in deep fissures where oleanders and carob trees had rooted, and on the other side of the river, a couple of kilometres away, another chain of mountains sloped down to the plain. Seen from the terrace, the coastline was just a diffuse transition from ochre to blue in the heat haze. They had gone down there shortly after the last night of *The Father* at the Royal Theatre. At the same time Harry had staged a première of *Uncle Vanya* in Oslo. In the weeks before they left they'd been together only when he flew down to Copenhagen for the weekend. She had been offered a role in a film, the first shots were to be taken soon, in early spring, but Harry had advised her to say no. He knew the director, and it was likely to be not just mediocre, but downright awful.

It had been raining for weeks in Denmark, Lucca thought she had almost forgotten what the sky looked like. When they got out of the plane she felt a warm breath in her face, and the almond trees were flowering in white and pink against the red earth as they drove through the dry landscape. In some places the land changed into a desert with deep crevasses and crumbling rock formations like the brains of huge, prehistoric animals. Soon they would have been there two months. They were planning to spend the summer in a house he would be renting beside the Jutland coast, before rehearsals started on *A Doll's House*. She was to play Nora.

When Harry was not directing a play he spent his time in Spain reading and writing. She didn't know what he was engaged on now. Wish lists, he had replied with a teasing smile, when she asked him. When you were young you wrote wish-lists, he went on, but he had gradually forgotten all the things he had wished for through the years. It was hard enough to remember them, all those years. She had not spoken to anyone but Harry for weeks, and all the days seemed alike, but strangely she had not felt bored. In Copenhagen there were always people to see, people of Harry's age. He was very attentive when they went out together, but even so she often felt just like a decorative appendage, instantly left out of the game because she was not born at the time their hilarious anecdotes had been launched.

Harry's friends were writers, painters or film directors, and usually they were as famous as he, but had been part of the élite for so long that their laurel leaves were pretty withered by now. Behind their comfortable complacency lurked a small, bewildered disquiet at getting fewer mentions in the newspapers than twenty years ago. They could spend hours discussing it, how bad the newspapers had become, just as they worried a good deal about the young having an easy time of it, and how little it took nowadays for them to climb dangerously close to their own exalted position. Up to a point they were quite generous at including her in the conversation, some of them even took the trouble to seem not at all formidable, and yet something sly and avuncular appeared in the sudden interest of the grey old codgers after she had been left on her own for a while.

She could feel their wives frowning at her when the men bent intimately over her while investigating what she might bring to the conversation. Most of them had known Harry's dead wife, but she was never actually mentioned. Lucca felt like an itinerant scandal, and when she was introduced she saw how their eyes flickered between disgust and envy at the indomitably lucky old dog. She had even been spared the attentions of the gutter press once when he was careless enough to take her to a première, and when she walked around town she sometimes felt she was recognised as Harry Wiener's talented young *lady friend*.

Harry was always the centre of attention, maybe because he was one of the few whose fame had not begun to fade at the edges. But that couldn't be the only reason, thought Lucca. People spotted him everywhere he went, and even when they had no idea who he was they were drawn to look at the elegant figure with his lined face, wavy grey hair and narrow eyes. He did not make any effort to arousc attention, on the contrary. He preferred to sit and listen while he observed the others, now and then folding the corners of his lips ironically around the colourless slit that served as his mouth. There was complete silence when he finally said something in his rusty voice and old-fashioned diction, which encompassed everything he said, even the most casual remark, with an exclusive and civilised atmosphere.

When they were in the car driving home one evening, after yet another dinner, she asked him why he bothered to spend so much of his time on that pack of burned-out old buggers. All they did was sit there nursing their bloodshot vanity, she said, sweating at the thought of being soon forgotten. She'd had too much to drink, because she was bored stiff. He laughed, looking at the road ahead. He was an old bugger himself . . . besides, everything was interesting to someone like him. She tugged the curls at his neck affectionately. At least he wasn't burned out, anyway . . . He smiled but did not give a direct answer. The most banal things, and the most sophisticated as well, he went on, are often the most interesting. He gave her a brief look. She probably didn't realise that yet, luckily. But even the utmost banality turned into a subject for sociology eventually.

They had met with Else once only, shortly before they left for Spain. Harry invited her to lunch one Saturday after he came back from Oslo. Lucca tried to dissuade him, but he just smiled at her. He really wanted to meet her mother. If she didn't like it, she could stay at home . . . Else had tried to hide her disapproval when Lucca finally gave in to her inquisitive questions and told her who it was she so often spent the night with. After a month she had more or less moved into the rooftop apartment with its view over the harbour.

She was nervous as she and Harry waited at the restaurant, and once more she was taken aback by his unruffled calm when Else walked in and looked around her with an anxious gaze and too much powder on her cheeks. Harry rose, shook her hand in a friendly way and pulled out a chair for her, taking no notice of her tense, hectic manner. Lucca had not realised he was older than her mother. Her own nervousness changed into wonder when she saw how agitated Else was and how coquettishly she tried out her feminine wiles on the famous man playing the role of son-in-law. An hour later when Else kissed her cheek and said goodbye, Lucca could feel that her thunderstruck condemnation had given way to something like admiration.

Harry worked in the afternoon while she took a siesta. When she woke up they would drive down to the sea. He thought the water was too cold, but she went in almost every day. She did not need a swimsuit, they had the beach to themselves. She felt childish as he sat watching her, but only until she came out and he stood waiting with towel and kimono, as she approached smiling, dripping and stark naked. In the evenings they sat talking or reading. He told her about people he had known, some of them names she had heard before, actors and writers, semi-mythological figures from another age. Sometimes she felt dizzy when she realised he was describing events that had taken place ten years before she was born.

He gave her books he thought would interest her. The house was crammed with books from floor to ceiling, and she had never read so much in such a short time. He opened windows and doors for her onto ideas and notions she'd never had before, but he didn't make her feel stupid, just very young. He did not lecture her nor did he ever use his age and experience as arguments. He contented himself with asking unexpected questions which produced equally unexpected answers from her. He guided without her noticing it, and let go of her again just as unnoticeably, so she had the feeling of having found her way on her own, she didn't know how. He merely looked at her meanwhile with his narrow dark eyes.

That was the way he worked, by hardly saying or doing anything. That was how he had made himself famous, the Gypsy King, as Otto had so scornfully called him. She could not understand how all those stories about his tyrannical cruelty had arisen. He had not raised his voice once during the rehearsals for *The Father*. Most of the time he sat in the auditorium or stood at the edge of the stage as if lost in his own thoughts, taking note of every single change of tone and each movement of the actors' features. Just occasionally he would come up to one or other of them and talk confidentially to each, at other times he would lay a hand on a shoulder, smile or raise his eyebrows with an expectant look. He seldom spoke to them all at once, and what he said was always so specific that none of them noticed the intrinsic lines in the picture he had envisaged from the start. Slowly they found their places in the picture, as of their own volition, apparently with no help from him.

She had sweat on her upper lip and her knees were trembling when she arrived for the audition one September afternoon. The porter was kind, he led her part of the way and pointed out a long corridor, but she still managed to get lost. When she finally found the rehearsal room the other actors were sitting at a long table watching her walk across the floor, the script pressed to her chest. She went up to Harry, who sat at the end of the table studying his hands, and apologised for being late. He waited for a moment before he took her hand without pressing it, as if indulging a childish whim on her part. He did not reply, merely smiled a little smile with his narrow lips as he regarded her out of the dark cracks of his eyes. He looked at her as if they had never met before, and it seemed inconceivable that she'd sat in his Mercedes one evening and asked if he might kiss her.

He was wearing an olive-green silk shirt that day, hanging loosely over the sand-coloured velvet trousers and his curly, steel-grey hair was carefully combed back from his forehead and ears. If there had been something frail and unprotected about him when he absent-mindedly received her in his roof apartment a few months earlier, in worn-out espadrilles and with his ruffled hair standing out at the sides in sleepy wings, that had quite vanished now. His motionless face was like a mask of baked clay. As she walked round shaking hands he sat leaning back at the end of the table caressing the silver lighter lying on his script beside his folded spectacles.

She knew their faces from the stage and the papers. Doubtless they were thinking that she must have lost her way. You didn't arrive late for Harry Wiener. The actor who was to play her mother, the captain's wife, sized her with a watchful glance over her reading glasses. For two generations of male theatre-goers the beautiful, generously bosomed diva had been the exemplar of feminine charm and mystery. There was something affected about her masculine reading glasses. Maybe she flirted with the idea that a little touch of ugly clumsiness would only add to her charming face and emphasise the mature dramatic sensuality of her eyes and lips.

The role of the captain was allotted to her male counterpart, the rebellious punk of the acting world, a notorious, rowdy drinker and seducer, with his eternal bedroom eyes, tousled hair and a voice like the morning after. Lucca could not see him without thinking of the line whispered in his ear by a buxom blonde in a television play from her childhood, in a somewhat outrageous bedroom scene for that period, as she rummaged in his unruly chest hair. *Big bad boy!* He smiled his very best professional bedroom smile as he pressed her hand until she was afraid it would be left in his horny paw. The big bad boy had turned grey and he too had acquired reading glasses, on a cord to prevent them getting lost. A small pot-belly had begun to show itself behind the tight-fitting denim shirt and he seemed to be constantly suppressing a belch.

She pulled out a chair and sat down beside the captain. He passed her a pencil. Watch out, it's sharp! he whispered with a sly foxy glance, as if he was a schoolboy and she was the new girl. Right, let's get going, said Harry Weiner, but he didn't put on his glasses nor did he open his script. He sat leaning back with crossed legs while they turned to the first page. He stayed like that throughout the reading, his head bent slightly forwards, eyes half closed and fixed on a point on the floor, listening to the actors reading their parts. If one of them started to stress a sentence, already trying to make their mark on how the role should be played, only then did he raise his head slightly and smile a little, inscrutable smile. That made the reader subdue his tone again and content himself with reading the words. When they had gone through the text and closed their scripts there was a moment's silence. Then he stood up, looked round and thanked them. They remained seated while he gathered his things and left. Again Lucca had the feeling of being in a classroom. As soon as Harry Wiener was out of the door conversation broke out all across the table.

That's how he was! The captain stretched out his arms backwards and smiled in amusement at the bewildered look on her face. He rested his hands on his knees with his elbows pointing outwards. Lucca shrugged her shoulders. She had expected him to say something to them about the play and the roles. He never did that . . . the cavalry captain held his breath a moment before breathing out through his nose. But just you wait! He might well seem a bit cold to begin with, and he was never much of a chatterbox, you could get quite frightened of him, but he was a *lovely* person. Probably the reason for his reserve today was because of his wife. It was bloody awful, she wasn't likely to see the new year. But he was taking it bravely . . . really there was something gentle . . . yes, gentle about him. You wouldn't believe it, said the captain, but he makes you feel safe, even if he gives quite the opposite impression. That's the secret, he smiled. Lucca nodded agreement, as if she was quite familiar with the situation. Harry Wiener put you at ease, but you didn't get to be friends. He knew how to keep himself to himself! The captain held up his hands. The diva leaned forward, her breasts in the informal sweatshirt pressed flat on the table. She put her head on one side and smiled lasciviously. Well, darling, so what was it like in Borneo? The captain turned towards her. *Brilliant!*

Sitting slightly apart Lucca wondered why it was that actors always talked to each other so affectedly. It was *darling* or *sweetheart* the whole time, and she secretly questioned if they were all gay. Even the women sounded gay because they seemed to mimic gay men's parody of women. She promised herself never to start talking like that. On her way down the corridor the diva caught up with her on high, clicking heels. The high-heeled shoes seemed like a feminine comment on the blue jeans, relaxed sweatshirt and ugly, mannish spectacles. It went *very* well, she said with a motherly smile, as if Lucca had been up for an exam. But do take *care* with your consonants! People don't *learn* to articulate properly any more . . . She held open the street door for her young colleague and put her head on one side again. Nice to have met you!

The captain had been right. Harry Wiener never exchanged jovialities with the actors that other directors might at the start of the day's rehearsals, to warm them up and maybe redress the ghastly old-fashioned authority they still represented. But although he did nothing to ingratiate himself with them or put them at ease, after a week Lucca discovered she felt perfectly safe with this undemonstrative, discreetly attentive man. She lost her fear of appearing foolish. Every bid, every suggestion was permitted, and if they could not be used, they dropped out by themselves, she didn't know how, for he never directly criticised her way of playing the part, a raised eyebrow was enough. Nor did he praise her, simply smiled now and then with unexpected mildness, almost gratefully, as she felt warmth spreading through her.

He preferred to express himself in simple and very physical images, always based on the current passage. Before and after rehearsing a scene he spoke to the actors separately. He seldom interrupted them when they were acting and if he did, it was with a specific question or a single word that might seem irrelevant or puzzling to the others, like a private code meant only for the one he was addressing, which helped the actor get back on the track. On the track of what? To begin with they didn't know. They thought they were approaching the unknown core of their character, but little by little they each discovered they were merely following the outlines of something they had known all the time without thinking about it, since it involved hidden aspects of themselves.

Lucca gradually came to respect the diva and the captain. She saw their concentration at work, and they saw her when she felt most vulnerable and naked. She had still not worked long enough to feel it on her own body, but she imagined their affected manner must be a shield. They were obliged to act in their own lives in order for them to be themselves on the stage. In the real world they had to allow themselves to play ironically and without commitment, employing the most grotesque and comical attitudes, because the stage was the only place where they could not allow themselves the least simulation or absent-minded, fashionable convention.

Lucca was completely exhausted after the rehearsals, and when she woke up in the evening having slept for an hour or two, she discovered she had spent yet another day without thinking of Otto. Thinking of him brought no particular feelings. She felt as if she'd had a local anaesthetic, and on the nights she had dinner with Else she hardly listened to what her mother said. Most of the time they left each other in peace, and there were days when they just met in the hall if one was leaving and the other coming home. Miriam called now and then, but if Lucca started to tell her anything she always noticed a shadow of envy beneath her friend's enthusiasm. For a year Miriam had had nothing but a minor part in a television series for children, disguised as a kangaroo. She had laughed at herself, but nevertheless she tried to present the role in a serious light when she explained how hard it actually was to hop around in a costume like that, legs together. She had been highly praised for it.

When Miriam thought they had talked enough about Strindberg and Harry Wiener she asked if Lucca still thought about Otto and, as if to make the most of it, she announced one day that after all there didn't seem to have been so much between Otto and the mulatto model he had been seen with. Lucca could sense Miriam didn't believe her when she said she hardly thought of him any more. She ought to go on suffering when everything else was going so well. Or had she fallen for the Gypsy King, in fact? When Miriam hinted at that for the third time Lucca shut her up. There was really more to life than everlastingly falling in love, she said, surprised to hear herself quoting Else. Work, for instance, she went on. That made Miriam change the subject.

Only at rehearsals did she felt completely alert. She no longer doubted that she had been given the role because Harry Wiener had faith in her talent. She had been reassured when she went to tea with him in his rooftop apartment, and her trust in him increased when he sometimes took her hand or put an arm round her shoulder as they talked. There was nothing in the least suggestive or underhand in his touch, it came as a natural extension of the conversation and his explanations when he went through a scene and showed her how he visualised her entrance and where she should stop.

She never spoke to him about anything but her part, and he left as soon as the day's rehearsal was finished. Nothing in his professional manner betrayed that she had sat on his sofa one afternoon talking about herself while outside thunder crashed and rain fell. It strengthened her feeling of laying herself bare on the stage, delivered to his eyes down in the semi-darkness of the auditorium. There was a small lamp on his desk, but its light illuminated only his torso, not his face. She wondered whether the other actors had been to tea with him too, and if he knew as much about their lives as he did about hers.

One day she was in the canteen with the captain and the diva, the two of them enjoying a teasing, comradely banter. They must have known each other since youth. Lucca felt an outsider. It was still strange to have lunch with them, although they were her colleagues. She had known their faces since she was a child, and here she was watching the diva pick up shrimps from her plate with her red nails and pop them between her red, red lips. She and the captain couldn't agree whether Harry Wiener's present wife was number three or four, and they helped each other count up the names of the women he had married, and those he'd had on the side. They even argued over the order. He changes wives as others change their cars, said the diva. She had been friends with the previous wife, that is, number two or three. *Wasn't* there one they had forgotten?

The captain filled up his beer glass. Anyway, Wiener would soon have to look around for a new one. He had foam on his nose when drinking. The diva removed it with an affectionate finger. Well, you *are* exquisitely sympathetic, she laughed with her moist lips and turned to Lucca. She had better take care or she would be the next! But maybe the crafty old bugger had already tried it on? Lucca felt her cheeks burn. Well, they'd better not go into that now! The captain made a poker face and raised an index finger at his friend. The young weren't like that – any more! The diva let out a whinny. One-love, she said and gasped for breath with a groan of ecstasy. But what was it he had called Wiener, that time they did *A Midsummer Night's Dream* . . . Yes, come on now! She gave his arm a pat of encouragement. The captain scratched his neck and raised his glass. She picked up the remaining shrimps from her plate and sucked mayonnaise from her fingers, looking at him expectantly. We call him the Gypsy King, said Lucca. The captain held out his glass and bent forwards as if his beer was going down the wrong way. They laughed.

As she cycled home she felt irritated with herself for blushing when the diva asked if Harry Wiener had made a pass at her. Had they seen through her? Was that how he tracked down new talent? But why then had she got the part? Was it only because it would be too painful if she put it around town how she had sent off such an old ape? Not because he was ashamed of his approaches, but because he was ashamed at being rejected. Had he given her the part simply to keep her mouth shut? That seemed too complicated, she thought and regretted having angled for such a cheap laugh with the hackneyed nickname. She had slipped that in to assure them she had not been to bed with him. But why was everyone convinced she had, Otto and Miriam and now the diva and the captain as well?

She could not make the image of the notorious womaniser match her impression of the calm, concentrated man with the lined face. Nor could she make her own image of him match the episode in his Mercedes when he had driven her home and quite openly made advances. Probably he had just felt lonely. His wife was incurably ill and he didn't know how long she had to lie suffering. Was it any wonder that he lost his bearings for a moment? Looking back at it now she felt he had opened a crack into something human in his otherwise controlled and impenetrable façade. Just as when he received her a month later, confused and half asleep in a frail and touching way.

Suddenly she pictured him again clearly, in the car when they stopped at the kerb outside the Egyptian restaurant. The vulnerable look in his eyes when he bravely gave himself away and asked for a kiss. He must have known what he was exposing himself to, the gossip and ridicule, but he had not cared. She kept on going back to the mixture of courage and vulnerability there had been in his expression. She couldn't possibly be just a firm young cunt, yet another in the series, if you were to believe the diva and the captain.

She recalled what he had said. That she was both talented and attractive, and she was wrong if she believed one had nothing to do with the other. When he said that she had thought he was merely trying to manipulate her or overwhelm her with his cynicism. But perhaps there was no difference, with a man like Harry Wiener. Maybe he had wanted to test her and see if she had sufficient substance and ability to resist. He must have seen something more in her that night. He must have seen the same thing he had patiently waited for from the start of rehearsals, down at his desk in the semi-darkness, until she too began to see it in the bright light up on the stage, as she gradually took possession of her part. Another side of herself which so far had remained hidden.

She slowly turned off the hot water until it became icy cold. For a moment her heart seemed to stop beating. She gasped but forced herself to stand still, eyes closed, completely stunned by cold. When she had turned off the water she stepped in front of the wide mirror fitted into the wall between the Moorish tiles. The window behind her was open, the mosquito net reflected the sun and the mountains faded behind a white fog. She had gained a little weight, her hips were rounder and her breasts bigger. For once she was brown all over, without the usual pale strips from her bikini. She lay naked, sunning herself on the terrace in the afternoons. No one could see her except Harry when he sat in the shade reading. The scratching sound of cicadas intensified outside the window, escalating rhythmically. She rubbed her face with her hands and pressed water out of her black hair.

She could still feel surprised when she looked at her black hair in the mirror. One day after rehearsal Harry had taken her aside and, as if in passing, asked if she would consider dyeing her hair black. It would make her look like the captain, her father in the play. When he saw her terrified look, he immediately laughed it off. It was just a thought. She forgot it again, but a week or two later when she was standing in front of the mirror memorising her lines it suddenly struck her that she ought to have black hair. Only when she'd suggested it did she recall it had been his own idea, but he made no comment, not so much as a twitch. He merely gazed at her as he considered it, until he nodded agreement, as if it was something she herself had discovered. She was both fascinated and alarmed. He said nothing when the play had been performed for the last time and she had her hair dyed black again because her own colour had begun to show at the roots. But at that point she knew he liked her with it.

She pretended not to have seen him when he came into the bathroom, at first only a silhouette against the shining mosquito net. He stepped into the light from the lamp above the mirror and embraced her from behind, laying his hands on her cool breasts. He gave a wry smile and met her eyes in the mirror. Beauty and the Beast, he said. She could feel his growing erection against her buttocks, through the linen trousers. She would have to go, she said. If she wanted to be on time . . . They had arranged for her to drive to Almeria and fetch their guest from the airport. He let go of her. She kissed his forehead and pulled the curls at his neck consolingly. Poor beast, she mumbled tenderly.

When she got into the car she realised she had no idea what he looked like, the man she was going to meet at the airport. She went back to the house. Harry looked at her ironically as she tore the lid from a cardboard box and wrote on it with a biro. *Andreas Bark,* she wrote. He nodded approvingly. Smart . . . She drove down the winding road from the village and out onto the main road. There was hardly any traffic. The landscape was grey and ochre-yellow in the sharp light. She put on her shades, stepped on the speedometer and turned up the volume on the radio.

She was on the stage in *The Father*. Half-way through the play she dried up. She could not remember a single line, and complete silence fell in the theatre, such silence that she couldn't even hear the prompter's whisper. The captain looked at her expectantly in the silence, and she felt her pulse beating softly behind her ear. The diva stood out in the wings gazing at her, dressed up as the white clown with a ruff, conical hat and white, painted face, smiling, with her head on one side. And suddenly a hole opened in her ear drum, that was how it felt when she heard Else's cultivated radio voice, reverberating like a loudspeaker at a railway station: *Take care with your consonants!*

The dream left a hollow, crushed feeling in her stomach, but she could not eat anything and managed only to swallow a cup of coffee when she went down to the kitchen. She sat looking out at the neglected garden. It had rained in the night and the sky hung heavy over the stripped tree crowns. The gale tore at their outermost branches and moved the greasy leaves around on the grass. There were two hours left before she had to be at the theatre. She decided to go at once. She did not know what else to do with herself.

The set design had been finished some days previously and she wanted to see what it looked like from the auditorium. She found her way through the labyrinth of corridors and emerged in the dimly lit theatre with its empty seats. There was light on the stage. Harry Wiener sat on a Victorian sofa covered with black chintz, he was dressed in black himself. The set design had the effect of being both realistic and dreamily strange. It was very simple, designed in black and grey except for a single armchair covered with red velvet. He sat deep in thought with one arm resting on the back of the sofa and his hand under his chin, looking down at the shabby stage floor. He had not seen her. She stood there gazing at him from a distance.

Again she remembered the sympathy she had felt between them when she was in his apartment, with rain foaming on the balcony and lightning brightening the sky above the harbour. The warmth of his manner when he spoke to her, and the frailty he exhibited when he greeted her, slightly dazed because he had fallen asleep on the sofa. It had made her forget her nervousness over meeting him. She had forgotten everything else as she sat there high above the city surrounded by his books, captured by the calm gaze resting on her as she told him about herself and listened to what he said about Strindberg in his subdued, hoarse voice. He had opened up to her, not only when he briefly explained that his wife was dying, but also when he talked of the captain in the play. Of man's unhappy love for woman and of how life belonged to women because they had the ability to pass it on. Of the deserted boy-child, who grew up to fear women and mistrust them because in his heart he cursed the mother who had once rejected him. Afterwards she had realised he hadn't spoken only of Strindberg and his captain, but of himself.

She had expected him to make some little sign to show her he remembered how they had sat and talked, but he kept her at a distance, as he did with all the others, kind, expectant and deeply concentrated on the work. With each week that passed she felt more defenceless, exposed to his eyes that apparently apprehended everything that stirred within her. He seemed to know her, but she herself knew so infinitesimally little about him. She felt in contact with him only when he occasionally came up to her and cautiously laid a hand on her shoulder as he put a question which took her unawares, anticipating what she felt without being able to express it clearly. But she was not the person he spoke to, it was the cavalry officer's daughter he had slowly drawn out in her from some forgotten, shadowy corner of her personality.

Perhaps he had invited her for tea to study her at close quarters before he set out to make use of her for his own purposes. Why would Harry Wiener be interested in her as more than a tool for his art? That must have been what he meant when he said she was both talented and attractive, and that one could not be separated from the other. He had been attracted to her as a sculptor might feel towards a lump of clay. He had asked to kiss her simply because he wanted to see what she looked like when being kissed.

He rose from the sofa, pushed it a little so it stood more at an angle, and sat down again. As he leaned back he caught sight of her. He smiled and waved her forward. Sit down, he said and patted the sofa cushion as she walked across the stage. He looked at her attentively. Was she nervous about the première? She said she was. That's how it should be, he smiled and looked down at his hand, carefully stroking the smooth chintz of the sofa. You're good, he said, that's why you're nervous. It was the first time he had praised her directly. He looked at her again. Still living with her mother? Lucca was amazed. She could not remember telling him where she lived. It had become quite difficult to find an apartment, had it? He had bought a freehold apartment for his daughter in Vanløse. Of course it was a dreary place, but she could afford the regular expenses there. He smiled kindly. What about her? Couldn't her mother help her with a payment? It was about the only way to get somewhere to live. Buying . . .

He stood up, the audience was over. She followed him into the wings, wondering what all that talk about owning property was for. Did he think the town was full of millionaires? Or had he asked about her accommodation situation because he wanted to be kind or had no idea what else to talk to her about, now she had burst in on him as he sat meditating before the rehearsal? He walked with head bent so she only saw the famous grey curls at his neck. Suddenly he staggered and stretched out a hand as if to find something to support him. She took his hand, just as he seemed about to sink to his knees. He put his arm round her shoulder and hid his face with the other hand. Everything went black, he said and removed the hand. He looked at her and smiled faintly, pale as paper. He wasn't getting enough sleep at present . . .

She stood there, still with his arm resting on her shoulder, looking into his eyes and without thinking she laid a hand over his and stroked it lightly. She recognised his gaze, it was the same as in his car that evening a few months before, the same vulnerability, but also something wondering and sad, as if he was not merely looking at her but also observing himself from outside. He let go of her shoulder and sat down on a box under the cables and control panels on the wall. Just go ahead, he said, closing his eyes. I'll sit here for a bit . . .

During the curtain calls after the première, as she stood among the other actors, each with their bouquet wrapped in cellophane, he finally allowed himself to be persuaded by the deafening applause to come up on the stage. He kissed all of them, even the male actors, on the cheek and when it was her turn he took her hand and walked forward on the proscenium with her in front of the others. The diva and the captain also started to clap, as well as they could with their huge bouquets, and soon all her fellow actors were clapping. Harry Wiener bowed one single time to the audience, still with her hand in his. She curtsied as she had seen the diva do, one foot behind the other, and when she straightened up the thunderous sound from the auditorium seemed stilled as he bent his face to hers. Thank you, he whispered and pressed her hand. When the curtain fell for the last time he had gone. The captain had been informed, the others crowded around him. Things were going badly with Wiener's wife, her condition was critical. Lucca stayed at the party only as long as she felt necessary.

It had been a huge success, but there was nothing very strange about that. The Gypsy King was condemned to eternal success, as Otto had once said with a sarcastic twist. The special thing about it for Lucca was that overnight she was transformed from a promising fringe talent into one of her generation's most shining dramatic lights, a new star in the theatrical sky, a brilliant cornucopia of emotional intensity, according to one critic. The newspapers were still fragrant with printer's ink the following night when she leaned against her bicycle in the town hall square and feverishly leafed through the culture sections, greedy for more. She was almost run down by a bus on the way home. She woke Else. They sat in the kitchen reading the reviews aloud to each other. Her mother put her glasses down on the pile of papers and said: There, you see! There is more to life than love! Lucca did not know how to reply.

December passed, and the days were almost uniform. Even the weather was the same, murky, wet and raw. She slept all morning and spent the afternoons watching television before she set off for the theatre. The garlands of light and Christmas hearts seemed alien and irrelevant. Miriam went to visit her parents in Jutland with her jazz boyfriend, and Else flew down to a Greek island. Lucca said no thank you, slightly brusque, when Else invited her to go too. What would she do there? Be with me, her mother replied, pained. But they were together all the time! Else looked at her sorrowfully. Were they? Lately she seemed only to be together with herself. It was almost impossible to get a single word out of her daughter. She would have to watch out or her work would take up her whole life.

Lucca smiled ironically but she could see Else did not understand why. She was about to say something about all the evenings she had spent alone as a child with some nanny or other, because her mother was broadcasting or out with a friend, but she held her tongue. Fortunately, she thought afterwards, glad that she hadn't allowed herself to be drawn into a quarrel she wasn't even anxious to win. Else threatened to call off her trip, but in the end she did fly down to the white houses and the blue, blue water, as she used to say, apparently doubting whether the word would be blue enough on its own.

Lucca felt confused when she thought about Harry Wiener. She thought of him with a mixture of gratitude and suppressed anger. She had become a success only because of his genius, she knew that, but all the same he had been the one to whisper his thanks during the curtain calls after the première, when he took her hand and presented her to the audience, his discovery. Thank you and goodbye, he should rather have whispered, for the next moment he had gone. He had got what he wanted from her. With his gaze and his voice he had surrounded her with a chrysalis of attention, he had almost hypnotised her and then woken her with a snap of the fingers. Now she could flutter around up in the light. When she was on the stage she became one with her role, everything in her was pervaded with its movements, moods and colour changes, but when she went home she was no more than a listless body that collapsed in front of the television empty of all thought.

The diva had seen what was happening to her. One evening after the performance when they sat together in the dressing room, she suddenly laid a hand on Lucca's arm. She really *mustn't* look so sad, she was the best ever! Lucca turned to her. Was she? Now, *stop* that, said the diva, starting to spread cleansing cream over her face with deft movements. Wiener had been absolutely ecstatic over her. She just must not take it personally. She must understand that she was here to be used. Indeed, he had used her, *squeezed* everything out of her, and she should be glad of that. Glad and proud. The diva leaned back her head as she put cream on her chin and neck. But she knew it well. One day you had all his attention, and you wallowed in it, you gobbled it up, and the next day you stood there and had to cope on your own. That was how it was! She smiled optimistically and put her head to one side, her face all white with cream, and suddenly she looked like the white clown in Lucca's dream.

Lucca smiled bitterly, thinking of the morning when she had met him before the rehearsal and seized his hand when he felt faint. As they faced each other in the wings there had been a moment when she believed he did look at her differently, and when he had whispered his little thank-you in her ear during the curtain calls, she had referred that to more than her performance. But what else should he have thanked her for? It was her place to thank him! How stupid she was! She felt ashamed when she thought how she had put her hand on his and stroked it as he leaned on her for support.

One morning a few days after the première Else knocked at her door. There was a telephone call for her. She said she was asleep. It was a journalist, said Else, something about an interview. On the way downstairs Lucca felt annoyed that Else had answered the phone. It must seem absurd for her to be living with her mother at the age of twenty-seven. The journalist wanted to come the next day, bringing a photographer. Her voice was irritatingly maternal. They arranged a time when Lucca was sure Else would not be in. She went through her wardrobe but couldn't decide what to wear. The search ended with an old T-shirt stolen from Otto. He would recognise it, she thought, since she was being photographed.

The journalist was a hefty lady of Else's age wearing a heavy amber necklace. She wanted to know what it had been like to be directed by Harry Wiener, and while Lucca was telling her, she had the feeling that it was really Harry who was being interviewed, through her. Harry Wiener was famous for never giving interviews. She was just as excited about the interview as she had been about the reviews of the performance, but everything was wrong, she felt, when she saw the picture of herself, which took up half a page, with her hands stuck out in the air like a jumping jack because she was explaining something. The printed words were not hers, but the journalist's. She could hear the wheedling, motherly tone as she read, and how the amber necklace rattled between the lines. Everything she had said was stuck together with sugary adjectives. It almost sounded as if she was head over heels in love with the great Harry Wiener, and the description of her was even worse. The boyish, gazelle-like Lucca Montale, who opened the door in her washed-out aubergine-coloured T-shirt, casual and enchanting with her mercurial gaze, her honey glow and the sparkling black hair which revealed her Italian background . . . she hurled the newspaper into the waste bin.

The day before Christmas Eve she went into town in the afternoon to go to the cinema. When she left after the film it was dark. She walked through the pedestrian streets, where people struggled past laden with all the parcels that twenty-four hours later would be unwrapped again by other people who had toiled along with similar parcels, just as red in the face with effort and irritation. Now all she needed was to run into Otto and his divine photo-mulatto, or whoever he had replaced her with if

Miriam was right that their affair had already ended. Once that had occurred to her she couldn't get it out of her head again. Of course she would meet Otto at any moment with Christmas presents under one arm and a gorgeous doll under the other, and then she would have to stand and smile all over her face to convince him of what actually was the case. That for weeks she had hardly given him a thought and had already begun to wonder why she had loved him so much.

She went round Magasin du Nord's food halls without finding anything to buy. Finally she decided on fillet steak. There were two steaks in each tray, obviously they thought no-one would be so extravagant as to buy fillet steak for themselves alone. But she could always eat the second one tomorrow, she thought, and now she was pushing the boat out she also put a tin of foie gras and a jar of caviar in her basket. As she approached the wine department she caught sight of a man standing with his back to her studying the labels. He wore a camel-hair coat and the grey curls at his neck fell over the turned-up collar.

She thought of turning round, he must have read that embarrassing interview, but she went on. The Gypsy King was not going to stop her drinking red wine on Christmas Eve. He glanced up from the bottle he held in his hand. He was pale and looked tired. She tried to smile but he did not smile back. Catching up with the shopping? he said finally. She held up her basket. My Christmas dinner, she said, launching into an over-elaborate explanation of why she would be alone, regretting she had disturbed him. He smiled wryly at her efforts and she stopped talking. Neither of them said anything, and when the silence grew too strained she found the courage to ask after his wife. She had not given her a thought since the première celebration. He put the bottle back on the shelf. She died this morning, he replied dully.

Afterwards Lucca could not have said how long they had been standing like that, looking into each other's eyes, she with her plastic basket, he with his hands in the pockets of his coat. He cleared his throat. She shook her head rapidly as if waking from a trance. He looked down at his shoes and then back at her. His wife had been alone, he had overslept. He looked away. They had phoned, he had gone out there as quickly as he could, but too late. He had come too late for her death.

For a moment his face seemed about to collapse. He turned his back and took a step or two between the shelves of bottles, and she heard a half-strangled throaty sound. She went towards him but stopped as he turned back again. He dried his eyes with the backs of his hands and looked at her. I'm sorry, he said. She said he needn't be. Would he rather be alone? He avoided her eyes and took another bottle from the shelf, desultorily studying the label. I don't really have any choice, he mumbled. But she supposed he needed something to eat . . . the words tumbled out of her mouth. He looked at her blankly. She pointed at her basket of fillet steaks. There are two of them, she said. He looked at her in surprise. Did she mean it? She shrugged her shoulders. He had better find something drinkable, then. He walked slowly along the shelf, carefully inspecting the labels, suddenly shy at having her standing there.

She made a bowl of salad while he fried the steaks. To start with they were a little stiff with each other. He said he had read the interview. She had said some nice things. She told him what she thought of the journalist. He smiled. A journalist like that wants to show she is someone too. You mustn't grudge her that . . . Now and again they fell silent and avoided each other's eyes, as if they took it in turns to regret she had gone home with him. They spoke about the performance, he said she had earned her success. If she wasn't too terrified he was thinking of asking her to work with him again next year. He felt like doing a new production of *A Doll's House*. It was fifteen years since he had last worked on the play, and he had actually considered it was *passé* since, according to their friend Strindberg, marriage had long since become 'a partnership with economic activity'. He smiled tiredly. But she had given him the courage to try. He had thought of her as Nora. She held her breath a moment. Yes, thank you, she said. He shook his head. She had nothing to thank him for.

When they had eaten they sat for a long time looking over the lights of the city. He told her about his wife, but not at length. They had lived apart for several years, she at the villa north of the town, he in the rooftop apartment. For years it hadn't been a real marriage, he said. There had been too much . . . how to put it? Too much and too little had been said between them. He put down his wine glass and walked over to the French window at the terrace. Either she should go now, or stay.

She stayed. Everything happened very slowly, as if through water, with long pauses when they just lay side by side until they had to give in to what they had so hesitantly begun. His body was different from any other body she had known. His skin was looser, but very soft, and his arms and legs were more sinewy than she had imagined. He did not let go of her eyes as she straddled him, and she recognised the open, vulnerable expression that had made her speculate so much. As if he marvelled over what she was doing to him, at the same time taking hold of her buttocks. There was something unfeigned, at once reckless and completely stripped bare over his face when he groaned and she felt that he came. She lay awake while he fell asleep in her embrace. It was a terrible thought, but she did think it. She thought that she was glad his wife had died before this happened. Since she was dying anyway.

The plane from Madrid had landed when she entered the arrival hall with her cardboard placard. She placed herself at the front of the group of people waiting. The first passengers came in sight with their luggage and looked around them, searching. People called out greetings and kissed each other. She recognised him at once, before he caught sight of her placard, it must be him. Andreas Bark looked pale, as Danes do when they emerge from winter and screw up their eyes against the bright light. He wore black jeans and a shabby leather jacket of the kind sported by the Copenhagen in-crowd of young artists and film-makers. But at least he wasn't shorn like the really hard-boiled arty types with their cropped pates that made them look like convicts. In fact he was not bad looking with his dark, unruly hair and prominent chin.

She waited until his gaze lit on her. His smile expressed surprise in a boyish, slightly flustered way. He knew very well who she was but he had not expected to meet her here. Andreas Bark probably did not read glossy magazines and obviously did not go in for gossip. He talked a lot as they drove, but his voice was pleasant. It had been snowing in Copenhagen when he left. I ask you! No wonder there was something abject, somehow aggrieved about the Danes. Each time you stuck out your nose for a whiff of spring you were put in your place with a shock of cold. He took off his leather jacket, he was sweating. He had spent the winter in Rome. His arms and wrists were surprisingly slender. Rome . . . wasn't it a place for old ladies? He laughed, but made no reply. He said he had seen her in *The Father*. The production had impressed him, its rhythm and clarity . . . And she had been good, he hastened to add, like something he almost forgot to mention.

They left Almeria behind them. At the end of the stony plain you could see the snow-clad ridge of the Sierra Nevada. Andreas gave free rein to his delight, genuinely bowled over. He caught sight of one of the mock-up towns left among the furrowed rocks after being used for a spaghetti western. Couldn't they stop by there? They walked among the wooden houses consisting of mere façades, with name-plates reading *Sheriff* or *Saloon* in faded lettering. The façades had wooden pillars and planked walkways, where the sheriff and the loafers of the town had sat tilting their chairs with their hat brims pulled down over their eyes. In the middle of the set there was a gallows with a rope that swung lightly back and forth in the wind. Andreas put the noose round his neck and stuck out his tongue. She laughed. He beckoned her with a familiar gesture, as if they already knew each other. From where he stood, beneath the gallows, you couldn't see the supporting beams against the backs of the flats. It was an authentic scene from a western, where the dust had just subsided after a horseman had ridden off.

Harry was disgruntled when they finally arrived back and joined him on the roof terrace. Did it really take so long to cover the hundred kilometres? Andreas was disconcerted at the grudging welcome and politely tried to defend her. He talked about their visit to the wild west town. He had led her astray, he said apologetically. She was annoyed that he was suddenly so smarmy. He had been more himself as they drove, she felt, but how could she tell? After all, she didn't know him. Well, Harry growled, it was time for a drink, anyway. Did he like white wine? Andreas shrugged his shoulders with an embarrassed smile. He liked everything. Harry stopped on his way across the terrace and turned towards him. Everything? That was quite a lot . . . They sat on the parapet while he went down. Andreas was less talkative than he'd been in the car. He avoided her eyes and studied the view. The riverbed was in shadow, the pink flowers of the oleander bushes glowed on the steep cliff sides. The cicadas rattled away as usual. Why were they suddenly lost for words?

Harry came back with a tray of glasses, a dewy bottle of white wine and a bowl of black olives. He placed the tray on the stone table and turned towards them. Come along then, children! He had recovered his good humour, and Andreas seemed more relaxed, but she could tell from his tone of voice how much he respected Harry, and took pains to find the right words. He spoke in a different way here on the terrace, his voice was more cultivated, and he did not smile boyishly as he had done at the airport. It was the master and his apprentice sitting in the flickering light under the canopy, drinking white wine and chatting about a Verdi opera Andreas had seen in Verona. Harry knew the director, a German. Andreas listened intently as Harry talked about the German director's staging of Schiller's *The Robbers* at the Burgtheater in Vienna.

Lucca was not listening. Andreas took a pack of Gitanes out of his bag and put a magazine on the table. Harry asked if he could have one. It was a long time since he had smoked a French cigarette. As many as you want! Andreas was a model of generosity. She picked up the magazine without asking leave and riffled through it. It was one of those so-called *men's magazines* with the latest in watertight watches and instructions on how to fasten a tie in fourteen ways, and how to find the most authentic run-down hotel in Havana with damp-stained columns in colonial style and mahogany ventilator fans. There was also an interview with a racing driver and a mountain climber, and at the end, between two whisky advertisements, there was one with Otto. She rose, saying she was tired after the drive. Harry looked up at her as if suddenly remembering she was there. She took the magazine to the bedroom and lay down on the bed.

Otto and his girlfriend were photographed in front of an American camper-van from the Fifties, rounded and shining silver. It was chocked up in the corner of a field. They went out there, said the caption, when they just needed to get away from it all. The girlfriend was a reflexologist. She looked sweet, she was four months gone. Lucca looked at the picture more closely. It must have been taken in the autumn, the sunlight was white and sharp, and there seemed to be a cluster of withered leaves hanging in the foreground. She counted on her fingers.

Otto had dropped Lucca in June. If the picture had been taken in October, he must recently have become a father. He hadn't wasted any time. He could not have known the reflexologist for more than a couple of weeks before she became pregnant, unless . . .

Otto confided to the readers that it had been like a revelation when he met the reflexologist. She was the woman in his life, and she had taught him what life was about. It had just been *wham*! He hadn't doubted they were made for each other. Lucca imagined what it had sounded like when he said *wham*! He explained that for years his life had felt unreal. Today he realised he had been through a depression. He had been concerned with external things, success and prestige, it had all happened much too fast. He had not had genuinely close relationships with anyone, and he had been about to lose his faith in love. Until he met the reflexologist. It had felt like being pulled down to earth and shot out into the galaxies at one and the same time. Otto felt as if only now was he starting to grow up. Now, when he was to be responsible for a new little person, totally entrusted to him. A little one like that, it was just a miracle. It was a boy, they had seen it when she had had a scan. He was already looking forward to the day when they would play football together . . .

Lucca put down the magazine. She thought of the American boy who had been given a red car for his birthday and sent his unknown father a drawing. She was glad she had persuaded Otto to send Lester that advent calendar. Otto . . . the twenty-fourth man in her life. She had really believed he was Father Christmas. It was less than a year since she had still believed that. At that time the Gypsy King was merely an old goat who had sneaked up on the pretext of his interest in her youthful talent. She took off her clothes and stretched out on the bed in the semi-darkness, thinking of Otto. He did not remember much, or else their memories differed. In any case she had made a mistake when she thought he was the one, hadn't she? . . . She pulled herself together and wished him luck.

A child. They had never talked about that. It was not something which could ever arise with Harry. He had said so, without her asking. He didn't want to be one of those pensioner fathers who were moved to tears over themselves, but who nevertheless took to the rocking chair before their children had passed their driving test. She felt he was right. There was more to life than children. There were enough of them anyway, more than all the adults in the world could provide with happiness. Her own childhood had not been particularly happy. She could say that now, matter-of-factly, without being upset. She had said it to Harry, and he had looked at her without comment. She was grateful he had not been sorry for her. Then she thought of Otto's pious chatter about the little boy who would depend on him completely. Poor child, she thought, and not only because of the thought of Otto as a father. He would probably be just as good or bad a father as anyone else. It was the dependence itself, the helplessness of the little child, that repelled her.

She heard Harry's hoarse voice behind the door when he came in from the terrace, saying something to Andreas. He walked downstairs, but the sound of his moccasins stilled halfway down. He had taken off his shoes, he must have thought she was asleep. She heard the dry skin under his bare feet rubbing against the tiles, his thoughtfulness made her smile. A gecko sat on the wall beside the door. Its white, rubbery, almost transparent body made her think of the foetuses she had seen in biology class at school, preserved in spirit. Anonymous abortions that would have been twice as old as she was if they had been allowed to live. She turned on her side and bent her knees. The mosquito net in front of the small window filtered the sun's afterglow, and the dim light was reflected in the smooth skin on her thigh and knee, surrounded by the soft swaddling of shadows.

She thought of Harry's gentleness in bed, his calm, confident hands and the vulnerable nakedness in his eyes when he let her do to him what she knew he was waiting for. Even when he was entirely defenceless, delivered over to her young, provocative body and his own desire for it, without his well-considered, civilised words, even then he was himself. Not someone different according to the situation, but wholly and completely himself. In contrast to Andreas Bark, who had been boyish, almost skittish, in the car and the wild west village, but who became precocious and anxious to please when he was in the presence of his master. She almost wished he was not there. She almost wished Harry would come to her as he did sometimes in the afternoons, when she lay in half darkness. He would stretch out beside her with closed eyes as if asleep. It was a game, when she caressed him slowly and his body began to admit what his unmoving face would not yet acknowledge.

She stretched out a hand and closed the window shutter so the room was totally dark. Only the hands and the circle of figures on the alarm clock shone green, far away. It was so dark that she saw no difference when she closed or opened her eyes. She remembered the first time she woke up in his bed. He was not there. She rose and pulled the curtains aside, at first slightly confused to be standing without a stitch on, looking out over the town from Harry Wiener's rooftop apartment. It was snowing, with big, woolly flakes. When she turned round he stood in the doorway holding a tray. He had made tea, he did not yet know she preferred coffee in the morning.

She sat cross-legged with the hot cup in her hands, looking out at the snow over the harbour. When she turned towards him, he was leaning against the wall regarding her sorrowfully with his narrow eyes. She began to think of his wife. She did not know what to say and asked if he would like her to leave. He smiled tiredly and sent a finger sliding down her spine. If you'd like to, do stay, he said. You will leave me one day anyway. She put the cup down on the tray and lay down with her head on his lap. Not willingly, she mumbled. We'll see, he replied, slowly stroking her coal-black hair.

Lucca was nervous as the plane came in to land at Charles de Gaulle airport. She was afraid Andreas would not be there as arranged on the telephone. She imagined he might have forgotten, preoccupied as he was when working. Maybe he had forgotten to look at his watch, maybe he had overslept because he had sat up writing all night. But she was also nervous at the thought of seeing him again. It was silly, they had only been apart for a fortnight and had talked on the phone several times. She was in the toilet when she heard the stewardess over the intercom asking the passengers to go back to their seats and fasten their seatbelts. She was putting on lipstick. There had been quite a lot of turbulence during the last part of the flight, it had spilt the coffee on her small folding table and almost made it drip on her clothes several times. Perhaps that was what made her nervous. The plane jolted again as she held the lipstick and pressed her lips down over her teeth, looking like a turtle. Her hand slipped and the lipstick left a long line on one cheek.

She was wearing a short beige dress she knew he liked. It was tight-fitting and fairly low-necked, and the skirt ended quite high up her thighs. He always had to touch her when she wore that dress. She had been in quite a state at the thought of getting coffee on it during the daft turbulence. Over the dress she wore a grey tailored jacket and a petrol-blue silk scarf he had bought for her when they lived in Rome. She had not looked so elegant for months, and it was equally long since she had put on any make-up.

As she was waiting to be checked in at Kastrup Airport she had felt like the typical provincial wife who had decked herself out just because she was travelling by air, but she wanted to look beautiful and sexy when he met her. She knew he had a weakness for girdles and high-heeled shoes with ankle straps. Besides, it was seldom now that she had the chance of making something of herself. At home she mostly dressed in dungarees and wellies.

She had finished painting the bookcase and all the books were in place, even down to alphabetical order. The living room had been the last job. While the bookcase was drying she had managed to fill in the hole around the stove pipe with mortar and then paint it over. It was an old cast-iron stove they had found at a scrap merchant's and hammered the rust off. She and Else sat by the stove drinking red wine after Lauritz had been put to bed. Else said all her doubts had been put to shame. She looked affectionately at Lucca and stroked her cheek. The glow from the open stove door softened her lined features. So she had got herself a home at last . . . Did Else realise the implications of what she had just said? It seemed unlikely. There was not a shadow of heart-searching in her tender expression. Lucca got up to open another bottle of wine. She wasn't used to her mother getting sentimental.

She thought of Else's remark again as she watched Copenhagen grow smaller and vanish in the clouds. She leaned back in her seat and observed the massed clouds, dazzling white above, making her screw up her eyes. So she had got herself a home . . . at last. Else had said it in a loving tone and she would have liked to give herself up to the affection in her glance and the hand that brushed her cheek. Instead she had moved her face away and gone into the kitchen for more wine. She believed she had long since put her bitterness behind her. Bitterness at Else and Giorgio making such a mess of their lives and her childhood. She could see Else was hurt when she took her hand away and looked into the flames in the stove.

As she pulled the cork from the bottle she reproached herself for behaving like a rejected child. But she had felt that her mother was pawing at the life she had herself created. The home she had in fact made, at last, with Andreas. As if Else was invading her happiness in order to warm herself the way she sat and warmed herself by the stove that Lucca and Andreas had had to hammer and scrape away at for days before getting rid of all the rust. Suddenly she was irritated because she was dependent on her mother to look after Lauritz while she was in Paris. She snapped at Else when she poured their wine and her mother asked how Andreas's new play was coming on. Else could not get over having a son-in-law who was an author and even starting to be famous.

Why couldn't she just share her happiness with Else in the home she had managed to get at last after all the wrong turnings and blind alleys? Why was she so touchy, now that she was supposed to have found peace in herself? She looked out of the small window at the wing. Suddenly she thought it looked like a diving board, a ten-metre diving board above a very large swimming pool filled with whipped cream. Surely the stewardess would soon bring her a plastic-wrapped swimsuit. The telephone had rung as she sat drinking red wine with Else. It was Miriam. They had chatted on the phone every day. Most of the time Lucca had just listened to her friend, who alternately wept, then furiously recited her jazz beloved's human failings, his egoism, his cowardice, his unfeeling and spoilt attitude to life. Miriam asked if she could come and see Lucca. A mutual friend had offered to drive her. Lucca explained she was on her way to Paris to visit Andreas.

After she had put down the phone she felt guilty again for not welcoming the deserted, heavily pregnant Miriam, and it did not improve matters that her excuse itself must seem like scorn. She hadn't time for her unhappy friend because she was flying down to her lover to walk around Paris arm in arm. But she felt even more guilty over her silent, inattentive reaction to Miriam's furious outbursts of sobbing. She could not hide it from herself. There was something repulsive about all that snivelling heartbreak. It was as if her friend was blowing her nose in Lucca's ear. She recalled how Else had stretched out a hand and caressed her cheek, as if she wanted to leave her fingerprints on her happiness and lick the butterfly dust from her fond fingers.

Suddenly she could not stand the idea of her mother lying

in the bed she and Andreas slept in every night. Perhaps Else would lie awake in the dark listening for a faint echo of their blissful sighs and moans from the walls. Through the years Else had been witness to all her failed relationships and affairs, and she had lamented them so enthusiastically that Lucca had sometimes suspected her of finding comfort and reassurance in her daughter's setbacks. She was in no doubt that Else rejoiced for her sake, but nor did she doubt that in her heart her mother envied her all that happiness and secretly thought it was really incredible after all the men she had gambolled with. She probably did not realise it herself, but Lucca had heard it as an undertone in her comments. Imagine, that she had got herself a home in spite of it all! When actually she did not really deserve it. How merciful life could be, after all . . .

She thought of Miriam who despite everything had believed so fervently in her jazz beloved that she had decided to have a child with him. She'd had the same faith in Andreas, in the certainty of his gaze and his voice one late summer morning in Trastevere when she told him she was pregnant. Was it just because she compared herself with her deserted friend that she felt so vulnerable in her own home? A few days before, when all the books were in place in the bookcase, she had looked around her not knowing what to do next. Now everything was as it should be. She called Andreas to tell him this, but she could feel she was disturbing him. Normally he called, in the evening. She asked him why he didn't just disconnect the phone. He mumbled that you never knew what might happen.

She missed him although there was less than a week to wait. She felt the lack of his presence, now she no longer had anything to throw herself into. The daily housework was quickly done, and the hours when Lauritz was at nursery school seemed longer than before. She sat and looked vacantly out of the window at the slanting ploughed furrows and the bare crown of the plum tree. She tried to read but put down the book after a page or two, unable to find any interest in the plot. She felt far too sensitive about the sudden emptiness. She had said that herself as an excuse one evening when she almost quarrelled with him on the telephone. They hardly ever quarrelled. Afterwards she could remember precisely what it was that had made her cross. He had seemed distant, as if he hadn't anything to say to her, but of course he was far away in his mind, deep in his play.

She told him about Miriam and said it was probably her snivelling phone-calls getting on her nerves. He replied that when all was said and done Miriam had brought it on herself. She said she missed him. He missed her too, he replied after a pause. She laughed down the phone at him and asked why he said that when it wasn't true. He had his work and the whole of Paris to romp around in when he was free. He didn't go out much, he replied. But shouldn't she get going on something soon? Now her role of do-it-yourself-woman was played out? It couldn't be much fun for her to be financially dependent on him. She was hurt. As if she was a little kept housewife, and had only been playing a game, covered with paint and mortar. During the hours when he had been writing she was actually the one who had buckled down to it, and she had done a great part of the work on her own.

She didn't say anything, didn't want to quarrel with him, not on the phone while he was in Paris out of range. When, on rare occasions they did quarrel, as a rule they ended up going to bed together and erasing all disagreement with caresses. They had never been angry for more than half an hour at a time, and she did not want the conversation to end on a bitter note when she could not snuggle up to him afterwards and feel everything was all right again. Besides, he was right. She ought to get going again, the question was, on what. She had not had a stage part since Lauritz was born, only one or two radio plays when he was little, and some dubbing for a Disney film. She had probably been forgotten, it would be almost like starting out afresh. She had said no when she was offered a job with Lauritz on a television ad for nappies, chiefly because Andreas had made fun of it and had been against their child being made use of commercially. Maybe it was stupid of her.

She had not been given the role of Nora in Harry's production of *A Doll's House*. Andreas had intervened. At the time she had not given much thought to it, newly in love as she was. She had merely thought it was the price she had to pay for the choice she had made. When she fell pregnant shortly after that, the role faded into insignificance. But she had paid the price.

When she and Harry had begun to show themselves publicly she could feel that people held their breath in shock and disgust over both her and the shameless old seducer. Lucca dared not think what they would have said if they had known she had been in his bed less than twenty-four hours after his wife died. But when the news spread that she had left Harry she felt people distanced themselves from her afresh. Suddenly everyone seemed to take his side, and the theatre magician's talented find was transformed into a calculating career prostitute who had ensnared the noble old artist in the midst of his loneliness and despair. They apparently forgot she had been given her role in *The Father* long before anything happened between her and Harry. Anyway, there were no more offers, and it felt as if she had been struck by a dangerous, infectious disease.

Harry had been right, then. She had ended up leaving him after all. But surely anyone could understand that sooner or later she would leave a man who was so much older. What if he had fought harder to keep her? To start with she had not cared much for his young disciple, and if anyone had told her he would be the father of her child, she would have laughed, both at the idea of having a child and the idea of having it with him.

She thought about that at Charles de Gaulle as she stood among the other passengers on the escalator in one of the plexiglass tubes. All these people, she thought. All of them had a place they called home, but how many of them would be able to say that they had been destined to get one particular home and not another? She thought about Otto again, that they had both had a child with just one year between them. What if he had not grown tired of her? Would those two children have been one and the same child, then? And what if it had not happened to be Andreas she ran into? It was hot in the tube, she was sweating and her impatience felt unbearable as she waited for her suitcase by the conveyor belt.

He was standing in the background in his shabby old leather jacket, which hung on him summer and winter. He waved and smiled, he looked like himself. Who else should he look like? She laughed at him and at herself. She could see he found her lovely and was glad she had taken pains with herself. He walked to meet her and tears came into her eyes as she put down her case and nestled into his embrace.

Wouldn't she take their young guest down to the beach so he could take a dip? He must need one . . . Harry had obviously forgotten she was a few years younger than their guest. It was the day after his arrival. Andreas seemed almost terrified at the idea. He muttered something about forgetting his swimming trunks. He and Harry were still seated in the shade on the roof terrace when she went up there after her siesta. Harry would not be deterred, Andreas could just borrow a pair of his. Now there was no way out. The young guest seemed quite disconcerted at the idea of putting on Harry Wiener's very own swimming trunks. What about you? he asked Harry. He made a deprecating gesture with his hands, he would stay here. Young Bark had drained him of energy, he was going to take forty winks.

Come on, then, she said, smiling encouragingly at Andreas, as if he was a shy child. They went down to the car. The village houses glowed white in the low sun and the shadows on the reddish rock slopes were long and distorted. On the way down Andreas pricked himself on an agave that stretched its tough leaves across the path. His arm was bleeding, but he said not a word, merely smiled although she could see it hurt. She was irritated because he would not even allow himself to say Ow! They drove down the mountainside. Is he tough on you? she asked. Tough and tough . . . he replied. As long as it brought improvement he was glad of criticism. A play script wasn't a finished work, after all, just as a score was not in itself music. It only came to life when the conductor, or in this case, the director, got hold of it and gave it his interpretation . . . It sounded like something he had taught himself to say.

She had sunbathed as usual that morning, in her bikini. It annoyed her, she was used to lying naked and getting brown all over. How modest . . . said Harry when he and Andreas came out on the terrace each with his coffee cup and each with his script under an arm. They went to sit in the shade. His teasing tone made her contrary and she took off her top before lying down again on the sun-bed. She caught sight of Andreas averting his eyes as her breasts came in sight, and she was sure Harry had seen it too. He smiled his foxy little smile. Could that really amuse him? She closed her eyes and listened to the cicadas, some close at hand, others further off, each chinking its rhythm, fast or lazy. She lay unmoving and enjoying the sunshine beating into her skin, making her sweat and feel heavy.

Harry treated Andreas in a different way from that he used with his actors. She felt he was being hard. He did not comment on anything he found good in the play, whereas he laid down in detail what did not work with no polite beating about the bush. For instance, how could it be that all the characters not only spoke alike but also just like their author? Andreas attempted to explain that he had tried to stylise the language in such a way that the characters, instead of expressing themselves in realistic language, used a poetic or grotesque form that flowed through them and at the same time defined their personalities. Harry cut him short. Perhaps they were meant to speak in tongues? Every character must have a *reason* for speaking and saying what he or she said. Besides, it was an advantage for the actors to understand their own lines. Not to mention the audience. After all, this was a play, not a poetry reading!

Andreas defended himself mildly by saying that the demand for simple, clear and unambiguous dialogue risked draining the play of finer nuances and tones . . . everything which in his opinion made the difference between art and message drama, he dared to add. Harry laughed hoarsely. Might he have one of his Gitanes? But of course! Lucca heard him fish a cigarette out of the pack and the little click of the lid of his silver lighter. Shortly afterwards she smelled the spicy scent of tobacco smoke wafting across the terrace.

Now listen . . . Harry's tone was friendlier now, almost fatherly. First of all he must never, never be afraid of being simple. Clarity, he said, clarity is all. On the stage nothing could be too clear. Where that was concerned there was no difference between Sophocles and a well-turned musical comedy. Tones, he said, he could very well leave those to poets, and as for nuances, they were something the impressionist painters had taken care of . . . wimps with full beards! When it came to the crunch the most archaic myths and the flattest pub jokes were constructed in the same way. And furthermore . . . he paused to inhale . . . he should not be afraid of losing his personal characteristics, his precious voice. *Style,* he went on, enunciating the word curtly and sharply, style began where you renounced yourself in favour of your story. If you had anything at all to tell. And he obviously had . . . otherwise they would not be sitting here, would they?

This was meant to be disarming, but she could see in Andreas that he was not at all sure Harry was right, and instead was picturing to himself how in a little while his master would slam the script shut and send him home. She had got up and was sitting on the sun-bed, dizzy with the heat. This time Andreas looked stiffly into her eyes to avoid having to look at her breasts. Harry looked at her too and smiled, but it was a smile she could not recall having seen before. A boyish smile like the one Andreas had given her when she fetched him from the airport and he was surprised to find her and not his guru waiting for him. Maybe it was the heat that confused her, but for a moment she thought the smile of the young man had nipped across onto the older man's face, while the boyish smile's rightful owner stared vacantly at her, afraid of moving his gaze as much as a millimetre downwards and humiliated at the thought that she had heard everything Harry said.

Everything went black when she got up. She turned her back on them and stood with head bent for a second or two before going down the stairs and into the bedroom. She put on one of Harry's shirts and went on down to the kitchen to make lunch. She ran the tap until it grew cold and held her wrists beneath the running water. It was a big dark room, the coolest in the house, with an arched ceiling and an open fireplace. A door gave way to a steep passage leading up to the village. The crack under the door was so big that the reflected sunlight from the alleyway fanned out over the uneven tiles on the floor. The light was reflected in the stream of cold water with a restless, silvery flickering. A bluebottle cruised lazily around the sticky ribbon hanging from the ceiling, thick with dead flies, but did not alight. She drank a glass of water. One of the sun rays struck an apron hanging on a hook, washed out pink, with printed yellow tulips.

According to Harry his wife had not been there for years, but her apron was still hanging up. There was a brown stain on it, where she must once have used it to hold something hot. Lucca had often felt like putting it on. She took smoked ham and olives out of the fridge and started to wash lettuce. The bluebottle kept on circling around the ham. She had found other traces of his wife around the house, a pair of old bathing slippers in the wardrobe and a small bottle of dried nail varnish on a shelf in the bathroom, and some faded women's magazines on the shelf beneath the bedside table, the newest ones four years old. Harry had told Lucca very little about her, and she had not asked. In the apartment in Copenhagen she had seen a photograph of an attractive, dark-haired woman with a triangular face, but the picture must have been taken at least fifteen years before, to judge from the dress. The bluebottle alighted on her upper lip, she spat and hit out with her hand. In the end she cut a small piece of fat from a slice of ham, put it on the chopping board and stood in wait with the fly swatter. She got it.

Harry was lively during lunch, almost jovial, and Andreas listened gratefully to his anecdotes. It irritated her to see him lapping it all up like a good little puppy getting his reward and comfort after Harry had given his script the full treatment. She was still amazed that this was the same guy who had seemed so free and spontaneous when they strolled around the wild west village. She went downstairs for her siesta. While she lay in the dark she thought of Harry's remark about her modest bikini and of his foxy face when she took off her top and Andreas averted his eyes. She pictured Harry's boyish smile again when she rose from the sun-bed after he had taught Andreas how to write drama. It did not suit him, that smile. It was not at all like him. It had the effect of an indecent exposure, as if he had taken down his trousers and shown off his bare bottom. At the same time there was something conspiratorial in his expression, as if he wanted to enlist her confirmation that the two of them shared something, whether it was his bare bottom, her young breasts or the beaten expression in his disciple's eyes.

Why did he put up with it? She came out with the question after a long pause in which neither of them had said anything. They followed the coast road past the bars and discothèques on the beach and the low white concrete buildings on the other side with boarding houses, shopping arcades and complexes of holiday apartments. It was still out of season and in most places the shutters were closed. He looked at her. He didn't mind being criticised. She returned his gaze briefly. He spoke in a tired tone, neither evasive nor forthcoming, as an obvious statement. He knew why he had written his play the way he had. Even if he was not particularly good at explaining it. But the old man might well be right in some of his criticism.

She was surprised to hear him speak of Harry like that. Perhaps it was in return for Harry's *young guest*. He laughed out loud. She looked at him again. What? He smiled in the same sudden way he had done when they drove from Almeria. He was all right, the old man . . . he *was* theatre, through and through! Andreas nodded his acknowledgement and seemed as he did so to shake off the humiliation, all Harry's didactic and ridiculing words, rather as you shake your head to get snow out of your hair. They passed the fish restaurant where they had eaten the previous evening, down on the beach. She would have to forgive him for making a fool of himself. What did he mean? Look out for the dog! he said quickly. She managed to avoid a skinny dog running across the road. Yes, what he had said about the part . . .

They had sat inside the garishly lit place because the wind had got up. She was beside Andreas, Harry opposite. You could see the spray rising from the waves in the light from the open windows. Harry leaned back with crossed legs, smoking, while they waited for their food. He told her about the play Andreas had written, and it sounded like a story he himself was inventing. Now and again he looked inquiringly at Andreas as if to assure himself that he did not get anything wrong. She loved to hear him talking in his deep hoarse voice, and she was so involved in listening to him that she was startled when the waiter arrived with their plates. Harry asked for an ashtray and the waiter went away. He pointed to the champagne cooler beside Andreas. Now he must see that his lady companion had something to drink. Andreas had been listening as intently as she had and turned to the wine bottle in confusion. Only to the brim! said Harry drily as he went on pouring.

The waiter came back with the ashtray and Harry put out his cigarette. They raised a toast. Andreas cleared his throat. He had been thinking of something. The part of the young woman . . . might that be a role for Lucca? Harry looked at him for a long time, and his eyes grew even narrower, as if he was thinking hard. He had considered it, he said finally, but had come to the opposite conclusion. It might well be seen as a trifle . . . he lifted his hands from the table cloth . . . overdone . . . if he gave the leading role in Andreas's play and in *A Doll's House* to his partner as well. He started to cut up his fish with great care. In any case we should never discuss casting in the presence of actors. He raised his eyes and looked out at the waves in the darkness, chewing. Andreas looked down at his fish.

She turned off the coast road along a track beside the cliffs that sloped steeply down to the surf. The water was jade green and blue black further out. No need to think of that, she said. Sure? She smiled soothingly. Of course . . . She drove round a point and negotiated a series of sharp corners down to the beach where she usually swam. It was framed by cliffs on both sides, forming a small cove. No-one else was there. She parked in the shade of a group of tall cacti.

When they had gone to bed the night before she had asked Harry why he was so worried about what people would say if he gave her the parts of both Nora and the woman in Andreas's play. Usually he did not care in the least what people said about him. She had been sitting up in bed, ready for a discussion. He stroked her gently under the chin. It wasn't actually his own reputation he was worried about . . . Besides, he went on, it was not the right part for her. He could not understand where Andreas had got that idea from. It wouldn't be right for her, and certainly not at this point in her career. She must trust him, after all he had read the play. Nora, on the other hand . . .

But what did she think of him, by the way? He raised himself on one elbow. She lay down on her back. He let a hand slide over her stomach and one breast. He seemed rather pleasant . . . and rather young. Harry smiled. He's older than you are, he said. Handsome enough chap, isn't he? She turned on her side, he withdrew his hand and pulled the sheet over his hip. Why did he say that? As soon as she had spoken the words she felt she had fallen into a trap. Harry smiled again and looked in front of him. Well, but he *was*, why did she make such a fuss about it? She didn't! He looked at her and kissed her forehead. That's all right then, he said and switched off the light.

She moved close to him, he laid a hand on her hip. I'm just an anxious old man, he said, and she could hear him smile in the dark. She gave him a push. Rather she was the one to be nervous. He turned onto his back, and she rested her cheek on his chest and let her fingertips circle over his stomach. Perhaps she was right . . . He sounded thoughtful. Did she know what his last wife had once called him? Her fingers had reached the hairs in his groin. No, not if he hadn't told her . . . She played with his growing erection. *Woman junkie*, he said, lazily caressing her buttocks. But the strange thing, he went on, the really puzzling thing was that even if he knew it himself, he was still carried away every time he caught sight of an engaging girl's face and a pair of lovely legs. She carefully weighed his hanging testicles in her hand. So when was he going to find a new young and unknown beauty? He laughed. She needn't worry. She could go on for a long time yet. When her youth came to an end he would have long since kicked the bucket.

* * *

For a moment she considered putting on her bikini top, but decided not to. He must be used to the sight by now. He stood a little way off with a towel round his waist as he took off his underpants. He stumbled a bit and almost fell down. His skin was white and he was so thin she could see his ribs and the muscles moving under the skin of his calves. He looked comic in Harry's bathing trunks, they flapped around him and she couldn't help laughing. He didn't seem to mind, he laughed himself as he pulled the drawstring to tighten them. She suggested they should swim out to the rock that reared out of the water at the end of the cove where the mountainside sloped vertically into the sea. He overtook her, he was a good swimmer. He crawled out with quick rhythmic strokes and soon disappeared round the point.

The water was calm and the sparkling folds on the surface changed from turquoise to mint green. The horizon was only a milky mist. Andreas came in sight at the top of the rock. He stood with legs together, bent down and dived head-first, and his body made a shining arrow in the low sunlight. When she got to the rock he was on his way up. He stretched out a hand and pulled her towards him. The sharp edges cut into her soles as she climbed after him. It was a long way down. They dived by turns once or twice. The pressure made her ears hum. She doubled up with her head against her knees each time she sank through the green shining mist passing into darkness beneath her. A moment later she stretched out again as she was pressed up into the vibrating white mirror. They sat on top of the rock drying themselves in the sun, looking at the beach. The mountain ridge and the car and clumps of cactus were nothing but flat silhouettes, and the light from behind shone in the dust on the car windows.

He asked what it was like to live with Wiener. He called him Wiener. It must be difficult to create your own space. She shaded her eyes with a hand, looking at him. Your own space? He shrugged his shoulders, the drops sparkled on his arms. She thought of the role in his play she would not get and the film role she had refused because Harry was sure it would be a bad film. Andreas smiled and nodded in the direction of the beach. He could do with a fag now. A drop fell from his wet forelock and landed on his upper lip, he removed it with his tongue. She asked if he wanted to go back. He could wait.

Actually she felt free, she said, with Harry. Maybe just because he was so much older. Andreas looked at her. How? She talked about Harry's calm, his lack of illusions, and repeated what he had said. That she would leave him one day. She looked down at her fingers stroking the rough surface of the rock. It might sound strange, but his saying that made her want to stay. He kissed her, and he did it so quickly that she hardly realised what was happening. She smiled in surprise, but when his face approached again she returned his kiss. His mouth tasted of salt and tobacco. She narrowed her eyes and took hold of his chin, which really was very prominent. Wasn't it about time for that fag?

They chatted about everything under the sun while they dried themselves on the beach and later in the car on the way back. As if it had not happened. She spoke of Ibsen and *A Doll's House* and what she thought of the role of Nora. He said it was brave of Wiener to put on that particular play. Women's liberation had lost its punch now, at least as something open to discussion, and you had to ask yourself if the play was still relevant. She said there was another side to Nora, but hadn't time to tell him what it was before the village came in sight round a bend. Soon they stopped below the house. The sun had gone down behind the mountains, the first street-lights had come on. Harry was in the kitchen stirring one of his Andalusian casseroles with chick peas and black pudding. She kissed him on the neck and went for her shower.

It was dark when she went up on the terrace. They talked quietly as they ate. Harry chatted to Andreas about Rome and let him describe it without showing off his own knowledge of the city, as she feared for a moment he would. When she was making the coffee in the kitchen Andreas came down with the dishes. He stood for a few seconds beside her but she did not look at him and he went up again. She served their coffee and said she wanted an early night. When Harry came into the room a few hours later she pretended to be asleep.

Andreas caught a bus to Almeria the next day. They had originally planned for him to stay on another day. He said there was an exhibition in Madrid he wanted to see before flying home. Harry drove him to the bus stop. She lay sunbathing on the terrace when he came back. He sat on the parapet beside the sun-bed looking down at the dried up river-bed, scratching his neck. He was in a great hurry . . . had he been too hard on him?

As the weeks went by it seemed more and more unreal to her that she had sat on a rock and kissed Andreas Bark. In her memory it had almost not happened. Everything was exactly the same between her and Harry. Before they went home they spent three days in Granada. He showed her round the Alhambra and described how the Catholic kings had driven out the Moors and the Spanish Jews in turn. That was how she discovered he was Jewish. He had not been circumcised. Thank God, he said, smiling. Think what I would have been like if they had cut my cock! He didn't care where he came from or what he was called, he said. No one was going to tell him who he was, and in any case, family was just one great crushing mill. They were in a roadside restaurant somewhere between Granada and Malaga. He bent over his plate of pork chops in sherry sauce. 'I know not how to tell thee who I am: My name, dear saint, is hateful to myself.' She laughed at his old-fashioned punctilious diction and wiped sauce from his chin with her napkin. She had just finished *Romeo and Juliet.* When they were back in the car it occurred to her that she might be the only one who allowed him to forget now and then that he was Harry Wiener.

One afternoon a few months later Lucca was sitting at a pavement café on Gammel Strand. She was waiting for Miriam. It had begun to drizzle but she stayed on under the umbrella breathing in the scent of wet asphalt. Harry had driven to Skagen in Jutland, they had arranged for her to join him a fortnight later. She had been planning to visit Else at the holiday cottage. She had not seen her mother since they went to Spain, but put it off every day and didn't feel like going up there. She enjoyed having the roof apartment to herself and being alone for the first time in six months. As she sat looking out for Miriam she noticed a woman standing on the pavement some distance away looking in her direction. Only after a while did Lucca realise the woman was gazing at her. She turned her head towards Thorvaldsen's Museum as if she was engaged in observing the frieze of pictures on the side of the building.

After her success in *The Father* and being photographed with Harry for the gossip columns she had grown used to people recognising her sometimes in the street, but she had never been stared at for so long before. When she turned round again the woman was standing beside her table. They must have been about the same age, but she seemed older. Her face was lined and pale and she looked unhealthy. Her greasy hair stuck to her forehead, carefully set in an unbecoming but very straight parting, and she had a dark moustache. She fixed Lucca with her gaze through the raindrops on her spectacles, digging her hands into the pockets of her woollen coat. It was buttoned right up to the chin although it was early July. Suddenly Lucca realised the woman must be mad.

She sat down opposite Lucca with an artificial smile. I know very well who you are, she said. You are my father's whore. You are the one who killed my mother . . . A waitress came up to take her order. Lucca waved her away and smiled at the woman. I haven't killed anybody, she replied calmly. She was reminded of what Harry had told her when they sat on the stage chatting one morning before rehearsal. This must be the woman he had bought an apartment for. He had mentioned his daughter only once, and as far as she knew he had no other children. You're lying, said the woman. You were fucking him when my mother was admitted to hospital! Lucca bent forward and lowered her voice as she tried to explain it was a misunderstanding, and that she had not started living with her father before her mother died. It felt wrong to say *living with*.

The tense shoulders in the woollen coat dropped, and Harry's daughter stared crestfallen. She couldn't understand it, she had seen them coming out of his building arm in arm. She looked up. It *must* have been her she had seen coming out the day her mother went to hospital. She had been tall and slim and black-haired . . . Harry's daughter raised her voice again and struck the table, making Lucca's cup rattle on its saucer . . . *Like you!* At that moment Lucca caught sight of Miriam. She stood up so abruptly that the chair fell over, called the waitress, passed her the change she had in her pocket and ran to meet her bewildered friend. Behind her she heard Harry's daughter call out in a despairing voice. Couldn't they talk? As she took Miriam's arm and walked on along the pavement she cursed his idea of having her hair dyed for the part in *The Father*. At the same time she wondered who she could be, the young black-haired woman Harry's daughter had seen him with. Was it the strange girl he had thought of when he made the suggestion? Had she been the substitute for an unknown woman?

The telephone rang next morning while she sat in bed reading *A Doll's House*, now and then looking over the harbour that appeared and disappeared again every time the wind lifted the curtains in front of the open sliding door. She decided not to answer it, afraid it was Harry's daughter. It went on ringing and in the end she stood up. It was Andreas. She was taken by surprise at hearing his voice and said Harry was in Skagen. He knew that. He was in Copenhagen, could he come round? Five minutes later the doorbell rang. She had to smile when she saw his silhouette behind the plate glass of the elevator door. She had seen the same silhouette exactly a year before on her way down the stairs after having tea with Harry. He wore his leather jacket and smiled his boyish smile, but he didn't seem shy.

Harry had called him a few days before, about his play, and during the conversation had told him she was in town. That was why he had come. He had to see her, and the next day he had caught the train, and here he was. She looked at him. You must be crazy, she said. He knew that. But he had thought of her a lot . . . it had been so strange, what happened on the rock that afternoon. Either it was nothing or . . . he had to see her again to find out what it was. If it was anything.

They sat on the balcony looking at the clouds over the harbour and at each other, suddenly shy. He had blurted it all out, and now he didn't know what to say. She wondered at his initiative and courage. She hadn't thought about him as much as he had about her, and she said what she thought straight out. She said she had not known what to make of what happened on that rock. As they sat there it felt as if she had spent the past six months in a kind of trance. She felt she was being honest as she said that.

They sat in silence for a few minutes. There was quite a strong wind and he could not get his cigarette to light however much he turned this way and that. She suggested they go inside. She went first, and in the middle of the room she turned to face him. It was as if they'd been forced to get up from those chairs out on the balcony. He looked at her expectantly, the man who had come by train all the way from Rome merely because he had been thinking of her and knew she was alone.

It surprised her that she did not feel any guilt towards Harry, and how easy she felt it was to talk to him when he called. She thought the ease was a sign in itself. She felt as if all the muscles in her body had relaxed after a tension that had gone on so long she had confused it with rest. She felt untroubled with Andreas. They did things she would never have done with Harry. One morning they went to Tivoli even though it rained, and rode on the Ferris wheel in the wet, grinning like children. One day they took the hydrofoil over to the island of Hven and hired bicycles. They lay kissing on a grassy slope, from where you could see the towers and power station smoke-stacks of Copenhagen in the distance. The same view she had seen a year before from the bathing jetty, on her last day with Otto. That day seemed as far away now as the city skyline seen from Hven.

Andreas went back to Rome a week later. She asked him to go. She had to be alone, she said, to be able to think. He gave her his telephone number. If she felt like calling him when she had done her thinking. That same day she packed her things and took a taxi to the villa in Frederiksberg. As she drove through town it occurred to her that her things took up no more room than they had done when she left Otto's apartment the year before. Two suitcases, some zip bags, some plastic bags. She had tried to call Harry, but he did not answer that afternoon. It was a relief. Instead she sent him a letter. Not a long one. He did not reply, and she never heard from him again.

Years later she asked herself if he had wanted it that way. Perhaps he had foreseen it was possible when he invited Andreas to come and visit them in Spain. She pondered on whether he had unconsciously wanted to hasten the inevitable, because he could not make the break abruptly himself. But it was only a thought. She had felt heavy inside when she heard the letter land in the letterbox with a dull thud, but it also made her more sure of her intentions, and she sensed that at last she was taking her life into her own hands. He wasn't her only sacrifice. She had left the script of *A Doll's House* on his desk.

She spent a week at home in the villa without anyone knowing she was there. She was just as alone as she had been the summer before when Otto threw her out and Harry called to invite her for tea. Just as alone, she thought, as when she was on her own in the evenings listening to Else speak to all and sundry over the air while she looked through the black and white pictures of young Giorgio in a square in Lucca, in front of a church wall speckled with the fleeting shadows of swallows. She talked to no one, nor did she give way to her need to hear Andreas's voice again. She was quite proud of that when she did finally call to tell him when her plane would land in Rome.

He had not shaved for several days, and her scarf caught in his long stubble when they embraced. You've still got this, have you? he mumbled, smiling pensively and touching the soft petrol-blue silk. It had been the first present he gave her, shortly after she arrived in Rome, one afternoon as they were walking up the Via Condotti. The stubble scratched her face and made her feel she was waking up. She had been going around like a sleepwalker, alone in the house when Lauritz was at nursery school, left to all the needless worries she had been embroidering because she had nothing better to do. They faded and vanished like the images of a meaningless dream when Andreas picked up her suitcase and they left the airport building to find a taxi. She repeated the funny things Lauritz had said and described how she had repaired the hole in the wall around the stove pipe and arranged the books in alphabetical order. So now Harold Pinter had his place beside *Pinocchio*! As she gradually ran out of things to report on they contented themselves with exchanging kisses on the back seat of the taxi, a little shy as they usually were when they had been away from each other and were picking up the threads again.

She nestled into his arms and breathed in the scent of his leather jacket as his hand slid up her thigh under the short skirt. He caressed the bare skin between the top of the stocking and her suspender belt. Only the taxi driver's ironic gaze in the back mirror stopped them throwing themselves at each other. She could see her forehead and her dishevelled auburn hair falling over his leather sleeve beside the driver's dark African eyes. Beneath the motorway, in an anonymous district of neglected housing blocks, she saw a half-demolished house and a crane with a lead ball swinging against a building where the front wall had been cut away. The multi-coloured squares of wallpaper and paint on the smashed storeys were all that remained of one-time apartments. A second later the wall was pulverised in a grey cascade of dust and broken bricks.

She had lived with him in Trastevere for a month when she woke up one morning to find his fingers running through her hair down to the scalp. He looked at her as if he had caught her in the act. But your hair is fair, he said. Her own hair colour had begun to grow out and displace the black dye she had worn for months. I am not the person you think I am, she smiled mysteriously and told him why it had been a black-haired woman he met in Spain. Was he disappointed? He looked at her teasingly. And he had been dreaming about a fiery gypsy lass . . . he had even travelled all the way from Rome to Copenhagen!

She shook her head so her hair fell down over her eyes. She could easily learn to dance flamenco. He kissed her and said it wasn't worth the trouble. A few weeks later, when her hair had grown and she really looked skewbald, she went into a barber's shop in Trastevere and asked to be shorn. At first the barber refused with a pained gesture, but when she left the shop she was as bare-headed as an Arab boy. Never before had she known the feeling of air on the top of her head and her temples, and as she walked along the street enjoying people's glances she felt as if her head was weightless and at any moment could take off like a balloon over the roofs of Rome.

The apartment was in a quiet, narrow side street to the Rue de Rennes. It was an attic apartment on two floors with one window from floor to ceiling looking out on a cramped courtyard. From the studio a staircase led up to a bedroom with French windows and a balcony with a view over the slanting zinc roofs and rows of chimney pots ranged close together. Everything was in shades of grey, the sky, the roofs and the walls. Behind a sooty party wall you could glimpse the Tour de Montparnasse far away, with lit windows in the evening. That was the only light visible from the balcony, in the middle of that enormous city.

She lay in the dusk listening to the distant sound of traffic. The air was cool on her bare shoulders, but she couldn't be bothered to get up and close the balcony doors. She wanted to lie feeling the air, listening to the sounds of the city while she waited for him to come back. He had gone shopping, she was too tired to go out to eat. She had got up early to catch the plane, Else had driven her to the station with Lauritz. He had cried on the platform, but Else had said she should just go. The train was about to leave without her, as she kneeled down to the boy and tried to comfort him.

She considered calling home, but decided to wait. It might make him miss her still more, now he most probably had stopped being miserable. The light from Andreas's laptop computer shone in the semi-darkness of the room. A shining white square floating among the dim outlines of furniture. He had not turned it off when he left for the airport, and as soon as they entered the apartment they fell into bed. But it had not come up to her expectations in the taxi, sitting with his hand between her thighs while she pressed her palm against the hard bulge in his trousers. She had kept her suspender belt and stockings on in bed, and the shoes with ankle straps, in the way she knew he liked and had maybe imagined her in the weeks he had been alone. When she dressed in the morning she had remembered to put her pants on outside the suspender belt. It seemed a bit comical to her now, when she took off her shoes and stockings and cuddled up to him under the duvet, wondering if he was disappointed.

It had not been as wild and passionate as she had wanted it to be. It had been the way it was when they were both tired and did not make love because they were completely swept away by desire but rather because they desired the idea of being close again instead of just falling asleep. He asked if she had come properly. She smiled at him fondly. It didn't matter. She was happy just to lie here and feel him beside her. He stroked her hair, she pushed her head under his chin. She asked if he had finished his play. Almost, he said. There was only the end to do now. When she went back to work, she said, she would like to have a part in one of his plays. It wouldn't need to be a leading part, she would be happy with a small one. She could come in with a letter!

She felt the need of a cigarette and got out of bed. The Tour de Montparnasse had turned into no more than a stack of little, shining cubes in the blue darkness. She switched on the lamp on the writing desk and took the carton of cigarettes out of the plastic bag from the airport. She couldn't find her lighter and there wasn't one on the desk either. She walked downstairs with the cigarette hanging from her lips, still naked, and thought that if she had a spotlight on her now she would look like a stripper coming down to ask one of the men in the audience for a light, as part of the show. There must be a lighter somewhere. Distrait as he was, Andreas always kept two or three plastic lighters going at the same time. She caught sight of his tweed jacket on a hanger behind the front door. The one he occasionally wore when he dropped his image of the young rebel. His Arthur Miller jacket, she called it. He did look a bit like Arthur Miller when he wore it, if you left out the horn-rimmed spectacles. It must be the prominent chin they had in common. As she searched through the pockets she heard a rustling sound. An envelope was sticking out of the breast pocket.

She might have just let it go, she thought later. She had never been through his pockets before, and never read his letters. She knew it was wrong, but she did it all the same. Was it intuition that made her take the envelope from his pocket, or was it ordinary, thoughtless curiosity? It was an airmail letter with a Swedish stamp, posted in Stockholm just over a week before. She could still have changed her mind as she held it in her hand. The letter bore no sender's name, but the writing on the envelope was a woman's, she could see, a young woman's. Andreas's name and address in Paris was written in felt tip and architectural capital letters, regular, very clear and with a weakness for calligraphic curlicues.

After she had read the letter three times she folded it up, put it back in the envelope and stuck it in the breast pocket of the tweed jacket, taking care to see that the stamp bearing Carl Gustav's puppyish playboy face was on the left side of the pocket, as she had found it. She went into the bathroom, kneeled down in front of the lavatory pan and vomited until she was empty. The cold of the floor and the spasms in her stomach made her shudder. She locked the door, sat in the bath and crouched with her knees under her chin and one foot on top of the other. She turned on the hot water and held the shower against her head until the scalding water made her cry out with pain. Only then did she start to weep. She turned on the cold tap, not too much, and sat sobbing under the hot stream of water that surrounded her like a steaming cloak. She closed her eyes and pictured the house she had seen being torn down on the way into Paris. The remains of a condemned suburban building with gaping window openings, flapping remnants of wallpaper and gnawed-off storey divisions that sank soundlessly in a cloud of pulverised bricks, a grey waterfall of dust.

She was still sitting in the bath weeping when she heard the front door slam and Andreas calling. She stopped sobbing. Soon afterwards he turned the door handle and said through the door that he was going to start cooking. She turned off the water and slowly stood up, stiff from sitting in the same position for so long. The steam had misted up the mirror over the wash basin. She wiped it with her hand and looked at her tear-stained face. Her eyelids were red and swollen. She wrapped herself in a towel and went into the kitchen. He raised his eyes from the steaks frying in the pan and looked at her worriedly. She said she had been sick. It must have been something she ate on the plane. He stroked her cheeks sympathetically, first one, then the other, and concentrated on the steaks again. She opened the window to let out the odour of cooking. He told her about a Japanese chef who had committed hara-kiri when the passengers on a plane had fallen ill because he had cooked with an infected finger. He showed her both his hands, grinning. No infection! She went upstairs to dress.

She had decided not to say anything. The decision had almost made itself when she heard him come in. She would wait and see what happened. She could not get down a single mouthful of the steak he served up for her. She managed a little salad, but drank up quickly when he refilled her glass. The red wine had a calming effect and soothed the clutching feeling in her stomach. She was impressed at his cold-bloodedness. He said he wanted to go up to Belleville next day and take photographs of the Arab district. If she felt better, he added kindly. She nodded. That would be good, she felt fine now. It had helped to empty out her stomach. He even stroked her hand, which lay beside her plate of cold steak.

They watched a film on television, she went upstairs before it ended. She undressed and lay down on the bed naked. She heard him pull the cord in the bathroom and water running in the wash basin, and shortly afterwards his step on the stair. She closed her eyes. The sound of steps stopped in the doorway. She told him to cover her face with thc blue scarf. He hesitated before complying. The light from the lamp on the desk penetrated the closely woven silk threads and took on their colour. She heard the sirens of an ambulance on the Rue de Rennes and someone shouting in the street. She lay like that, without a face, delivered to his gaze, with empty eye sockets and a dark slit between her lips where the silk was sucked in each time she drew breath.

When she woke up next morning Andreas was working at the dining table in what had once been a studio and was now furnished as a living room. She made coffee and placed a cup beside his computer. He caressed her thigh vaguely without looking up from the screen. She took her own coffee up on the balcony. She leaned over the railing, looking at the occasional pedestrians. It was a long way down. Would you pass out before you hit the ground? The sun was shining and if she pulled her coat round her shoulders it was warm enough to sit outside. She leaned back with closed eyes.

It probably did not occur to him that she would go through his pockets. Actually it was her own fault that everything between them was suddenly changed. But to him it might be just a harmless affair, otherwise he would mention it. She was not sure though. In the letter at least it did not sound like a digression, a single bonk to freshen things up a bit. How passionate they were, the words written in neat, architectural block letters. They were even garnished with graceful little drawings as proof of the sender's feminine charm, here a bird, there a star and a naked lady, rather à la Matisse. She wrote that the colours around her had grown brighter since she had met him. She couldn't sleep at night, she was afraid of going off her head. She had been living in a daze for too long, in a relationship that made her feel she was invisible. Just as he had, if she had understood him rightly. When she stood in front of the mirror it felt as if the mirror was looking at her with his gaze. As if she was seeing herself for the first time.

Lucca had sat for a long time studying her while Andreas was out shopping. She could well understand when she saw the polaroid picture that fell out of the envelope. His correspondent was pale and had blue eyes and curly, jet-black hair. A gypsy with blue eyes, of course that had been irresistible. After all, he did have a weakness for black hair. She sat on a double bed, her hair glittered in the morning sun which reached exactly to her breasts. Andreas had hardly been the one who had taken the photo, if so he would have kept it. She must have sent him a picture taken by someone else. But who had snapped her naked in an unmade bed? Andreas must have wondered about that too.

Even though the letter lacked any prosaic details as to who or what the woman was in real life, Lucca could work out that they must have met in Malmö during the rehearsals for Andreas's play, which had been so important for him to attend several times a week. Perhaps she was an actor. A Swedish colleague! Lucca remembered his impatience in the morning, when he was leaving and had promised to drive Lauritz to nursery school first. How irritated he had been when the boy sat over his porridge half asleep. There were several references in the letter to something Andreas had said or written to her. In one place she actually quoted him. He was right, she wrote. Sometimes you did have to believe your own eyes. Otherwise you risked everything around you becoming as fleeting and unreal as a film. She too would like to meet him again. Unfortunately she could not get to Paris for the week after Easter.

Lucca shaded her eyes with a hand and gazed at the Tour de Montparnasse, rising from among the slanting zinc roofs and thronging chimney pots like a big, dumb prick of smoke-coloured glass. Did she feel shattered? She put the question in the same way as if she had leaned over the balcony rail and seen herself lying in the street in a pool of blood. She was beside herself. The expression had never seemed more apt, but it did not only cover the sorrow that kept on trickling out inside her from a gash so agonising she could hardly breathe. She was beside herself because she was observing herself like an outsider.

She recalled Andreas's words about believing your own eyes. He had said almost the identical thing in Harry's apartment in Copenhagen when he had gone rushing up from Rome, and later in Trastevere when she had told him she was pregnant. So those were the words he used for celebrations. But then again, why invent the wheel each time? They worked, those words. His own home-made version of love's magic formula, which apparently created what the words suggested, like a self-fulfilling prophecy. Had not the same words brought them all the way to Paris, she on the balcony, he in the studio bent over his play, while their little son might be making a snowman out of the Easter snow at home, with his grandmother?

Of course there had been more to it than words. Ambiguous feelings and mysterious glances, a peculiar restlessness, an unexpected ease and the alluring powers of physical attraction. But the words had made the difference, encouraging her to dare give herself once more. His words about believing what you saw, instead of being sceptical and cautious because you were no longer a spring chicken and had tried all this before. And yet the words had no more weight or meaning than those glances and feeling jittery, intoxicating carnal dizziness. The words were the same, just as the glances and feelings had been, from time to time. Only the faces had changed on the way. The faith in what you saw, that Andreas had spoken of, was itself faithless. You could believe in so much and so many. He had probably been sincere when he said it.

She thought of what the dark curly-haired charmer had written in her letter, despite her romantic rapture. She could not come to Paris after Easter, unfortunately. Something was apparently more important than looking into Andreas's wonderful eyes again. Had that made him stop for a moment and think about the one at home wielding her paint brush and mortar trowel? Did he give a thought to the fact that they had a child? She had hoped the years would gain the weight the words lacked. Lauritz was living proof that there was more than words and sensations between them. Or was he? Their child and their home had not prevented Andreas from saying those same words the years had made so precious, to someone he had known for a mere few weeks.

The weather was mild and spring-like as they walked around the Arab quarter in the afternoon. The scents of spices, the shrill music of tape recorders and the hoarse Arabian voices almost made them forget they were in Paris. They talked about it. That it was like walking through a North African town. Colourful fabrics, videos and cheap kitchen equipment were on sale. Andreas took pictures of people, all portraits. The women giggled or turned away, the men posed with hands to their sides and stomachs pushed out. She kept a little distance between them, without losing sight of him. Everywhere people were doing business, and notes were exchanged between brown or black hands. The women's palms were painted with henna and their silver jewellery glinted palely in the misty sunlight. They wore long garments and some had tattoos on their faces. Most of the men wore European clothes. They looked at her, some of them out of the corners of their eyes, others directly, with an impudent air that made her feel she was being pawed at.

She regretted putting on her short skirt. The voices, the glances, the music and crowds brought her out in a sweat, and she told Andreas she would go back to the boulevard and wait for him at a café they had passed.

She sat down on the glass-roofed terrace and ordered coffee. Only a few customers were in the café or on the pavement outside. She looked at the patchy bark of the plane trees, resembling the pattern on camouflage suits. Each breath made her feel she was encased in armour. She wanted to weep but was not sure she would be able to even if she permitted herself. A pantechnicon was parked on the other side of the street. The removal men carried furniture out of the house and into the vehicle. An entire home passed by on the pavement as if assembled at random. So that was how they had chosen to arrange things, the unknown people who had lived on one of the floors over there. Two of the men helped each other carry a large gold-framed mirror, and as they struggled with it, turning it first one way, then another, fragments of clouds, cars, trees and shutters whirled through the gold frame in quickly shifting glimpses. When thc mirror caught the sun for a moment a sharp spot of light leapt jerkily over the asphalt and its dazzle forced her to close her eyes.

Twenty-four hours earlier he had been in Charles de Gaulle airport waving and smiling when she came in sight. He must have forgotten his Swedish girlfriend for a moment, it wasn't possible for anyone to smile with such tender devotion and think of another woman at the same time. She shook the little packet of sugar, tore off the top and watched the lump of sugar settle on the beige-coloured foam of the coffee, then sink slowly through the surface. Maybe he really was able to remember and forget on command, as if he had a television set inside himself and his will was a remote control that could zap back and forth between channels that were separate from each other. Wife and child on one channel, Swedish romance on the other. Could he be the same person on both channels?

Perhaps you could really change yourself as easily as the words changed their meaning according to who said them to whom, and when they were said. You had the same face, the same body, but inside you were a different person, according to whether the woman you were with was black-haired or auburn. Now what was it his exotic princess had written in her letter? That she had lived in a daze without being seen as she was. Just as he had . . . Until she met him and felt he woke her with his gaze and reminded her of the person she was in her heart. Lucca picked up her teaspoon and stirred the small coffee cup. She went on stirring long after the sugar had dissolved. The words were not only those of his lover and himself, they were also hers, Lucca's. She had almost said the same words to him when they were getting to know each other.

He had turned up one day as an option, although at first she didn't see him that way. She had believed Harry was the one she was meant to be with. The Gypsy King, who had opened up a vulnerable crack in his frighteningly self-confident mask, seeing an unknown side of her and liberating it on the stage. She had imagined that what he did with her on the stage could happen in real life as well, and for a few months it did. Recalling her two years with Otto she shook her head over how naïvely she had confused her own dream images with the Otto who hauled her so painlessly into his life and then dumped her again. Harry's cynical honesty had been a release, and although sometimes his experience and status oppressed her the imbalance was cancelled out as soon as they were alone. In bed she saw in his eyes the insecurity she had seen for the first time in his Mercedes, when he tried to seduce her, and the second time on his balcony, with lightning flashing over the harbour.

Andreas disturbed her settled life with his boyish smile, his sudden kiss on the rock and his rash arrival a few months later. She suddenly realised she must have over-interpreted her enchantment by the legendary Harry Wiener. If Andreas travelled all the way from Rome for the sole purpose of seeing her again, that in itself was a question she had to answer not just with words but with all her being. And two weeks later when she was reckless enough to fly down to join him, she had come to believe that his eyes were the only ones that could net her in after the aimless flutterings of her early youth. Just as she had believed Otto's eyes were hard and blue enough to make their image of her more solid than a confused reflection from a mirror in the sun, flitting aimlessly around like a firefly in broad daylight.

But she herself had been little more than a mirror. A homeless mirror which two breathless removal men had been at a loss to know how to deal with. They had collected the mirror from a house in the Copenhagen suburbs without any directions for where it was to be taken. A lady had telephoned. Unfortunately she could not be there when they came, she had to make a broadcast. The key was under the mat. The removal men had set off, unsuspecting, and whenever a passer-by threw a vain or worried glance at himself in the mirror they thought they might finally get rid of their heavy, gold-framed burden. But no, each time the stranger walked on in the opposite direction, if he did not simply vanish from sight, because the weight of the mirror caused the removal men to stagger, or because the one in front thought it best to go to right or left. New faces and views constantly skimmed over the shining surface, on which no one and nothing left any lasting trace.

They discovered it was easier to carry it horizontally like a bed, and they got quite a long way like that, while the mirror only reflected the clouds in the sky. White as a sheet, said one removal man to the other. Like snow, said the other, like newly fallen snow. To pass the time they talked about how lovely it was to go out of your house on a winter morning when it had snowed in the night, and how you could hardly bring yourself to tread on the snow no-one had yet walked on. They had stopped to rest and for a moment it seemed really like standing on the threshold of one's house and watching the virginal snow. But they couldn't go on standing like that holding the mirror, which resembled both a bed and a snow-covered landscape. The removal men began to lose heart but they did their best to cheer each other on. After all, the mirror was bound to find a home at last. They didn't really believe that any more, but they kept on saying it.

Lucca . . .

She looked up from her coffee cup when she heard Andreas calling. He stood among the tables with his camera held up, so she could not see his eyes. Click, it went.

The plane circled in above the tangled web of Copenhagen street lights. In an hour she would be in the train on the way home. Else and Lauritz would be waiting at the station as arranged. She did not know how to get through it without cracking up. She could already hear Else's words of consolation. Andreas was having an affair, so what? It was bound to happen to one of them sooner or later. Had she really imagined they would live together until their hair turned grey without one or the other having a fling on the side? It was quite predictable, Else would say, after you had lived together for a few years. If she was wise she would keep mum and see it through. He would soon tire of his Swedish fairy-tale.

Lucca wouldn't be able to explain to her mother what she was feeling behind the pain and the outrage and her wounded vanity over Andreas falling in love with someone else. She could not even explain to herself what she felt beneath the emotions everyone would anticipate. Through the general, inevitable pain she glimpsed a black abyss whose depths she could not contemplate, nor could she see what lay at the bottom of it, if it had a bottom. For a moment she imagined that the darkness among the threads of lights beneath her did not hide buildings but a bottomless chasm into which you could keep on falling. How was she to make her mother understand that it was not merely Andreas she feared to lose?

They had strolled around in the Marais quarter looking at the Jewish shops and had spent a few hours at the Picasso museum. In the evening they went to the cinema and afterwards ate at a Vietnamese restaurant. It rained the following day, he worked, she read. She was sure he did not suspect anything. She had behaved as usual and imagined she would have done if she had not felt the need of a cigarette and searched in the pocket of his tweed jacket for a lighter. It was not hard to picture. The hard thing was to play the part completely, so he did not glimpse as much as a crack into the void where she was beside herself with pain and bitterness, dizzy at suddenly seeing everything at a distance. A distance she felt simultaneously with the suffering, and which made her suffer still more, not on account of Andreas, but of herself.

She went to Charles de Gaulle on her own. She wasn't sure she could go through with an emotional parting scene in the same place where three days earlier all her worries had paled when she saw him smiling and waving. He insisted on seeing her to the airport bus at L'Etoile. He kept asking whether he should go with her, but it did not alleviate her pain at all to see how guilt tore at him and made him exaggeratedly considerate. She looked at him as if he was no-one in particular as she waved a final time. As he turned and walked back towards the Arch of Triumph she looked at him just as she had done at Almeria airport when she held up a placard with his name on. He had appeared smiling among the crowd of passengers, as unknown and strange as they were.

She had a long wait in baggage reclaim at Kastrup. Her stomach ached at the thought of arriving home, putting down her suitcase in the kitchen and sitting down to eat with Lauritz and Else. She considered calling home and saying she had been delayed. But what would she do with herself? She did not want to go to Miriam's and take it in turns to weep. She smoked a cigarette while waiting. I loved him so much, she said to herself. It was not out of revenge that she put it in the past tense. She had been happy without thinking about it, without having to pursue her own thoughts and feelings all the time.

The letter from Stockholm had made her wake up, as if her years with Andreas had been only a dream. When people had asked her whether she really was as happy as she sounded, the question had taken her by surprise. It told her she had long since been released from herself. But that was all in the past. Now she was back again, locked up in her own head, puzzled over where she had been all this time.

Lucca . . .

She turned. She did not recognise him at once, the man who had spoken her name.

He had changed. He had grown a full beard, his hairline was receding and there were touches of grey in his beard and curly hair, but he was just as stooping and thin as before, and he wore spectacles again, oval and unframed. She noticed that in the taxi. You've stopped wearing your contact lenses, she said. He smiled, shy at her commenting on his appearance. Barbara had made him wear contact lenses. He said it in a way that told her they were no longer together, but she asked all the same. He met her eyes as he shrugged his shoulders and tried to smile like someone who has overcome the blows he had received. She leaned back and looked ahead.

He had just come back from Reykjavik. One of his compositions had been performed at a festival for new Scandinavian music. Although I don't feel so young any more, he added. He might have been right there, sitting with his well-trimmed beard and unframed glasses, grizzled and in a herring-bone coat. Was it Daniel? The short-sighted, unworldly Daniel she had once made so unhappy. She pictured him at the piano in his little apartment, as she stood at the window and made an end of it.

She told him about Andreas and Lauritz, about the house they had renovated, and how relieved she had been to move out of town and forget all the brooding over her career, totally absorbed in watching her son grow, seeing their home taking shape . . . Well, it must sound boring . . . He shook his head. He didn't think so. Incidentally, he had seen her on stage, in *The Father*. He had followed her progress. She borrowed his mobile and called Else to say she would be delayed. They walked beside the canal, he insisted on carrying her case. The reflections from the old street lamps trembled on the restless black water. The wind had got up, the boats rocked beside the quay and tugged at their mooring ropes, making them creak.

She watched the cobblestones sliding to meet her through the lamps' circles of light. I wasn't very nice to you, she said. He made light of it, it was so long ago. They walked for a while in silence. How strange it is, he said, that we should meet, out of the blue! Yes, she replied, I meet you every time I am deserted. It leaped out of her. He looked at her in a way that made her lower her eyes. She told him how Otto had dropped her a few hours after she ran into him and Barbara one evening in a bar. He had thought she was the kind who did the dropping. She shrugged her shoulders. She had thought so too. He smiled ironically. If only he had met her the next day instead! She smiled back. Well, he was not free then. The cold made him shiver. Every time . . . he said cautiously. Did that mean? . . . He looked at her inquiringly. She told him briefly about Paris and the letter. What kind of daft shit had she married? She looked at him. Sorry, he just felt . . .

Daniel's houseboat was at the end of the quay. He crossed the gangway first, put the cases down on the deck and gallantly took her hand. It was an old barge. There's no electricity, he said on the way down the stairs. She stood still while he lit the oil lamps and a gas stove in the middle of the floor. The piano was on a dais at one end of what had once been the hold. At the other end there was a galley and a door into the cabin where he slept. She recognised his grandmother's teacups on a shelf above the kitchen table, with a rowing boat in moonlight and a romantic couple. The handle was missing from one of the cups. The place was covered with varnished boards that shone in the glow from the lamps and candles, and there were small portholes in the walls from which you could look out over the canal and the quay. He uncorked a bottle of wine, they sat on safari chairs. A chest between them functioned as a table.

He was quite frank. He had had one or two brief relationships since Barbara left him, but they had never turned into anything permanent, he was probably not fit for that. He poured out the wine. Gradually he had grown used to living alone. It had its advantages, he could do as he pleased. She told him how surprised she had been when she met him with Barbara. Just imagine how surprised he had been himself! She took off her shoes and pulled her feet up in the chair. The red wine and the slight rocking beneath her had a calming effect.

Barbara had found herself a stockbroker. He smiled, but without bitterness. That probably suited her better . . . But he did not regret their relationship, she had been rather sweet, and she had helped him to get on. She had made him believe he was not entirely impossible. But he had been impossible back then, he could see that quite well . . . Lucca smiled. He raised his eyes and she regretted her smile when she saw the expression in his eyes. Now he had to smile himself. It's like a disease, he said, being hopelessly in love. And you almost go crazy, he went on, because you can't get it into your head that your disease isn't infectious.

Had it gone on a long time? He shrugged it off. A year and a half, two years, until he met Barbara. She cured him. He laughed and shook his head at himself, raising his glass again. Lucca tried to remember the girl with the big red lips and bulging breasts. That was what it took, obviously. But two years . . . exactly the same time she had been with Otto. In all that time Daniel had been thinking of her even though he knew it was hopeless. She almost smiled again but stopped herself. He looked as if he thought it was quite funny himself when he thought back on the heartbreak of his youth. But who had ever loved her so faithfully, knowing well he hadn't the ghost of a chance to have his love requited?

It was odd to be on Daniel's houseboat drinking red wine. Their chance meeting and the unusual surroundings matched her feeling of observing her life from outside, as if she was someone else. She felt strangely untouched by what had happened in Paris, as if she was divided in two. Her twin sister took all the pain on herself and gave herself up to all the unanswered questions about what would happen if Andreas left her, and what was wrong with her to make him fall for a Swede with black curls and blue eyes.

How different they were, she and Daniel. He had gone on

loving her long after their relationship had ended, although he knew she had met someone else. His love had not lessened when he no longer had her near him. It had merely grown stronger and more faithful in her absence, away from his reach. The loss of her had filled him to the brim with love, when she was no longer there to receive it. It had grown and grown, and he had been at bursting point because he could not get rid of it. Whereas she had started to think of her love for Andreas in the past tense as soon as she realised she could no longer count on him.

Daniel had loved her in spite of himself and in spite of her, until it was driving him mad, his love turned into a disease. She was not like that. What made her twin sister suffer was not the fever of emotion, apart from jealousy at the thought of the polaroid picture of the pale beauty sitting on an unmade bed with a halo of morning sun in her unruly hair. What hurt wasn't anything inside her, but the feeling that something had been amputated, leaving only a bleeding wound.

Reading the terrible letter had been like the stroke of an axe, and that axe had been so sharp and slashed so hard and unexpectedly that several minutes passed before she felt pain and realised that a part of herself had vanished. Even more time passed before she understood that it was not like losing an arm or a leg. Not until next morning when she sat sunning herself on the balcony and trying to imagine what it would be like to jump off, not until so many hours later did it strike her that the axe had cut her in two. One who could actually have swung her legs over the rail, and another to whom that was merely an unreal idea. One was already in the train bound for home, leaning her forehead against the window as she stared despairingly into the darkness. The other sat on a safari chair on Daniel's houseboat drinking red wine.

She rose and looked at her watch and realised it would have looked more convincing if she had looked at it before getting up. She said she would try to catch the last train. He fetched her coat and held it out for her while she put her arms in the sleeves. He carefully lifted her pony tail so it fell over the collar. When she turned round he looked quite frightened at his own intimate gesture. It had been good, she said, to see him again. He smiled and looked into her eyes. It had . . . She walked towards the stairs, he followed. She had already taken two steps up when he said it. She stopped and turned round. She wasn't sure she had heard aright. He wished she didn't have to go. He looked at her without blinking. Bravely, she thought, as he raised his hands to the side a little with an apologetic movement. Now it was said. He caught hold of her without faltering when, slightly theatrically she had to admit, she let herself fall into his embrace.

She still had her coat on when she lay back on his bed. She closed her eyes as he kissed her. It was an unusual feeling, she had never had a lover with a full beard. He unbuttoned her with practised fingers. She recalled how she had admired his confident hands when they struck even the widest chords. He stripped off her pants and tights. As he kissed her nipples she regretted not leaving. She suddenly felt she was a retrospective reward for his faithful, fruitless love.

The bed rose and fell in time with the rocking movements of the boat, and she felt the rough prickling of his full beard on the thin skin of her thighs. In a detached flake of a second she saw the waving tufts of pine needles. She locked her thighs around his neck and felt his scratchy beard and the firm grip of his hands round her ankles, and once more she was carried on a pair of broad shoulders in the same rocking rhythm among the tree trunks towards the dunes and the sea.

It rained all the way from Copenhagen. The raindrops crawled sideways across the windowpane as houses, trees and fields rushed past under the low clouds. When she stepped off the train she noticed a young girl humping a heavy bag. The girl broke into a run when she caught sight of a tall man in his forties coming towards her. They had the same colour hair, chestnut brown. The man embraced her slightly clumsily and took her bag. Probably a divorced father, thought Lucca and followed them out of the station where they got into a car. She tried to picture what it would be like if she and Andreas took turns to have Lauritz. She couldn't imagine living alone in the house. But where then? She thought how she had moved away, first from Otto and then from Harry, with her cases and bags. There were no taxis. She rang for one and stood in shelter for a long time in the cold, gazing at the depressing, unchanging square with its provincial shops and parked cars.

Else sat in the kitchen reading the paper. She hadn't yet cleared the breakfast things. As usual Lauritz had shaken out more cornflakes than he could eat. The orange flakes had gone soft in the yellowish milk. Else put her head on one side with a worried look in her eyes. Lucca put down her suitcase and leaned against the fridge door as she slid down onto the floor and began to weep. Her mother rose and went to kneel beside her. What had happened? Lucca pulled herself together, got to her feet and walked into the living room. She tore off her coat on the way and let it fall on the floor. Else followed her, they sat down on the sofa. Lucca bent over. The weeping broke out of her throat again in cramped contractions, as if she was vomiting. Else put an arm around her and stroked her back.

Lucca explained in disconnected sentences interrupted by sniffing. Else clasped her close. I suspected as much, she said, stroking her hair. Lucca snatched her hand away with an angry movement, rose and went to one of the windows looking onto the garden. What did she mean, she thought as much? Else made no reply. It had stopped raining. Lauritz's little plastic tractor lay overturned on the muddy lawn. The branches of the plum tree dripped. She turned round. Else stood beside the stove, she bent down and picked the coat up. What do you mean by that? repeated Lucca, herself surprised at her accusing tone. Else laid the coat over one arm and stroked it slowly with her hand. Say it then! shouted Lucca as she went to sit on the sofa. Else sat down beside her in the opposite corner.

Now she must try to calm down a bit. She had not exactly gone around expecting it, but she had to admit she had had her ideas through the years. You're sure to be cross with me, she said, pausing. She brushed dust off the stove with the flat of a hand. In a way she had been asking for it herself. That was probably an awful thing to say, but . . . She looked firmly at Lucca. Now I'm being honest, she said. Lucca looked out of the window again. She could see the neighbour's horse in the meadow beside the drive, unmoving except for its tail fluttering limply like a pennant. She had worshipped him far too much. Else's voice had grown cool and confident, it was the voice she used on the radio to all and sundry. A small bird flew over the black field, itself black against the grey sky. It rose and fell in arcs, as if it wanted to imitate the curves of the plough-land.

She had become subservient to him. What did she think it was like, to be worshipped in that way? She had completely neglected herself for the sake of him and the boy. Lucca squeezed up her eyes. The rainwater had gathered in pools on the lawn, and the grass blades were reflected in the quiet water, black against the greyish mirror image of the sky. She breathed evenly again. Good Lord, there were enough suckers about who thought it was lovely to have a sweet, home-loving woman always ready and waiting. But Andreas was no sucker, he was an intelligent and sensitive person, and an artist too. He needed challenges, even opposition, and she had not given him any. When all was said and done he was only a man, and men tended to grow tired of women who clung to them and only yearned and sighed for confirmation. It was no surprise to find he had succumbed to temptation. Lucca looked at her. What do you want me to do then? she said. Else fell silent and looked at her for a long time, as if reading her face for an answer. Get yourself a lover, she said.

Lucca pulled up her feet and stretched out for a cushion, she clutched it to her stomach with her arms crossed over it. She looked down at the floor. The cloud cover was thinning, and pale sunlight lit the floorboards in softly outlined squares. What about you? she asked. Else smiled. What did she mean? Lucca hesitated for a moment before going on. What about the time she was with Ivan and suddenly started wearing completely different clothes and changing all the furniture? As for her friends, she had exchanged even them for Ivan's advertising chums. Else looked past the stove into the kitchen. She had even demanded a church wedding although Ivan didn't want that at all. She who had always held bourgeois traditions to scorn and talked of marriage as a form of prostitution. That hadn't hindered her from parading as a fifty-year-old bride with a white veil and naughty underclothes.

Who said Ivan didn't want a wedding? Else's well-modulated voice suddenly sounded dry. Lucca prodded the cushion cover with a nail. He had said so himself . . . Else cleared her throat and looked at her. When? Lucca laid down the cushion, put her feet on the floor and crossed her legs. She swallowed and met her mother's eyes. She explained that she had gone into the country one summer's day not knowing Else was in town. She described how she had had dinner with Ivan and talked to him more easily than ever before, and how for the first time she had understood what Else saw in him. Until she had gone to bed, drunk with all the white wine he had poured into her, only to be woken up by his paunch rubbing her back and his stiff prick between her thighs.

She went on despite the tears that ran down Else's cheeks. She had noticed how he looked at her in the mornings when she was on her way to the bathroom, but she had to admit she was pretty surprised to wake up with her stepfather in her bed and her stepfather's prick between her thighs. That was why she had gone to Italy so suddenly to find Giorgio. And maybe in the end that was the reason, and not so much because he had found himself another tight delicious twenty-year-old, for Ivan finally making off. For fear of her letting the cat out of the bag some day.

Else had got up. She stood for a moment without moving, one hand resting on the cold stove pipe, before going into the bedroom. Soon afterwards she came back with her suitcase. She went into the hall to put on her coat. Lucca said there would not be a train for another hour. Else wanted to leave at once. Neither of them spoke in the car. Lucca went onto the platform with her. Maybe, she said, maybe you were asking for it. Maybe you worshipped him too much . . . Else turned round and slapped her soundly. Lucca staggered. Her cheek still burned as she walked to the exit. She turned in the station entrance. Her mother was sitting on a bench with legs crossed and her head leaning back. An elegant, lone female figure at a station in the provinces. Lucca could not see whether her eyes were open or closed.

A week later she stood on the opposite platform holding Lauritz by the hand and waiting for the train from Copenhagen. It was a dry day but windy and the passing clouds made shadows appear and fade again by turns. Lauritz played with the shadow of the roof as they waited. He placed himself with the tips of his toes in line with the edge where the shadow was succeeded by sunshine on the asphalt. He was equally excited each time another cloud had passed the sun and he still stood balancing like an acrobat with his toes on the boundary between light and shadow.

She still had the feeling of being cut in two. One who feared Andreas was going to leave her, and one who had started to disengage herself from the moment she had read the letter from his lover. But they no longer lived side by side, her two halves, they took turns to rule over her feelings and thoughts. She had hardly slept since getting back from Paris, and as she stood waiting for Andreas she was dizzy with exhaustion.

Lauritz did not understand why she lay in bed weeping, or why she pushed him away when he tried to comfort her. She grew irritable and reacted harshly with cross words to his persistent attempts to make contact. At other times she completely ignored him and sat for hours gazing dejectedly out at the garden and the field, torturing herself with elaborate fantasies about Andreas and the black-haired letter writer. When she was in that state everything about the boy seemed unbearable, his very existence seemed like a hindrance to her, a parasitic organism that drained her of energy and life. She came to regard him as a frightful mistake who suddenly represented everything that had made Andreas tire of her. All the routines, all the dull cud-chewing, all the washed-out and sloppy details of daily life.

But Lauritz was still more confused a few minutes later when she took him on her lap and hugged him or sat on the floor building a house with his Lego bricks, completely involved in the activity. It was not only guilt at her unexpected hatred of him that made her so attentive and devoted. She was kind to him again because she was thinking of Andreas in the past tense. She doubted that her love for him had been anything other than a craving, a self-obsessed dream. When she embraced her son she also passed into herself, into the vacuum Andreas had left when he took his love away from her and gave it to someone else. There was nothing left there, not even the shadow of love, and maybe her love had been just a shadow of his. As she buried her nose in her son's soft neck and licked the fair down, she imagined herself another life somewhere else, alone with Lauritz. He was the only one whose love she did not need to doubt, and the only one she knew she loved more than herself.

Her thoughts about Daniel and what had happened on his houseboat went through the same fluctuations as her feelings for the boy. When she slammed the door in Lauritz's face and lay down on her bed to weep she heard Else's words again, inflamed with venomous female spite. Get yourself a lover! She despised herself for having yielded to Daniel's pleading dog's eyes. Their chance reunion had broken open the poor man's old wound again. She had ministered to his needy loneliness merely to take revenge on Andreas and create a balance in their shared account, but that had just made her an even greater traitor. She felt she had not only betrayed Andreas but herself as well.

Daniel called one evening after she had put Lauritz to bed. Could she speak freely? It offended her to be drawn into the low-voiced mood of intimate conspiracy. She quite forgot to ask how he had got hold of her number. Did she feel very bad about what had happened? No . . . she just hoped he was not sorry about it himself. He was not. He still cared for her, so why should he regret it? Because . . . said Lucca, but did not finish the sentence. He understood. She must not think that he in any way . . . Now he was the one who interrupted himself. She didn't. He gave her his mobile number, but she didn't write it down. He hoped she would call him one day. He shouldn't rely on that, she answered coldly.

When she had replaced the receiver she immediately regretted not having noted his number. Lauritz called from his room.

He asked if it was Andreas. Yes, she said. Andreas had not telephoned since she came back from Paris. That in itself was proof, she thought and kissed the boy's cheek. Later when she sat in front of the stove gazing dully at the glowing coals, she pictured her life without Andreas, but not alone. It was just a foolish fleeting daydream, but for a moment she saw herself and Lauritz on the houseboat with Daniel. She stood on deck hanging out washing on a line. The boy was fishing with a rod, and Daniel sat in the hold strumming on his piano. Furious with herself, she kicked shut the door of the stove so the cinders dropped down inside.

Lauritz called again. She went to him. He asked why she was making a noise. It's because I miss your dad, she said. He did too. He would like to make a noise too. Do, then, she said. Lauritz crawled out of bed and turned his box of Lego bricks upside down. She asked if it helped. He didn't know yet. She tucked the duvet round him and told him gently to try and fall asleep. When she could hear his even breathing, she went outside. The moon was almost full and its pallid light fell leaden and faint over the grass and the branches of the plum tree.

Nowhere, she thought, nowhere in the whole world did she belong. She felt no pity for herself at the thought, she merely thought it, slowly stating the fact as she watched the lights of a car pass the end of the gravel road. A dog barked further away. A subdued soughing came from the woods. But not so far away someone had loved her in spite of himself and in spite of her. After all those years he was still so fond of her that he was not afraid of humiliating himself yet again.

She recalled what Harry had said one night about his career as a seducer. How he had long ago seen through himself and yet kept on pursuing one unknown beauty after another. As if his knowledge and his desire were unable to communicate. But perhaps it was not only desire that had made him reach out time and again for a new, strange face. Perhaps it was hope as well, which something inside him had refused to give up, although his experience told him it was useless to go on hoping for a meeting that would change everything. She would like to believe that was why he had reached out to her the night before Christmas Eve when she turned up unexpectedly.

As she stood in front of the house hunching her shoulders against the cold she decided that Harry had been a victim both of his own hope and of hers, when she met Andreas. Had Daniel's phone call made her hope again? After all, she had been receptive to him despite the knowledge of how many times her hopes had been disappointed by one man or another. If she thought of Daniel it was possibly in spite of herself, but it was also thanks to the hole Andreas had left in her. It made her suffer, that hole, not so much because of him as of its own yawning emptiness. But it was not only the emptiness in which something was missing, it was also the opening where someone else might show his face. It hurt to go on hoping, but would she ever be able to do anything else?

Stretching out her hand as she lay in bed, she felt the T-shirt Andreas had slept in. She put it to her face and breathed in the faint smell of sweat, his smell. She began to weep again. She could not explain to herself why she felt so sure it was over. She had no inkling of what would follow. There was nothing to imagine, nor was there anything to hope for.

He looked pale, and he avoided her eyes when he stepped out of the train and Lauritz ran to meet him. The boy's delight and hundreds of questions lasted all the way home. When they were inside Andreas said he needed a rest before dinner. They had still not exchanged more than generalities. She opened a bottle of red wine while cooking. Lauritz lay on the living room floor with a fire engine Andreas had brought him. The feeble but constant sound of its siren made her feel like screaming and smashing something, but for once she controlled herself. When the food was ready she had drunk the best part of the bottle. She went into the bedroom to wake Andreas. He sat on the edge of the bed looking out into the twilight, he had not heard her. He turned round with a start and tried to smile.

All seemed as usual after he had returned from a trip. The boy fired questions and Andreas talked about what he had done. He asked who had called and what had happened while he was away. He had finished his play. Quite finished, he said, with an exhausted air. After dinner he brushed Lauritz's teeth and put him to bed. She cleared away and sat down again while he read a bedtime story. Her eyes fell on the notice-board where they had put pictures of themselves and Lauritz. She looked at the one he had taken of her in the café in Paris. He had given her the film to take home for developing. She sat for a long time meeting her own surprised, searching gaze that seemed in itself impenetrable, as if it was not her. When at last he joined her she had drunk a bottle and a half of wine. She went to kiss Lauritz goodnight. He stroked her cheek and asked if she was happy now. Yes, she said and felt a smarting sensation around her eyes. I'm happy now . . . She hastened to switch off the light and stood for a moment in the darkened room until she was sure she was not going to cry. The telephone rang in the living room. Andreas had already risen but she managed to get there first. Did she know it was Daniel? She had guessed it was. He asked if he was interrupting. Yes, she said. He had thought a lot about her. Could they meet? She asked where he was calling from. The boat, he replied. She raised her voice as she said goodbye and put the receiver down before he could say more.

Andreas looked up as she went into the kitchen. Who was that? He had lit a cigarette. My mother, she said and sat down opposite him. The cigarette smoke made her feel sick. He looked out of the window. It was pitch dark now. What is it? she asked. Her voice sounded thin and unnatural. He turned to her. He had lost weight, and he had a pimple on his forehead, red and swollen. I want to live alone, he said. She was perfectly calm now. Was there someone else? He looked away. No, he said. She did not take her eyes away. Why did he want to live alone, then? He watched the smoke of his cigarette, curling upwards in the lamplight. Because he didn't love her any more.

She rose from the table and went out into the hall, put on her coat and made sure the car keys were in the pocket. He followed her outside. She could not just go off, they must talk about it. He had been thinking a great deal about this . . . She slammed the car door in the middle of his sentence and started the car. He shouted her name as she drove down the drive. It was cloudy and the road was dark. She thought of calling Daniel from a phone box but decided to surprise him instead. She looked at the clock beside the speedometer. She could be in Copenhagen in an hour.

Epilogue

One morning in October Robert woke up while it was still dark. He peered at the hands of the alarm clock. It was twenty past five. He sank back on the pillow feeling sleep rising from below again. He pictured the water trickling out of the soil between the grass blades under their boots as they walked along the isthmus towards the reed-bed further out. It had begun to drizzle. He had taken her hand to show her the way along the strip of land between the shallow stretch of sea and the flooded meadows. She put her head back to feel the light prickling of the rain on her forehead and cheeks. The dark glasses were spotted with drops. She had folded up her white stick and put it in her coat pocket.

Lucca had never been out to the headland. She wondered why they had never been there, she and Andreas. They had been able to see the sand bank and the rushes from the beach where they went to swim. Listen, she said, stopping, and now Robert too heard the airy, rhythmical whistling of wing beats. He looked up and turned round, but did not catch sight of the flock before it was far out on the horizon, where the calm water and clouded sky converged along a blurred edge of reflections.

The alarm started to beep. He had been on the point of falling asleep again. Half past five. He must have set it at the wrong time. He did not usually get up before seven. He was about to switch off the alarm when he caught sight of the packed travel bag standing in front of the wardrobe. They had planned to leave at six o'clock to catch an early ferry. He rose, put on his dressing gown and opened the curtains. It had rained all night, the trees were laden with rain. He met Lucca in the corridor. She wore her sunglasses, she never showed herself to him without them. She had heard his alarm even though Lea's room was at the opposite end of the house. He asked if she would like the bathroom first. She made an evasive, sleepy gesture and went back along the corridor, her hand brushing the wall. She had grown used to the house by now.

She often heard sounds he had not caught. Her hearing had grown sharper as she trained herself for blindness. That was her own expression. He took night duties so he could drive her to the Institute for the Blind once or twice a week. She was a good student, and so far the only impediment was her firm refusal to have anything to do with dogs. She couldn't stand dogs, particularly Alsatians, she would not dream of making friends with one. But she had started to learn Braille. One morning she sat in the kitchen moving her fingertips over the breadcrumbs on the table. What does it say? he asked. She smiled secretively. I'm not telling!

He went into the bathroom and took off his dressing gown. He leaned against the basin as he brushed his teeth and now and then glanced at himself in the mirror. A solid tousled man in his forties with foam round his mouth. He felt as heavy as the weather, but within the weight of his body he felt a lightness he had not noticed for a long time. It was the prospect of travelling that made him light, the thought of the endless motorways that would take them south, away. If he drove hard they could get through most of Germany before midnight, perhaps right down to the Stuttgart area.

He had scarcely been anywhere abroad since his divorce from Monica, on the contrary he had worked so hard for the past two years that he usually had some holiday due to him. Once only he had taken Lea to the Algarve. It was pretty awful, but she had seemed to enjoy herself. As a rule she went away with Monica and Jan, and he had not felt like going alone. He could not see himself trailing around some picturesque town and going to a restaurant in the evening. A solitary tourist secretly spying on the inhabitants, grateful if anyone smiled at him.

It was his idea for them to go away, and Lucca had agreed at once. He felt the trip might get something in her to loosen its grip. Something that had firmly embedded itself and made her life, during the past months, seem like a closed circle. She had been staying with him since he visited her at the orthopaedic hospital. He had surprised himself by his sudden whim, when he saw how deep her despair was, and invited her to stay with him. He had not known what to say when she asked why he made such an amazing offer. Too much room. That had been his modest reason. That he was someone who had too much room. But it was still the best explanation he could hit on.

Luckily she had not asked him again. He did not think it was because she had started to take him for granted. She behaved more like someone afraid of upsetting the temporary and precarious state of things with too many questions. She often kept to herself in Lea's room or on the terrace, until it grew too cold to sit outdoors. When it began to get dark early he found her several times sitting out there in her coat or wrapped in a rug. Sometimes he asked her to come inside. He did not like the thought of her staying outside in the dusk so as not to impose on him. At other times he left her alone, relieved that she did not feel obliged to be sociable.

As he rinsed the toothpaste from his mouth his gaze fell on some of her things that had found their place on the bathroom shelves, bottles of perfume and skin lotion, her nail file, hairbrush, shower cap and bag of sanitary towels. There wasn't a name for their chaste life together. You could say she was his guest. Since the accident he had gradually been drawn into her life, until he discovered he had moved far outside his medical sphere of action. The expression made him smile as he tidied away some used cotton wool sticks she had dropped on the floor beside the waste bin.

She had not seen Andreas or as much as talked to him on the phone since he came back from Paris and confirmed what she already knew. Robert was still playing the part of messenger, and several times he'd had to ask Andreas to be patient and stop ringing. Give it time, he kept saying to the grief-stricken man, but he could feel Andreas growing ever more despondent at the thought that he might have left it too late to repent and show goodwill. Robert himself had no idea what the future would bring. He defended Lucca's decision to isolate herself from everyone except her son without wholly understanding her fierce resolution, and he did not press her to explain herself. The accident had stopped her in her course, and no one could tell how long her stupor would last. She did not even know that herself.

At times he felt like a living fortress against what she must feel was a siege. Andreas kept on insinuating himself with his eager guilt, impatient for her to relieve him by at least meeting him and hearing how fluently he could talk about his error. She made no comment when Robert passed on what he had been asked to tell her. She never asked what he knew about Andreas's trip to Stockholm. Nor did she ask him to respond to the messages her mother and Miriam got him to deliver.

Robert had long telephone conversations with Else when she called to hear how things were going, and to ask if Lucca wouldn't at least come to the phone. He had to smile when this woman with the cultivated voice tried out her mature charm on him in the hope that he might happen to reveal the nature of his relationship with her daughter by his tone of voice or some unconsidered word. He also spoke to Miriam and heard her baby wailing in the background. Still less could she comprehend why her friend had no use for her now that everything in her life had fallen apart. Else hinted darkly that they'd had a kind of row, but that it was of no importance now. He pretended not to know what she was talking about. Robert also concealed his knowledge from Andreas, although he sometimes almost interrupted his grief-stricken monologue when he went out to the house in the woods to fetch Lauritz or take him home again.

They would sit in the kitchen where the pictures of Lucca still hung on the notice-board. The sighted Lucca, building the house or swinging her son around or sitting at a Parisian café and smiling, her eyes surprised and yet aware. Andreas could be so full of remorse and self-pity that Robert found it hard to keep quiet. He remembered the shame he had heard in her voice and read on her face when she told him what had happened on Daniel's houseboat. He could see and hear that her shame related not merely to Andreas, to whom she had been unfaithful, or Daniel whom she had misused. Something had been shattered that night, a week before she had driven herself into disaster, and Robert was the only one who had any inkling of it. He was relieved each time he drove home without having betrayed her confidence, even though he had seen Andreas in all his misery, sincere but also hollow.

One evening it was Daniel on the phone. He presented himself as an old friend and said he had been given Robert's number by Else. He asked how she was. He did not say Lucca, but *she*. His intimate tone surprised Robert, seeing they had never talked to each other before. How many times had he phoned the house in the woods and slammed the receiver down because Andreas answered? Or waited until the connection was broken off because no one answered? Daniel paused. Are you . . . he asked and interrupted himself before trying again. I mean . . . you and Lucca . . . Robert almost sympathised with the irrepressible need for clarity beneath the other man's heavy-hearted stammer.

Lucca sat in an easy-chair wearing headphones. He went over to her and laid a cautious hand on her shoulder. She was alarmed, for once she had not heard him, she who otherwise heard everything. He could faintly hear the crescendo in the last movement of Brahms's third symphony. He said it was Daniel, and as he spoke he wondered at himself for not telling the caller as usual that Lucca did not want to speak to anyone. She hesitated a moment before rising and walking over to the telephone, orientating herself as was now her habit by brushing the furniture with her hand en route. He took care not to change the position of anything when he did the housework. She waited to pick up the receiver until he had gone out of the room and closed the door behind him.

He went into the kitchen and started clearing up the dinner things. One of the plates clattered as he put it into the dishwasher, and at the same moment he heard a corresponding clatter from the other end of the house, like an echo. She squatted in the middle of the room surrounded by tulips, water and fragments of glass. She used one hand to search for the pieces and collected them in the other, curving it like a cup. Two of her fingers were bleeding, he led her into the bathroom. She had a deep cut on one fingertip. I'm sorry, she said. I just needed to smash something . . . When he had bandaged the cut finger and put a plaster on another, she collapsed onto the lid of the lavatory seat. What was I thinking of? she mumbled. What could I have been thinking of? She bent forwards and began to weep. He looked at her for a moment before going into the scullery to get a dustpan and brush.

He stood waking up under the shower for a long time. It felt as if the hot water slowly made his fatigue crackle and fall away from him in invisible flakes. His own life was the same, almost. He went to the hospital every morning and came home in the late afternoon, but whereas previously he had spent his leisure hours vegetating and listening to music, now he helped Lucca get accustomed to her new existence. He had stopped playing tennis, and not only because he had no time. His friendship with Jacob had cooled after he had let him wait in vain at the tennis courts one summer day, and after Jacob had stood in his garden an hour later and seen him through the window talking to Lucca on the telephone. One day when they were together in a queue in the hospital canteen Jacob asked Robert what he was up to with his former patient. Someone must have seen them together in town, although Lucca seldom went out, for fear of meeting Andreas.

To spare her pride he tried to help her as little as possible. He cleared up discreetly after her small accidents and behaved as if he had not noticed them. Now and again, before she was familiar with the house, he took her arm cautiously when she was about to run into a door or crack her head on the open door of a cupboard, and the episode with the flower vase was not the only time he had to put a plaster on her, like a clumsy child. She said that herself. That it was like learning everything over again, just like a child. At first he'd had to help her in the bathroom in the morning. He guided her under the shower and took her hand to show her how to regulate the water. Her nakedness made them shy and very correct.

He turned off the shower and opened the window to let out the steam. It resembled the smoke from a fire as it billowed up and blew away into the cold damp murkiness. It had been dark when they arrived at his house for the first time. He asked her to wait in the hall while he went in and switched on the lights. She asked him to show her the house. He took her arm and led her round. She wanted to know what each room looked like, and he described the furniture, the pictures on the walls and the other things. She smiled when he got to the ping pong table in what should have been the dining room. As he described it in detail, he suddenly felt he was seeing his home like a stranger.

Later in the evening she grew hungry, and he suddenly realised he had not done any shopping. He offered to make an omelette. She insisted on breaking the eggs and beating them. She needed to cook again after months of insipid hospital food. He set a bowl and a tray of eggs on the kitchen table and put a whisk into her hand. When she knocked the first egg on the edge of the bowl, the yolk slid down onto the table, and so it went on. In the end she had broken almost all the eggs in the tray and half the shells lay in the bowl with the yolks that had been lucky enough not to land on the table. She broke down, convulsed with sobbing as she bent forwards, the tips of her hair dipping into the pool of egg yolk on the table top. He cleared up after her, washed the bowl and suggested she start again. This time she succeeded. She whisked the eggs, he fried the omelettes. Don't worry, he said. I'm not sorry for you. She turned her dark spectacles towards him. That's good, she said in a muted voice.

He did not know how she passed the time when she was alone in the house. He asked her when he got home one afternoon and found her sitting on the threshold of the terrace. I'm remembering, she said. He taught her to work the stereo, and she sorted his extensive record collection into piles on the floor, which she memorised, as she tried them all out to find the music she liked. She kept returning to Chopin, but one day when he arrived back in the afternoon, the passionate voice and crisp guitar of José Feliciano reached him out in the drive. He had forgotten that one. It was filled with childhood memories, she told him. Her mother had been mad about José Feliciano, and now he had become a kind of colleague as well. When she had played *Che serà serà* for the fifth time he suggested that she might like to try what it sounded like listening through his earphones for a change.

He sometimes called her when he was on night duty. They did not talk about anything special, but he lowered his voice nevertheless if the night nurse walked past. He asked what she was doing, and said whatever came into his head. Perhaps that was the biggest change. Someone being in the house when he was not there. The fact that he could call home. He mostly thought about the change during their nocturnal telephone conversations. Things had become quite natural by now, when they were in the house together. When they came to an end of their conversation she always thanked him for phoning. Her politeness made him feel sad. As if he had only called because he knew she was sitting there alone.

Every time after he had driven her to the training session at the Institute for the Blind he would walk around the centre of Copenhagen, browse in music shops or sit in a café. Sometimes he went to see his mother, at others he waited for Lea outside her school. She had given him a teasing look when he fetched her from the station for the first time after the summer holidays and explained in the car that he no longer lived on his own. To start with she wouldn't believe that Lucca wasn't his new girlfriend. She only began to believe it when she found one of Lucca's elastic hair-bands on her bedside table. When Lea came, Lucca slept in an empty room previously used as a store-room. He had tidied away the junk, piled the packing cases at one end and made up a mattress at the other.

Lea felt uncertain about Lucca when they were introduced. She had never before been with a blind person and was shy about her dark glasses and searching manner of turning her face in the direction of anyone speaking. She made an effort to seem natural and behave nicely, but it did not help that she was handicapped, this strange woman who had moved in with her father, even though they were not lovers. As if that wasn't odd enough anyway. Conversation at the dinner table languished. Lea's replies were only monosyllables, and Lucca withdrew into herself. Robert felt like an unsuccessful clown desperately rushing around the ring trying in vain to elicit a smile from the audience.

It helped when he fetched Lauritz the next day. The boy's joy over the reunion made an impression on Lea and she began to relax with Lucca. Lea and Lauritz played blind man's buff with her in the garden. Standing inside he wondered at her cynical ease as he heard them laugh and saw her reeling around after the children. She was touched, he could see, to sense how Lea treated the boy as if he were her little brother. She succeeded in winning Lea's confidence, he didn't know how, and when he saw them sitting on the lawn together, he did not disturb them.

It was one of the last warm days of August, and after lunch they went to the beach. Lea took Lucca's hand and led her out to the other side of the reef where it was deep enough to swim. He stayed on the edge of the sea with Lauritz. While the boy tumbled around in the waves he watched Lucca, standing with her arms crossed, in water up to her waist. Lea kept encouraging her and finally she gave way and stretched out her arms, lifting her feet off the bottom. They swam slowly side by side towards the posts. Robert admired her courage. She laughed, at once nervous and released. He wasn't sure he would have dared entrust himself to the water without sight.

The sky was visible now, but it probably would not get much brighter. An October day with low-lying clouds and sticky withered leaves on the damp asphalt. When Robert had dressed he went into the kitchen and switched on the coffee-maker. Lucca must have fallen asleep again, she liked to sleep late. He put out bread and cheese and went to wake her up. The door of Lea's room was ajar. He opened it cautiously, without a sound. The grey daylight met the wall and shone on the glazed poster above the bed, blurring all but Michael Jackson's small, arrogant face in a milky haze. Lucca's hair was spread out on the pillow-case with its pattern of swallows and cheerful stylised clouds. Her eyelids were closed and her lips lightly parted, she was breathing peacefully.

She had put on a little weight while staying with him, her face was no longer as bony and drawn and still showed a touch of summer colour. It was a long time since he had seen her without her dark glasses. A long, white scar above her left eyebrow seemed to be the only trace left by the accident. Her serious expression reminded him of the photograph Andreas had taken of her at the pavement café in Paris, when she knew their relationship had ended. Her lips were parted in the same way, as if she had been surprised in the middle of a word, not by the photographer but by sleep.

The corners of her mouth curved. I'm not asleep, she said. I woke up when you came in. He protested. He had no shoes on and the door had opened without a sound. It wasn't you, I heard, she said, it was the coffee-maker. Listen . . . Now he too could hear the faint snorting and gurgling sound. He went down the drive to fetch the newspaper from the letterbox. When he came in again he heard water splashing on the tiles in the bathroom.

He had a cup of coffee and read the paper, but when he put it down he had forgotten what was in it.

She came into the kitchen and sat down opposite him. She had buttoned her blouse crookedly, but he did not remark on it. She let her hand roam over the table until she found the bread basket and the butter dish. She asked when they would be in Italy. Her damp towelled hair fell in front of the dark glasses. Tomorrow afternoon, he replied, and noticed how accurately she scraped up butter with her knife and spread it on the bread. Anyway, we should be in Milan by tomorrow afternoon, he went on. She searched with her hand again, found a slice of cheese, put it on the bread and brushed her hair away from one cheek before taking a bite. Milan, she murmured, chewing.

How about Lucca? she asked as he locked the front door. Maybe late the next morning, he said, carrying their luggage to the boot. Maybe late in the evening . . . He had suggested going to Lucca merely because it occurred to him and so as not just to suggest a trip into the blue. Perhaps that was why she had acquiesced to his suggestion without hesitation. When he hit on the idea he had thought she might find it easier to reflect on her future if she got away. At least she would not have to use so much energy on defending herself. But he too felt the urge to go, exhausted as he was with shielding her isolation. He explained to Andreas that she needed to get out of his reach before she could think of him without feeling under pressure. Had she said that? No, said Robert. It was something he had thought out for himself. Andreas agreed he was right.

Neither of them said anything when he started the car. He drove through the industrial district, past the hospital and further on to the viaduct with slip-roads down to the motorway's north- and south-facing lanes. I never saw Lucca, she said finally. She said it in a matter-of-fact way. He replied that they didn't need to go there if she didn't want to. She let down her seat so she could lean back. No, she said, I need to know I have been there.

It began to rain again a few kilometres south. The rainwater whistled under the tyres and the red rear lights of the cars glistened on the wet asphalt. I'm not nervous, she said. He smiled. Then why did she say that? She pondered for a while. Because I ought to be, she replied. To drive that far, and to drive for so long with someone I hardly know, in a way. He turned into the fast lane. It's strange, she said, to know such a lot about someone I have never seen. He replied that he had only told her so much about himself because she couldn't see him. She nodded. That was why she had dared to talk about herself. Because she couldn't see him. It precluded her from forming an impression of how he looked at her.

It had occurred to her a little while earlier, when he opened the door of Lea's room to wake her up. When he stood looking at her because he thought she was asleep. Had she felt spied on? No, it wasn't that. On the contrary, she had realised that it no longer affected her if she was looked at. Her face had become irrelevant, something separate from herself. That's probably why I am not nervous, she laughed. Because of that and because you are not in love with me. If I thought you were I would never have told you my story, and if you were, you would certainly not have told me yours. She paused. Stories, she went on, stories give out too much light. You can't hide from them. He smiled. She often made him smile, and each time it struck him that he was alone with his smile. You're right, he said, in the end they always catch you up. Yes, she replied after a pause. They have no escape routes . . . even if my own story is about one long flight.

After she fell silent he sat for a long time thinking over what she had said. They had grown used to keeping silent in each other's company, when one of them paused in the narrative. It no longer worried them, but there was something significant in the silence between them now, in the car. They were outside everything, sitting here among the other cars on the motorway, where the towns they passed were no more than white names on blue signboards. It was the right place to be, he thought, in a car on a motorway, for they had met the same way, as unknown to each other as the cars on the road, beyond all relationship. Perhaps she was right, perhaps they had no need to feel nervous. Gradually they had immersed themselves more deeply into each other's life than one normally does, but at the same time he had felt as if they were conversing by satellite, across an enormous distance. They were close to each other and yet apart, and maybe they could only become so close because they were restricted to words alone.

Each knew more about the other than many other people did, but her blindness protected both of them. Particularly when the details grew so intimate that they would never have believed they would tell them to anyone. She was spared seeing how he reacted to her story, and he could speak freely about himself without the surveillance of a searching, sympathetic or reproachful glance. They felt free because they could speak without worrying or having any hopes about the impacts of their narratives. And yet they went on behaving like two people who have just got to know each other, considerate and cautious. She behaved modestly like the guest she was, modestly because she felt he didn't want her to express her gratitude too fervently. And he restrained his way of helping her, afraid of exaggerating and making her feel indebted.

Their restraint was not lessened by knowing so much about each other. So far they had barely commented on their own story or the other's, nor had they talked of how unusual it was, revealing so much to a stranger. They were content to listen and ask about specific matters. It was almost as if they had made a rule for it, albeit unspoken. He felt sure she thought about this too, sitting beside him, leaning back against the head-rest. That she had just broken the rule which in the past months had made it possible to speak without fear of being exposed to judgement or pity.

Their evenings had passed with one or the other telling more of their story. She lay on the sofa, he sat in an easy-chair. Sometimes he had not even looked at her. He had gazed out into the summer evening or the first evenings of autumn, listening to her voice or hearing himself speaking. They had been like two strangers who meet in the dimness of a quiet hotel vestibule and fall into conversation. Two strangers who take into account that they have no previous knowledge and therefore need an explanation for everything. Two homesick tourists who have stayed in the hotel instead of going on the excursion to Luxor or the Cheops pyramid, because they prefer to sit listening and noting the congruencies and divergences between their otherwise quite ordinary stories.

Her story had emerged in a gliding progression of events and ideas, people she had known and places where she had been. To begin with he could feel she was embarrassed when she touched on things she had never confided to anyone, and feelings she had never before expressed in words. She could blush in mid-sentence or hesitate before continuing, but at the same time he sensed the pressure of the untold things waking at the sound of her voice and impatiently insisting to be expressed and given a place in her narrative. As it gradually unfolded she quite forgot to distinguish between what was acceptable and what was revealing or directly unattractive. One event or emotion drew another with it, her tone gradually grew calmer and more confidential, and he discovered that he too was no longer too startled or embarrassed to listen to her intimate revelations. Only in the pauses when silence fell between them could he see how she suddenly directed her mind's eye towards her story, amazed, sad or ironic, as if she were a stranger meditating for a while on its tortuous course, its blind alleys and delusions, the agitation and restless craving of emotions.

Something similar took place in him when he heard his own voice narrating. He did not see himself in his story but another, and he saw that other from behind, unable to fathom his deeper impulses. His secret, intimate feelings became secretive even to himself. And it was as if she read his thoughts. You don't know why things happen, why they come to be as they are, she said one evening, after he had made a long pause. No, he replied. You can never really know.

An escape . . . could her story be concentrated into that one word? Was it an attempted flight that had been halted by the Dutch truck that evening in April? As he followed the peaceful rhythm of the traffic he felt it sounded like an answer to something he had said the previous day when they walked out to the headland. They had gone as far as they could get, right out to the end of the reed beds. She asked him to tell her what it looked like, and he described the tall reeds and the tussocks of grass and the rowing boat moored to a post in the inlet, reflected in the quiet water. They had passed the rotten post where he used to sit. She balanced on it, supporting herself with a hand on his shoulder. The faded pack of Gitanes had vanished. He told her about it and said Andreas must have been out there one day.

Apart from the humble and practical messages he passed on he seldom mentioned Andreas, but now and then he asked if it wasn't time for them to talk. Each time she gave him the same answer. Not yet . . . he asked again out on the headland. She stopped. Was he tired of having her as a guest? No, he said, but I feel you are running away . . . It had started to rain in earnest and he suggested turning back. They took shelter from the rain in the shed made of tall, tarred planks, the only break in the flat landscape. The grey light penetrated the gloom through the spaces between the planks, where the inlet and the sand bank stretched horizontally, broken by the dark into vertical bands. He saw a big seagull flying across the strip of sand, disappearing and appearing again in the cracks. Not any more, she said. I am not running away any more. But to go home . . . that would be a flight.

He glanced at her briefly. What about their trip then? She turned her dark glasses towards him. He switched on the windscreen wipers and concentrated on the road again. The rain was like fog around the wheels of the lorry ahead of him. Wasn't that an escape too? Her being here with him in the car driving south? She waited a few moments before replying. No, she said. What should they call it then? Going back, she said. All the way back. To the beginning . . . He overtook the lorry and pulled in again. Yes, he replied. That's probably the only way to go.

It rained through most of Germany. The countryside was unvarying, woods, fields, factories and woods again, blurred and blue-grey in the misty rain. The names of towns told them how far they had come. He read them aloud to her when they passed yet another signboard. She took a cigarette from the pack under the window and put it between her lips. They had just passed Hanover. On the satellite picture of the weather forecast the night before, a gigantic spiral of cloud was moving in over northern Europe in a slowly ticking movement. So tonight the astronauts couldn't see the lights of the cities. She smiled with her lips clamped round the cigarette and ignited her lighter. She was always nervous when she lit a cigarette. During the first weeks she had scorched the tips of her hair several times or set light to the filter, but he had accustomed himself not to interfere.

She lit the cigarette, inhaled and slowly blew out smoke. The astronauts? Yes, he said, describing a picture he had once seen in the newspaper. It had been taken on a clear night, from space, and you could clearly distinguish the contours of Europe surrounded by dark blue, with shining spots for each big city on the continent. The picture had illustrated an article on light pollution. He hadn't understood that word. How could light pollute? She agreed. She had seen that picture too. It was one of the most beautiful pictures she had ever seen. Like a reflection of the firmament, she said. As if each city was a star. Yes, he replied, taking his hand off the gear lever and pulling out the ashtray. And imagine, if one day the lights of cities should reach some distant, inhabited planet, long after the cities and their inhabitants had disappeared. She nodded. Poor things, she said, if they found out the lights were not stars, but cities. Then they would believe they were not alone in the universe.

Robert disagreed. Would we feel sad if we thought the stars were cities? On the contrary, life would feel better for them, he said, with the thought that light years away, fools like themselves had existed who would surely have been just as confused. She smiled. How could he be sure they would be just as confused? He shrugged. He couldn't imagine life without confusion. Unless you spend your life without knowing it, she replied. But then nothing would matter much, of course. Yes, he said. But it's worse if you believe you are alive, even though your thoughts are merely the delayed light of a dead star. But, my dear doctor! she exclaimed and tapped out her ash outside the ashtray so the flakes drifted down over her left knee. She didn't know he could be so philosophical. He didn't know that either.

He put on a tape of Beethoven's late string quartets and sank into the music as they passed industrial complexes and the looping junctions to big cities. All those emotions, he thought. The music vibrated with them, rough, smooth, hoarse or trembling, singing in the warm soundboard of the instruments, like slim crystal glasses vibrating from the circling of a damp finger. So many emotions were involved there, but they had lost their faces, they were no longer elicited by something or directed towards anyone, swallowed up by the transforming power of music. Their anonymity was the price of his own feeling, sitting in his car surrounded by strange cars and road signs, factories and cities, and yet being recognised and exposed. They sat silently listening to the music linking the cities as did the endless asphalt. It had different meanings to them, the same music, as it vibrated through their heads, and that could only be because in itself it meant nothing at all.

The ease he had felt in the morning at the prospect of going away had been superseded by a drowsy flatness, but he did not feel heavy as he usually did when he was tired. Nor was it the monotonous driving that exhausted him. His ease had changed into a strange, weightless feeling, and it seemed as if the restless or lingering string instruments echoed inside him as in a cavity surrounded by porous walls. Suddenly it seemed unrealistic to be sitting in his car beside his one-time patient on the way to the town whose name she had been given. In the past few months he had not had time to fall back into vegetating as usual. When he got home from work she was there, whether they talked or she sat by herself on the terrace, and at weekends Lauritz came and filled the house with his toys and his high-pitched babbling. He saw more of her son than of his own daughter, and the boy was becoming dangerously attached to him.

When they returned to the car after tanking up and having coffee at a service station outside Wurzburg, she put on the radio before he could go back to Beethoven. She zapped between programmes until deciding on a station playing pop. He never listened to that, but he thought it was her turn to choose and when they had driven another hundred kilometres the mindless pop music had merged with his strange, at once relaxed and melancholy mood. Now and then they chatted a little. She asked about details of what he had told her, or answered herself when he asked her to say more about some of the men she had known.

As he heard his own voice and listened to hers above the soft, stupefying pop, he recognised the feeling that had struck him when he was on the beach watching Lea swimming alongside the reef, the last Sunday before the summer holidays. It was the same feeling that overwhelmed him a few weeks later when Lauritz had stayed the night with him for the first time. He hadn't gone into the house when he came back after driving the boy home. He sat in the car thinking of what Andreas had told him about his trip to Stockholm. His abortive attempt at flight from the life he now spoke of so devoutly was almost unbearable. As Robert alternately slipped into the overtaking lane and back into the line of cars driving south through Germany, he again recalled Lucca's eyes in the photograph from Paris and the vague, intangible recollection her expression had woken. Like a mute reminder of something left undone, but what? Some act of negligence, he had thought, an unredeemed pledge, but of what and to whom?

It wasn't so much the thought of how Andreas had smoked his cigarettes and gobbled up plums as he untangled himself from one illusion only to get wound up into another. It was not that which had paralysed him so he stayed on in his car listening to the sprinklers in the quiet gardens, staring at his own idiotic plastic chairs reflected in the window by the terrace. Nor was he suddenly struck by paralysis at the melancholy realisation that Lea would soon be a young woman who had no further need of him. That was not why he felt dumped on a siding when he waved to her out there between the poles and later, as the train moved off and he walked along the platform beside it to keep in sight of her face for a second or two longer.

Behind Lea's face in the train window and Lucca's at the

pavement café, others appeared. He saw Monica's face again, looking over the water and smoking a cigarette, one late afternoon on the beach a year or two before they were divorced. He saw his mother sitting on her balcony looking out over the railway towards the heating system's blank red-brick wall concentrating the last sunlight. He saw another Monica blushing as she bent over him beneath a woollen blanket in the Alps, and he caught sight of Sonia's inflamed young face behind Monica's, bent over in the same way while she rode him like a mechanical toy horse. And behind them he was looking Ana in the eyes again, her dark gaze watched him through all the others' as she lay down with loosened hair on the dim patterns of a dark red carpet, that winter evening when they were young and she finally gave him what he had wanted for so long he had forgotten why, and wanted it so frenziedly that she had not been able to quell his insatiable hunger.

He had been too young when he lost Ana, too young to lose something he had wanted so terribly much. He had withdrawn into a cave deep inside himself. It had terrified him to witness his own body amusing itself with anyone who came along. He had not dared come out until Monica pulled a woollen blanket over her head to protect their first kiss from the cruel light of the snow-clad mountains. By then he had learned to be more patient, less basic in his desires, but perhaps his body had grown used to being on its own. At any rate, it had gone off again when Sonia appeared in the barrister's garden showing off her strong legs and slight breasts and doing her tai chi until he was totally mesmerised.

An incident of no importance had chanced to devour what meant everything, not with the insatiability of desire, but with that of silence. In fact he had not been as greedy as a lot of people, but what had been his had ended by slipping out of his hands again, because he let go, or because he was no longer capable of holding on with his previous conviction. As he watched them, the faces from the story of his life appeared before him and grew thin and transparent, Ana, Monica and Sonia, even his mother and Lea paled in his mind. Finally they fused and disappeared like reflections when a gust of wind whips up the surface of the water into sudden ripples. Again he visualised the flat landscape he had so often walked, the sand banks and reeds, the lonely shed of tarred planks, the birds' signs on the sky and the tufts of grass on the inlet, their inundated stalks.

After midnight he drove into the car park of a motel between Stuttgart and Tübingen. Lucca had been asleep for the past hour. It was stupid to have driven so far when they were both tired, but he had been caught up into the trance-like monotony of driving and kept succumbing to the temptation to drive another hundred kilometres. As he switched off the engine and stretched out in his seat, fatigue came over him. He sat for a while looking listlessly through the drops on the windscreen, sparkling in the light from the motel's yellow sign. The restaurant behind the white net curtains was in darkness, with only bluish neon strip lights to relieve it. He spoke her name several times, at first quietly, then with more insistence. Finally he laid a hand on her shoulder and shook it gently. She woke with a start, frightened and confused. He told her where they were. That far . . . Her voice was thick with sleep. She apologised for having slept instead of entertaining him. He carried their bags in one hand and took her arm as they hurried through the rain.

The motel was furnished in sham romantic style, as if guests were supposed to imagine themselves in a hunting lodge, a casino and a solid Christian home blended into one. While they were signing the register he said she should be glad she couldn't see how ghastly it was. She did not react, it was not very funny, but it had become a habit with them, these slightly cynical references to her handicap. She stood swaying slightly, on the verge of falling asleep. They had rooms side by side. He showed her the bed and the door into the bathroom before going to his own room and collapsing in his clothes.

He hadn't even taken off his shoes, he must have fallen asleep at once. At first he had no idea where he was, he lay on his side with his shoes tangled up in the blanket, watching the distant lights of passing trucks. It was a long time since he had remembered a dream. As a rule his dreams faded as soon as he woke up and he only saw a few dissolving, disconnected details. But this dream he remembered absolutely clearly. He pulled the pillow under his ear and sniffed in the scent of washing powder in the cool, smooth pillow-case.

It had been a colourless dream in shades of grey, white and black. He had never been in Africa, but that was where he was, he didn't know why nor what kind of room he was standing in. He kneeled down in front of a boy with curly, close-cropped hair. A boy of four, perhaps five, not dark brown but grey like everything else in the dream. The boy had no eyes. There was nothing in their place but thin grey skin. Someone spoke to him behind his back, he did not know who. He could not see the person who spoke, nor hear if it was a man or a woman. The voice told him what he was to do. It said he should reach out and rub the skin where the boy's eyes should have been. He rubbed cautiously with his knuckles and felt the tense membranes breaking at the light touch. As the flaps of skin curled up, two dark boy's eyes appeared. Then he woke up.

At first he did not know what it was, the clenching feeling in his diaphragm, which made him double up with his forehead against his knees. He could not breathe, and for a few seconds everything in his body locked in a vice-like grip, until the cramp gave way to an overpowering force that chopped through him in hard, rhythmic stabs. Then he felt sobs breaking from his lungs and throat, hollow, deep and impossible to check.

A little later his muscles slackened, the weeping stopped and he was able to sit up. He dried his eyes and looked out at the silhouettes of parked cars. His watch showed the time to be half past two. He found a cigarette and lit it. The door beside the window led out to the car park. He went outside, it had stopped raining. The cold wind went straight through his shirt, but he kept on walking up and down beside the line of trucks and trailers. There was a wood beside the motel. He had not noticed that when they arrived. The tops of the tall pine trees were faintly outlined against the night sky above the dark windows of the building.

He did not wake up until half past nine. Lucca answered at once when he knocked on her door. She sat with her coat on beside the open window. Her bag was on the bed, packed. They were silent in the restaurant. The end wall was decorated with antlers, and a subdued Viennese waltz sounded from the invisible loudspeakers. He fetched their breakfast from the sideboard. There were no other people and the car park was almost empty. He asked if she had slept well. As she turned her face towards him he could see himself and a section of the wood in her dark glasses. I heard you, she said quietly. He directed his gaze through the corridor of pine trees, their dark trunks vanishing into the dimness. Her cup clattered on the saucer, and he felt the warmth of her hand on his. I am your friend, she said. He looked at her. My friend? She nodded. Yes, she said with a wry smile. Your friend in the dark . . .

When they were in the car he unfolded the map over the steering wheel and traced the road south to the Swiss border and on through Zurich, St Gotthard and Milan. She put on the tape of Beethoven's string quartets. He asked if they could hear something else. Like what? He searched out the route to Genoa and down the coast through La Spezia to Viareggio, where they would turn inland again. Whatever you like, he said, folding up the map. Tunes of the day, he added, starting up. She moved the red needle along the FM band until she found a station with good reception. He was grateful to her for not saying anything. Her silence was neither awkward nor frightened, she merely let him be. She kept quiet as you do beside someone in a state of deep concentration.

It was not that he concentrated on anything besides driving. Thoughts passed through his head like birds, and he made no attempt to hold on to them, but he was fully awake. An hour later they were on the way through the Alps. The lethargy of the previous day had been replaced by a clear, sharp feeling, like a reflection of the white light that dazzled him when they emerged from yet another tunnel, forcing him to screw up his eyes.

They reached Viareggio in late afternoon. The sky was overcast and there was an offshore wind. The blue-grey colour of the water changed into a lighter milky green under the frayed foam as the waves arched themselves and collapsed. She walked in front of him prodding the sand with her white stick. He stopped to tie his shoelace. The wide beach was completely deserted. A black dog ran around wildly with its tongue hanging out of its mouth and bared teeth, as if biting at the wind. Far to the north behind her solitary figure in the fluttering coat he could see the rocky island off La Spezia and the promontory that sloped upwards and merged into the Apennine Alps. The highest peak was white, not of snow but marble. He straightened himself and caught up with her. Minute drops of salt water covered her dark glasses in a fine layer. Like marble dust, he thought. They walked back and along the promenade past the imposing façades of hotels and pavilions between the promenade and the beach. Hardly anyone was about. There was only the dull rumbling of the breakers in the background, the sound of their heels and the tapping noise of her slim stick.

It was somewhere round here, said Lucca, somewhere along this stretch, she saw him for the first time. Robert tried to imagine a young version of the woman with the mature cultivated voice he had been talking to once or twice a week. A young Else in her suit standing at the edge of the curious crowd watching a film being shot featuring Marcello Mastroianni. There must have been spotlights behind the camera even though the sun was shining. They depicted the scene to each other as they walked along the row of wind-blown palms. It developed into a game in which they took turns at elaborating each other's fancy.

Else must have been fascinated by the blend of sunlight

and white spotlights enveloping the actors in a magical sphere impossible to break into, like a dream. And there, carrying a long boom as he adroitly followed the camera's movements along the rails, she suddenly caught sight of the dark young man, who perhaps, in a pause between two shots, had already observed the elegant, Scandinavian girl on the other side of the white, the magic circle. It was no longer Mastroianni she looked at, it was Giorgio, but she did not know that. She did not yet know his name, nor could she know he would be the father of her daughter. Merely because, during a stroll along the promenade in Viareggio, she had been attracted by the artificial glare around the crowd of spectators.

And up there, said Robert, pointing, as if it would help, up there behind one of the closed shutters she undressed for the first time in front of her lover, while her husband lay vomiting on one of the other floors because he had eaten some oysters he should have left well alone. Yes, said Lucca. In the afternoon, most likely, with the slanting sunrays from the shutters caressing their young, curious bodies just as in a film. And cut! All of a sudden her life was changed, she loved someone else, and no one in their wildest dreams could have imagined that her story would take such a completely different turn. By chance, said Robert. Yes, she responded. I'm an accidental girl!

The light was fading as they left Viareggio and drove east through hills covered with pines and olive groves. One crest appeared behind another in the twilight. The hills resembled the moveable scenery in a puppet theatre with minute silhouettes of wide pine crowns and pointed cypresses. It was dark when they arrived in Lucca. He drove around the town along the city wall and through one of the gateways to the old quarter. They parked in the square in front of a church. The marble façade shone yellow in the light from the street lamps. She was silent. He wondered whether this was the church where Giorgio had sat when he had his photograph taken one day in early youth, happy and unaware while the low-flying swallows threw their whirling shadows on the marble façade. They continued on foot along a narrow street without traffic. People thronged the street, the shops were still open. The walls resounded with steps and voices, and beneath their murmuring he heard the tip of her slim stick when it grazed the cobblestones. He asked if he should describe the town to her. No, she said, slightly irritated. Have I ever asked you to describe yourself?

They went into a café, she ordered espresso and grappa. He was surprised to hear her speaking Italian. He asked for a beer. They had been quiet for a while when she rose to her feet. I'm going for a walk, she said. Should he come with her? She would rather he didn't. And if she got lost? She shrugged her shoulders. Then he'd have to look for her. As he sat alone watching the inhabitants of the town in their winter coats coming in to sit at the bar, he began to understand why she did not want to know what the place looked like.

He could have described the square tower with trees growing on top of it, or the church façade consisting of columns of which not a single one matched the others, some with animal reliefs or geometric patterns, others twisted or carved to look as if they were tied in knots. He could have described the angel standing atop the gable looking down on passers-by with a teasing smile, and he could have mentioned the narrow staircase on the back of the gable, apparently gratuitous unless it was meant for the angel to climb because he didn't want to terrify people by flying. But all of this would have been nothing but pictures to her, his own pictures, of which she could only form vague and imprecise ideas.

Why should she be interested in the beauty of the town? After all, she could not see it. He thought about what she had said. It was true, she had never asked him what he looked like. Only when he went to see her the first time without his white coat and she wanted to know what he was wearing. She had no inkling of his face. To her he was a voice and what the voice told her, and the expectant, listening silence in which she herself could speak. Her town must be like that to her. A name and the echo of steps and voices blending with her thoughts among the invisible walls. He remembered how he had stood at the door of Lea's room the previous day looking at her because he thought she was asleep. Her own face was no longer of any concern to her. She had come to regard it as something outside herself. Like a mask, he thought. You don't see it when you wear it. Why worry yourself about it if that's the only one you've got?

He pictured her walking around with her tapping stick among the other pedestrians in the narrow old streets, how she noted each street corner and marked it on a plan in her memory. When he had waited half an hour he began to get worried. He paid and went in search of her. The shops were closing, traders let down the shutters in front of the windows and he thought she must be able to hear the same rattling sound perhaps only a few streets away. The moon had come out, almost full, above a medieval tower whose only decoration was a white clock-face of marble. The moon and the clock looked like images of each other. He would have liked to describe the likeness to her, and for a moment felt sad at the thought of her prohibition of pictures.

He had been walking a long time up and down the streets, growing more and more anxious, when he caught sight of her, framed in a gateway with a strangely curved façade. The entrance led to a square surrounded by terraced houses, all painted yellow, with small windows at different heights. She stood perfectly still among the passers-by in the middle of the square, face raised. He stayed at the entrance. He remembered reading about the square in a guide book. Once it had been a Roman arena, and later on houses had been built in a circle following its circumference. There was nothing remarkable about those houses. They were quite ordinary, with washing hanging on lines and shutters open to apartments where people were cooking or watching television. The remarkable thing about the space was its long elliptical curves.

He closed his eyes and listened to the steps approaching or withdrawing in fleeting, contrapuntal figures. The walls behind the open windows resounded with voices, squealing chair legs, domestic machines and churning television sets, and the sounds blended into a complex murmur above his head. It probably sounded like that every evening, when the occupants of the houses had come home. A scooter crossed the square. It was an ordinary evening in Lucca, with nothing particular happening. An evening when they would just be together, the people who lived here, whether they were happy or unhappy or something in between. Robert waited until the scooter had passed before going up to her. She turned towards him and smiled. Well, there you are . . . He took her hand. I can find my way very well, she said. I know you can, he answered.